THE
EMPTY
KAYAK

THE
EMPTY
KAYAK

A Queen City Crimes Novel

Jodé Millman

LEVEL
BEST BOOKS

Author Photo Credit: Evangeline Gala

First edition

ISBN: 978-1-68512-287-4

Cover art by Level Best Designs, Jodé Millman, and OPENAI

This book was professionally typeset on Reedsy.
Find out more at reedsy.com

To my sons, Max and Ben—the rays of sunshine in my life.

Praise for the Queen City Crimes Mysteries

Praise for *The Empty Kayak*

"Three strong women follow their own inexorable paths to justice in *The Empty Kayak*, and it's a pleasure to cheer them on. *The Empty Kayak* is not only a compelling and believable mystery, but a sharply drawn portrait of women's friendships."—Joseph Finder, *New York Times* bestselling author of *House on Fire*

"Twisty personal relationships build to a satisfying, stunner finale in *The Empty Kayak*."—Lisa Black, *New York Times* bestselling author of the *Locard Institute* series

"Poignant in places, nail-biting in others, the tension and turmoil add up to some fine high-stakes suspense."—Steve Berry, *New York Times* bestselling author of *The Last Kingdom*

"Millman's narrative is evenly paced and gracefully rendered, with suspense sustained throughout. *The Empty Kayak* utilizes familiar mystery elements to strong effect. Millman keeps readers guessing with potential leads, red herrings, and dead ends."—The Booklife Prize

"In Jodé Millman's propulsive thriller *The Empty Kayak*, a drowning investigation leads to legal wrangling. The prose is emotive and sensory…and in effect, the book doubles as a study of how women assume power, while also showing how such roles affect their lives and relationships."—Foreword Reviews

"*The Empty Kayak* by Jodé Millman is a wonderfully tense mystery with a strong focus on relationships and careers destroying lives…The suspense draws you deeper into this gripping tale; you won't put it down until you're done." (5 Stars)—Readers Favorite

Praise for *Hooker Avenue*

"A worthwhile beach read for summer vacation."—*USA Today Network*

"In this ambitious sequel, Millman certainly doesn't skimp on the action—every page seems to reveal a new drama or explain an old one, and the tale's pace never lags."—*Kirkus Reviews*

"Dark, dangerous and deviously suspenseful, Hooker Avenue kept me turning pages late into the night. I adored the fascinating cast of characters and the rich Hudson Valley setting. A truly terrific book!"—Alison Gaylin, *USA Today* Bestselling, and Edgar Award-winning author of *The Collective*

Praise for *The Midnight Call*

"A Must-read." —*USA Today* Network

"The tricky legal maneuvering intrigues…Millman writes with verve."—*Publishers Weekly*

"Jodé Susan Millman's *The Midnight Call* is an impressive debut. Deft plotting peels back the payers of this deliciously creepy and convoluted suspense novel in which surprises abound and nothing is as it seems. Don't think you know how this plays out—just put yourself in Millman's capable hands and enjoy the ride."—Karen Dionne, *USA Today* and #1 International bestselling author of *The Marsh King's Daughter*.

BOOK AWARDS:

The Midnight Call
   2021 – Independent Press Award—Winner – Legal Thriller
   2020 – American Fiction Award —Winner —Legal Thriller
   2020 – Independent Publishers Book Awards—Winner—Bronze IPPY Award
   2020 – Golden Quill – Desert Rose RWA—Finalist for Suspense
   2020 – Write Touch Readers Award – Wisconsin RWA—Finalist
   2020 - Reader's Favorite —Honorable Mention
   2019 – National Readers Choice Award – Oklahoma RWA—Finalist
   2019 –Clue Award— Shortlist
   2014 – Clue Award—Finalist
   2014 – Chantireviews.com —"Best Police Procedural"

Hooker Avenue
   2022 – Independent Press Award—Winner – Crime Fiction
   2022—American Fiction Award – Finalist
   2022—Clue Award —First Place Award
   2022—Bookshelf Awards—Honorable Mention

Chapter One

Detective Ebony Jones felt as though she was toting around a thousand-pound weight, which grew heavier and more torturous with each step. Her cargo, a petite one-year-old, nestled her dark curly head against Ebony's shoulder and wriggled on Ebony's bum left hip, the one with the .38 caliber bullet fragments lodged in it. Even the slightest pressure from the child's body sent relentless jolts of electricity sizzling down her leg. Between the squirmy kid and the merciless pain, Ebony's trek up the sidewalk was a living hell. And the situation was about to get worse. Much, much worse.

The toddler's green eyes locked onto Ebony's, so trusting and innocent that they tugged at her jaded cop's heartstrings. Lily Martin's face was muddy, her fuzzy pink hoodie was soaked from the sudden rainstorm, and she was missing one sneaker. But it wasn't Lily's bedraggled condition that made their journey up the front walk so unbearable; it was the heartbreak that would follow after Ebony rang the doorbell. And Lily's mother answered.

The Tudor-style City of Poughkeepsie home belonged to Jessie Martin, Lily's mom and Ebony's on-again, off-again best friend. Since kindergarten, over twenty-five years ago, the two women had been BFFs, but once they pursued conflicting careers in the law, Ebony as a cop and Jessie as a criminal defense attorney, their relationship had deteriorated. Around every corner, clients, cases, and the legal system had thrust obstacles in their path, testing their friendship. Sometimes, Ebony wanted to pack it in and move on, but deep in her heart, she yearned to reconcile with Jessie. The present

1

catastrophe wasn't going to help that cause.

On her trip to Jessie's, Ebony had stewed over the appropriate way to tell Jessie that her ex, Lily's father, Kyle, was missing. There would be so many questions—*how, when, where, why*. How could Ebony explain the outcome of Kyle's disappearance when she didn't know for sure whether he'd survived the freak accident?

Ebony limped up Jessie's bluestone path, laden with a cauldron of emotions. Sorrow. Guilt. Anger. Disbelief. Fear. And reluctance, to name a few. She still couldn't swallow the reality. Kyle Emory was missing, and, if she was honest, presumed dead.

Midway down the walk, Ebony glanced over her shoulder at Zander, who had remained curbside with their unmarked black Explorer. He was tall and slender, and leaned against the hood of the car. Zander's brows were drawn together, and he watched her with hawk-like precision. As partners, they were supposed to deliver death notifications in pairs, but he'd made no move to join her on the threshold.

Chicken, she thought. Or was he being uncharacteristically empathetic, given her close relationship to Jessie?

Delivering the news of a loved one's death—or possible death—was the most onerous part of her job, and fortunately, she'd never discharged this duty before. Why did the first time have to be Jessie? This was going to be a day, a moment, that would be branded into Jessie's heart and mind forever.

The need to perform the death notification properly, professionally, prompted Ebony to ask herself how she'd prefer this horrific news disclosed to her.

It wasn't as if she was notifying a stranger. She knew Jessie as intimately as she knew her own kid sister, Carly. And similar to her arguments with Carly, she and Jessie had always forgiven each other eventually. Ebony only hoped being the messenger of a suspected death didn't permanently sever their already fragile bond.

But Jessie was a lawyer; a smart, strong, and fierce criminal defense attorney. She'd understand. She'd want honesty. No bullshit.

Straight but gentle, Ebony reminded herself as she scaled the porch stairs, clasping Lily to her side. Upon reaching the landing, she exhaled a deep breath, pressed the doorbell, and waited.

An eternity passed before Jessie answered the door. Jessie's eyes flitted from Ebony to Lily. Jessie's broad smile vanished as a ripple of worry lines surfaced on her forehead, and her ears flushed pink. Hal Samuels, Jessie's fiancé, stood behind her, looking equally surprised. They were dressed for early autumn hiking with scuffed tan boots, plaid flannel shirts, and faded jeans. They radiated happiness. Every time Ebony saw Hal and Jessie together, she was reminded that a homicide investigation had reunited them and that new beginnings could grow from despair.

"Eb, what are you doing here? How did you get Lily? Is she okay?" Jessie craned her neck to peek past Ebony's shoulder toward the street. "What's going on? Where's Kyle?"

Ebony cleared her throat. "Jessie, we have a situation."

Hal dipped his head in recognition. The former District Attorney, and now Dutchess County Court Judge, seemed to acknowledge her gravitas and cupped his hands on Jessie's shoulders as if propping her up in anticipation of an imminent disaster.

Jessie's mossy green eyes burned into hers, and she snatched Lily away from Ebony as though protecting her child from a mistress of evil.

"What do you mean? A situation? Tell me what happened to Lily. Is she hurt?" Jessie peeled off Lily's wet hoodie, socks, and muddy sneaker, and ran her trembling hands over her daughter's plump body, checking for bumps, bruises, and cuts. Finding none, she continued, "Has Kyle been in a car accident? Where is he? Is he okay?" As expected, the questions tumbled out, heavy with worry.

Despite the pain in her leg, there had been something comforting about having the baby's legs locked around her waist and the soft body cuddled against her. The warmth. The maternal stirrings. The irresistible scent of baby shampoo. The sudden emptiness in Ebony's arms only exacerbated the burden of her visit and reminded her that the worst was yet to come.

Ebony's entire vocabulary lodged in the back of her throat like a fish bone. Her mind analyzed the techniques for being sensitive, caring, and

3

supportive, as protocol and friendship required. She stood frozen in time and space, cognizant that the truth would make the tragedy real for both of them.

"Ebony, please come in," Hal said, guiding Jessie across the foyer. "Take a seat in the living room."

She followed them into the living room, where vibrant flowered sheets blanketed the sofa and chairs, protecting them from tiny, sticky hands. Ebony recalled that almost four months ago, she and Zander had barged into this room, attempting to pressure Jessie's client into testifying in what had proven to be a landmark serial killer case. But Jessie had obstructed them, her customary modus operandi when dealing with the police.

The same floral sheets billowed as Ebony occupied an armchair that faced Jessie, who had Lily nestled in her lap upon the couch. Hal settled in beside them and leaned forward with his hands clasped and his elbows resting on his knees.

Ebony coughed at the dust motes floating in the air and cleared her throat. *Straight but gentle.* "Jessie, I have some bad news." She sucked in a long breath and exhaled slowly to prepare herself. "We believe Kyle may have drowned in a kayaking accident this morning on the Hudson River. We haven't found him, but we're out looking for him. I'm so sorry."

Jessie's eyebrows shot up as she absorbed the words. *What?* Her dilated pupils seemed to demand.

"Jessie, did you hear me? Kyle disappeared this morning."

"What do you mean, you believe he's missing? Don't you know if he's dead or alive?" Jessie's face flushed, and her grip on Lily tightened. "Kyle had Lily with him. How could he have been kayaking? Who was watching Lily?" Jessie's voice increased in pitch until it was a squeak.

Hal slid close to Jessie and slipped his arm around her shoulders, shoring her up against the blow. "Let's take it step by step, Jess. You must be in shock. Ebony, can you please start at the beginning? I'm sure that will answer some of our questions."

"Before I get into the details, do you want me to call your mom and dad? They can help with Lily while I fill you in. I can send Zander over to retrieve them."

Jessie balked at the suggestion and clutched the fidgety baby tightly to her breast. Hal tilted his head backward and jutted his chin toward the door, signaling his consent.

Taking the hint, Ebony shot off a text to Zander. *Please pick up Ed and Lena Martin and bring them here.* She gave him their address, and he texted back. *10-4. On the way.*

Although she owed Jessie an explanation, she wanted to delay getting into the details until Ed and Lena arrived to take care of Lily. The poor tot had been through enough at the scene.

"When did you last see Kyle?" Ebony asked.

"This morning. He came by around nine to pick up Lily. It was his Saturday with her."

"Did he mention where he was headed?"

"No. I didn't ask. We're supposed to sign the custody papers this week, and since we were getting along, I figured I'd cut him some slack." Jessie paused. "I'm working on my trust issues with him."

"So, he didn't tell you he was going kayaking at Kaal Rock?"

"No. He was there by himself? He had Lily with him?" A sense of disbelief colored her voice.

"Did he indicate he was meeting... friends?" Ebony asked. She needed to proceed step-by-step. *Straight but gentle.*

"No, what friends?"

"Does the name Olivia Vargas mean anything to you?" Ebony kept her tone calm, although her stomach clenched into a knot.

"Ebony, you're scaring me. Who is this person, and what is happening?"

"Apparently, Kyle was engaged to Olivia. They became engaged three weeks ago on Labor Day. They were supposed to be getting married on Valentine's Day next year."

"What the hell? You're telling me Kyle's missing, and he was engaged?" Jessie shouted. Lily startled and bawled as though she understood the significance of Ebony's announcement. Jessie rose and paced across the living room carpet, shushing her daughter and planting kisses on her curly head. "It's okay, Lilybean. Hush, hush."

Hal narrowed his eyes and made a time-out sign. "You're asking a lot of questions and not revealing any facts about what happened to Emory." He paused. "Stop beating around the bush and start at the beginning like I asked." Hal's demeanor had pivoted from being a supportive partner into a cool and controlled prosecutor ready to cross-examine an adverse witness. "What does this Vargas woman have to do with the kayak? And Kyle's disappearance?"

"I'll explain after the Martins arrive," Ebony said.

As they waited, an uncomfortable silence filled the room.

Ebony shifted in her chair as the hinge of the front door squeaked, followed by the shuffling of feet. Jessie's parents, Lena and Ed Martin, accompanied Zander into the living room, and Jessie's anxious expression greeted them. Then, in one swift movement, Hal gently pried Lily from Jessie's embrace and deposited the toddler into her grandmother's waiting arms. Ed opened his mouth to speak, but Hal interrupted him by whispering into his ear. Ed sighed and disappeared with Lena and their granddaughter in tow.

With the arrival of Jessie's parents, Ebony could quit procrastinating and get down to business.

Zander perched on the arm of Ebony's chair and crossed his arms over his chest.

"Okay. Here's what we know," Ebony said.

Chapter Two

Ebony's black Explorer screeched to a halt in the parking lot of Kaal Rock Park, and she glanced out of the windshield, not knowing what to expect. She and Zander had initially responded to the codes "10-50" and "10-33" for a vehicle accident requiring immediate attention, but then the dispatch officer had modified the call to report a distressed canoer at the City of Poughkeepsie riverfront park. There were only two other cars in the lot, one with a double *J*-shaped rack on its roof, and there was no boat in sight, only people pacing along the shoreline and milling around on the grass.

The sky was overcast, and the murky gray-green water of the Hudson River churned with white caps. The lack of sun dulled the vibrant copper and red leaves fluttering on the maple and oak trees and the slender grassy strip of the riverside park, washing them as lackluster as Kaal Rock.

The namesake shale outcropping on the northern end of the park was the length of a football field and soared two hundred feet above the ground, almost grazing the underbelly of the eastern leg of the FDR Mid-Hudson Bridge, which dissected the park. The imposing cliff, and its dominion over the Poughkeepsie waterfront, awed Ebony. The landmark lived and breathed and possessed the historical secrets of the region — from the prehistoric glaciers slashing through the valley to the landing of Henry Hudson on this spot over four centuries ago.

There had been proposals in the past few years to revitalize the deteriorating park by creating a promenade along the city's waterfront connecting it with Waryas Park upriver on the far side of the outcropping. Those plans had evaporated, leaving the grounds underutilized, and creating another magnet for nighttime drug deals, sexual liaisons, and gun violence.

Now the mighty rock had borne witness to another potential tragedy, and Zander and Ebony were duty-bound to investigate. In the back of her mind, she knew that this might be their last major case together if they both passed their upcoming promotion exams. But she forced that thought from her mind and focused on the task at hand.

They exited their car, and the hum of the wheels whizzing across the suspension bridge overhead penetrated Ebony's bones like the purr of a cat sleeping on her chest. Downhill from the picnic area, three people had congregated on the rocky shoreline. Two men and a woman pointed toward the bridge stanchions in the deep water while others congregated on the lawn near the sky-blue restroom pavilion, trying to calm a young woman. The brisk breeze conveyed the weight of her heartbreak upwind in their direction, and Ebony steeled herself for whatever horror was about to be revealed.

Ebony and Zander flashed their badges as they approached the nearest group, but before they could introduce themselves, a middle-aged Hispanic couple accosted them. At five feet, nine inches in her bare feet, and with her lug-soled work boots and unruly blonde Afro, Ebony towered over the petite pair. The husband, of an athletic build, sported a finely tailored herringbone blazer, and his thick black hair was sprinkled with silver. His wife was stylishly dressed in a navy cashmere turtleneck, pressed denim slacks, and knee-high boots. She'd pulled her long wavy hair into a low ponytail held in place with a fancy designer scarf.

"Help him, he's out there," the man said, waving toward the water beneath the bridge.

"Who's out there?" Ebony's attention shifted to the river, but she saw nothing.

Shit. A hole opened up in the pit of her stomach. This was more than a capsized canoe.

"Our daughter almost drowned. Please call an ambulance for her right now." The woman glanced toward a young, dark-haired woman who had collapsed on the grass. "She's going to catch pneumonia. Please do something."

The pieces came together in a horrific picture of what had happened. Two people had gone out. Only one had returned. What had happened out there? Where was the other person?

"Keel, Keel!" the young woman wailed, beating the grass with her fists. Despite being wrapped in a thick wool blanket, she trembled uncontrollably, and Ebony thought she heard the woman's teeth rattle as they chattered.

A millennial man and woman knelt beside the hysterical woman, offering her a drink, but she flung it away with a swipe of her hand and pleaded, "Keel! Help Keel! He's in the water." Muffled by tears and gasps, her cries were barely coherent.

"Olivia, honey, calm down. The police are here. They'll find Kyle. Would you like us to locate your phone? Would that make you feel better?" the millennial woman asked.

"My phone?" Olivia glanced up as sparkling droplets trickled down her cheeks. "Where's my phone? Did I lose it? Oh my god, please find it." She began to bawl again.

It was evident that the woman's companion had fallen into the drink, but what the hell was going on? Why were Olivia's companions trying to divert her attention with the phone? Was she more concerned about her phone than the person in the water?

Zander peeled away from the gathering and strode toward the trio at the shoreline. A tall man in an orange puffer vest ran over to him and dragged him closer to the shore. Zander nodded and tipped his head, apparently listening as the speaker gestured toward the middle of the dark water. After extracting his phone from his pocket, Zander snapped a few photos and bowed his head over his phone.

"Do something! Don't just stand there!" The mother's voice rose in volume, drawing Ebony's focus back to the distraught victim.

"Ma'am, an ambulance is on its way, and the fire department is launching the rescue boats parked downriver at the Shadows Marina. Both should be here shortly. Let's try to stay calm." Ebony paused. "How long has Keel been missing?"

"About a half-hour, I think," the mother said.

A half-hour? She and Zander had only received the call about five minutes ago. What had taken this group so long to report the accident? With the chilly water temperatures, hypothermia could set in within minutes, and with the swift current, there was no way to predict where Keel might be. Or whether he was still alive.

She and Zander could assist the survivors onshore, but they were helpless to search the river for the victim. As each second ticked by, the odds of saving the accident victim grew slimmer. Where the hell were the fireboats and ambulance? What was taking them so long?

Ebony's head was spinning. She had a job to accomplish. She needed to investigate the relationships between this woman, her family and friends, and the missing person. And determine whether this had been a horrible accident or whether something more sinister had occurred. Was this Mother Nature's handiwork, human error, or had there been foul play? As visions of feet trampling around the park destroying evidence filled her thoughts, she decided she needed to secure the scene until the other investigators arrived. But before Ebony could commence her investigation, she needed to start at the source and calm the survivor's hysteria.

Ebony exhaled with frustration and knelt beside the sobbing figure. The woman was attractive, in her late twenties, but her burgundy mascara had pooled beneath her blood-shot eyes and streaked her cheeks reddened by tears. She was a survivor of a terrible trauma, one of many whose lives would be altered by this tragic accident.

"My name is Detective Ebony Jones. I'm here with my partner, Zander Pulaski. Do you understand? We're here to help you. I need you to tell me what happened this morning, so let's start with your name. What is it?"

The woman wiped her face with the corner of the blanket and looked toward her. The glazed-over stare disappeared as clarity returned to her hazel eyes. "Olivia. Olivia Vargas."

"She's my daughter," the mother interrupted. "Olivia's too upset to speak right now. Can you wait until after the paramedics examine her? Maybe they can give her something to relax her nerves."

Olivia tugged the blanket tighter around her shoulders. "It's okay, Mamá."

"No, it's not. You've had a terrible shock. There's no reason the detective can't wait."

Ebony immediately read the cues. Left unchecked, an overbearing mother with a passive daughter would insert herself into their investigation, wreaking havoc and impeding the processing of the crime scene. She and Zander needed to assert control over the witness before Mamá got out of hand. "Please, Mrs. Vargas, let me speak to Olivia so we can get this all sorted out."

"But she and her fiancé were out on the river...."

Ebony heard a whistle and glanced up to observe Zander wildly waving his phone. He motioned toward the river, and then she saw it. The bottom of a small, red watercraft, either a canoe or kayak, bobbed in the middle of the river. The current had dragged it downriver about halfway between the bridge and the marina, and it was moving fast. Her vision shifted toward a blue kayak beached on a sandy patch about a hundred yards south of their location. It was lying there peacefully, untouched by the tempest that had attacked the red kayak, as if someone had gently pulled it from the water and tilted it on its side to dry.

"Olivia, you were kayaking on the Hudson, but you weren't alone, were you?"

Olivia shook her wet head and shivered. Her shoulders bobbed up and down as she hiccupped and blew her nose on a silk handkerchief embroidered with the initials *CV*.

"Who were you out there with? What was his name?"

Mrs. Vargas piped in before Olivia could respond. "I told you. She was out there with her fiancé. We'd come down for a family picnic earlier in the morning. It was a beautiful day, and then...."

After five years as a City of Poughkeepsie Detective, the only detective of her sex and color, and one of five women cops on the force, Ebony had learned to halt irritating people dead in their tracks. By being polite and professional, she'd tamed her chauvinistic colleagues, a courtroom of sleazy attorneys, and a slew of uncooperative witnesses, and there was no reason it couldn't happen with Mrs. Vargas. More flies with honey, she thought.

"Mrs. Vargas, I know you're eager to help, but I need to hear Olivia tell the story. We'll take your statement later, and I'm sure you'll be invaluable to our investigation. However, right now, please let Olivia tell me what happened. Otherwise, we're going to have to take her down to the station straight away." Ebony paused, trusting that Olivia's mother had received the warning. Mrs. Vargas uttered an annoyed *humph* and retreated into the arms of her husband. "Olivia, when was the last time you saw your fiancé?"

"We were out in our kayaks when a storm blew in from the west, and the waves knocked Keel into the water. I tried to help him, but he disappeared. I couldn't find him." Olivia covered her face with her hands and slumped forward. "I yelled and yelled." She sobbed again.

"*Mi cariña*, don't worry. They'll find *tu amante*. He's an excellent swimmer. I'm sure he's fine," Mr. Vargas said tenderly, dropping into a crouch beside his daughter. "Do you want Max or Auggie to look for him?"

"Oh, Papa!"

Mr. Vargas stroked his daughter's raw cheeks, and she gazed at him, her wet eyes glistening with hope. Here was a father who doted on his daughter and who would sacrifice anything for his little princess, even the safety of his two sons.

"Sir, that's not going to happen. There's been a suspected drowning, and this area is now an accident scene." At the word *drowning*, Olivia wailed. "There are procedures to follow, so please leave everything as it is. The fire department will be here in a few minutes, and they're trained to deal with marine casualties. As difficult as it is, I need you to remain with your family until our team has questioned Olivia and all the witnesses. Backup will be here shortly to assist with the investigation."

"Detective, I understand. I was just trying—" His voice faded away.

"I appreciate that," Ebony said, bestowing a sympathetic smile. The full-body tension exuded by Mr. Vargas suggested the burden of managing his panic-stricken offspring and his domineering wife. Ebony understood that love and desperation provoked people into doing and saying crazy things to ease the suffering of loved ones. Perhaps the tight father-daughter connection could expedite a clear path to Olivia. So, if Ebony enlisted Mr. Vargas to occupy his wife, she could interview Olivia immediately, preserving the reliability of her witness statement.

A baby's whimper interrupted her thoughts. The whine simmered softly but then exploded into a full-blown siren, echoing off the rock wall sheltering the park. Ebony's focus drifted toward the young woman standing with Zander on the riverbank, cuddling an infant in her arms. Judging from the baby's size, he or she was about a year old. The woman in the orange vest pivoted toward her, and Ebony watched the baby's chubby-cheeked face scrunch up and its body tense in distress. And yowl.

Ebony blinked in disbelief. In her daily life, she had as much contact with kids as she did with cadavers. To her, all babies looked alike, but this kid was different. The dark curly hair. The tiny elfin ears and rosebud lips. The red Nike sneakers she'd given as a baby gift.

Holy crap. It couldn't be.

Chapter Three

Ebony's heart hammered in her chest at the sight of the crying infant. The late summer sun appeared to also recognize the child, bursting through a sliver in the clouds to create a bright patch of green grass. In the middle of the pool of sunlight, a dazzling beam glistened off the baby's dark hair.

"Olivia, please listen carefully. What is your fiancé's name?" Ebony asked.

In her gut, Ebony knew the answer, but she needed Olivia Vargas to confirm her suspicions. *Kyle Emory*. Her thoughts raced, hoping her mind was playing tricks on her. Maybe the baby wasn't Lily Martin, the daughter of her best friend, Jessie.

She scrutinized the physiques of the two men standing with Zander on the rocky riverbank. Maybe Kyle was one of those guys. With the broad shoulders and narrow hips of an Olympic swimmer, the guy wearing an orange vest was taller than Zander's six-foot frame. The other man appeared to be of average height and build, like Kyle, and he was rocking a woolen beanie and plaid shirt like she'd seen Kyle wear.

Even if she eliminated the taller fellow, Ebony was too far away from the group to identify Zander's familiar crooked nose and the two-day stubble on his pointed chin. As a former college basketball shooting guard, she estimated they were standing at least a basketball court and a half away from her—about one hundred and fifty feet. It was far enough away for faces and details to be blurry and for the possibility of a mistaken identity.

Ebony realized she'd sucked in her breath, waiting for Olivia to reveal the name that would alter so many lives, including hers.

14

"Keel. Keel E-mory."

Ebony felt as if her heart had stopped. A dead vacuum filled her chest, and she gulped down the cool, brackish air to fill the emptiness inside her.

"Do you mean Kyle Emory was your fiancé? And that's his daughter Lily over there?" The revelations were steadily becoming a nightmare for the people she loved. Jessie. Hal. Lily. Ed and Lena Martin. The Emory Family. None of them knew it yet, but their world was about to implode.

A shot of adrenaline coursed through her veins. More than ever, they would rely upon her to solve the mystery of Kyle's disappearance, and, although unlikely, bring him home alive. Every prior case had led to this moment. It was her duty, her honor, to serve her friends, her family, and her community, and she refused to disappoint them, and herself.

No matter the obstacles, she'd find Kyle.

A fresh tide of sobs seized Olivia as though crushing her heart and spirit into pebbles like those on the sandy beach where her blue kayak lay. The blonde millennial woman swept Olivia up in her arms, and Olivia buried her face in her friend's chest.

"I wish I was dead," Olivia moaned.

Ebony jumped to her feet, and the blood rushing to her head made her dizzy. She staggered, catching her balance. "Zander!"

Zander stopped his conversation and looked in her direction as she beckoned him to come. They needed to get the complete story from a reliable source, and Mr. Vargas seemed like the logical choice.

"Are you all right, Detective? You look like an *espiritu maligno*, an evil spirit, has paid you a visit," Mr. Vargas said.

"I'm fine. May we have a word with you in private, please?"

"Of course. Please call me Carlos." He turned to the blonde woman embracing Olivia. "Serena, sweetheart, please stay with Oli while Viv and I speak with the detectives."

Zander dashed toward Ebony as she escorted Carlos and Viv to the north side of the blue stucco restroom pavilion, out of the earshot of the rest of their party.

"What did you find out?" Ebony asked Zander. His expression was grave and she could tell he knew that the victim was Kyle Emory. She also knew she could rely upon him to maintain his professionalism, and not reveal her connection to the victim's ex-girlfriend to the witnesses.

"I spoke with Olivia's older brother, Maximo, and his wife, Ana. They reported that at approximately eleven this morning, Olivia and Kyle Emory raced toward the western bridge pier in their kayaks, and then about a half-hour later, a rainsquall appeared out of nowhere. They said that the waves were about four feet high, trapping Olivia and Kyle out on the river. They wanted to stay and make sure Olivia and Kyle were safe, but the wind and the rain were so intense that they had to take cover. The last time they saw the couple, they were heading toward the bridge." Zander paused, and Ebony glanced toward Carlos, who scowled in confirmation.

"Yes," Carlos said. "We arrived to picnic about ten o'clock. Oli and Kyle had brought their kayaks for a quick trip before we went apple-picking across the river in Highland this afternoon. Kyle and Oli left Lily with us while they were out on the river. We thought they'd be gone for twenty minutes while the rest of us set up the food and drink."

"I had a bad feeling about this, and I warned Oli not to bring the kayaks. Did she listen to me? No. And now her fiancé has disappeared. *Mi pobrecita!*" Mrs. Vargas said, choking back the tears.

Zander continued. "Max stated that when the rain started, everyone took shelter in the pavilion to wait out the storm. They were inside for about fifteen minutes."

"And when we came out, we heard screaming and saw Oli paddling toward us, but Kyle was nowhere to be seen. When she reached the shore, she was hysterical and told us Kyle had fallen into the river and been swept away. Then she called 911..." The drone of motorboat engines revving on the river interrupted Carlos.

"You saw her. Oli's usually so happy and full of life, but she's a mess. She's been crying so hard she can't catch her breath," Mrs. Vargas punctuated her words with gestures toward her daughter as though blaming Ebony and Zander for Olivia's ills. "And Kyle, I can't imagine what that poor boy is going through or where he is. Isn't it your job to find him?"

Zander gestured toward the river where the fire department's rescue vessels, the *Marine 1* and *Marine 2,* chugged slowly beneath the bridge heading north and then looped around to return south underneath the bridge span. They appeared to be starting at the center of the river and performing a visual search crisscrossing the surface area in a north-south, east-west grid.

"About time," Mrs. Vargas said with a sharp note of impatience in her voice.

While nothing was going to make Mrs. Vargas happy, Ebony had to agree. Every minute counted in searching for a person in the water, and it seemed like a long time had passed.

"Maybe we'll have some news soon. Did you notice anyone else down here either before or after the accident?" Zander asked.

"No," Mrs. Vargas said. "We were the only ones here all morning." She paused. "But a white SUV drove into the parking lot, turned around, and sped away."

"When was this? Did you recognize the driver?"

"While Kyle and Oli were on the water." Mrs. Vargas' ponytail swished as she shook her head. "No, I didn't. I only noticed them because I had gone to our car to grab a sweater." She waved toward the pearl white BMW sedan that Ebony recognized as one of the pricey new hybrid models. "Maybe they saw me and changed their minds. I did smell marijuana."

The afternoon sun peeked out from behind the clouds, but a brisk breeze served as a reminder of the deadly storm. Ebony tilted her head upward to inspect the underpinnings of the bridge, and then toward the closest bridge stanchion. The stacked stone block piers rose from the choppy, opaque waters and merged with twin steel towers rising two hundred feet above the Hudson to support the bridge deck. She estimated the closest pier was about a third of the way across the bridge, about a thousand feet away from the shore. She knew little about kayaking, but being in a storm on the treacherous river could spell danger for even the most experienced boater.

"Just to confirm the timeline, you folks arrived at the park around—" Zander said.

"Ten," Carlos interrupted. "Kyle and my son Auggie picked Lily up around nine, and we met up at Kelly's Bakery for coffee before coming down here."

"And Kyle and Olivia set out on the river around eleven. The squall hit around eleven-thirty, and the rest of you assembled in the pavilion until eleven-forty-five?"

"That's right," the Vargases replied in unison as Zander scribbled notes on a pad. He glanced up as the wail of sirens announced the approaching emergency medical response team and backup.

"Thanks for your help. Our team is arriving. Wait here. Our colleagues will need to speak with you," Ebony said.

"What about Oli? She needs us," Mrs. Vargas said. Her husband slipped his arm around her shoulder as if to secure her in place, but she shrugged him away.

"Vivanna, she'll be fine. Serena is with her, and the ambulance will arrive in a minute."

Ebony thanked the troubled parents, and she and Zander climbed the concrete steps to greet their team in the parking lot. The vehicles screeched to a halt, leaving a trail of fine dust along the steep driveway leading to the accident scene.

At the top step, she glanced toward the river at Lily Martin cuddled safely in the arms of a stranger. Soon, Lily would be in her arms on the way home to Jessie. Ebony would protect Lily with her life, if necessary, but she couldn't protect her from the pain of growing up without her father. Nobody could.

Chapter Four

The fragile corporeal ties that tethered Jessie to earth slipped away as her body and soul floated to the ceiling of her living room. She was weightless, defying gravity's attempts to strike her down. From her airborne perspective, she observed herself withdraw from the company of Hal, Zander, and Ebony. Her arms reached out to clutch Lily to her breast, and upon discovering them empty, she glanced about wildly, madly, searching for her child.

"Jess?" Hal asked, calling her back to earth. "Are you all right? Lily's fine. She's with your folks in the kitchen." He rose, approached the bookshelf next to the fireplace, withdrew a bottle of brandy from a high shelf, and poured her a generous snifter. "Here, drink this."

She complied, and the sweet syrupy liquor shot a burst of heat through her, melting the iciness permeating her bones.

"Better?" he asked, gently tucking a flyaway curl behind her ear.

"Yes, thanks," she said, turning toward Ebony and Zander. "You said Kyle's kayak capsized in the river, but there's been no sign of him?"

"No. When we left the park, the fire department's rescue skiffs had just arrived to search the area and retrieve his kayak," Ebony said.

"Kyle could be alive. He may have swum to the shore. He could have drifted up or downstream to one of the parklands along the coast," she said. "Are they being searched too?" Jessie paused. "We should go down to the river and help find him. Hal, let's go help. I can't sit here and do nothing."

Jessie could tell from the way Ebony entwined her long fingers and rolled her wrists that she was analyzing what she should reveal and what would remain confidential behind the thin blue line.

"We hope that Kyle survived the storm, but you can't help right now," Ebony said. "Kaal Rock Park and Poughkeepsie's eastern shoreline north to Marist College are accident scenes, and your entry is prohibited. Forensics is processing the scene, the patrol team is interviewing the witnesses, and the fire department has their boats in the vicinity searching for him. There's absolutely nothing you could do, even if you could enter the park. I know it's difficult, but it's best to wait here. Our team will notify us of their progress."

"This is absurd. I want to help. I need to help. Hal, can't you contact Cindie Tarrico and see if there's something we can do? I can't sit around here and wait for the phone to ring."

Jessie had never been good at waiting. She needed to stay active and not let the grass grow beneath her feet. When she and Kyle had been together, she'd been the organizer and the first person ready to go out the door for the evening. He'd been the one primping in front of the mirror while she tapped her wrist as a signal to get going. Kyle remained that way with Lily now, doing things on his own schedule, including *when* he picked her up for visitation. *When* being the operative term for his unreliable parenting.

"We're all worried about Kyle," Hal said. "However, we have to consider the ethics and propriety of requesting a favor from my successor at the DA's office. Regardless of this crisis, it's inappropriate for us to interfere with an ongoing police investigation, and it wouldn't bode well for Cindie, either. We need to sit tight and allow the police to do their job."

Jessie had heard this edict before from Kyle. He'd spoken the same words about a year ago, on the night of her friend Ryan Paige's murder. Kyle had pleaded with her to let the police investigate the crime after her former mentor and high school teacher, Terrence Butterfield, had admitted his guilt to her over the phone. She hadn't listened to Kyle then, and a shit storm had erupted, trapping Jessie in the center. Her misplaced loyalty had cost her a law partnership, her relationship with Kyle, and had threatened her life and the life of her unborn daughter.

But this time was different. This accident involved Kyle. Lily's father.

Although they'd both moved on with their lives, they remained connected by Lily. They'd agreed that Lily would live with Jessie, but Kyle would co-parent with an equal say on the important issues—schools, religious upbringing, sleep schedules, diet—and recently, he'd seemed to accept the responsibility with newfound fervor. She felt like he'd become a participant in Lily's life, not just an observer. If he wasn't found—if he had died—Lily would miss the chance to know him, and Kyle would never experience her growth.

Hal must have noticed her shoulders droop in disappointment, and he added. "I'll call the chief to see if he's requested the drones, the state troopers' divers, or the Coast Guard to search the river."

Ebony shifted in her seat, poised to type additional notes on her phone. "This is a terrible accident, and I know you're in shock, but maybe you could supply some background about Kyle. I only knew him through you."

Ebony had never made her dislike for Kyle a secret. She'd thought he was manipulative and self-absorbed, and that Jessie was compromising by marrying him. Ebony was particularly aggrieved by Kyle's temper tantrums after Jessie had postponed their wedding when she'd discovered she was pregnant. Kyle had needled Jessie about the delay, and he'd been an unsupportive partner, abandoning Jessie during her third trimester. Ebony had repeatedly criticized Kyle's infantile behavior, and despite her good intentions, the disdain had inhibited Jessie from confiding in Ebony as she once had.

"I know nothing about Kyle's background, so maybe you could fill me in," Ebony said. She scratched the back of her neck, where her hair grazed the collar of her leather jacket. "It would be helpful for us to collect medical and dental information about him. Just in case."

Just in case was a poor choice of words. Of course, Ebony and Zander would find Kyle. Perhaps they were withholding a lead, but as a criminal defense attorney, Jessie understood the importance of medical, dental, and DNA information in identifying suspects and bodies. If she could help them, she'd gladly cooperate.

In the past, Ebony had avoided the topic of Kyle Emory, but now that it was essential to her investigation, she wanted to hear all about him, Jessie thought with a mixture of resentment and anxiety. She'd hoped that Ebony would have been more sympathetic or tactful, but Ebony was dedicated to her job, prioritizing it over her family, love, and friendship. While this trait annoyed Jessie and polarized them as friends, she respected Ebony's commitment to the force and her community.

"Do we need to do this now?" Hal asked. "We should spend some time alone as a family."

"No, Hal," Jessie said. "What else are we going to do? Stare at the walls? Watch the news? Surf the net? It'll be a welcome distraction to discuss Kyle, and maybe I can help. What do you want to know?"

"Tell me about Kyle's kayaking ability."

"I didn't know he could kayak or had a kayak. This must be a new hobby." Jessie scoffed. "You should look at our basement. It's loaded with the discards of his former interests—musical instruments, golf clubs, skis, and softball gear. You're welcome to see if there's anything worthwhile down there. But I knew nothing about kayaking... Or his fiancée."

"You once mentioned Kyle grew up on the water. Where exactly?" Zander asked.

"He lived in Albany, but his grandparents owned a house midway up Lake George at Bolton Landing. That's where he spent his summers until he went to college. He talked about boating and fishing with his grandpa and swimming in the lake with his friends. Kyle loved to swim, and he was a strong swimmer." She paused, thinking that his talents might pull him through this trial, landing him safely on a sandbar or park along the river. "I never met his grandfather. He died about six years ago, right after we met. They'd been close, and his death hit Kyle hard."

"Was Kyle prone to depression? Was he on any meds for any medical conditions?" Ebony asked.

"No." Jessie's body tensed at the affront to Kyle's mental stability. He was *not* suicidal. He would never have taken his life. He had so much to live for—Lily, his prestigious vice presidency at the Barclays Center, his new condo in Brooklyn, and resolving their relationship issues. Kyle had started a new life, apparently including a new fiancée. Even if he'd been depressed, which he hadn't been, Jessie never would have confided in Ebony about Kyle's mental health issues. She was too judgmental. "No, he didn't take his own life."

Ebony pressed her lips flat and jotted notes on her phone while Zander scribbled on his notepad.

"I'm serious. We had our disagreements, and Kyle could be a jerk, but he wasn't usually moody or mean-spirited. Lately, he seemed happy, content, and we were getting along great. We'd reached an agreement over Lily's custody and the house, and we were both ready to move on. We'd gotten past the acrimony, and we were becoming friends, or at least friendly."

Hal nodded in agreement.

Jessie's eyes prickled as tears welled up in memory of the man with whom she'd shared the last six years. The guy who'd cried at his grandfather's passing, who'd boldly introduced himself to her at an NYU entertainment law conference, who'd wined and dined her when he was working at Madison Square Garden, and who'd sacrificed his career to accompany her to Poughkeepsie to manage the near-bankrupt Mid-Hudson Civic Center.

No, Jessie thought. She would not shed tears for Kyle. Not yet. Kyle was still alive. He wouldn't kill himself. Kyle could handle the currents of the Hudson and the winds of any storm to come home to Lily.

"Can you tell me about Olivia?" Jessie asked quietly. She nestled against Hal's shoulder, and he slipped his arm around her, drawing her close to him.

"There's not much to tell. We had a preliminary discussion with Olivia Vargas, but since she was in shock, it was difficult to have a cogent conversation." Jessie cocked her head, imploring Ebony to dish on Kyle's new love. "She's in her late twenties, attractive, with an athletic build. She and her family claim she's Kyle's fiancée, although she wasn't wearing an engagement ring."

That was odd, Jessie thought, fingering the two-carat Tiffany engagement ring Hal had given her. Kyle had made their engagement into an extravaganza by popping the question at the MSG center court during halftime

23

at a Knicks' game. His proposal had been unexpected, bewildering Jessie since they'd known each other for less than a year. She'd believed Kyle had been her rebound guy after Hal had broken her heart and married Erin. Yet, when Kyle had dropped to one knee before a crowd of thousands, Jessie had searched her heart. Kyle meant much more to her than a passing fancy, and she'd accepted his proposal, fully committed to him.

Kyle had been sentimental about the antique pear-shaped engagement ring, as it had belonged to his fraternal grandmother. He'd never asked for it back, and she'd locked it away in her jewelry box, assuming he wanted her to keep it safe for Lily. Maybe the return of the ring and his announcing his engagement to Olivia were loose ends Kyle had intended to resolve next week after they signed the settlement papers.

"Have you told his parents yet?" she asked. Kyle was the oldest of three siblings, and his parents, Tom and Bev Emory, would be devastated by the news.

Across the glass coffee table, Ebony fiddled with the badge on her belt. "No, I was hoping you could help me with the task."

Jessie felt as though Ebony had sucker-punched her in the belly. "What? You want me to call them and tell them their son is missing and presumed drowned? Lately, our relationship has been strained, so I'm probably not the best messenger."

"Detective Jones, aren't death notifications a police responsibility? It's presumptuous to put Jessie in such a trying situation." Hal glowered at Ebony. "It seems appropriate that you and Detective Pulaski deliver the news to Kyle's family."

"We thought it would be easier coming from Jessie, but perhaps not. Do you have the Emory's contact information?" Ebony handed Jessie her phone, and Jessie entered Tom and Bev's address and phone number.

Before returning the phone to Ebony, she peeked at the notes inscribed on the screen. Ebony had written the words "blues," "moody," and "temper," cop-speak for depression or bipolar disorder.

"Do you think they knew Kyle was getting married?" Ebony asked.

"We haven't spoken recently, but I'm sure Bev would've mentioned it last week when she called to wish Lily a happy birthday." A sense of bone-weariness drained Jessie of all energy as the stress-induced adrenaline rush waned. Any desire to further cooperate had dissipated at the sight of Ebony's notes intimating Kyle's moodiness and depression, which were completely at odds with Jessie's assertions. "On second thought, we've got a lot to deal with. I think we'd like to be alone for a while, and I'm sure you'll let us know when you hear anything."

"If you could email us any medical information, that would be helpful," Zander said, rising and tucking his pad into the pocket of his slacks. Following his lead, the rest of the group rose. "I'm sorry about this situation, Jessie."

"Let's hope for the best," Jessie replied.

A flicker of sympathy flashed across Ebony's stony features, and she started toward Jessie as though intending to offer her a hug; however, Ebony appeared to change her mind. She turned on her heels and retreated toward the front hallway.

Jessie watched, dumbfounded. At that moment, Jessie needed Ebony to make the first move. She needed her best friend's arms wrapped around her, comforting her and reassuring her everything would be all right. Even if it was a lie. That's how friends supported each other in times of need. Lying to spare the other's feelings. Lying to make things better. Lying to pretend that a dying friendship was alive and thriving.

Lena, Jessie's mom, popped her strawberry-blonde head into the archway of the living room. Her cheeks were flushed, and her makeup was smeared from crying. "Would anyone like coffee or tea?"

"They were just leaving," Jessie said flatly.

"No thanks, Mrs. Martin." Ebony turned toward Jessie. "We're truly sorry about Kyle, and we'll be in touch soon." She and Zander strode across the hallway and out the front door.

Hal leaned against the doorjamb, watching them walk toward their car. "Thanks," he called and waved before shutting the front door.

At the thud of the closing door, Jessie flinched and stroked the gaping hole in her chest. Although it was an illusion, the emptiness and the cold sweat consuming her were real. Chilled to the bone, her limbs trembled as if she was standing naked on a Catskill mountaintop surrounded by swirling snow and bitter winds.

Hal gathered Jessie in his arms and pulled her tight against the soft flannel shirt covering his sturdy chest.

Chapter Five

Cindie Tarrico breathed on the gleaming brass door plaque bearing her name, *Lucinda Raymond Tarrico - Dutchess County District Attorney*, and polished away the fog with the sleeve of her black sweatshirt. She didn't care if the grime stained her clothing; she'd throw them in the washer when she got home later. It had taken the maintenance staff a month to tighten the sign's last screw, and she wanted to make sure her nameplate was as bright and shiny as her enthusiasm about her new promotion.

She scanned the vast suite on the fifth floor of the county annex seeking someone to share in her excitement, but she was alone. Cindie had scheduled the special furniture delivery for Saturday afternoon so as not to interrupt the operation of her department. And to keep nosey staffers out of her business.

Cindie sighed with the pride of accomplishment. With the plaque in place, she finally felt like the District Attorney for Dutchess County in the State of New York. She protected three hundred thousand citizens within the eight hundred twenty-five square mile area situated one-hour upstate from New York City, which included thirty square miles of the majestic Hudson River. Fortunately, Dutchess had experienced fewer violent crimes than its northerly and southerly neighbors of Putnam, Ulster, Orange, and Hudson Counties. However, gun control, drugs, human trafficking, gangs, and assault and battery remained problematic. As the newly minted DA, she would grapple with those pressing issues, along with the rise of hate crimes, robberies, and domestic violence.

Recently, there had been grisly bloodshed during the murder of Ryan Paige, the teenage son of a local business magnate, and the serial killing spree of Duvall Bennett, so she expected Dutchess to skyrocket to the top of the statewide "most crimes" list. Those tragedies had occurred during the tenures of her two predecessors. She was beginning her term of office with a squeaky-clean slate.

When the governor had appointed Hal Samuels to fill a mid-term judicial vacancy in Dutchess County's County Court, Hal had advocated for Cindie to be his replacement. It had shocked her when the governor approved the assignment. As Hal's chief assistant, Hal had mentored her in criminal procedure and trial tactics, and she'd forever be indebted to him. However, he'd left his office a disgusting pigsty. The disarray was unusual for Hal, as he was fastidious in his grooming, his work, and his ethics, but the office space was another story.

Dusty, yellowed *New York Law Journals* collected by his predecessor littered the worn leather couch. The army green metal desk was a rat-chewed monstrosity, and the horsehair stuffing from the visitor's chairs had seeped out, depositing piles of sawdust on the threadbare rug. Even the dust caking the ornate woodwork dated back to the building's construction in the early twentieth century. Cindie guessed Hal had been too busy with his administrative duties to redecorate during his brief, homicide-ridden tenure, but she couldn't tolerate the disarray.

Yesterday, before the installation of her nameplate, she'd enlisted the maintenance guys to strip the office to its bare bones and polish every surface until it glowed. Now, Cindie waited in the lemon-scented room for her new furniture and carpet to arrive. It was empty of its contents, except for the built-in mahogany bookshelves, a few boxes of law books and personal stuff, and the phone console sitting on the floor.

Cindie wanted to make a good impression when her staff, the never-ending stream of criminal defense attorneys, and the county executive came to call. There was no better way than a clean sweep of the past. She didn't want them to stereotype her as a middle-aged fifty-five-year-old poseur who'd inherited the position; rather, she wanted them to see her as a seasoned prosecutor who'd earned the top slot. And one whose exquisite taste meant business.

An hour later, Cindie greeted the delivery staff and directed them to lay the sage green rug and place the Mission-style furniture in exactly the right spots.

"Thanks," she said, slipping the burly lead mover a generous tip as her cellphone vibrated, announcing a text.

Hon, you wanted me to interrupt you and remind you to stop at the cleaners before you head home. Love you, P.

Paul. He was so reliably wonderful. The perfect husband. The perfect dad. And the perfect arm candy for the surrogate judge's retirement bash tonight. Although Paul had packed on a few pounds during their thirty years of marriage, he still had the most gorgeous curly brown hair. They'd make quite a pair as they shimmied on the dance floor tonight; Paul in his tux and she in her black sequined dress cut low enough to be sexy and short enough to showcase her shapely legs.

She texted him a heart emoji, and her phone vibrated again.

"What did you forget, my darling? To remind me about the bagels and cream cheese for breakfast tomorrow?" she asked the phone.

The sender of the new text surprised her. It was from the City of Poughkeepsie Police Chief Matt Shepardson.

Sorry to bother you on the weekend. There's been a boating accident below the bridge at Kaal Rock. Just letting you know we're on the scene. Will update you later. Matt.

It wasn't unusual for her office to prosecute aquatic DWIs, unlicensed operators, and minor collisions, but during her decade in the department, there had never been a serious river accident.

She glanced out her fifth-floor window toward the twin silver towers of the Mid-Hudson Bridge. Gulls and geese soared overhead, and she spied the visible sliver of the serene river below. Although magnificent, the Hudson River could be a giver of life and a taker as well. Sadly, this time it appeared it was the latter.

The alarm on Cindie's smartwatch buzzed. It was three o'clock, and she had plenty of time to prepare for tonight's event. She'd swing by the park after she finished unpacking and before the cleaners and market.

After hanging her nursing and legal diplomas, Cindie arranged the last law books in alphabetical order on the bookshelves, intermixing them with family photos and trinkets her kids had created over the years. Her mother would have called them "dust collectors," but she cherished them as much as her Master's in Nursing and J.D. degrees. She cupped a blue ceramic duck in her palms, recalling her son with curly brown hair like his father's. Her phone rang again.

She blinked twice at the name on the screen and answered.

"Cin? Hi, it's Hal." His voice sounded as tight as a rubber band, ready to snap.

"Hal, nice to hear from you. This is a surprise."

"Sorry to bother you, but we have a family situation, and I'm hoping you might have some information." He paused, and she noted the reluctance in his voice. "We received news that Kyle Emory, Jessie's ex, was in a kayaking accident on the Hudson. All we know is that he became trapped in a storm on the river this morning, and he's missing. Detectives Jones and Pulaski stopped by the house but couldn't give us any details about the accident. I was wondering whether you had any news."

"What? The victim is Kyle? I'm sorry to hear that. Matt Shepardson texted me about a boating accident but said nothing more. I'm at the office, and I was planning to stop by the accident scene on the way home, so I'll call you after that. I'm happy to share any information, so long as it doesn't impact the investigation."

"I understand. I don't want you to violate any ethical boundaries just because it's me. Your job comes first, and I can always bug Matt for updates."

"I'll talk to you later, and please tell Jessie I'm thinking about her and Lily."

"Thanks again. Talk to you later," Hal said and hung up.

Her mouth tasted metallic. She swallowed hard to quell the acid rising in the back of her throat. She'd never met Emory, but she'd heard plenty about him and his shenanigans from Hal. Kyle's parental and financial irresponsibility had nearly driven Hal mad with concern about Jessie.

Regardless, no one deserved to drown. It was a bizarre coincidence that Kyle was the person missing in the Hudson. Once again, Hal was helping Jessie cope with another problem stemming from the deceitful Mr. Emory. No wonder he'd sounded stressed. Cindie wondered whether she would feel more sympathetic if the victim had been a stranger or someone other than Kyle Emory.

She shivered, brushed aside her prejudices, and slapped on her District Attorney hat. In time, Matt Shepardson's team would determine whether a crime was involved.

So much for her clean record.

Chapter Six

A dead silence engulfed Ebony and Zander's SUV on their return trip to Kaal Rock Park. Ebony rested her head against the car window, watching the city whiz by and wrestling with the pinch of guilt that had escalated into full-blown remorse. She needed to do her job, but she should have been more compassionate with Jessie. Being a cop was difficult enough without straddling the fine line between duty and friendship.

She and Jessie had negotiated this dance many times before.

Last year, when their former high school teacher, Terrence Butterfield, had murdered the teenager, Ryan Paige, Jessie's attempts to aid Butterfield had raised questions about her relationship with the murderer and the crime. To dismiss the charges, the defense had claimed that Jessie had violated Butterfield's attorney-client privilege by informing the police about the killing. Although Jessie had been exonerated of all wrongdoing, her interference had almost blown their case, creating a rift between the two friends.

More recently, Ebony had connected the dots in a series of cold cases involving the disappearances of eight prostitutes around the Hudson Valley. Jessie had refused to disclose the whereabouts of her client, a key witness in identifying a suspect linked to the crimes. As a result, the investigation had stalled until Jessie and her client finally relented, enabling the serial killer Duvall Bennett to be brought to justice.

For some reason, she and Jessie never escaped the tension created by their respective roles as cop and defense attorney. Ebony arrested the perps, and Jessie set them free. With Kyle's disappearance, the gulf between them widened.

Ebony shoved the moroseness from her mind. She and Zander had been away from the park for an hour, but it felt like an eternity. Bearing the tragic news had created the sense that time had stopped, but now, they'd returned to the accident scene encompassing a half-mile of waterfront and the entire Hudson River. She was back in the action, where she belonged, rather than focusing on the emotional fallout of the disappearance.

Her team had locked the rusty iron gate into Kaal Rock Park, but when a patrolman recognized them, he shifted the barricade and waved them through. The flurry of activity at the bottom of the hill was reminiscent of a disaster movie. An army of black-and-white patrol cars, the shiny red hook and ladder, and the emergency services vehicles from the Poughkeepsie Engine Company No. 7 firehouse jammed the lot. An ambulance, with its blue and red lights flashing, had parked on the grassy lawn next to the restroom pavilion.

Uniformed patrols had divided the Vargas family members into small groups and were scurrying around, taking statements. The white jumpsuit-clad forensics team had unfurled rolls of bright yellow tape and had staked it along the rocky shoreline. Members of the team were combing the vicinity, taking photographs and videos, and drawing diagrams. At the sandy beach area, a team was loading the blue kayak onto the waiting trailer of a police van.

Out in the river, white caps fractured the brackish surface of the Hudson. The fire department's *Marine 1* zigzagged through the waves beneath the bridge alongside the New York State Troopers Underwater Recovery Team. *Marine 2*, the new rigid-hull inflatable rescue boat, bumped across the choppy surface, aiding in the search and rescue effort. Overhead, the high-pitched whine of a surveillance drone echoed off the tall tower of Kaal Rock.

Near the blue pavilion, the rear doors of the ambulance stood open. Olivia Vargas and her parents perched on its back steps conversing with a paramedic, and Officer Victoria Robinson, another minority sister on the force.

"That was brutal," Zander said as they descended the steps toward the ambulance.

"Brutal doesn't even describe it," Ebony replied before they reached the group. "Vic, any updates?" Ebony respected the full-figured Vic and her down-to-earth warmth when interviewing crime victims. She stifled a smirk, recalling Vic's wicked sense of humor at last year's holiday bash and Vic's shameless razzing of their brothers in blue, including the chief.

"They've retrieved the victim's red kayak, but they haven't found Mr. Emory yet. The divers have been deployed for the search and rescue operation. When you get a chance, give the chief a call. He's looking for a status report from you."

"Detective," Carlos Vargas said cheerfully, interrupting them. He stretched his arm to pat Zander's shoulder in a fraternal fashion. "Did you deliver Lily to her mother? I'm sure she was distraught at the news. We've never met Jessica, but Kyle has told us how dedicated she is to their daughter. We hope she has family to support her during this terrible ordeal." His lips curled into an ingratiating smile. "We mentioned to Officer Robinson that our daughter is freezing and in shock, and we'd like to take her home. She's starting to exhibit symptoms of hypothermia."

The paramedic grimaced and shook her head.

Carlos Vargas' words contained the undertone of a command rather than a request, and it was apparent he was used to controlling the situation. While Zander had waited outside Jessie's house for Ebony, he'd run a preliminary background check on the Vargases, and so far, he'd only received the reports on the parents. Carlos Vargas was the vice president of a global program for an international pharmaceutical firm in Tarrytown, N.Y., and was an MD and had a Ph.D. in chemistry. He and his wife, Vivianna, an oil painter renowned for her colorful, abstract depictions of modern Hispanic life, lived in upscale Garrison, N.Y.

"Dr. Vargas, I'm sure Officer Robinson has been thorough, but we'd like to speak with Olivia before we let you leave." When Carlos stood firm in his place, Ebony added, "Alone, please."

The request wasn't unreasonable or overreaching. Olivia seemed more calm and alert than when they'd last seen her. Her cheeks were raw from crying, but the glassiness had vanished from her bloodshot eyes. She'd shed her wet clothing, which had been sealed in an evidence bag, and had changed into Tyvek police coveralls.

The afternoon was warm and breezy, more long sleeve T-shirt than windbreaker weather. Yet, swaddled in a metallic Mylar blanket, Olivia shivered uncontrollably. Ebony suspected the woman's overreaction was designed to manipulate her doting parents.

"We understand, detective. We're happy to cooperate with your investigation. But please, Oli's had a terrific shock, and we don't want her to become ill." Carlos kissed his daughter on the forehead. "*Mi cariña*, we'll be with Max. If you need anything, just call." The Vargases trotted toward their son and daughter-in-law, who were being interviewed by another officer at a nearby picnic table.

"Olivia, Detective Pulaski, and I are sorry for your loss. I knew Kyle. He was a good guy and a good father. Neither you nor he deserved to get trapped in the storm, and we will do everything we can to find him. However, we need your help to put the puzzle pieces together. Do you feel up to it?"

When Olivia batted her hazel eyes and nodded, Ebony directed Officer Robinson to take notes of their conversation and for Zander to press the record button on his phone. He set it beside Olivia on the ambulance steps.

"Olivia, my name is Detective Ebony Jones, and as I already mentioned, this is my partner, Detective Zander Pulaski. We are going to ask you questions about the boating accident that occurred today. Do we have your permission to record this conversation?"

Olivia nodded again.

"We need you to say 'yes' or 'no' for the recording. Okay?"

"Yes, detective, you have my permission."

"Let's start with some background information. What can you tell us about your relationship with Kyle? How did you meet?"

Although she smiled, a single tear rolled down her cheek. "Do you see the couple standing with my brother, Auggie?"

Ebony observed the millennial couple sitting atop a picnic table covered with the remnants of the spoiled outing. They clutched each other, and the beanie guy paced frenetically alongside.

"Well, it's a sweet story. Kyle and I met at their destination wedding last March in Bermuda. The groom was Kyle's college roommate, and the bride was my cousin, Serena. Kyle was a groomsman, and I was in the bridal party. Like a *Hallmark* movie, we fell in love. It all happened lightning-fast." Olivia paused, and the color drained from her flawless olive skin. "Oh, my god. Kyle is gone." Her shoulders shook as she broke into a fit of sobs.

Zander, Ebony, and Officer Vic exchanged worried glances, not knowing how to react.

"Ms. Vargas," Officer Vic said, assuming a seat beside Olivia and clasping the woman's hands. "We're doing everything we can to find Kyle. There's a massive area to search, and he may be okay. Let's think positively until we have reason to believe otherwise."

Robinson's speech seemed to reassure Olivia. She wiped her swollen eyes, and continued. "What were you asking me?"

"About you and Kyle," Ebony said. "When did you become engaged?"

"Again, it was really sudden. We got engaged over Labor Day at my family's barbeque."

"Did you set a date?"

"I'm freezing. Is it possible to get some tea or coffee?" Ebony signaled to a nearby paramedic, who left to fetch the coffee. "I'm sorry. I don't know if it's my nerves or being in the storm, or losing Kyle. The whole situation seems so unreal. One minute we're gliding along having fun, and the next, there's a thunderstorm, and he's in the water." The paramedic returned with a steaming cup of coffee and another shiny Mylar blanket. Olivia wrapped the blanket around her shoulders and took a long sip from the paper cup.

"Hon, there's no need to apologize. Just take your time and relax. We know you're upset and want to go home. You'll be there soon enough," Officer Vic said.

"What can you tell us about the events this morning?" Ebony asked.

"I already told Officer Robinson the whole story."

"We know it's difficult, but we'd like to hear it. If you don't mind?" Zander asked.

"My family arrived at the park around ten, after Kyle had stopped to get Lily. I didn't go with Kyle for the pickup because I haven't met Lily's mom yet. Kyle met us at Kelly's Bakery, and we came here. About a half-hour later, Kyle suggested we paddle out on the river, and he bet me he could beat me out to the bridge tower. We unloaded the kayaks and set off from the sandy shore. Over there, where my kayak was." Olivia gestured downriver past the red kayak on the trailer.

"As we reached the stanchion, a storm came out of nowhere. The waves were over our heads, and we tried to stay together, but the wind blew us apart. Before I knew it, Kyle was splashing around in the water, calling for help. And then he was gone." Olivia's breath hitched as she blinked to hold back the tears. "I looked everywhere. I called his name, but the wind was howling. With the rain coming down in sheets and the enormous waves, I could barely see ahead of me, and I clung to the pier for my life. When the storm died down, I saw Kyle's kayak had capsized. But I didn't see him anywhere. I didn't know what to do. I couldn't abandon him, so I paddled around, looking for him and screaming his name. After a while, the sky darkened again, and I was afraid of another storm blowing in. So, I gave up and paddled back in. Then I called for help." Olivia rocked back and forth as the tears returned. "It's all my fault. I never should've left him. We were going to start a life together, and now he's gone."

"Honey, it's not your fault," Officer Vic said. "It was an accident. You couldn't have prevented it, and your life was in danger, too. You're lucky to be alive."

"I realize I'm lucky, but Kyle isn't."

"We don't know that," Officer Vic said, her voice sympathetic.

"I know. I was the one on the river with him. One minute, Kyle was there. And the next, he wasn't." Olivia pointed to the fire rescue boats on the river, which had been joined in the hunt by civilian outboards, sailboats, and cabin cruisers. Her face turned a greenish-gray, and tears streamed down her face. "Look out there. It's been hours." She sniffled. "If they'd found Kyle, they wouldn't still be searching. Kyle's gone. He's gone." Olivia exploded into hysteria, and her parents charged back to her side. Swept up in her mother's arms, Olivia buried her face in her mother's bosom, overcome with breathless sobs.

"Detectives, don't you think Oli's been through enough for one day? If you insist on continuing, I'm going to contact your boss and our attorney to complain about this harassment," Dr. Vargas said. His wife caressed their stricken daughter and sneered at them.

"Sir, we mean no disrespect," Zander said, stopping the recording on his phone. He seemed to sense that his words bore more weight than those coming from either Ebony or Vic, the two female cops. "We have your contact information, so we'll let you go now. I'm assuming Olivia will stay with you for the time being, so we can schedule an interview at a later time." Zander handed his business card to Vargas. "We'll be in touch if we have any news, and if you need anything or have questions, please contact me."

Carlos Vargas smiled smugly as though the two men had reached a silent understanding. "Come, *mi cariña*. Let's go home."

"Mamá, how do I look? Is my face puffy and red?" Olivia's voice whined. "I don't want anyone to see me like this." She ran her fingers through her disheveled hair as she jumped down from the ambulance steps.

"No, *mi querida*. Don't worry, you look fine," Mrs. Vargas replied.

Vargas, his wife, and Olivia huddled together as they shuffled toward the white BMW Sedan in the parking lot.

"It takes all kinds," Vic mumbled under her breath.

Ebony and Zander exchanged a glance with a raised eyebrow.

Perhaps the trauma had warped Olivia's mind, but her anxiety over her personal appearance was wildly out of character for someone who had just lost her fiancé. She acted as if the media awaited her, and so far, Ebony believed the police department had kept the press at bay.

Before getting into the car, Olivia glanced back at them, and one corner of her lip twisted into a smirk.

CHAPTER SIX

Something's off here, Ebony thought. Olivia's shifting reactions to Kyle's disappearance had piqued her suspicions. One minute Olivia was grieving and distraught, and the next, she was worried about her lost phone. She and Zander needed to know more about Olivia Vargas, her relationship to Kyle, and the Vargas clan. Hopefully, her team had collected sufficient evidence to jumpstart their investigation.

Chapter Seven

The metallic quarter-hour chime of the grandfather clock reminded Jessie of the seconds, minutes, and hours passing without news about Kyle. It had been three hours since Ebony and Zander's departure, and the wait was as excruciating as anything she'd ever experienced. Like the sweeping hands on the clock, her emotions had cycled through denial, helplessness, panic, numbness, and back to denial again. None of them plugged the gaping hole in her chest. Or stopped the sorrow in her heart for the people Kyle had left behind—his parents, his siblings, and Lily.

But she'd never surrendered to acceptance. She'd never believe Kyle was dead until they'd identified his body. With no body, hope remained. And Jessie clung to hope like a buoy.

As a distraction, Jessie busied herself with mundane household chores and settling Lily down for a nap, doing anything to keep from thinking about Kyle or discussing him with her parents and Hal. Fortunately, Hal and her father had been shocked into silence, but her mother could talk any topic to death. Especially Kyle, which was the last thing Jessie desired. Her father and Hal's hovering weren't helping either.

Seeking refuge in the basement, Jessie grabbed the damp laundry from the washer and pitched it into the dryer. She examined a tiny top with the words "Daddy's Girl" embroidered over a pink tiger. Last week, Kyle had blinked away the tears when Lily had called him "Da," and only days ago, he'd bought the frilly pint-sized shirt.

Maybe he'd finally gotten the hang of being a parent, she thought.

Tossing the shirt into the dryer, Jessie steeled herself not to cry. There was nothing to cry about until she had more information. Then she'd let the tears flow freely. Hopefully, tears of relief.

They had to find him. He was Lily's father, and Lily couldn't grow up fatherless. And Jessie couldn't live without harmony between them. She wanted Lily to grow up surrounded by a loving, caring family, as she had, with two parents rooting for her along the way.

"Please, God. Please bring Kyle home safely." She promised if they found Kyle alive, she'd work harder to make their relationship better, stronger. "Please let Lily see her father again."

The doorbell rang, and Jessie sprang up the basement steps to answer the front door. It was probably Kyle's parents, who had texted they were driving down from upstate.

Bev and Tom Emory stood on the front porch looking stunned and exhausted. At their feet sat a pair of worn overnight suitcases. Their grief-stricken faces begged for entry, which Jessie couldn't refuse. They were family—Lily's grandparents. Despite strained relations, Tom and Bev were welcome in her home. Perhaps Lily's boundless energy and bubbly personality were the panacea everyone needed to survive the trial ahead of them.

Bev stepped forward and enveloped Jessie in her plump arms, inviting Jessie's tears to fall. Jessie couldn't refuse.

Ed appeared, grabbed the bags, and ushered Tom into the foyer. "How was the drive from Albany?" he asked, shutting the door behind them.

"Not much traffic on the Thruway, so we made excellent time. An hour and seventeen minutes," Tom said, examining his military field watch. Lanky Tom Emory, with his sparse white hair, reminded Jessie of the stiff, bespectacled farmer in Grant Wood's painting, *American Gothic*. In contrast to her easygoing father, Tom spoke with the precision of a man specializing in mechanical engineering. He stuck to the facts and only expressed opinions supported by science. Kyle used to joke that living with his father was like having the IBM Watson computer as his parent.

"Come into the kitchen. Lena's got a pot of coffee on," Ed said. Without waiting for an answer, he seized Tom's elbow and spirited him away.

Bev Emory was the opposite of her husband. She was a round, squishy ball of hugs and love, but you didn't want her as an enemy. Then, Bev transformed into a vicious, unforgiving tiger mom, swiping her claws at anyone threatening her clan.

Jessie had dodged Bev's nasty swats after she'd postponed her wedding to Kyle, had refused to give Lily Kyle's surname, and again when she and Kyle had split up. Nevertheless, the crushing tightness of Bev's embrace seemed to declare a détente.

After several minutes of rocking in mutual grief, Jessie extricated herself from Bev's crushing clinch. "I'm so glad you came down. Of course, you're welcome to stay for as long as you like." She wiped her wet cheeks with her sleeve. "How did you find out about Kyle?"

Bev whipped off her tartan cape to reveal a stretchy paisley jersey tunic and black leggings, which exaggerated her plump figure. In her early sixties, Bev had let her hair go gray. Her roots were silver, and she'd dyed the bottom half of her curly bob a startling henna color. No one could say Bev Emory embraced life quietly.

"Two sheriffs from Albany County came to tell us. Tom knew one of them from the fish and game club, and they were very kind. But they couldn't give us any details, except that Kyle had been in a kayaking accident early this morning, and he was missing. Have you heard anything?"

Jessie guided Bev into the den and plopped down cross-legged on the soft leather sofa. She gestured for Bev to join her, which she did.

"Nothing since two detectives brought Lily home around noontime. This morning, Kyle picked Lily up around nine to spend the day with her. The detectives mentioned Kyle had gotten caught up in a storm when he'd been kayaking on the Hudson with his fiancée and her family down at Kaal Rock Park."

Bev's eyebrows flew up, and her mouth dropped open. "His what?"

"His fiancée? You don't know her? Her name is Olivia Vargas, and that's all I know about her."

"That's impossible. Kyle would've told us about her or at least mentioned her to Dani and Petey. Those three are thick as thieves, but they can't keep secrets from their old mother. Especially Dani. I spoke with her and Petey and asked them not to come until we hear something."

Jessie silently sighed with relief at the respite from entertaining Kyle's younger siblings. The fraternal twins were another example of Emory opposites, while Kyle was a combination of his folks. Danielle mimicked their outgoing mom, while Pete mirrored their stern mathematical dad. She had preferred hanging out with fun-loving Dani, who ran a recording studio in White Plains and always had the latest entertainment gossip, rather than droll Pete, who was in construction management in Buffalo.

"How are they taking it?"

"You know Petey. He didn't utter a peep while Dani blubbered like a baby. Speaking of babies, where's Lily?"

"She's napping, but she'll be up soon. Let's join my parents and Tom in the kitchen. Come on," Jessie said, rising from the couch. Inside her pocket, her phone vibrated. She withdrew it, and when Ebony's caller ID appeared, she answered it. "Hey, Eb. What's going on? Have you found Kyle?"

She listened to Ebony's update. They'd retrieved both kayaks, and the forensics team was processing the vessels. Olivia's family had provided preliminary statements about the accidents and had confirmed they'd introduced Kyle to kayaking in early summer.

"Jessie, apparently Olivia and Kyle met at a wedding in Bermuda last March. His college roommate got hitched to Olivia's cousin, and according to Olivia, it was love at first sight." Jessie kept her face expressionless as Ebony expelled a long exhalation. "Then they got engaged two weeks ago over Labor Day. It seemed like the wedding was on the fast track."

Fast track? Kyle wasn't impulsive. He was the opposite—excruciatingly slow about every decision they'd made together. Kyle reminded her of a crab, plodding in every direction except straight ahead. Never taking the direct path. Lily's unplanned but joyous arrival had thrown Kyle into a tizzy for weeks. Gradually, he'd accepted the idea of having a child, but he'd never fully committed to the responsibility.

And he was frugal. When planning their wedding or buying the house, she'd had to balance their checkbook twice before he acted. He'd driven her mad.

Then it dawned on Jessie. Olivia could be pregnant. Was a new baby the reason for the rush to the altar?

As her thoughts stumbled around the possibility, Jessie blurted out, "I remember the wedding because Kyle canceled his visit at the last minute as usual." Oops, Jessie thought. Her eyes darted toward Bev, who had pursed her lips at the snide remark. "Is there anything else?"

"Sorry. It's going to take time to review the witness statements and examine the evidence, and the divers are still scouring the river. The water's choppy today, and they're trying to cover as much water as possible before dark. I'll let you know as soon as I hear anything."

"Can you answer a question for me? Your team has been out on the river for at least four hours. Are you still considering it a search and rescue, or has it become a recovery mission? Please be honest with me."

"As you said, it's only been four hours, and it's too early to make that call. Keep the faith, will you?"

Jessie's attention drifted out the den's window. Outside, the sun shone brightly, and the gentle breeze stirred the red and gold-tinted maple trees in the yard. The days remained long, with sunset around seven o'clock. There was still plenty of time to find Kyle before nightfall.

"Thanks. And the Emorys are with me, in case you're looking for them."

"We're shorthanded, and with the accident investigation monopolizing our staff, the chief alerted the Albany Sheriff to contact the Emorys. I'm glad they're with you. How are they doing?"

"As well as can be expected. Eb, thanks for calling, and we're standing by."

"I know it's rough, but hang in there." An awkward silence suggested that Ebony desired to add something more intimate, but she didn't. Again.

It was best to end the conversation before it became even weirder, Jessie thought. "Take care."

"You, too."

Click. The line went dead.

Bev's doe-colored irises drilled into Jessie with the burning question. "Any good news?"

"Sorry. Nothing we don't already know."

Bev had a right to know about Kyle and Olivia's relationship. But Jessie would keep the rushed engagement, her suspicions about their urgency, and Ebony's suicide theory to herself. There was no reason to upset Bev further, not until Jessie knew more.

The room darkened, and Jessie's vision pivoted back out the window as the blue sky vanished. A single black storm cloud passed over the sun, stealing the sunlight. In the yard, a brisk wind kicked up, making the maple leaves shiver and reveal their light undersides.

Inside the warm den, a chill crept up Jessie's spine. Another tempest brewed within her home, threatening to devastate everyone who knew and loved Kyle.

For whatever reason, Kyle had kept parts of his new life hidden from his parents and from her. When they'd lived together, Jessie had believed she and Kyle had been open and honest with each other. Her love had blinded her, and it wasn't until their relationship ended that she learned about Kyle's true nature. He'd been a man of secrets and lies. A master of the art of deception, and his concealing his engagement was another example of the same old deceit.

Those secrets and lies had shattered their relationship. Now, in all likelihood, they had destroyed his life.

Chapter Eight

Evening swiftly approached. Across from Kaal Rock Park, the sun dipped behind the rolling crests of the Hudson Highlands, skirting the western bank of the river, setting the sky afire in a gold and blue glow. On the shore, Ebony shaded the glare with her hands, observing the flotilla of law enforcement boats disbanding for the night. Some sped north toward Hyde Park, Norrie Point, and Kingston, while others turned downriver to the marinas in Poughkeepsie and New Hamburg, leaving a crosshatch across the black waves.

The search had been suspended for two reasons. First, after seven hours of combing every quadrant of the river beneath the bridge, they'd abandoned hope of finding Kyle alive. And the second, the bright underwater searchlights couldn't penetrate the murky river, rendering their efforts useless. Even during the bright sunlight, the tidal river's opaqueness inhibited divers from seeing their hands in front of their faces. At night, it would be impossible.

Ebony's limbs were heavy, as though her body was being compressed into the rocky shore beneath her feet. There would be no good news to share with Jessie tonight.

"Hey, we'll know more shortly," Zander said. He nudged her shoulder and gestured toward the police vessels heading homeward.

Boats belonging to the New York State Police Marine Unit's Underwater Recovery Team and the City of Poughkeepsie Fire Department sped past them on the way to the Shadows Marina a half-mile south of Kaal Rock. The last remnants of sunlight glinted off the state's slick aluminum craft with a cabin large enough to accommodate a team of divers, winches, radar, and sonar equipment. Following behind, *Marine 1*, the city's fiberglass skiff, was half its size. Yet, with two GPS fish finders, thermal imagery, side sonars, radar, and four crewmembers on board, it led the search team in this recovery operation.

Ebony's firefighter boyfriend, Drew Johnston, was assigned to the Hooker Avenue firehouse that manned *Marine 1* from Memorial Day to Labor Day, so she knew the ship and its crew. Drew had mentioned that so far this year, the fire department had assisted over fifty stranded sailboats, cruisers, and jet skiers who had suffered mechanical troubles or had run out of gas on the river. The fireboat never used to answer those distress calls because they provided emergency services, not law enforcement or water safety patrols. But this summer, *Marine 1* had been on duty 24/7. And it seemed to her that Drew had been, too.

Since their colleagues were wrapping up for the evening, Ebony and Zander hustled down to the marina to meet *Marine 1* as she arrived. Drew would be onboard, and he could provide them with an update on their progress.

They parked in the lot next to the pair of idling fire department rigs assigned to the investigation. The dock's lights flicked on as Ebony and Zander strode down the metal gangway onto the narrow floating platform serving as *Marine 1's* berth for the season. The floating dock's slick deck pitched and rolled in the boat's wake.

Beside her, the sure-footed Zander posed with his pricey Italian loafers casually spread apart as she struggled to maintain her balance on the slippery surface. She rolled her weight to avoid any sudden jolts to her bum left hip and being tossed into the river.

Gathering her nerve, Ebony peeked over the edge of the dock. Her knees buckled at the sight of her muted reflection in the grey-green surface. Water can be so beautiful, yet so destructive, she thought, shivering to ward off the chill snaking up her spine. Ever since she was a kid, opaque water had given her the creeps. She was a solid swimmer in pools or the clear, bathtub-warm waters of the Caribbean, but not in dark water. She needed to see her feet, touch a solid surface, or feel the sand between her toes. The Hudson offered none of those securities.

The night sky had turned blue-black, and the onboard spotlights of the shiny crafts approached, accompanied by the oily smell of diesel and the putt-putt of engines.

Marine 1 entered the docking range, and Ebony stepped out of Drew's way as he hopped off the skiff to tie up the boat. Drew's firm hands easily caught the rope thrown by his crewmate, and he guided the ship into dock as the captain cut the motor. Growing up in Coastal South Carolina, he'd been raised on boating and was proficient with maritime bowline knots and clove hitches, a talent Ebony found exciting in the bedroom. Drew tugged on the rear rope, pulling the boat toward him.

"Hey, toss me the line," Zander shouted. Catching it, he expertly tied the rope to the port stern cleat attached to the pitching dock.

"Impressive. You are full of surprises, aren't you?" Ebony asked.

"All part of my Boy Scout training," Zander said.

The state troopers' boat entered a slip farther down the platform, and her exhausted divers spilled onto the dock. They stripped off their scuba gear and tanks and grumbled in low voices.

"Hey, Sugar. I'm surprised to see you here," Drew said. He was referring to his pet name for her, Sugar Boo. It was his intimate reference to her sexual prowess; that she came as slow and sweet as brown molasses. "Zander, dude, what's up?"

Since last week, Drew had been on-duty at the station house, and this was the first time she'd seen him in days. Her pulse raced at the sight of him, and she gave Drew a peck on the cheek and then peeked into the boat's illuminated back deck. A red kayak lay tipped on its side in a pool of water. It appeared to be intact, with no visible signs of storm or accident damage.

"We fished the kayak out of the water, but no operator." Drew frowned. "We arrived around twelve-fifteen, right, Tim?" He deferred to Lieutenant Timothy Decatur, *Marine 1's* Captain. His commander nodded. "We were on the river for six and a half hours before we called off the search for the night. Our sonar and thermal scans showed nothing. No body. No clothing. Only the usual—fish." He straightened a boat bumper to ensure the siding of the boat didn't scrape against the dock's metal edging. "The drone found nothing, either. And with the water temps being seventy degrees, hypothermia could've set in after two hours of being in the water. Maybe Emory could've lasted longer if he'd been properly dressed."

Images of Olivia, wet and shivering beneath the blanket, popped into Ebony's mind.

Drew's crewmates appeared sedate as they buttoned down the boat for the evening. They slipped on latex gloves and loaded the kayak into a massive transparent plastic evidence bag. After sealing it, they lifted it onto the deck.

"Couldn't you have stayed out on the water longer?" Ebony asked.

"The water was choppy, and we struggled against the whitecaps. Between the dwindling light, the strong incoming tide, and the water being as thick as pea soup even during daylight, we weren't making any headway. Best to call it a night."

"Did the divers find anything?" Zander jumped to accommodate the sharp rise and fall of the deck caused by the wake of a cabin cruiser pulling into port.

"Not that I know of. I don't know if you're familiar with the topography of the river." Zander shook his head. "The Hudson is a deep-centered channel river. About seventy feet in from the shoreline, the water's twenty to forty feet deep, but then there's a steep drop-off to three hundred feet in the center. The Hudson makes such a good commercial waterway because it can accommodate huge tankers, like the ones that travel up to Albany carrying oil. Like that one." Drew motioned toward the shadow of a tugboat with its blinking white lights and purring motor, pushing a mammoth barge the length of a city block upriver. "Unfortunately, the victim capsized beneath the bridge in the deep channel zone. You can't see anything in the murky water. As a result, it would be tough for divers to find him, even with their infrared technology. That's not what you wanted to hear, is it?"

"So, it's not a rescue. It's a recovery?" The question was rhetorical, but Ebony needed to ask it.

"I'm sorry," Drew whispered.

The fine hairs on Ebony's arms prickled in response, and she rubbed her arms for comfort.

There was nothing else to say. Kyle was presumed drowned.

"Any chance we can review your sonar readings and data?" Zander asked.

"Sure, I'll email them to you later, okay? We need to finish up with *Marine*."

"Are you and the divers going back out tomorrow? You're not giving up?" Ebony didn't bother to hide the desperation in her voice. Both Zander and Drew understood what was at stake.

"No way. We'll be back at the crack of dawn. So I'm going to crash at the firehouse tonight. You don't mind, do you, Sugar?"

Of course, Ebony minded. For the past few months, they'd been working hard on rekindling their romance, which was strained by their demanding work schedules. She balked at the idea that this would be the fourth night in a row he'd stayed away overnight. But she had no choice in the matter. His job was his job.

She didn't enjoy sleeping alone and was too wired to sleep tonight. Plus, their hundred-pound shepherd would hog the bed, anyway. When Drew wasn't home, Wrangler took advantage and curled up beside her on the bed, and Ebony never had the heart to boot him off.

This wasn't the time to discuss their domestic issues, so she shook her head again. "I'll miss you."

"I'll miss you, too. But I know you've got that mutt keeping you warm." She gaped at her fireman, mocking shock. "Yeah, from his fur on the blanket, I know all about that hairy beast hogging my side of the bed."

"Now, kids. Play nice. If there's nothing more, we'd better return to the station and clock out," Zander said, checking the time on his smartwatch.

"You're right. We should log out before the chief wants us to do something else." This time, Ebony kissed Drew on the lips and waved to his mates. "Night, sweets. I'll talk to you later. Bye, guys."

The firefighters interrupted their cleaning to wave back at her.

At the foot of the gangway, she stopped to admire the view. Tonight was a new moon, so the sky was pitch black. The red, white, blue, and green lights outlining the top cable of the Mid-Hudson Bridge twinkled in the darkness. The headlights of cars and trucks streaming across the bridge deck drew a delicate white line from the east to the west, and the floodlit bridge towers shone like ancient steely giants guarding the shorelines.

Just north of the Mid-Hudson Bridge, a pearly necklace of lights illuminated the Walkway Over the Hudson pedestrian bridge from shore to shore. She could barely discern the American flag flapping in the breeze midway over the river.

She exhaled slowly, releasing the tensions of the day from her body. The Mid-Hudson Bridge appeared to be floating upon a bed of inky blue water streaked with reflections of the rainbow lights. The bridges, river, and night were amazing. She wanted to remain in this spot forever, silently soaking in the valley's splendor surrounding her, but the beauty of the night was marred by Kyle's disappearance in the deep water beneath the shimmering lights. While they admired the view, Kyle couldn't, and he might never enjoy this magnificent sight again.

Ebony believed Kyle was out there somewhere, but where? How could such beauty hide death within the depths? Would the divers ever find him? Had the current sucked Kyle into the bottomless channel? Or had the fickle estuary swept his body out to sea? Beneath the pearly lights on its surface, what secrets was the river keeping?

An icy wind kicked up, twisting her thoughts as dusky as the night.

"Eb, are you coming?" Zander asked, his voice sounding far away.

The lapping of the water on the rocky shore returned Ebony to the present and the tragedy it held. As she followed Zander across the creaking gangway to their car, she wondered what she was going to tell Jessie.

Chapter Nine

Cindie admired her new digs one last time before she left, shutting the door with the new nameplate. As she turned the key in the lock, the phone rang again. It was Paul.

"Cin, I heard a call over the police scanner about an accident on the river."

Paul and his ridiculous scanner. Ever since he'd been selected as the neighborhood watch captain, his ears had been glued to the device. With their neighborhood under siege from a barrage of catalytic converter thefts, he saw danger everywhere. Nowhere was safe anymore.

"Matt called about a boating accident on the Hudson, and, yes, I'm going to stop by Kaal Rock. Don't worry, I won't be late for the party."

"No worries. Just be safe. I worry when you visit crime scenes."

"I know, but it's a potential drowning, not a homicide. I'll fill you in when I get home," she said. "Gotta go."

Since her errands were located uptown, she'd head there first. Then she'd hit Kaal Rock Park as her final destination, leaving plenty of time to head home and dress for the banquet.

It was nearly seven o'clock by the time she pulled into Kaal Rock Park, where she stumbled upon an atypical accident scene. By the time she'd arrived, the witnesses had been dismissed, and emergency services had departed, but the forensic team and a team of patrol officers, photographers, and technicians were still scouring the shoreline. On the river, the aquatic teams were disbursing and heading home. From the controlled chaos, it appeared as though the entire Hudson River had become the accident scene.

Cindie pinned her DA's shield to her denim jacket, wondering how anyone could possibly process a river as an accident or crime scene? The first question was, had a crime been committed? So far, there was no proof of one; everything pointed toward a horrible accident.

The unique fact pattern of the missing kayaker sounded like an exam question from law school. Is there a crime without a victim? Was there a crime with no wrongdoing? Did a crime exist without the four elements of a crime? To establish a crime, there needed to be: 1) a criminal act, 2) a criminal intent, 3) concurrence of the act and intent, and 4) a causal relationship between the criminal act and the end result.

They didn't have answers to some of those questions. Not yet.

Hal had mentioned when the noontime thunderstorm had blown in, the weather had capsized Kyle Emory's kayak. Had there been a criminal act? No one knew. On the surface, there appeared to be no crime, only a boating accident. A senseless and avoidable catastrophe. Regardless, it was a tragedy the police and the marine patrols were mandated to investigate.

It was far too early to drag her investigators into the fray. Her department was already overburdened with prosecuting incidents exhibiting all four of the criminal elements.

If, as Cindie believed, Mother Nature had been responsible for Kyle's disappearance, her department would never become involved.

For friendship's sake, she'd ask a few questions and hopefully get definitive answers to pass along to Hal. Jessie's family was going through hell, and it was the least she could do as a friend and a colleague.

In the gathering darkness, Cindie approached a tech in a white hazmat jumpsuit crouched at the water's edge, sifting through the silt of a sandy beach area. "Find anything?"

The young woman lost her balance and tumbled back into the water. "Crap!" she yelled.

"Sorry about that. I didn't mean to frighten you. You looked so intense, like you'd found something." Cindie extended her hand and pulled the woman to her feet.

"It's okay. Falling into the Hudson is better than landing in a pile of manure at a local dairy farm," the tech said and gave a light, airy laugh.

Her bespectacled eyes peering above a respirator mask pivoted to Cindie's badge, and she added, "Ma'am. I'm Officer Maya Moore."

"What did you find?" Cindie prodded.

Maya motioned a blue glove toward the ground. "You can see the grooves in the sand. It's the track from the fiancée's kayak."

"What fiancée? Can you bring me up to speed? All I've been told is there was a presumed drowning."

Moore explained the circumstances of the accident and that the survivor and witnesses had given their statements to the investigators and had been sent home.

"I can tell from the depth of the track's groove whether she paddled into shore and pulled in the kayak or she jumped out in the water and pushed it into shore."

"Does it matter if the accident happened in the middle of the Hudson?"

"Who knows? But it's like a footprint, and I need to preserve the evidence before the tide washes it away. You never know what's relevant in an accident scene investigation. One little detail can make the difference between life and death." Moore grabbed a bag resting on the grass next to the beach, rifled through it, and extracted a can of hairspray. "This type of case is difficult because the Hudson is an estuary and is a tidal river that's fed by the ocean. High tide was at noon, and the current has shifted out to sea. The next low tide is around midnight, so I have to preserve the evidence before it's swept away."

The tech paused and shook the can. "Did you know that the Hudson is called a 'drowned river' because although it was created by the glacial melt, the sea waters flood the river valley each time the tide rises."

"A drowned river?" Cindie shuddered at the name filled with foreboding. Her eyes darted away from the ominous riverfront and upward to the bridge. "Are there any video cameras in the park or under the bridge?"

Moore returned to the shoreline and knelt on the wet sand. "No, that's another problem. We don't have a digital record of the accident. Since the kayaks and the survivor can provide part of the story, we need to collect whatever other physical evidence is available. You don't mind, do you?"

The tech motioned for Cindie to step backward.

Cindie moved to give Officer Moore space to make a casting of the groove. First, the tech shook the can, and next, she gently coated a large area surrounding the imprint with the thick polymer to protect the sandy track from shifting. Moore didn't stand directly over the spot and spray the hairspray close in. Instead, she directed the spray toward the track because the pressure of the spray could blow the sand around.

"Ingenious," Cindie remarked. "You let the hairspray settle in and harden."

"Yeah. Then, voilà! I lift the cast I've made of the track," Officer Moore said, admiring her handiwork. "Like I said, the evidence may be irrelevant, but I'd rather be safe than sorry."

"Where's the crime scene leader? I have a few questions for them." Cindie looked over her shoulder at the officers milling around the lawn.

Moore glanced toward the restroom pavilion near the parking lot. "I don't see Detectives Jones and Pulaski now. You can check with the officers over by the building. They may be able to help."

Cindie knew Detectives Ebony Jones and Zander Pulaski, but not well. Last spring, they'd been the dynamic duo responsible for uncovering the link between eight missing prostitutes and the serial killer Duvall Bennett. Thanks to their keen intuition and determination, they'd apprehended Bennett and had enabled Cindie's team to obtain convictions for eight consecutive life sentences for murder, plus additional time for the assault and battery of another sex worker, Lissie Sexton, who had escaped Bennett's clutches.

Hal's fiancée, Jessie Martin, had enlisted Sexton's cooperation, which had blown the case wide open when she'd identified Bennett as her attacker. Now, almost six months later, another tragedy engulfed Jessie—the presumed loss of her child's father. Cindie wondered how much suffering the poor woman could withstand. Luckily, Jessie had Hal and her family for support, but nothing could compensate a child for losing her father, regardless of his irresponsibility.

Cindie thanked her and crossed the wet grass to the pavilion. She introduced herself to an officer whose badge read "Robinson" and who was comparing notes with her colleagues. "I'm wondering if you could help me. I'm looking for Detectives Jones and Pulaski. Are they around?"

"They went to Waryas Park to see if there was any news about locating the victim." Robinson pressed the walkie-talkie clipped to her black bulletproof vest and relayed the message over the air.

The voice of Zander Pulaski replied over the speaker. "Please tell Ms. Tarrico we'll call her with an update if we find anything. Do you copy?"

When Cindie nodded, Robinson replied, "Copy."

As Cindie walked toward the parking lot, she stopped and turned back toward the water. There was something about Officer Moore's comments that gave her pause. *Only the survivor would know what had really occurred that afternoon.* Moore had been referring to Kyle's fiancée. She would know about the circumstances of the accident and what happened to Kyle.

Certainly, it was a tragedy. But Jessie, Lily, and the Emorys were entitled to the details of the afternoon. No matter how horrible. If she'd lost a loved one in the river, she'd want to know the grisly details and that every resource had been exhausted to uncover the truth. While it appeared the police had covered all the bases, Cindie made a mental note to request a copy of the incident report from Chief Shepardson. Just to make sure.

"Officer Robinson," Cindie said, "I'd appreciate it if you could keep me in the loop. Thanks."

Officer Robinson waved as Cindie walked toward her car and away from the drowned river.

Chapter Ten

Wild bursts of a frigid north wind pummeled the overgrown rose bush outside Jessie's bedroom window. After the summer's perfusion of red blossoms, the skeletal remains of thorny branches and dead leaves scratched on her windowpane as though seeking refuge from the cold.

Jessie shivered and tugged the comforter up around her, hiding from the racket. It was well past midnight, and she hadn't been able to sleep. It was foolish to think she could. Her mind kept spinning with "what if's." What if Kyle was alive, hurt, and abandoned on a freezing shoreline somewhere along the Hudson? What if the search teams had given up too soon last evening? What if Ebony and Zander weren't revealing everything? What if they found Kyle dead? What if they never found him?

What if she never saw Kyle again? What if she never got to tell him everything she'd wanted to say?

What if? What if? What if?

Her temples ached, clouding her thoughts. Over the years, Kyle had betrayed and lied to her, but he was the father of her child. While she'd prided herself on being able to read a potential client when they walked through the door, she never seemed to understand the men closest to her, except Hal and her dad. Love had made her blind to Kyle's flaws, and those of her high school teacher Terrence Butterfield, who'd turned out to be a killer and who had almost cost her life and Lily's. But her apprehensions weren't about her relationship with Kyle; they were about justice for Lily.

Jessie checked the time on the cellphone charging on her nightstand. A comforting photo of Hal and Lily greeted her as the time, two-thirty, floated over their smiling faces. Abandoning any hope of sleep, she slipped out of bed, slid into her robe, and padded downstairs barefooted. The chilly hardwood treads shot a shiver up her spine.

The house was quiet, and the kitchen counter lights shone on a note bearing her name. She read it.

Jessie, sweetheart. You were very gracious in offering us shelter, but we didn't want to impose. We're staying at the Spring Court Inn and know you'll contact us should you hear anything. We'll talk in the morning. Love, Bev.

Earlier, about eight o'clock, Jessie had collapsed into bed after putting Lily down for the night. Tom and Bev must have left shortly afterward. It was just as well. Playing hostess and pretending everything was copasetic had exhausted her, but without the daytime distractions, her mind whirled, robbing her of sleep.

An open bottle of Merlot was in the fridge, so she reached inside, grasped it, then uncorked it and poured herself a half-glass. In a swift movement, Bono leaped onto the counter and nudged his wet, black nose against her hand, nearly spilling the wine.

"No, you don't. This is for Mama, not kitty."

"But what about Papa?"

Jessie startled at the sound of Hal's sleepy voice drifting down the shadowy hallway. He belted his terrycloth bathrobe over his bare chest and the boxers hanging low on his hips. Entering the dimly lit kitchen, he yawned and stretched his arms wide. The cat jumped down from the counter and skedaddled.

"Sorry, I didn't mean to wake you. I couldn't sleep," she said.

"That's understandable, and I wasn't really asleep either. With you tossing, turning, and kicking off the covers, it was impossible."

"I guess you're just a light sleeper. It must have been the wind keeping you awake." She handed him the note, retrieved another glass, and filled it to match hers.

"Yeah. You were upstairs when they escaped. I tried to stop Bev, but she wouldn't listen to me. Frankly, they make me uncomfortable, like I'm an interloper around here. But I'm sure they'll get over it." He sipped the wine. "They're an odd couple, aren't they? Bev is warm and fuzzy, and Tom is an iceberg."

"They're an odd couple? Look at us. Boozing it up at two in the morning in our pajamas." She paused and stared into the deep red liquid in the glass. "I wonder if they blame me for Kyle's disappearance…if we hadn't broken up, he'd still be alive and all that."

"Stop. You're being ridiculous, and even if they need someone to blame, that's their problem, not yours. I'm confident Ebony will find him. You have to trust her."

"I'm tempted to call her to see whether she's heard anything."

"It's a bit early for that. Besides, she said she'd call if they had any news, as did Cindie."

"I keep replaying the scenarios in my mind, and it's driving me nuts. We're all worried about Kyle, of course, but I still don't understand how Ebony ended up with Lily. She never mentioned it at all. Who was watching Lily when Kyle was kayaking? Did he leave her with strangers? Who were these people with Kyle, and what was their connection to him? Had he ever left Lily with his 'fiancée' before?"

Hal covered her trembling hand with his. "You're getting way ahead of yourself. Lily is fine, and we can ask Ebony those questions when we talk to her later. Let's keep positive thoughts about Kyle and hope they find him. It should be daylight soon, so the water search should resume in the next few hours. I'm sure we'll know more later today."

She slugged the wine. It was sweet and smooth on her tongue. Almost a sedative. Maybe it would encourage sleep or maybe hype her up even more. Either way, she'd enjoy the fog dulling the edges of her razor-thin nerves.

"I know you're upset, but there's nothing we can do except wait," Hal said. He rose, went to the pantry, selected a bag of cheese crackers, and returned to the table. He popped one into this mouth and offered Jessie the bag. "We can't search the river, and the shoreline's off limits, so our hands are tied."

Jessie grabbed a handful of crackers and munched on them thoughtfully. "It's frustrating. I'm not used to sitting around waiting for things to happen.

I need to contribute to the cause. You know, fight the good fight."

"There's no fight right now. Hopefully, there won't be. But you're more than suited to the task if there is." He took another sip and popped a few crackers into his mouth. "Mmm. Wine and cheese. Did you tell Jeremy what's going on?"

"I texted him, and he and Gayle sent their prayers. He mentioned if I needed to take time off, I should let him know. I hope it won't be necessary." She sipped. "I'm grateful to have an empathetic law partner like Jeremy, but I don't want him carrying the sole burden for too long. We're busy, and he has his health issues to contend with."

Criminal defense icon Jeremy Kaplan had given her the opportunity to reinvigorate her legal career when no one else would touch her. Her downfall had partially been his fault since he had falsely accused her of violating the rules of professional conduct last year when he'd defended Terrence Butterfield. Jeremy had redeemed himself through their brief partnership, and she refused to betray his trust.

"I wouldn't worry about Jeremy. He can handle the office for a few days. Concentrate on yourself."

"Yeah, but—" Jessie felt woozy as the elixir worked its magic, relaxing her mind and the tension in her lower back. "You're right."

In the warm haze, Jessie pondered options that wouldn't step on Ebony's toes. She required someone with unhampered access to information about Olivia Vargas, her family, and their relationship to Kyle. Someone without scruples. Or a person who owed Jeremy a favor.

"If anything arises, I could contact Carey Wentworth. He's a sleazeball, but he's well connected," she mused aloud. Wentworth's nicotine-stained teeth, greasy hair, and polyester clothing made Jessie's skin crawl, but Wentworth was the best PI in the valley.

"We've used Carey at the DA's office when our investigators hit stonewalls. Jess, I can hear the gears shifting in your head, but you're getting ahead of yourself. And you might not like what you discover. Sometimes it's better to leave sleeping dogs alone."

"I think we need to know more about Kyle's fiancée, that's all."

Hal clucked his tongue in apparent frustration and rested his chin on his fist. "I'm beat. Want to give sleep another try? We've got a few hours before Lily's up." He grabbed her hand and pulled her to a standing position. "Come on. Let's go."

The kitchen clock read three o'clock, and the early hour prompted Jessie's eyelids to become leaden. She quickly drained her glass and groaned. "All right. But no promises."

"No promises you won't sleep or that you won't steal the covers?"

"Both," she said, snapping off the light.

Chapter Eleven

Ebony's bed was toasty warm, and so were Drew's roving hands. He sleepily slipped them around her waist and tucked her against his muscular body. Drew loved spooning with her. He could do it for hours, and he possessed a talent for stoking her flames better than any man she'd ever known. He was a firefighter, after all.

Drew had surprised her around midnight, right after she'd received a text from the chief scheduling a meeting early the next morning. He'd sneaked into their bed and fallen asleep as soon as his sandy-colored head had hit the pillow. She guessed Drew had either tired of the testosterone-filled firehouse, or he'd surrendered to his desire for her and their comfortable mattress. Regardless, she was glad he'd returned home.

Heat emanated from Drew's body. It penetrated his t-shirt and her short nightshirt down into her skin, creating a thin layer of moisture where their bodies made contact. If they'd been naked, their bodies would have become glued together as one; instead, Ebony blissfully snuggled into place like a key inside a lock.

Ebony was due at the chief's office in an hour, and reluctantly, she tossed back the covers and rolled out of bed. But Drew was too quick. He grabbed her hand and tugged hard, forcing her to collapse on top of him, face to face. Drew's steel grip enclosed her in a hug while his lips tenderly explored her neck, shoulders, and lips.

"Aren't you supposed to be out on the river?" she asked.

He kissed her skin intermittently as he spoke. "The lieutenant reassigned me to the noon shift, so I have plenty of time," he purred. "Come on, Sugar.

Stay in bed with me, please. Five more minutes. I'll even do that thing you love so much." Drew's Southern drawl dripped with honey, and he sneaked his knees between hers, separating them.

Oh, god. He's killing me, Ebony thought, dreaming about his special moves in the sack and the tempting stiffness pressing against her thighs. Mustering her strength, she wiggled free from his grasp and rose from the bed. She glared at him.

"Sorry, babe. I'm running late. It's naughty to tempt me when I've got to work, but I'll be home as soon as I can. So, put a pin in your seduction."

Drew mimed a childlike pout, and she considered leaning in for a conciliatory kiss. However, Ebony suspected it might lead to him sticking his key in her lock, and she really didn't have the time.

After hurriedly showering, dressing, and preparing breakfast for both herself and Wrangler, Ebony was ready to go. She paused at the front door and shouted, "Please take the dog out, and I'll see you soon. Love you." Before she could change her mind, she dashed out the door.

She took solace in the sunshine and sparkling blue skies along the three-block stroll past the renovated row houses, lofts, and churches to the police station. Today would have been the perfect autumn day to hike along the jagged cliffs overlooking the U.S. Military Academy at West Point and the picaresque Storm King Mountain across the river. But, like hot sex with Drew, it wasn't to be.

* * *

The chief's beat-up Ford pickup and Zander's electric coupe were parked in the lot when she arrived. The scent of fresh-brewed coffee guided her through the lobby and central beehive to Chief Shepardson's office, where he'd set out a brunch of coffee, tea, and pastries on his credenza. Usually, Ebony was served an earful about some rule she'd bent or her incomplete paperwork, but never delicacies. Today, the chief must be out to impress the DA.

For close to a decade, the chief's commendations, awards, and Naval

Bronze Star hanging on the wall behind his desk had reminded Ebony of his sterling service to the community. This morning, she studied the photo gallery on the opposite wall above the spread. This was the chief's personal side of the room, the mementos he viewed over her shoulder. The gallery displayed the history of a young officer becoming a husband, father, and grandfather, and the commander of the largest city force in the Hudson Valley.

Chief Shepardson had started his career in Poughkeepsie. Now, close to sixty-five, his tenure would soon end. Observing the chief brush the powdered sugar of a donut from his starched shirt, a knot twisted Ebony's gut. She refused to accept the chief's inevitable retirement. Over the years, they had butted heads, but Shepardson had been her greatest supporter. He'd been a demanding teacher who'd given her the space to spread her wings and reel in her crazies. And he'd championed her taking the upcoming sergeant's exam, two months away.

Ebony prayed he'd hang around for another decade. But if not, she hoped his successor would be as benevolent as Shepardson had been with her.

"Morning, Eb," Zander said. Dressed stylishly in a suede bomber jacket, vintage Nirvana T-shirt, and jeans, he balanced a plate loaded with goodies.

"Hey, Z." Ebony grabbed a cup of tea and a croissant as District Attorney Tarrico arrived.

Ebony didn't know the new DA well, but she admired her after her recent prosecution of Duvall Bennett, the serial killer. Tarrico was chicly dressed in gray corduroy trousers and a marled turtleneck sweater, with a touch of makeup. Flashy Elton John-like glasses camouflaged the bluish crescents beneath her eyes. Ebony's face warmed with embarrassment. After staying in bed too long with Drew, her rushed morning had left no time for her beauty routine, and she'd thrown on the first clothes she could grab —jeans and a denim work shirt— from the top of the laundry basket.

The chief covered his mouth to hide a yawn, and he waited for Tarrico to grab a plate before starting the meeting. It must have been a late night, as each of them exhibited some form of exhaustion except Zander, who was suspiciously chipper.

"Cindie, Jones, and Pulaski, I appreciate your interrupting your weekends for this meeting. We've received new forensic information about the Emory investigation, and we need to jump on this case."

An adrenaline rush juiced her heart and her brain snapped to attention. I knew something was fishy, Ebony thought.

Chief Shepardson distributed manila folders to the group, and Ebony removed a packet of documents containing accident scene sketches and photographs, maps, witness statements from the Vargas family, and photos of Kyle's and Olivia's kayaks. Olivia's kayak was identical to Kyle's red one, except its top was blue and green, and a black nylon skirt enclosed the cockpit. Both were ten feet long and had padded backrests, front and rear storage compartments, phone holders, and drain holes and plugs in the kayak's topside deck.

"Forensics has examined the kayaks," the chief said. He picked up one of the documents, squinted at it and returned it to the pile on his desk. "It appears there may have been a defect with Kyle Emory's kayak. Let's examine the photos of his boat first."

A defect? That's odd. Sounds like a crack in the hull, which could be a product liability case. Or physical damage caused by the storm, Ebony thought.

The group shuffled through the papers and withdrew a series of photos of a red kayak with a white bottom. Its shell appeared to be composed of thick plastic, and midway between the stern and the bow, there was an open cockpit containing a seat. Two black storage compartments secured by bungee cords were inserted at both ends of the kayak's top deck. The smaller hatch was in the front, and the larger one in the back. The kayak looked bulky, simple, and cheap, like those available at a big box sporting goods store, unlike the sleek fiberglass or wooden models Ebony had seen at her uncle's lake house in Connecticut. From the photos, there were no obvious cracks, scratches, or dents in the craft.

The second photo showed someone holding a nickel next to a comparably sized black hole in the kayak's top deck. It was a close-up, so it was hard to pinpoint its exact location on the boat other than that it was near the cockpit opening. There didn't seem to be anything sinister about the black hole. The manufacturer had rimmed it in molded plastic, making it appear to be part of the boat's original construction.

After a few moments, the chief continued. "The kayaks are the same model from the same manufacturer, the Pelican Water-Runner 100K Kayak. As you can see from the bottom, it's pretty clean. So Emory's is a newish boat."

Ebony wondered whether the chief had any knowledge of kayaking or whether he was regurgitating what forensics had told him.

"Sir," Zander said, "I've done a bit of kayaking, and this looks like a lower-end recreational model. The kind you'd use in a lake, not the Hudson River. You'd probably want a more sophisticated touring model for the river's strong currents."

"That's what forensics said, too. Anyway, in the second photo, there is a small black hole in the surface of the kayak's top deck. There're usually four or six of these holes in the front and back of every kayak. Apparently, they are drains to allow the water to flow through the hull, to stabilize and steer the boats."

"Actually, sir, they're called scupper holes. They can also be located in the footwall, sidewalls, or tank well close to the waterline. They're designed as a safety feature to drain water away from the kayak's upper deck so it doesn't accumulate there. If too much water gets onto or into the kayak, the excess water affects the buoyancy. The water weighs the kayak down and pushes it farther into the water."

"Thanks, Pulaski." The chief sounded annoyed at the interruption and continued. "The holes are plugged with plugs or stoppers to prevent water from draining into the kayak."

"Scupper plugs," Zander interjected. "They usually make the plugs of plastic, and they come in all sizes and shapes to fit securely into the scupper hole. They stop the water from entering the boat when there's rough water, like during a storm."

"Thank you, Detective," Cindie said, echoing the chief's impatience. "We appreciate your knowledge on the subject, but could we please let Chief

Shepardson tell us what forensics found? Detective Jones, any comments? You've been quiet."

"No, ma'am. I'm just digesting Zander's lecture," Ebony replied.

"As I said, there are four scupper holes on the deck of Emory's Pelican, and forensics noted there were only three plugs. One of the front plugs is missing," the chief said.

There was dead silence in the room.

An alarm bell sounded in Ebony's mind. Having a hole in a boat anytime could be deadly even if the opening was small, but especially during a storm. Her mind churned, trying to figure out the possibilities. Had Mother Nature pulled the plug, or had humans intervened?

"What does this mean?" She turned to Zander. "Did Kyle set out with three plugs, or could he have lost the fourth one during the storm?"

"Probably not. Why would only one be missing? They're supposed to be fitted tightly into the scupper holes," Zander said.

"This raises a whole lot of questions that require further investigation. From a technical perspective, I'm unsure how the missing scupper plug impacts our investigation," Shepardson said. "But forensics is working on it. In the meantime, we have to consider the possibility that someone intentionally tampered with Emory's kayak."

Ebony's mind immediately discounted Kyle's disappearance as an accident or product liability issue and leaped straight to murder or suicide.

"Sir, when we interviewed Jessie Martin yesterday, she suggested Kyle was prone to moods. Should we pursue suicide as a plausible theory?" Ebony asked.

"We can't rule out anything. The missing plug could have been defect, or Emory or a third party could have removed the plug, or he could have lost it during the storm. We don't know what happened, so it's best to start with the witnesses." The chief scratched the silver-speckled stubble on his chin. "The Vargas family might shed some light on the events leading up to the presumed drowning. We have their initial statements, but given this recent development, they're worth revisiting to gather any details we may have overlooked."

Ebony skipped through the pile to the accident scene photos depicting the waterfront of Kaal Rock Park festooned with the yellow streamers that announced a tragedy. Growing up in Poughkeepsie, Ebony had visited this spot a thousand times. Her family had loved picnicking at the lush park along the water's edge, which had felt ten degrees cooler than their landlocked city backyard. And as a teen, she, Jessie, and their crew had hung out on the riverbank, drinking beer, breaking curfew, and making out with their boyfriends in the back seats of their cars. Doing all the mischievous things teenagers weren't supposed to do.

Ebony wondered whether uptight Zander Pulaski, a fellow Poughkeep-sian, had engaged in similar hijinks. He was a townie, but the cliffside refuge drew kids from all over the valley. Zander probably still brings his chicks here, she thought, observing him. He caught her staring and wrinkled his nose in question, but she flicked her eyes away.

"We have eight witnesses, including Olivia, her parents, her brothers, sister-in-law, cousin, and the cousin's husband," Ebony weighed in. "Their statements mostly concern the thunderstorm, their location during the storm, and their observations afterward. We need to turn back the clock and determine what occurred prior to the weather turning sour."

Cindie Tarrico, who'd been a silent observer, set down her mug and piped in. "Matt, we should establish a timeline of the events leading up to the accident. Until your team speaks with the Vargas family, we won't know how far to go back. It could be the morning of, days, or weeks before." She dusted a crumb off her slacks, folded her arms, and leaned against the credenza.

"And sir, if we present this as a weather-related accident, won't they be suspicious about why we're following up?" Zander asked.

"We'll simply inform them it's an ongoing accident investigation. There's no reason to provide details. Yet," Tarrico said.

"We should also run background checks and RAP sheets on them," Ebony said. "And what about interviewing Emory's family?" They would need to include Jessie on the suspect list, but Jessie was intuitive and smart, plus a criminal defense attorney. She'd easily piece the puzzle together.

68

Besides, Ebony wouldn't actually be lying to Jessie. She'd attempt to be straight with Jessie while concealing her true motives. Their mission wouldn't be easy, but confidentiality was required. Even between friends. Or potential murder suspects.

"Cindie, what do you think?" Chief Shepardson asked and then bit into a jelly donut, his second. The strawberry goo squirted onto his white uniform shirt, and he dabbed a napkin on the crimson stain, smearing it like blood oozing from his belly.

All heads swiveled toward District Attorney Cindie Tarrico to receive her mandate.

Chapter Twelve

Ebony observed District Attorney Cindie Tarrico sit up straight when the chief addressed her. The slight tick at the corner of her peach-colored lips had been barely noticeable, but it had been there. Had the DA reacted to the tragic drowning or the identity of the victim?

Any drowning was a disaster, but Kyle Emory wasn't the most popular person in the room.

Ebony's mind drifted to a year ago when during Ryan Paige's homicide case, Kyle had proven himself to be the ultimate scumbag. He'd withheld his reporting of Ryan Paige's murder to the police, letting Jessie take the fall as the informant. Like the toppling tiles of dominoes, Jessie's world had collapsed around her. She'd nearly lost her career, and Kyle had abandoned her late in her pregnancy. The stressful situation had nearly killed Jessie and her baby.

It seemed like every appalling event in Jessie's life could be traced back to Kyle Emory's spitefulness and jealousy of Jessie and her success. But his malicious deeds had backfired when Jessie had dumped him for good. It had been about time.

However, there was no reason to celebrate Kyle's disappearance or allow it to impact her job. She was a cop, duty-bound to ignore her personal prejudices. Like every victim, she owed Kyle and his family her best efforts in finding him and investigating the accident.

And she owed it to her best friend and her best friend's daughter to learn the truth. If she and Zander solved the mystery of Kyle's disappearance, maybe it would bring her and Jessie closer. Maybe. She had to try, not only for Jessie but also for herself.

The chief pulled a handkerchief from his pocket and blew his veined nose with a honk as Cindie Tarrico spoke, returning Ebony's attention to the present.

"At the scene, a tech commented about how one little detail could make the difference between life and death. I'm not rushing to judgment, but it seems ludicrous that a missing nickel-sized piece of plastic could be deadly, but it certainly raises a lot of questions. And because we have so many moving parts in this investigation, we must cast a wide net." To emphasize the point, Tarrico balled her fingers into a fist and unfurled a digit for each item she recited until her uplifted palm was empty. "We have a missing victim, a survivor, multiple witnesses, the weather, the unique accident location, the defective kayak, and the accident itself. At the moment, there's no hard evidence of a crime being committed, so we need to proceed as we would in any accident investigation."

Tarrico looked around the room as though she were gathering her thoughts. "For the past few years, we've been fortunate. We've had no arrests or serious incidents on the river, but that's not to say it never happens. We mostly prosecute drunken boat operators, but Kyle Emory's disappearance is a dreadful and unusual situation. I'm relying on you, Jones and Pulaski, to perform your due diligence to determine whether any laws have been broken and, if so, to apprehend the perpetrators. Still, our departments lack the technical expertise to analyze the aquatic accident scene, which demands that we engage experts to assist us. Let me give this further consideration before I make any recommendations."

Zander and the chief nodded in agreement.

Ebony saw where the DA was headed. If this were a fatal car accident, the district attorney and the defense, and the plaintiff's attorneys would enlist accident reconstruction experts to recreate the scene for presentation to the judge and jury. She'd seen it happen dozens of times. Why should they treat this river accident differently from any other? How would they locate an aquatic forensic expert familiar with the Hudson? Generally, those firms serviced coastal areas used to boating wrecks, like Maine, Florida, and the Carolinas or on the West Coast. Not upstate New York.

"Our investigation remains ongoing because we still haven't found Kyle Emory, which is troubling," the chief said. His expression tensed, deep vertical lines separating his bushy brows. "Any way you analyze this incident, it's horrific."

As the DA had mentioned, the incident involved multiple facets, yet Kyle's disappearance remained at its heart. At this moment, the divers and boats were continuing their searches. With each passing minute, the truth was becoming more obvious. Kyle might never be found because he could have sunk to the river's muddy bottom or been swept north to Albany or south to the Atlantic by the fickle tides.

Ebony wondered what Jessie and the Vargas and Emory families were thinking. Kyle's kin must be going out of their minds. Ebony would be if she were in their shoes.

Everyone needed answers. As the lead detectives on the case, it was time for them to take action.

Ebony sipped her lukewarm tea and knotted her fingers together to stretch them, cracking her knuckles. "Our game plan is for Zander and me to review the witness statements and interview the witnesses again. Forensics will continue to analyze the accident scene and the kayaks, and the boats will continue the water search." She wondered for how long the search would continue. When would it be time to call it quits?

"Forensics spotted an ID sticker on both crafts from The Hudson Outfitter. Put them on your list. If they bought the kayaks at that store, there should be receipts and invoices. It might provide a lead about the missing plug," the chief said.

"I know the place. It's in Beacon, so we'll hustle down there pronto," Zander said. "In the meantime, what about expanding aerial surveillance? We've used drones, but we could enlist the state police chopper?" Zander checked his smartwatch. "It's been almost twenty-four hours. Do you think it's too late?"

"I'll contact Troop T in Newburgh about using their chopper, but we've got the Hudson blanketed with our boats, the sheriff's, and the state police's. Plus, civilian volunteers are on the hunt, too. It can't hurt, though."

"The investigators in my office may have other suggestions about what we need." Cindie Tarrico crossed her arms and sat up tall in her chair. "Once this gets out to the media, every action we take will be examined under a microscope. There's no room for error, and we need to get this resolved post-haste." She paused a beat. "Matt, I appreciate being included at this early stage. If my office is required to prosecute a crime or give counsel to the victims' families, my involvement will make our jobs easier. We don't want anyone thinking we aren't taking this incident seriously."

Ebony speculated that Tarrico was referring to the systematic failure of their departments to discover that eight prostitutes had vanished throughout the valley. Only Ebony had linked the cold cases together, recognizing the pattern of a homicidal maniac.

Despite their oaths of office, Tarrico and Shepardson were politicians, and neither could afford another slip-up.

"Agreed. It sounds like we have our agendas, so let's proceed and keep in touch. Again, sorry for ruining your Sunday, but thanks for coming in." He turned toward Ebony and Zander. "The ball's in your court, and we know you won't disappoint us. Take the rest of the day off and start fresh tomorrow."

Ebony and Zander thanked their superiors and left the building together. Zander whipped out his iPhone, texting as he walked toward his car. Meanwhile, Ebony fought the urge to jog home to the sexy firefighter she hoped was still in her bed.

Chapter Thirteen

The next morning, Zander had beaten Ebony to the riverfront coffee shop where they'd agreed to meet before work. In the dense fog, she barely made out his car in the parking lot, but he was nowhere in sight. She'd hiked the short distance from her apartment, and with each step toward the Hudson, the mist had thickened. It was like being trapped inside a thick cloud, with only the hollow cry of the bridge's foghorn guiding her to Zander.

Nestled next to the train station, the café offered rapid-fire service to the commuters hopping on the Manhattan-bound trains. On clear days, patrons enjoyed expansive views of the waterfront, but this morning the cloudbank obscured the river, the mountains, and the Mid-Hudson Bridge.

"Hey!" Zander shouted from one of the prized window tables.

"Hi," Ebony said, sliding into the seat across from him where a steaming mug marked her place. "Thanks."

He flicked a hand in acknowledgment, but his attention returned to the witness reports and photos spread on the tabletop.

"Have you ever kayaked?" he asked. It was a rhetorical question because he knew she barely set foot on any surface not adhered to the solid earth. "I'm not an expert, but a missing nickel-sized plug couldn't sink a kayak. The scupper hole doesn't admit much water into the boat."

"The cockpit of the blue kayak has a skirty thing. Doesn't that keep out the water?"

"Yeah, but most recreational kayaks like Kyle's and Olivia's don't have skirts. They're used for rougher water expeditions. Kayaks are designed to stay afloat, and we know Kyle's had capsized when the fire department retrieved it."

"So you think this is a drowning case? Simply Kyle's bad luck." Ebony hoped it was true because survivors seemed more willing to accept death by a natural disaster rather than by homicide.

"I'm saying between the weather, his inappropriate street clothing, and the lack of life jacket, Emory got screwed. Not by a stupid hole in the kayak deck." He picked up a sugar pack and swatted it against his palm. "My theory is that since his kayak wasn't designed to roll over and right itself, he either fell out and was swept away or got trapped underneath it."

"If that's the case, we still have unanswered questions. Like why Kyle wasn't wearing a life vest, and did they have advanced warning of the storm?" she asked. "Did you think there was anything dodgy about Olivia Vargas?"

"Eb, sometimes shit happens. You know that. Emory's may be one of those unfortunate occasions, but while he lived, he had a hot babe of a fiancée."

Shit happened. A load of shit, which had strained her friendship with Jessie and their lives. They could now add Kyle's disappearance to the list, but at least Ebony could redeem herself by solving this mystery.

"How long have you been kayaking?"

"About as long as we've been partners. The past two years have been on a regular basis. My skiff is the next level up from Emory's, and even though I've taken a few training classes, I'm still a novice. I'm learning how to read the water and handle easy rapids. No white water, though."

The answer surprised Ebony. Maybe she didn't know Zander as well as she thought. Or he, her. She was also learning to read the water, conquering her fear of what lay beneath the dark surface. She'd never mentioned it to Zander, but Drew, an avid fly fisherman, was teaching her to be an angler. Standing in her waders with waist-high water rushing by, Ebony was locating fish by reading the surface bubbles and practicing to land her fly in the perfect spot to entice a bite.

Part of living in the Hudson Valley was enjoying its freshwater lakes, rivers, and streams, and one of the first lessons Drew taught her was to be safe around the water. Dress appropriately. Take it slow in the water. Shuffle versus step across the slippery bottom. Always remain with your partner. And watch the weather.

Too bad Kyle hadn't followed the basic water safety rules. It was too late for him now.

"Your experience will be handy in unraveling the logistics of Kyle's accident," Ebony said.

"I'm sorry to predict that in the end, we'll discover Kyle's death was an accident caused by human error. He should have stayed with his kayak and worn the proper protective gear." An uncharacteristic melancholy washed over Zander's expression, dulling his usual ocean-blue eyes to grey. "I never met Emory, and he may not have been the world's greatest guy, but nobody deserves to die gasping for breath in a watery grave."

"There must've been something good in him; otherwise, Jessie wouldn't have loved him as she once had." Ebony realized she'd referred to Kyle in the past tense, presuming he was dead. As Jessie's friend, she'd hoped to remain optimistic. Though as a cop, the preliminary evidence pointed toward Kyle's demise. Their investigation was the only way to establish the truth.

"We should continue our fact-finding with Dr. and Mrs. Vargas. They seemed tuned into their kids and could provide insight into Kyle and Olivia's relationship," Zander said.

Ebony shuffled through the paperwork on the table, extracted Olivia's statement, and scanned it. "Olivia teaches middle school in the Bronx and lives in Brooklyn, but I'm betting she's taken leave and is temporarily staying with her folks." She thumbed through the pile for Carlos's report and tapped her finger on the front page. "The Vargases live in Garrison. That's not too far, maybe forty minutes south. Let's clock in at the station, make a few calls, and take a ride. We may snag three birds in one swoop."

"Sounds like a plan." Zander's eyes latched on to hers, an intensity returning to his gaze. "Eb, this Emory situation must hit close to home. Can you handle it?"

From the outset, Ebony had been repressing the past, however, Kyle's presumed drowning had dredged up emptiness within her soul. Nearly twenty years ago on Ebony's thirteenth birthday, her Aunt Alicia had vanished. Alicia's lies and drug addictions had torn her family apart, and for years, the pall of the mystery had robbed Ebony and her sister, Carly, of the frivolities of being teenagers. Neither the private investigators, the media campaigns, the billboards, nor the flyers had yielded results.

After six autumns, the truth had washed up on a Long Island beach. Early morning joggers had found Alicia's unrecognizable body in the dunes. Following the DNA match and a proper goodbye, her family had let Alicia go. Ebony couldn't. Perhaps Aunt Alicia had been the reason she'd become a cop. To help others in need.

Zander's allusion exemplified that they each contributed a rare perspective into Kyle's investigation. Ebony brought empathy from experiencing the hellish limbo of a missing person's case. Zander embodied the experience of the dangerous, exhilarating water sport at the core of the accident.

If they were lucky, they'd find Kyle alive and well. If not, two watery graves had claimed the lives of people she'd known—one of them, a cherished aunt whose death haunted her every day of her life.

Ebony swallowed hard. "I'm good," she lied.

Chapter Fourteen

Ebony had called ahead to the Vargas home, and despite the lack of a street number, they knew they were in the right place. On their witness statements, Carlos and Vivianna Vargas had listed their home addresses as "White Oaks," and there was the name, engraved upon the gleaming brass plaque affixed to a stone pillar on the right side of the road. Tall white fencing stretched as far as they could see, and Ebony estimated the sophisticated security system had cost as much as the fleet of patrol cars back at the station.

"Pretty fancy-schmancy," Zander said as the security gates slid open, and the motorized CCTV cameras tracked them down the winding driveway. He drove slowly so they could absorb the lay of the land. The heavily wooded landscape had changed color, displaying a patchwork of red, orange, and gold. A family of white-tailed deer stared as the SUV passed by, and they seemed to be the Vargas's only neighbors on the isolated mountaintop.

"It feels like we're a million miles away from everything," Ebony said. As they entered the clearing, a compound consisting of a mansion, farmhouse, gatehouse, five-car garage, horse stalls, pool, pool house, and tennis court came into view. "Other than the Vargas family, I wonder who else lives here and how much acreage they have."

"Good questions. It's weird, but with Dr. Vargas being a pharma bigwig, I suppose he prefers his privacy. I'm sure we'll get the full story soon enough." Zander gestured toward the blue-shingled main house, a gabled mansion with wings sprouting in every direction. Dr. Vargas, dressed in a buttercup-colored cashmere sweater and navy khakis, waved at them from the patio.

Zander parked in the driveway next to a white BMW with dark-tinted windows, and they exited the car to join their host on the front steps.

Carlos Vargas looked haggard, more so than when they'd last seen him two days ago. His pallor had turned gray, and the puffiness beneath his soft brown eyes reflected a lack of sleep. Ebony suspected she'd been correct about Olivia's moving in and that she'd been running her poor daddy ragged. No doubt Mrs. Vargas was always a handful.

Carlos clasped their hands in welcome and ushered them into the manor house. "Welcome, detectives. We hope you have news for us. We haven't been able to concentrate on anything other than Kyle for the last forty-eight hours."

His strides were long and confident as he escorted them through the grand two-story foyer and into the living room quadruple the size of her apartment. At the far end of the long room, the morning light streamed in through floor-to-ceiling windows, reflecting off a black lacquered grand piano. At their end, a marble fireplace as large as Ebony's VW Bug balanced out the room. Carlos motioned for them to sit on the modern white leather sectional sofa facing the fireplace, and he took the matching club chair beside it.

"Detectives, can I offer you something to drink? Coffee, water, or something stronger?"

Ebony never understood why people felt compelled to offer them beverages the moment they walked in the door. Did she and Zander always look parched upon their arrival? Or was the polite ritual merely an icebreaker?

She and Zander exchanged mindful looks and declined. They rarely accepted the libations.

"We'd like to ask you and Mrs. Vargas follow-up questions about the accident. Also, we'd like to contact your children and niece," Ebony said. When she shifted to get comfortable, the stiff leather cushion squeaked beneath her.

"Viv is working in her studio over in the garage. I can text her if you like. And the kids." He rose and walked toward a western-facing window with a vista of the mountains, seeming to organize his thoughts. His voice dropped to a whisper. "Olivia is asleep upstairs. She's been having a terrible time, and our doctor prescribed her sedatives and sleeping aids, so she's knocked out for a while. *Pobre mi cariña*."

The distraught man wrung his hands, probably more in concern for his ailing daughter than her missing fiancé.

"This is a heartbreaking situation, but you still haven't told me if you have news. I'm assuming if you did, you would have led with it."

"Before we confirm anything, sir, we need you to understand we are taking this accident investigation seriously. To help with it, we'd like to contact Max and Auggie," Zander said.

"They are both working right now, but they'll be home this evening."

Ebony considered whether "home" meant dinner with the folks or in residence at White Oaks, which would contradict the addresses supplied during their police interviews. "Sir, do your kids live at White Oaks?"

"Auggie had a place in Tribeca, but he moved into our guest cottage a month ago. He's on the road a lot, so it made little sense for him to pay rent. Max and Ana have a cottage in Garrison Village but live here during the weekends. It's easier to commute to the city from Garrison." He blew out a long breath. "Olivia shares an apartment with some girlfriends in Brooklyn, but she was moving in with Kyle. Right now, she's staying here. We're unsure what her plans are going forward. It all depends upon what you find."

The Vargas family impressed Ebony as being a close-knit pack, but were they banding together in grief, support, or to stifle the police inquiry?

Viv Vargas burst into the room, her dark hair tied in a ponytail and dressed in an artist's smock splattered with the colors of the sunset—purple, yellow, orange, and red. She reeked of the piney scent of turpentine, and paintbrushes, rags, and tools protruded from her deep patch pockets.

Ebony had researched Viv's works online, and Viv's whimsical renderings of Latino culture sold for tens of thousands of dollars, and she'd exhibited her paintings in museums and galleries around the world.

"Carlos, I saw a car pull up. Oh, I see we have guests." When Viv observed the identity of the visitors, her demeanor became cool. "Detectives, do you have news about Kyle?" She shed her smock and took her place beside her husband, arms crossed over her chest in defiance. "You know our daughter has been devastated by this accident, and we're entitled to transparency about Kyle's disappearance."

Ebony refused to play Mrs. Vargas's wily game. "Unfortunately, there's nothing new to report. Forensics is still examining the kayaks and the waterfront area, and boats are searching the Hudson. We'd like some background about the day of the accident. Can you tell us about the evening prior to the accident?"

Mrs. Vargas deferred to her husband to respond.

"We wanted to get an early start on Saturday morning, so Oli and Kyle and Ana and Max spent Friday night here. They arrived before dinner, we had a family meal, and went to bed early," Carlos said.

"Was it just the immediate family for dinner?" Ebony asked.

"Yes, but Cody stopped by for coffee and dessert. He came by to visit Auggie," Viv said.

"Who's Cody?" Ebony asked.

"He's—" Viv said. Carlos coughed, and his wife's eyes flicked toward him, flashed with secret understanding, and then returned to Ebony. "Cody grew up with our children, and he and Auggie spend a lot of time together."

Viv's restrained manner intimated that Cody possessed a deeper connection to the family than she was letting on. Ebony let it pass but jotted the name on her phone.

"What about your niece and her husband?" Zander asked, oblivious.

"We made plans to meet them for coffee before we went to the park. They were driving up from Piermont, and it was easier to meet them in Poughkeepsie."

"There were seven of you leaving from White Oaks, correct? What were the transportation arrangements?"

"Since Kyle had to pick up Lily at her mother's house, he transferred her car seat into my BMW, and he and Auggie traveled together. Olivia, Viv, and I drove Kyle's car with the kayaks strapped on top to Poughkeepsie.

They stow their kayaks, the roof rack, and gear out in the barn because they don't have the space in the city."

Ebony recalled Kyle's ancient BMW, which he'd driven as long as she'd known him. The clunker had been a bone of contention between Jessie and Kyle because he'd been too cheap to spring for a new one, although he could easily afford it. Ebony had often imagined their disagreements over buckling Lily inside the deathtrap. It surprised her that the elegant Dr. and Mrs. Vargas would have set foot inside his rusty wheels with its chipped black paint, cracked windshield, and ripped upholstery.

"Can you describe the events of the morning leading up to your departure?" Zander asked.

"Oli, Kyle, Carlos, and I got up early, around six, took showers, and came downstairs after dressing. Auggie was at his place, so I don't know what he did, and Max and Ana stayed in the farmhouse by the stables. Everyone gathered in the kitchen around seven, and I made a hearty breakfast before we left around eight-fifteen. We all met up at Kelly's Bakery in Poughkeepsie at nine for coffee," Viv said.

"Did you check the weather before you started out?"

"Sure, we had the morning news playing on the kitchen's television, so we caught the forecast. They'd predicted a perfect day for outside activities upstate, like picnics and hiking. Temperature in the mid-seventies and sunny all day." Viv shook her head in apparent disgust at the meteorologist's erroneous report. "The weather was magnificent when we left, and I don't understand how they got it wrong. WAKE UP NEWS is usually so reliable."

Ebony wondered whether Kyle or Olivia had double-checked the weather apps for Poughkeepsie before commencing their excursion or whether they had relied on the early morning New York metro weather report. The Hudson Valley was notorious for its changeable weather, and the locals could often be heard saying, "if you don't like the weather, wait five minutes." Visitors might not know the idiom; however, Kyle was another matter. He'd lived with Jessie in Poughkeepsie for several years, and he should've known better.

She made notes on her phone as the Vargases spoke, and she suspected her next question could be a loaded one. "How do your sons get along with Kyle?"

"Good." Viv's tone was snippy, as if the question had been an insult. She shot her husband a side-glance. "That's a ridiculous question. Oli loves that man more than I can express. She can't wait to be his wife. And the boys treat Kyle like a brother. How dare you suggest—"

"Yes. Kyle's like a member of the *familia*. Why do you ask?" Carlos raised his dark eyebrows in question and rested a hand on his wife's arm to quiet her.

"We're trying to understand the relationships between the parties and their observations around the time of the accident," Ebony replied, keeping her expression stoic. "Can you tell us about Kyle and Olivia? Do you spend time with them?"

"Olivia already told you it was love at first sight. Since they met last spring, they've been inseparable, except for work, of course. He's so caring and patient toward our daughter. I love Oli, but she can be demanding...and rebellious." Carlos flinched as Viv delivered a sharp elbow to his ribs. "Oli wants what she wants when she wants it." He rubbed his side. "*Querida*, you know it's true."

"But her students adore her. They've been texting and calling non-stop since yesterday." Viv paused. "Oli is the school's choir mistress and is dedicated to her students. She even helps them make their music videos for auditions and social media. She's so proud of them, and—"

Carlos cleared his throat, interrupting his wife.

"Had you ever seen Kyle and Olivia argue?" Ebony made a note.

Carlos' glance shifted to his wife, then back to Zander. "*Nunca*. Never."

Viv curled her fingers, studied the purple and red oil paint staining her nails, and then balled her artist's hands into fists. "That's an impertinent line of inquiry. It's disrespectful to our family, especially under the circumstances. Olivia worships Kyle. All couples have disagreements, but nothing you'd call a *fight*." Her words were as sharp as the tip of the palette knife in her smock's pocket.

The Vargases weren't going to fess up about any conflicts between the happily engaged couple, so she'd better change course immediately. Otherwise, they'd be out the door on their asses.

Zander's expression tightened. "We're sorry, but it's a standard question in every investigation," he said. "Can you tell us what you observed during the moments prior to the storm?"

Carlos was quiet for a long moment as though disengaging from the conversation in irritation. But he wasn't. In his pressing his lips together, Ebony sensed the wheels of his mind spinning as fast as a centrifuge. Dr. Carlos Vargas appeared to be practiced in the art of controlling his emotions. Unlike his wife, he could manipulate any situation in his favor. "I'm not sure what you're looking for, detective," he replied.

Okay, asshole, we'll spell it out for you, Ebony wanted to shout. But Zander beat her to it.

"Can you please walk us through your observations from the time you parked your vehicle until the police arrived," Zander said.

"But we already told Officer Robinson everything."

Viv Vargas inched closer to her husband until they stood shoulder to shoulder, creating an impenetrable wall.

Us against them, Ebony thought. It was Zander's turn.

"We'd like to hear it again. If you don't mind," Zander said.

Carlos sighed heavily in surrender. "We arrived at Kaal Rock Park around ten a.m. in Kyle's BMW with the kayaks in the roof rack. Kyle and Auggie arrived in my car with Lily, and Serena and Andrew, and Max and Ana arrived in their separate cars. Max and Ana had driven separately because they were meeting friends for dinner in Woodstock that evening. We parked, and the boys unloaded the kayaks from the roof rack and carried them to the shoreline beach. The women gathered the picnic supplies and set the food and utensils on the table. This was about ten-thirty."

Viv Vargas swayed her head in agreement like a bobblehead doll.

"Which boys unloaded the kayaks?" Ebony asked.

"All of the guys. The kayaks were pretty bulky, so it took Max, Auggie, Kyle, Andrew, and myself to lift them off the car roof rack."

Carlos described his grabbing the coolers and Kyle and Olivia setting off shortly thereafter. "Honestly, Viv and I weren't paying them much attention. We were sitting with Ana, who had Lily in her lap, and the baby had us enthralled. She's such a cutie, and smart, too."

"It's been a while since we've had an infant around. Max and Ana haven't taken my hints about making me an *abuela*," Viv interjected, her face flushing.

"Give them time, *querida*," Carlos said. "Then the storm arrived, and we took shelter. Olivia is an experienced kayaker, so we figured she and Kyle would park beneath the bridge until the storm blew through. We never expected the torrential rain, but it stormed for about fifteen minutes."

"I texted Oli to see if she was okay, but I didn't receive a response," Viv said.

"When the rain stopped, we went outside and walked down to the shoreline. We saw Oli paddling her kayak, but we didn't see Kyle. The water was choppy, and there were tremendous whitecaps. We thought maybe Kyle had fallen in the drink, or he was holding onto his kayak." Carlos shook his head. "But that wasn't the case."

"She was crying and screaming, and we could hardly understand her. Oli was soaked to the skin, freezing and in shock," Viv said.

"Is that when you called 911?" Ebony asked.

"No, Oli called them. When she returned to shore," Viv said proudly, as though her daughter was a hero.

"How long after the storm did Olivia return to shore?" Ebony asked, her heart racing. She couldn't believe what she was hearing. Olivia had a phone with her in the kayak and during the storm, but she didn't immediately call for help. Zander would have a better idea, but it had to be a fifteen-minute paddle from the stanchion to the shore. Enough time to make the difference between life and death.

"I don't know," Carlos said with sadness in his voice. "Things became chaotic after the storm. We were relieved Oli was okay, but Kyle's disappearance shocked us. It's all a blur... and then you arrived at the park shortly thereafter."

"We understand, and we appreciate your sharing these details with us. It can't be easy," Ebony said.

"It's not," Viv said. "And our daughter's drug-induced stupor makes the situation even worse. When she's not asleep, she babbles about disappointing Kyle and her students. She feels guilty about leaving him behind and missing work." Her acerbic tone accused Ebony and Zander of causing the accident and its collateral damage.

"Before we go, could you show us the barn where the kayaks were stored?" Zander asked.

The damn leather sofa squeaked as Ebony stood up.

Carlos led them across the yard and past the paddock toward an immense whitewashed two-story barn. Downstairs, there were five empty stalls, each door bearing the name of its former resident. There was no odor of sweet hay mixed with manure, only the unexpected scent of turpentine and linseed oil. The only evidence of the former stable mates was two burnished leather saddles and crops mounted on the walls. Kayaking gear had replaced the dressage equipment, making it appear more like a sporting goods store than a barn.

Ebony and Zander examined a showcase containing ribbons and silver cups mounted on the wall opposite the stalls and a photo collage of Olivia on her horse.

"That's Oli on her favorite pony, Patches, when she was in high school. She used to be quite an equestrian, and we had Olympic hopes for her. However, Oli had other aspirations. She wanted to audition for *American Idol*, and while her singing lifted my heart, the judges were not impressed." He shook his head.

Ebony went toward the closest stall, which was filled with kayaks similar to Olivia's and Kyle's recreational models. Five of them were stacked on their toes, arranged against the wall like colorful bowling pins. Their empty cockpits gaped at her as if in fright, and their black plugs were all in place. Her vision skittered around the floor, hoping to spot the telltale plug, but she found nothing. Damn. If the plug had been there, it would have been obvious against the beige cobblestones swept so clean that her muddy boot prints desecrated the flooring.

"Do you lock the door to the barn?" she asked, veering off from Carlos and Zander to tour the interior perimeter of the building.

"It's unnecessary. Only those who are admitted through the security gate enter the compound."

The stalls on the right were accessible, but the storage closets and office on the left were locked. Ebony stood in the corridor that ran past the stalls and squinted as she peered up into the shaft of sunlight streaming through the hayloft opening from the second floor. The turpentine odor was overwhelming there.

So far, there was no sign of the plug, but there were still other places to search. In the remaining stalls, wetsuits were draped over wooden racks next to piles of fluorescent yellow life vests, an assortment of paddles, swim fins, and goggles. In an adjacent compartment, a car kayak carrier rested against a wall. Her eyes settled on a black camera suitcase imprinted with the SportsPro logo placed in the corner alongside a rusted toolbox.

Ebony knelt to examine the camera case and noticed it bore a sticker from The Hudson Outfitters. The stall was dark, so she switched on her flash to capture a photo of the label. In the flash's glare, she spied a piece of paper tucked between the SportsPro box and the wall. Curious, she slid it from its resting place. It was the cash receipt from a local sporting goods shop, not Outfitters. Since this find could be treasure or trash, Ebony stashed it inside a plastic evidence baggie and slipped it into her pocket.

"Detective Jones, are you looking for something?" Carlos asked.

She popped up and exited the stall, having completed her search. With disappointment, she'd concluded that the plug wasn't inside the pristine barn, but the sales ticket might be relevant to their inquiry.

"No, I'm fascinated by old barns. What's upstairs?"

"We remodeled the barn a few years ago, and Viv stores her paintings up there. Would you like to see them?"

"Thank you, no, but that explains the unusual scent. Your barn and compound is quite impressive."

"White Oaks represents Viv's handiwork. She prides herself on keeping the place nice and tidy."

I bet she does, Ebony thought. If forensics dusted for fingerprints, they would find nothing. The old barn was too spotless, as though someone was hiding secrets.

"Have you ever had any intruders?" Zander asked, selecting a carbon fiber paddle and examining it.

"*Nunca,* never. You must have noticed our state-of-the-art security system. We value our privacy."

"Thank you for the tour," Zander said, replacing the paddle and strolling toward the barn door. "We've taken enough of your time, and we appreciate your help. If you think of anything else, please call me."

"Sir, one more question before we go. Do you and your wife kayak?" Ebony asked.

"Yes, of course, we do." Carlos forced a fake smile as he motioned toward the paddock.

"Thanks again, Dr. Vargas," Ebony said.

"Detectives, please forgive my wife," Carlos said as he escorted them to the parking area. "She's as passionate as her daughter. When they throw themselves into something or someone, they commit with their complete hearts and souls. They are heartsick beyond despair. The boys and I are, too. Again, please let us know as soon as you hear anything."

Ebony slipped into their SUV. Through the windshield, she took one last look at the grand manor house at White Oaks. Her vision drifted toward the broad window in the front center gable. The white curtains fluttered as though they were being spied upon, but it could have been her imagination.

She and Zander drove in silence as he navigated the winding driveway toward the main road. At the entrance, a shiny black Porsche with dark-tinted windows and white pinstripes sped into the White Oak's driveway, pelting their car with pebbles as it whizzed by.

Zander whistled, checking out the sports car in the rearview mirror. "Nice wheels. That Targa costs about a buck and a half. More if it's the fiftieth-anniversary edition. Must be nice."

Ebony was half-listening. After their visit with Dr. and Mrs. Vargas, there was one obvious reason for their inquiries about this guarded family and their relationship with Kyle Emory, which wasn't her imagination.

One tiny reason about the size of a coin. The missing plug. And every occupant at White Oaks had possessed the opportunity to pull it and make it disappear.

Chapter Fifteen

Two days had passed, and still no details from Ebony.

Even the brief texts simply saying: *Sorry, Nothing New, E* failed to ease the knots clenching Jessie's belly. The lack of information left Jessie in a surrealistic haze, as though she'd dreamed the entire episode. Further, her exclusion from the investigation only increased her frustration. She was a player, not a spectator, and the waiting was unsettling.

Rehashing Ebony's cursory missives, she reached a decision. If she investigated the culprits, the Vargas family, perhaps it might ease her concerns. Knowledge was power.

A Google search on Olivia Vargas revealed an active and extensive social media life. Olivia was a music teacher at Rosa Parks Middle School in the Bronx, and she lived in Brooklyn. She'd attended New York University for both her undergraduate and master's degrees in music education. Her birthday was August 17th, which made her a Leo, and Olivia was twenty-nine years old, seven years younger than Kyle.

In every image, Olivia was stunning, as though she'd been digitally mastered by artificial intelligence. Waist length, lustrous dark hair. Glowing olive skin. A heart-shaped face with captivating hazel eyes and an infectious smile. An athletic-toned body, the kind that men died for.

It was understandable why Olivia's followers numbered over seventy-five thousand on Instagram alone. Every aspect of her life was in the public spotlight. She unabashedly offered her acolytes glimpses of her boot camp-style workouts, her travels, her music, her trendy wardrobe, and her posse of friends enjoying fabulous parties. She'd also produced a series of music videos where she sang and danced with her students to the latest hits. Amid the recent birthday bashes and picnics, Kyle cuddled with Olivia, grinning like an idiot. There were even photos of them launching from Kaal Rock Park on Saturday before the storm hit.

These playful posts stung as fiercely as if someone had doused alcohol in an open wound. When they'd been together, Kyle forbade Jessie from displaying their life and Lily on social media. He'd even goaded her into removing the photos from her feeds. To smooth the choppy waters of their relationship, she'd assented.

In countless videos, Olivia shilled natural skincare products and cosmetics from a brand called *Honey Face*, and demonstrated their vast line derived from artisan beeswax, honey, and botanicals. Scantily clad, Olivia invited her audience into her cheery bedroom while she applied Honey Face makeup. She claimed to go from "drab to fab" in five easy steps. In the evening, she removed her makeup and undertook her nighttime beauty regimen.

Jessie had read that micro-influencers with around one hundred thousand followers focused on a particular niche by creating quality content and interacting with their followers. Their "likes" converted into big bucks, and Olivia Vargas appeared to be no exception.

The social media tidbits were informative, but they were a superficial Fantasy Land. Jessie needed to find out the truth about Olivia. Who was she, really? Did she love Kyle, or was she exploiting him?

Jessie couldn't understand Kyle's rush to marry Olivia. Or how had Kyle felt about sharing his half-naked, Insta-fame-seeking fiancée with the world. She'd never know, but there was more to Olivia Vargas than met the public eye, and she needed to dig deeper.

Despite Hal's warnings, Jessie could solicit guidance from Mo Esposito, Jeremy Kaplan's devoted secretary, for a referral to one of Jeremy's private investigators.

With Lily asleep and the house otherwise empty, Jessie called her law office. After one ring, Mo answered.

"I'm sorry to hear about Kyle," Mo said, her voice choked up with sympathy. "Jeremy mentioned you'd probably be home for a few days."

"Thanks," Jessie replied. "We're waiting to hear from the police, but so far, nothing." Mo didn't comment, so Jessie continued, "I'd like to do a background check on Kyle's fiancée, Olivia Vargas."

"You don't need to say anything else," Mo replied sharply. "Carey Wentworth's your guy. If you use him, be forewarned. Carey's hygiene borders on derelict and his services don't come cheap. I'll text you his contact info."

"Jeremy doesn't need to know about this. I just need some questions answered."

"Like I said, you don't need to say anything else. Your request is going into the vault."

Jessie imagined Mo sitting at her desk surrounded by files and discarded super-sized cups of diet cola, pursing her thin lips and zipping them shut.

A text pinged with Wentworth's information, and she thanked Mo.

"Don't mention it. Seriously, never mention the referral because Carey will snitch to Jeremy. Those two go back to high school, and Jeremy might take issue with your interfering with an ongoing police investigation."

"I'm not interfering. I—"

"I don't want to know. And for a change, please stay out of trouble," Mo moaned.

Click. The line went dead.

Ridiculous. Jessie wasn't interfering with a police investigation. She owned the right to research the woman Kyle had planned to marry. If they discovered Kyle alive, the wannabe celebrity would be Lily's stepmother. God forbid.

The idea nauseated her. Olivia tucking Lily into bed. Olivia kissing Lily goodnight. Olivia participating in family holidays and milestones. Olivia taking Lily shopping, to lunch, or to the movies.

Jessie scrolled through Olivia's social media posts again. Why had Kyle chosen Olivia? Besides her big boobs and pretty face, what made Olivia Vargas so special?

She wasn't jealous of Kyle's newfound happiness. Good for him. Jessie had achieved it with Hal, too. Her annoyance stemmed from the secrecy surrounding his engagement, his life, and Ebony being the person who'd dropped the bombshell during the course of Kyle's accident case. Ebony! Of all people.

Why had Kyle neglected to mention Olivia? What was he hiding? Had he ever been honest with her about anything?

Fortunately, Jessie had learned about Olivia before they'd signed the custody agreement. Goddamn Kyle.

Fueled by a blinding white rage, Jessie punched Wentworth's number into her cell and waited for him to answer.

Chapter Sixteen

Mo hadn't mentioned the supersonic speed with which PI Wentworth conjured his alchemy. As she checked her email before dinner, the fine hairs on Jessie's arms tingled at the appearance of a file from PI Carey Wentworth, accompanied by the pricey bill for his services. Wentworth's report had better be worth the thousand bucks he'd charged her.

Tempted to read the results immediately, her finger hovered over the file, but she stopped. Before being sidetracked, Jessie needed to feed Lily and her cat. Bono's incessant yowling and the angry flick of his tail expressed his demand for dinner right away or else.

"You're right, Mr. B," she said, topping his bowl with kibble. "Patience is a virtue. After Lily's bedtime, I'll have plenty of time because it's you and me this evening. The big guy is in White Plains at a judge's meeting." Jessie scratched behind the cat's soft ears as he purred, chowing down his meal.

After supper, an unexpected visit from Grandpa Tom and Grandma Bev, and putting Lily to bed, it was time to dig into Wentworth's report.

Cuddled up on the fluffy down comforter on her bed, she plumped the pillows and leaned back. Bono sprang to her side, kneaded the blanket into a cozy nest, and settled in. His soft purring reassured her she wasn't stalking Olivia Vargas alone.

To steady her nerves, Jessie sipped a fortifying glass of Rioja, and exhaling a long breath, she clicked on the file entitled "Olivia Vargas." As it downloaded, she ignored any trepidation about Wentworth's data collection methods. By reputation, he mined most of his gems from public records, but others harkened from shadier sources. Better to leave the dirty work to a professional like Carey Wentworth, PI.

Although aiding Kyle was beyond her purview, it was her duty to protect Lily at all costs.

She reviewed the report about *Olivia Sanchez-Madera Vargas.*

PERSONAL INFORMATION FOR YOUR EYES ONLY

Olivia Sanchez-Madera Vargas

Birthdate and place: (dob August 17,1993) Westchester Medical Center, White Plains, N.Y.

Address: 250 Atlantic Avenue, New York, N.Y.; White Oaks, Garrison, N.Y.

CRIMINAL RECORD: No arrests or convictions. No sex offender status.

DMV: Valid NYS Driver's License NYS # 124583

Vehicle Registration - 2023 Lexus Hybrid Sedan, Black

License suspended two years ago for non-payment of NYC parking tickets. License reinstated after two months.

EMPLOYMENT: Rosa Parks Middle School (2018 to present), Music Education Teacher. On track to receive tenure.

New York State Teaching Certificate—Professional Certificate - Active status.

EDUCATION :

Masters of Arts in Music Education, New York University, Steinhardt School

Bachelor of Arts, New York University, Music Education (Dean's List)

St. Rose High School, Chappaqua, N.Y. (Private, Catholic High School)

FINANCES: Credit Score – 586

Accumulated Credit card debt - $17,500.00

Lexus auto loan—Westminster Savings Bank $34,000.00

Mortgage—Westminster Savings Bank $475,000.00. Co-signer on loan.

No student loans.

No Bankruptcies of record.

Combined Westminster Savings Bank, Savings and Checking Account balance (account numbers redacted) - $1753.34

Credit reporting agency notes several delinquent payments on credit and car loan payments.

Salary - $62,000.00 – New York State Retirement System—Tier 6, joined (2018)

IRS and New York State Department of Taxation and Finance Searches pending.

MARITAL STATUS: Married to Raul Esperanza on July 3, 2019, at the Old Dutch Church of Sleepy Hollow, Sleepy Hollow, N.Y.

Search outstanding on Raul Esperanza.

COURT PROCEEDINGS:

Plaintiff. *Esperanza vs. Esperanza.* (Index # 2023/325) Judgment of Divorce is pending in Dutchess County Supreme Court. Plaintiff-wife alleges the grounds of cruel and unusual punishment. Husband counterclaimed for Adultery. Husband dropped counterclaim and consented to an uncontested divorce.

Judgment is pending before Honorable Antonia Coppola. Judgment will allow resumption of plaintiff's maiden name, Vargas. The parties have not filed a Separation Agreement or proposed property settlement with the court.

REAL ESTATE: Co-owner of property secured by mortgage: Raul Esperanza in 72 North Walnut Street, Beacon, N.Y.

BUSINESS INTERESTS: Treasurer of The Hudson Outfitter, Inc., 72 North Walnut Street, Beacon, N.Y. Incorporated with the New York State Department of State on August 1, 2019. Registered Agent: Gloria Reyes Castellano, Esq., White Plains, N.Y.

SOCIAL MEDIA PROFILES: @Oliviahoneybabe

Instagram - 75,000 followers

Facebook- 83,000 followers

TikTok - 23,000 followers, up to 500K views.

LinkedIn- 975 connections

YouTube Channel - varies, can be up to a 500K views.

Paid beauty influencer for *Honey Face Natural Cosmetics* since 2021. Fees paid monthly, plus commission, with an average of $25,000.00 per year for her services on their social media platforms.

FAMILY:

Carlos Vargas, M.D., Ph.D. (age 60) In Chemistry. Employed by ChemMed, Tarrytown, NY. Position—V.P. Global Program. Born in Bogota, Columbia, and became a naturalized citizen in 1991.

Vivianna Sanchez Vargas—(age 59) Visual Artist. Medium—Oils. Born in Bogota, Columbia, and became a naturalized citizen in 1991. Exhibitions: "Through the Eyes of the Village." Albuquerque, NM, San Francisco, CA, San Diego, CA, New Orleans, LA, Atlanta, GA, Naples, FL, New York, N.Y. Visiting Professor, Savannah College of Art and Design.

Maximo Vargas (Brother) (age 31) V.P. Westminster Savings Bank, New York, N.Y. Married Ana Santos in 2014. Head designer for an athletic leisure clothing business, Lotus Wear, New York, N.Y. No Children.

Augusto Vargas (Brother) (age 27)- Business Development—Go-To Sports Betting, Inc., White Plains, N.Y., Single, Secretary of The Hudson Outfitters, Inc.

Family residence: "White Oaks," Croton-on-Hudson, N.Y. Occupied by all family members, except for Olivia.

EQUESTRIAN AWARDS: Placed in Interscholastic Equestrian Association Finals in Dressage. Middle School and High School.

Jessie shut her eyes, listening to her heartbeat gallop like the hooves of Olivia's thoroughbreds. She longed to escape the nightmare of her life, but the report had delivered a powerful blow to her chest. Every muscle burned as though she'd raced the Belmont Stakes twice over. Wentworth's report revealed the hard facts about Olivia's life, but not who she was as a person. Jessie didn't know where to begin or what to think.

While she'd been employed in the corporate and real estate law division at Curtis and McMann, Esquires, Jessie had reviewed background checks to vet the parties involved in multi-million dollar real estate deals. In high-stakes negotiations, it was necessary to understand the strengths and weaknesses of the firm's potential clients and the truthfulness of their representations.

As the DA, Hal had also researched prospective jurors. He'd asserted that it was imperative to comprehend a juror's mindset in advance rather than second-guessing their motivations, post-trial.

But seeking Olivia's dossier was unrelated to any business dealings. It was personal. Nothing was more personal to Jessie than protecting her child. Sure, she felt empathy for Olivia's loss and guilty about the digital spying, but certain harsh realities about Olivia Vargas smarted.

First, the woman was *married*. Olivia Vargas wasn't even her legal name. Until Judge Coppola signed the divorce decree, she remained Olivia Esperanza. With the judicial shortage and stifling case backlog, it could take months before the judge finalized the divorce. And Judge Coppola probably wanted the property issues resolved before she signed off.

It was disconcerting and inexplicable that Olivia was rushing to marry Kyle when she remained married to another man.

Second, Olivia Vargas earned an outrageous sum of money for a twenty-nine-year-old. Between her teacher's salary and her influencing, Olivia cleared close to a hundred grand. Plus, she owned property and was an officer in a business in Beacon, N.Y. Conversely, Olivia bore substantial debts and was a dead-beat, a scofflaw. Jessie wondered where the money went. Drugs? Clothing? Travel? Gambling? An extravagant lifestyle?

Finally, Olivia Esperanza enjoyed every advantage in life: an affluent family and an excellent education. Superficially, it might seem honorable that Olivia's career was music education, but her having any contact with Lily remained difficult to swallow.

The mystifying secrecy swirling around Kyle and Olivia's relationship also remained troublesome. Did he know about Olivia's marital status? Or did Olivia keep secrets from Kyle, too?

There was more to Olivia Vargas than was outlined in Wentworth's report, but Jessie couldn't put her finger on it. Something smelled like pungent horse manure. The report painted a picture of Olivia, but it was blurry, incomplete. Also, in New York, there was a seven-year limitation on information appearing in background checks, leaving the possibility of hidden secrets in Olivia's past. Thus, any arrest, traffic violation, bankruptcy, or court proceeding before Olivia was twenty-one didn't appear. Were there more inconsistencies to worry about?

"Bono," Jessie said, snapping the computer lid shut. "There's nothing more to do tonight. Let's sleep on it. We'll get a fresh perspective in the morning."

The cat raised his head, twitched his whiskers, and lowered his head back onto the bed.

She set the computer on her nightstand, and a text popped up on her phone.

On the way home. Will try not to wake you. Love you... H

She replied. *Drive carefully. Love you 2.*

As Jessie extinguished the bedside lamp, another ping sounded on her night table. In the darkness, she grabbed her phone, and the glowing screen revealed another new message.

Free tomorrow? I have some questions for you. E

"Great. Now I'll never get to sleep," Jessie muttered, her mind whirling with questions of her own.

Chapter Seventeen

Jessie's early morning text didn't surprise Ebony, but its cryptic contents did. It was so Jessie.

Kaal Rock Park at 7:30. I'll bring the chai.

Ebony wrestled with whether to invite Zander along, but she elected to go solo. Dragging him along would stifle the conversation, especially if Jessie perceived they were ganging up on her.

At Kaal Rock Park, Jessie stood at the river's edge, just shy of the flimsy yellow plastic barricade. Since it was early, neither the boats nor forensics had returned to their tasks. She and Jessie were alone with the park to themselves.

A gentle wind blew, and the gulls and geese circled overhead as the sun disappeared behind a cloud and then reappeared with a burst of brightness. Jessie faced away from the parking lot toward the river, seemingly oblivious to Ebony's approach from across the lawn. Ebony couldn't tell whether the brilliant sunlight sparkling on the water, the traffic on the bridge, or the crime scene tape had captured Jessie's attention. Whatever the reason, the majestic backdrop was a panorama of contradictions—beauty and death on the Hudson.

As Ebony drew closer, she observed Jessie pick up a stone and toss it into the frothy water. In a barely audible whisper, she muttered the Kaddish, the mourner's prayer, in Hebrew. The reverence of the moment was unmistakable. In Judaism, they considered it a mitzvah, a blessing to mark a grave with a stone, and Jessie was marking Kyle's watery grave, one from which he might never return.

Jessie turned and started when she observed Ebony waiting a few feet away. "Hey! I wasn't sure you were going to show, but I'm glad you did."

Ebony waited for the lump in her throat to subside before she leaned in hard. "I hate to be a bitch, but this is a restricted area. You're not supposed to be here."

"There was no one to stop me, and the gates were open."

They walked to a picnic table and took seats on the dew-stained wooden bench. Jessie handed her a paper coffee mug marked with the letter E from the table. "Here, this is for you."

"Thanks. I'm sorry about Kyle, but this area is off-limits right now."

"I know, but I had to come here. I had to see it. I've been to this place a hundred times, and I never tire of the view. Now, I know better." She motioned toward the tape that quivered in the stiff breeze. "Do you have any information you can share with me? I won't mention anything to anyone, Hal or the Emorys, if you say so. I'm living in limbo and going kind of crazy." Her voice quavered as though she was losing her grip on reality.

Ebony remained quiet, torn between whether to spill about the kayak's missing plug and keeping her trap shut. There was no harm in telling Jessie, but there was something holding her back. For the time being, she wouldn't say anything. Not until she'd gotten what she'd come here for.

"Jessie, you're my closest friend, and we've hit a rough patch lately, but I've got a job to do. I need to understand more about the day of the accident. Can you help me?"

"Sure, what the hell? What do you want to know?"

"Is there anything else about Kyle that might be relevant to our case?" Ebony clasped her hands together and rolled her wrists in an unconscious nervous movement. When she realized her action, Ebony stopped, hoping Jessie hadn't noticed her tell.

"Nope. I wish there was. I believed I knew Kyle, but I'm realizing I didn't at all. He kept so many secrets." She paused. "And what about you? Do you have anything to tell me?"

The pain on Jessie's face tugged at Ebony's soul. It would only exacerbate the rift between them if she slapped Jessie with an "I told you so." Ebony wanted to make amends, repair the damage, and not alienate Jessie even further. Lately, they had their differences, their conflicts, but since kindergarten, they'd been connected like sisters. Despite the tension of their professional lives, they both recognized that if their lives were on the line, the other would be there in a split second.

"There is one thing. And it's not for publication, do you understand?"

The breeze ruffled Jessie's auburn curls, and she dipped her chin in agreement.

"Forensics discovered a problem with Kyle's kayak. I can't give you any details yet because we don't understand the defect's significance."

Jessie's eyes widened, and the color drained from her face as she absorbed the news. "Are you telling me there was a product liability issue, or sabotage, or—"

"I'm not stating any conclusions other than we discovered an abnormality with the kayak. We don't understand what this means, so don't let your imagination run wild. It could mean something or nothing."

"I guess that contradicts your suicide theory, doesn't it?" Jessie paused, and she studied her hands, wringing them as though thinking. "How many people were with Kyle at the park? Did everyone have access to the kayak? Have you interviewed them all? What have they said? Have you spoken to his fiancée?"

"This discovery has pushed our investigation into an entirely new direction, and yes, we're interviewing the witnesses. As soon as there's any news, I'll pass it along."

"At least you know I'm blameless in Kyle's drowning." Jessie scoffed.

Thank god, Ebony thought. She couldn't live through Jessie having to prove her innocence in another murder investigation.

"I don't have any more to share about Kyle, but the fiancée is married," Jessie said, taking a sip from her cup.

"Who's married?"

"Olivia Vargas. She's filed for a divorce, which hasn't been granted yet."

"How did you discover that, Jessie? I told you not to meddle." Ebony struggled to mask the sharp edge of a migraine stabbing her temples. It was the throbbing pain Jessie's impertinence seemed to summon. "Any interference could land you in serious trouble."

"Hell, no. It's a matter of public record. Anyone can log into the Dutchess County Clerk's database and perform a search," Jessie said. "I was curious about Olivia Vargas, so I took a shot. There were no judgments, tax liens, or criminal convictions in our county, only the pending divorce. The actual documents are confidential, but the clerk's minutes listed that she'd filed a summons with notice for divorce, but no final judgment has been signed."

"Sorry, I shouldn't have been so quick to accuse you." The ache in Ebony's forehead dulled as she regretted her rush to judgment. Sometimes, Jessie got lucky. And sometimes, she underestimated Jessie's innate legal talent. Although perhaps Jessie wasn't revealing the entire picture. "And?"

"They filed it this past June 27th."

"You're killing me here. Who's her husband?" Ebony insisted.

"Her husband? The defendant is Raul Esperanza."

"Never heard of him, but I'd better add his name to our witness list."

Chapter Eighteen

Cindie despised waiting in the telephone queue to speak with the prescription nurse at her physician's office. Trapped in a sinkhole of South American pan flute music, each note plunged her deeper into the "on hold" abyss. As the music droned on, she sat at her office desk, taking her new laptop for a test drive.

Her corneas felt as sandy as the Sahara Desert. Mid-September had triggered the autumn allergy season, and she'd just returned from the ladies' room after ditching her contact lenses. Between her inflamed eyes, the lack of sleep, and the missing kayak plug, she was having a banner morning. She'd been in the criminal law game for a decade and had grown numb to the small-town drug dealers, gamblers, drunks, and robbers. Major crimes, like murder and rape, had been Hal's forte, not hers. He'd been at his best when pitching his theories about a brutal homicide to a jury, but prosecuting violent felony crimes made her squeamish.

Organization skills were her strong suit. Her talents shined in managing the lawyers, investigators, support staff, and the hundreds of cases being prosecuted by the largest district attorney's office in the Hudson Valley. After five years as ADA Hal Samuel's first chair assistant, she'd graduated to his ADA when he'd been promoted to DA last year. He'd conferred the nitty-gritty office operations on her, allowing him to bask in the courtroom's spotlight.

Cindie preferred the arrangement. She was a behind-the-scenes gal who didn't seek recognition. She received enough at home from Paul, their two kids, and in her community endeavors.

Now, as DA, she was the head administrator. While Hal complained about office operations robbing him of his trial time, Cindie loved it. Hal had prepared her to be the heart and soul of the Dutchess County District Attorney's office, and she pledged to continue the eradication of the mess bequeathed to Hal by the prior administration.

It was the influence of her medical career which had honed her talent. For fifteen years, she'd served as the physician's assistant to the well-respected family practitioner, Martin Myers, MD. She'd organized his charts, ordered his supplies, managed his schedule, and cared for his patients. Myers had been in his mid-sixties when she'd joined his practice, and as time passed, she'd observed his forgetfulness and his growing impatience with his staff and patients.

Cindie had covered for him—double-checking his prescriptions, the tests he'd ordered, and ensuring he'd reviewed the patient charts before his appointments. But as hard as she tried, she couldn't supervise his every action. It took one error, one misprescribed medication, to hospitalize a child with a life-threatening allergic reaction to penicillin. To Cindie's horror, Myer had overlooked the clearly labeled allergy in the boy's chart.

It had been a blessing when, after a half-century of medical service, he'd sold out to a medical conglomerate. The merger, and the child's malpractice suit, had signaled it was time for Cindie to move on. Studying the law had helped diminish the heartbreak, the guilt plaguing her every hour of every day. Instead, she focused on pursuing justice and truth and serving her community.

As a PA, she'd brought life into the world and helped it depart, too. Natural death didn't bother her. Unnatural, brutal death did, like Kyle Emory's was shaping up to be.

The queasiness and questions incited by Kyle's disappearance had kept her up last night. Was the missing plug an accident or an intentional act? Who would undertake such a horrible, premeditated act? And why?

Unable to sleep, Cindie had put the inky predawn hours to good use, combing the web for aquatic forensic experts. For over an hour and with two cups of coffee, she'd struggled to frame the correct keywords on her laptop in the kitchen. Then, finally, she'd hit on *Aquatic Deaths and Homicidal Drowning Investigations. Hudson Valley.* By the time the sun peeked over the leafy horizon outside her window, one name had popped up.

Joanna Medina, MD, Ph.D. in Criminal Psychology. Dr. Medina had published a slew of articles on drowning deaths, and operated an institute in Kerhonkson, N.Y. to teach and certify law enforcement and public safety officials about diving protocols, water and boating rescue and recovery, and subsurface anti-terrorist training.

Kerhonkson, Cindie had mused, taking a slug of coffee. What a peculiar place for an aquatic expert to live.

Kerhonkson was a rural, one-street town situated along the Rondout Creek, a tributary of the Hudson. Tucked in the Southern Catskills "Borscht Belt" past New Paltz, Kerhonkson's claim to fame was a one-legged tap dancer named Clayton "Peg Leg" Bates. Bates had been a Black American groundbreaker and hotelier who had performed on stage and on television from the 1920s to 1990s. Not much else happened in Kerhonkson, which could explain its attraction to Dr. Medina.

The flute music stopped, and Cindie held her breath in anticipation. She heard silence, a click, and the mocking dial tone. Tempted to smash her phone against the wall, she thought better of it.

"Screw it," she said, returning her attention to the website for Medina & Associates, Inc., and its cute logo of fish cavorting on the ocean's sandy floor. The site was a sourcebook for public safety diving training, and there were articles about underwater vehicle extraction, and the recovery of bodies-in-the-water investigations.

Clicking on Medina's resume, the photo of a woman about her own age, with short blonde hair, an angular face, and glasses, popped up. A ten-page resume of her education (BA- Boston University, MD-Harvard Medical School, Ph.D.-John Jay College of Criminal Justice), certifications, speaking and teaching engagements, and research and publications accompanied the photo.

Cindie's itchy, weary eyes scanned an entry, which appeared to be custom-made for Kyle's case: *Certified Expert Witness in Bodies-Found-in-Water* and *Aquatic Death Investigation in CT, MA, FL, and NY*. Joanna Medina even provided a list of the litigation where she'd consulted on homicidal drowning, and criminal and civil cases where she'd served as an expert witness. Her certifications with the U.S. Navy, Coast Guard, and Quantico weren't shabby either.

Out of curiosity, she clicked on a link to a *New York Times* feature about Medina foiling a terrorism plot in the waters off the Ellis Island National Museum of Immigration and the Statue of Liberty. According to the article, Medina had led the divers' team in neutralizing explosives installed beneath the Ellis Island ferry dock. For her heroism, the governor had awarded her the New York State Medal of Valor.

Cindie vaguely recalled the incident, but she'd never heard of Medina until last night. There'd been no reason since her office had never investigated an aquatic disappearance before.

Medina, her husband, and their partner, Sissy Mackum, had formed the company fifteen years ago. From the calendar of events, their services were in high demand. As the named partner and medal winner, Medina was the rock star of the trio.

Armed with her research, Cindie's heart leaped, anticipating meeting Joanna Medina, the real-life superhero who lived in the neighborhood. She would contact Medina and feel her out about Kyle's disappearance. Unfortunately, there was a major flaw in her logic. There was no victim or case to present to Medina. Any discussions would be hypothetical, and to a world-renowned expert like Joanna Medina, a waste of time.

At present, Shepardson's team found no evidence of foul play. And Kyle could reappear at any moment. Yet, the uneasiness in Cindie's gut persisted. Call it prosecutor's intuition or paranoia, but something about the missing plug tugged at her. She didn't want to wait.

The Poughkeepsie Police Department was treading water in unfamiliar territory, and Medina might offer suggestions about their investigation. She might steer them in a direction they'd never imagined.

So what if Cindie appeared to be a fool? She had everything to gain and nothing to lose. As did Kyle Emory. And it was her responsibility to ensure every inch of the Hudson and its shoreline were thoroughly and properly searched to find him.

Cindie picked up the phone and placed the call.

Chapter Nineteen

Kyle had left the basement of their Platt Street home a depressing mess. In the far corner, he'd ditched his skis, boots, golf clubs, fishing poles, vinyl record collection, record player, musical instruments, and assorted boxes from his parents' basement. What was Jessie going to do with the stuff now? Keep it for Lily to throw away?

Among the detritus, she'd unearthed a water-stained carton marked "Kyle's Room." The bold handwriting belonged to Kyle's mother, Bev, and warned hands-off her oldest son's private property. Jessie inspected the moldy carton, torn between invading Kyle's teenage years and leaving the memories in peace. Before she could change her mind, she ripped back the tape, opened the flaps, and peeked inside.

Neatly stacked within were swimming trophies and medals, baseball trading cards, photos, a vinyl-clad Book of Common Prayer, Kyle's high school diploma, and his high school yearbooks. Bev's handwriting may have been on the outside, but fastidious Tom had organized the contents.

Jessie removed a framed swim team photo of athletic young men and women standing poolside beneath a banner proclaiming them as "New York State Champions-Albany, N.Y." To get a better look, she wiped away its dusty film with the hem of her t-shirt. Shiny gold medals on blue ribbons dangled around their necks, and the teens grinned as if they'd won the Olympics.

Even in the poor basement lighting, Jessie could tell which kid was Kyle. He was the team captain, lording over the back row. Average height, but strapping, she recognized his inquisitive brown eyes, slender nose, and crooked smile. Wanting to better examine the memorabilia, she gathered the photo and yearbooks and lugged them up the cellar stairs.

At the far end of the hallway, the grandfather clock chimed three-thirty in the afternoon, and inside her pocket, her phone vibrated with a sound notification from the nursery. Setting the items on the granite kitchen countertop, she rushed to investigate.

Through the slender crack in the nursery door, Jessie spied Lily standing in her crib, boxing with the farm animal mobile dangling overhead.

"Someone's having a good time, Lilybean. Are you trying to catch Old MacDonald's cows? And are you ready for snack time?"

* * *

Downstairs in the kitchen, Lily gnawed on a cookie, clutching her bottle in the opposite hand.

"I want to show you something. These are books with pictures of your daddy when he was a boy. Let's check them out," Jessie said.

These unilateral conversations were commonplace with Lily, and even if Lily didn't reply, Lily's penetrating expression convinced Jessie that she understood. Theirs was an indestructible bond, and together, they would survive Kyle's death or anything else life threw at them. No one could ever replace Kyle in Lily's life, but they had each other, Hal, and his eight-year-old son, Tyler. And she promised Lily and Kyle that she'd spend the rest of her life making Lily feel secure and loved.

The three yearbooks resting on the table depicted Kyle's Albany High School years, and Jessie selected the green one with the blue mascot, a falcon, on the cover. The spine cracked as she opened the musty leatherette cover and skimmed through the photographs until she'd located Kyle within the sophomore class.

"Look, here's Daddy, when he was—" Jessie calculated he would have been sixteen years old in the photo. "Sixteen. Just learning to drive a car and about life." Stifling a giggle, Jessie held the page up for Lily's review.

Kyle sported an Aerosmith t-shirt, and his untamed shoulder-length dark curls tumbled across his forehead, making him appear as if he'd just risen from bed. He squinted, and his forced white smile revealed his unease at being photographed and an awareness of the unwanted attention the yearbook might bring. This Kyle was a boy on the cusp of manhood, uncomfortable in his own body and unprepared for the impending, unavoidable changes; a slouchy teen destined to drive the adolescent girls wild.

Lily withdrew the bottle from her mouth and scooped a handful of Cheerios from the highchair tray.

Kyle also appeared with a shiny, shaved head in the composite shots for the swim team, clutching the narrow neck of a standup bass in the orchestra, and mugging for the camera in the student council. The curlicue handwriting of teenage girls blanketed the inside covers, wishing him "a great summer" and "hoping I see you around."

"Your daddy was a heartbreaker," Jessie said with Lily's gaze glued on her.

Through these photos, the past reached out to the present, providing her with a glimmer of Kyle's hidden backstory. Swimmer. Classical Musician. Student Leader.

Next, she selected the maroon book with a silver falcon on the cover, Kyle's junior year, a year that had wrought dramatic physical changes in him. Time had chiseled away his cherubic appearance, leaving sharp, handsome planes and high cheekbones. He'd styled his dark hair short on the sides, leaving a tamed wave of curls above his prominent forehead. At seventeen, there was noticeable stubble on his chin, foreshadowing the thick, trimmed beard Kyle had worn when she'd last seen him. He sat tall, his broad shoulders as straight as a board. His chestnut eyes flirted with the camera, beckoning the viewer with a curl of his lips.

As Jessie raised the book for Lily's inspection, another photo fluttered to the tile floor. She retrieved it and placed it on the kitchen table. The selfie depicted Kyle on a lake, standing in a rowboat with three other sleek, suntanned boys. Fishing poles, a six-pack of beer, and a bag of weed were stowed among the towels and paddles in the bottom of the aluminum hull.

"This must be at his grandparents' place on Lake George," Jessie explained to Lily. "They would be your great-grandparents, Colonel Geoff and Maimie Gaines. I never met them, but Daddy adored them." She examined the backside of the photo. "There's no date on it, but it looks about the same time as the yearbook picture. Doesn't it?"

The front doorbell rang, and Jessie tucked the photo inside the maroon cover and placed it on top of the others. "Coming," Jessie yelled as she removed Lily from the highchair, slung her across her hip, and jogged to answer the door.

Jessie wasn't expecting any visitors today, so discovering her father, Ed, on the porch was a pleasant surprise. The track of the autumn sun had shifted lower in the sky, and the sun hovered right above her father's head, making her squint at him. The days were getting shorter, the evenings were cooler, and soon, the sunset threatened to arrive. Sharp shadows sliced her emerald lawn, which glowed in a colorful jumble of fallen leaves.

Ed brandished a brown paper bag from her favorite bakery, Kelly's. "I know it's close to dinnertime, but I've brought the chocolate croissants you enjoy. I thought you deserved a treat."

Jessie kissed her father's five o'clock shadow and invited him inside. "I was thinking of taking Lily for a walk before it gets darker. Care to join us?"

Ever since the news about Kyle, her father had been overprotective. He was a solid man, a family man, and a community man. As Poughkeepsie High principal, local parents relied upon him to protect their kids. Besides Hal, she leaned on him more than anyone else in the universe. Her dad was and had always been her rock.

"Sure. I've been sitting all day, and I could use a good stretch of the legs. I'll grab the stroller from the mudroom and meet you ladies on the back porch," Ed said.

Jessie bundled Lily in a navy hoodie and jean jacket, grabbed her own camel hair poncho and the baby bag, and joined Ed on the bluestone patio in the backyard. Only the fluffy yellow and red snapdragons and shoulder-height white dahlias remained in the garden, reminding her of summer's warm days and autumn's cool nights ahead.

"I know Hal's been busy with court, and I thought you could use some company. How long are you planning to take off from work?" he asked.

Jessie buckled Lily into the expensive Italian stroller her parents had splurged on for their newest granddaughter. "Jeremy told me to take as much time as I need, so I don't know. Before I return, I'd like there to be a resolution on Kyle's case, but who knows how long that'll be?" She pushed the stroller across the patio, and Ed assumed control once they hit the gravel driveway.

"Honey, there may not be a resolution. We may never understand what happened to Kyle. I hope you can live with that outcome."

"I'll have to. But his *accident* is shrouded in mystery." Jessie gestured with air quotes. "We still don't know whether he's dead or alive, but I'm beginning to fear the worst. If it has happened, we don't know how Kyle died. Was it suicide, which I don't believe, or was there foul play? I was clueless about his engagement, and the more I dig, the more I realize Kyle was a stranger."

"What are you talking about? You lived together for five years, and I don't believe you didn't know him. Kyle was a nice, quiet, hardworking guy who was a smidge uptight. Your mother and I liked Kyle, and we were sorry when your relationship ended. His jealousy of your friendship with Terrence and your professional success spread like poison through his veins, ruining the life you had built. Too bad. It was his loss."

Jessie gave a loving squeeze to her dad's muscular arm as he pushed the stroller. "Dad, you're describing him like the serial killers we hear about on the news." She lowered her voice, mocking a newscaster. "He was a quiet man, and we never suspected he could slaughter his family with a machete."

They laughed. The stroller hit an uneven portion of the sidewalk as they rounded onto Adriance Avenue, causing it to pitch and roll. Lily sang, "La-La-La," oblivious to Ed's righting the carriage on its course.

"You know what I meant. Kyle wasn't dynamic. He played his cards close to his vest. Not like..." Ed paused.

Her father was about to compare Kyle to Hal. Heartbroken when Jessie's older brother Ethan and his family moved to Silicon Valley a few years

113

ago, Ed had adopted Hal as a surrogate son. They were similar. Both were free-spoken men of integrity, dedicated to their families and public service. Kyle had never connected with Ed, and it had stung. Rather, Kyle had sidled up to her mother, Lena, the head cheerleader of TEAM KYLE, and she'd pressured the pair to reconcile until Jessie and Hal's engagement.

They crossed the street, and Ed pointed out squirrels to his granddaughter. "Lilybean, that big fat squirrel is gathering acorns for the winter. From the looks of it, it's going to be a long, cold one."

Memories of the endless, bleak Hudson Valley winters dominated by ice and snow sent a shiver up Jessie's spine. She tilted her face toward the last remnants of the golden sunlight sparkling through the leaves, soaking it into her skin. At that moment, her phone vibrated in her pocket, interrupting her reverie. She withdrew it and, not recognizing the caller, she let it go to voicemail. She'd check the message later.

"What I meant was," Jessie said, "Kyle's secrets give credibility to Ebony's suggestion about Kyle's suicide. But in my heart, I don't buy it." Relief flooded Jessie as she spoke aloud about the conclusion she'd long harbored. "I found a box of his stuff in the basement from when he was in high school. Kyle was a state champion swimmer. I'm not saying he didn't drown, but I don't believe he took his life. He had too much to live for. Lily. His fiancée. We'd settled our custody and money issues. It doesn't add up."

"A couple of months ago, Kyle stopped by to see your mother after he'd dropped Lily at your house. He mentioned he was seeing someone, and he was happier than he'd been in a long time. Although he hinted the circumstances were complicated."

Everything was complicated with Kyle, but Jessie questioned exactly what he meant.

"Why didn't you mention this before?"

Ed shrugged. "It didn't seem important, and we figured Kyle would inform you if the relationship turned serious."

"I guess you were wrong about that," Jessie said. "But you're not wrong often, old man."

"You can analyze the circumstances surrounding Kyle's disappearance forever, but what good will it do? Honey, in the end, this could've been a horrible accident, honey. He got caught in a storm. End of discussion." Ed removed his Yankee baseball cap and scratched his gray hair. A pained expression flashed across his face. "I would hate to see you jeopardize your law partnership with Jeremy and your new life with Hal by chasing after ghosts. Sometimes you have to let things go."

Sometimes, she and her dad were so in sync she could read his mind. He was thinking about his former best friend and staff member, and her teacher, mentor, and confidante, Terrence Butterfield, and their two decades of fishing trips, baseball games, and intense, philosophical debates. No one, especially Ed, would ever comprehend how a popular, charismatic teacher had become a psychotic killer. Occasionally, like now, Ed's guilt and hurt surfaced. But Ed had let it go.

"What if there was foul play? Don't I owe it to Lily to help find out the truth?" Jessie asked.

A fire truck sped past, turning the corner and heading downtown toward the central business district.

"Weeeeeee-ooo!" Lily squealed as Jessie peeked inside the carriage to find Lily applauding in delight. "Weeeeeee-ooo!"

"That's for the police to determine, honey. But I know you. You'll plow ahead and try to help, but please keep Kyle's death in perspective. I know you feel an obligation to Lily, but before the accident, both you and he had moved on. Don't let any guilt over your breakup drag you into his death. You have too much to lose, and Kyle isn't worth it."

Her father wasn't being cruel. He was being her protector. And he was correct.

At the time of his death, she and Kyle had entered other committed relationships. For years, Jessie had dreamed about marrying Hal, and next June, those dreams would become reality. Yet she owed Lily the truth about Kyle's death.

A bit more snooping couldn't hurt, could it?

Chapter Twenty

Ebony rolled down the car window and inhaled the autumn air, heavy with the perfume of damp earth, decaying leaves, and a hint of bonfire. She and Zander were driving south toward Beacon along the back roads. On the straightaways, she glimpsed the Hudson and the fertile fruit and vegetable farms and vineyards. Mostly, they wound through the housing, commercial, and industrial developments sprouting like mushrooms on the vanishing farmlands of southern Dutchess County. She remembered when the land had been rich with dairy farms, before the minor league baseball stadium, the malls, the distribution centers, and the commuters flocked upstate for a better life.

Arriving in Beacon a half-hour later, Zander parked on Main Street in front of The Hudson Outfitters behind a slick silver two-seater Mercedes. Although it was a weekday, the town crawled with leaf peepers eager to post snaps of the dazzling bronze, gold, and red tapestry on their social media feeds.

Ebony and Zander had called ahead to make an appointment with the store's owner, Cody Shaw, and with any luck, he'd keep it.

Ebony had never heard of Shaw, but Zander assured her Shaw was the valley's expert on small watercraft and the great outdoors. The goofy grin on Zander's face indicated his excitement about meeting the celebrated outdoorsman and host of a weekly public radio show.

To bone up for their interview, she'd streamed a recent podcast episode of *The Hudson Outsider*. Shaw discussed autumn extreme sports like rock climbing and whitewater kayaking, while exuding the persona of a rugged expert who could handle limitless danger. She knew the type. Reckless. Unreliable. Egotistical. Shaw had sounded that way over the phone, too, so she knew what to expect. If he showed up.

The store was also as Ebony had imagined. With its expensive backpacks, lanterns, and clothing in the window, and the rustic barn wood framing the interior walls, it oozed with the hyper-masculinity of an Adirondack lodge. Alternative rock tunes blasted over the sound system, and kayaks dangled overhead on invisible nylon lines like the blue whale at the American Museum of Natural History. As her feet sank into the plush red and black buffalo check carpeting, she spied a young man with dark shiny hair sitting in a club chair before a cobblestone fireplace. He typed on a laptop and didn't bother to look up when she and Zander approached him.

"Auggie Vargas?" Zander asked, apparently recognizing the man from the day of the accident. "We're looking for Cody Shaw, but what are you doing here?"

Auggie peered up, blinking. "Detectives, this is a pleasant surprise. Cody's in the back room checking a shipment." He glanced around to ensure they were alone in the store. "We don't advertise it, but I'm his silent partner in Outfitter. In fact, my folks don't even know." He shut the laptop and set it on the table next to the chair. "Cody's awesome at promotion and marketing, and he knows the inventory like nobody else, but he's not so great with finances. But me, I don't know shit about the outdoors or stock, but I've got a head for figures." He smiled a sparkling, cheerful smile, a genuine smile, as he sprang to his feet. "I'll go get him. Wait a sec."

The young man disappeared through a door in the back of the store, leaving them listening to the Red Hot Chili Peppers and staring into the crackling artificial fire. There was something hypnotic about the dancing yellow flames, which made it difficult to look away, even from the fake ones.

Ebony liked Auggie. He reminded her of a puppy with boundless energy and the desire to please. She surmised Auggie was the underrated runt of the Vargas litter, muscling his successful brother and spoiled sister out of the way for his parents' attention. He needn't have been, though. From their background check, they'd discovered that besides owning a minority interest in Outfitter, Auggie held an MBA from Harvard Business School and was the director of business management for an online sport-betting firm. He knew numbers all right and was working hard to become a millionaire before the age of thirty.

The door swung open, and a charismatic rock star presence blew into the room, trailed by his minion, Auggie Vargas. From Zander's raised eyebrows, he sensed it, too. Tall, tan, and sinewy, Cody Shaw strutted toward them, brushing his shoulder-length sun-streaked hair out of his ruggedly handsome face. His plaid shirt and jeans were crumpled, not in a vagrant way, but as though he'd spent the night camping under the stars. As he drew closer, she noted Shaw even smelled woody and piney, as though an evergreen forest had sprung up inside the store.

Before Ebony stood a radio personality and a regular contributor and featured cover boy for *Outside* magazine. She'd also discovered that Shaw was a social media influencer for some of the items hanging on the store's walls, such as natural sunscreen products, hiking clothes, camping gear, and whitewater excursions. She'd chuckled at his promotional videos, where he seductively stared into the camera, proclaiming, "Hi, I'm Cody Shaw. Let me be your guide on the adventure of a lifetime."

The corners of Shaw's mouth upturned. He batted the velvety brown eyes beneath his long, dark lashes, aware of his effect on people. "I'm Cody Shaw. Can I help you?"

Ebony shivered, dispelling the fantasies of sharing a bliss-filled tent with him overnight where neither of them slept.

Zander cleared his throat and made the introductions. "As I mentioned on the phone, we'd like a word with you about the apparent drowning of Kyle Emory. Is there somewhere we can talk in private?" Zander glanced at Vargas.

"Man, I understand. I've got to go anyway, so I'll catch you later," Auggie said, grabbing his jacket off the back of the chair.

"Mr. Vargas, we'd like to speak with you, too. Here's my card; please call me tomorrow." Zander held out a card. Auggie smiled amiably. He and

Shaw shook hands in a fraternal fashion, bumped shoulders, and he left the store. The cowbells on the door handle jingled when the door shut behind him.

"I'm a fan of your show," Ebony said. Flattery appeared to be a currency in this sporting goods shop.

Shaw's practiced smile widened. "Detective, do you kayak or hike?" His baritone made the simple question reek of pheromones.

"No. Detective Pulaski is the avid kayaker here. Aren't you Zander?"

Seeming to recognize a kindred spirit, the two men embarked on a conversation about equipment, weather, and whitewater excursions. Shaw led Zander around the shop, stopping to highlight the photographs of his death-defying feats. Ebony wasn't listening to them, but she overheard technical terms like "bent shaft paddle," "J-Cradle," and "wet exit," which meant zero to her. She hoped Shaw's charisma hadn't seduced Zander and that he maintained his objectivity during their investigation.

After ten minutes, Shaw segued from his kayaking trips in New Zealand to his backpacking throughout the U.S. National Parks. To grab their attention, Ebony cleared her throat, but they ignored her, making her regret mentioning Zander's interest in kayaking.

"Excuse me, Mr. Shaw," Ebony said, interrupting the love fest. "We have a few questions about the sale of two kayaks to Olivia Vargas and Kyle Emory. What's your relationship with the Vargas family?"

"I've known them since I was a kid. They're a great crew and avid kayakers. Auggie and I have been best buds for as long as I can remember, and now we're business partners."

His answers echoed Viv Vargas' words, implying a more intimate relationship between the two men.

"What about Kyle Emory?" Zander asked.

"It's awful what happened to the dude. I feel partially responsible because Livvie brought him into the store a few months ago, and I sold them their Pelican kayaks. They said they were using them in lakes and ponds. Recreational stuff. They never mentioned open water paddling." He snagged Zander's arm again and dragged him aside, pointing up toward a yellow tie-dye PVC kayak hanging from the ceiling. "I sold them both this recreational model. It's a nice, safe, stable, lightweight beginner boat with molded footrests and onboard storage. If they were going onto the Hudson, they should've upgraded to the sea model, which is designed for long-distance touring and playing in rough waters, and they cost twice as much." He gestured toward a shiny, sleek black fiberglass boat hanging from a distant rafter.

"When was that?" Ebony asked.

This guy was slick, she thought. Shaw was deflecting the responsibility to Kyle and Olivia, making them the fall guys. He must have been coached by his lawyer, agent, or both to distance himself from any liability for the accident.

"I'd have to say April or May. I can check the sales records on the computer if you like."

"Thanks. That would be helpful. Did Emory say whether he was an experienced boater?" Zander asked.

"I know Livvie was because we've done several trips together and also with her family. She's Class III, an intermediate paddler. As for Emory? Not so sure." He paused, twisting his neck, looking for an answer. "I think he'd mentioned he'd been out on the water as a kid, so he wasn't a complete novice. His grandparents had a summer place on Lake Champlain or someplace in the northeast. Livvie seemed to be nuts about him, with his medium athletic build and big gig in the city. I wondered about his enthusiasm for the sport or whether he was doing it just for her."

Another travel photo hanging beside the fireplace attracted Ebony's attention. A group dressed in swimsuits, helmets, and life vests posed on a sandy riverbank with a river raft in the background. With their arms draped around each other's shoulders and leaning on their paddles, they grinned at the camera. Nestled against Shaw with her hair sopping wet, Olivia beamed up at him. Auggie, Max, and Carlos were also in the photo, along with two other guys about Shaw's age.

Ebony had misread the situation. Cody didn't have a thing with Auggie. Cody and Olivia had been a couple, which explained his sizing up Kyle. She wondered whether he still fanned the flames of desire for Olivia and why Viv had reacted so strangely. "Nice picture. Is it a recent one?" she asked.

"We snapped that one on the Arkansas River in Colorado last summer. Man, that Royal Gorge was a stunner, and we hit some Class IV rapids that made my heart beat out of my chest. Livvie was a real trooper on the trip, being the only chick in the raft. Her mom had to bail because of an art exhibition, and Max's wife couldn't get off work. So it was just Livvie and the guys, including my two brothers, who joined us on the adventure. We had a blast."

Ebony reexamined the photo of Olivia surrounded by a flock of handsome men. The family resemblance between Cody and his brothers was obvious—three golden Adonises with matching physiques and blinding smiles.

"Your rafting trip looks like it was an amazing expedition for the Vargas and Shaw families," Zander said, unable to hide his envy. "I've always wanted to run the rapids but haven't had the opportunity."

"You will someday, bro. Don't give up." Shaw slapped Zander on the back. "And their name's not Shaw. Shaw is my stage and business name. I mean, who would want to buy camping equipment from or listen to a podcast by a Latino guy named Raul Esperanza? Nobody. But Cody Shaw, everyone wants him." Cody glimpsed his reflection in the mirror hanging over the mantle and preened, twisting his long strands of hair into a ponytail.

Raul Esperanza. The tiny hairs on Ebony's forearm stood on end. It was the same name mentioned during her conversation with Jessie. This minor celebrity, Cody Shaw, aka Raul Esperanza, was Olivia's husband. Her soon-to-be ex-husband. Despite being married to Shaw, Olivia had staked Kyle on the runway, ready for the altar.

Her eyes flicked toward Zander. His slender face paled as the seismic quake rocked their investigation, and his piercing gaze locked onto hers.

Broadcast personality, entrepreneur, and outdoorsman Cody Shaw had become a person of interest.

Chapter Twenty-One

Ebony wandered around the store examining Shaw's photo gallery, cataloging Olivia's photo-ready smile in a half-dozen pictures with her husband. Shaw and Olivia were parasailing at a Caribbean beach, windsurfing off the Monterey Peninsula, and waterskiing on Candlewood Lake. Ebony leaned closer to examine a snowy mountaintop photo of them dressed in matching Day-Glo ski garb, petting a drooling St. Bernard with the Matterhorn silhouetted behind them. The gallery caused Ebony to wonder whether any were honeymoon shots of the now-estranged couple, and why Shaw kept them on display. Usually, when a marriage died, all photos and memorabilia found their way into the trash. Or worst, as she'd witnessed with the serial killer, Duvall Bennett, who'd decapitated his pretty ex-bride in their photos.

She sensed someone behind her and found Zander at her shoulder.

"What about this one?" he asked, examining a photo of Olivia and Shaw snorkeling at sunset with the manta rays.

"Oh. We were on the big island of Hawaii," Shaw said, sneaking up beside them. He gestured toward an *Outside* magazine cover featuring him dropping over a gushing waterfall in a kayak. "In this one, I was shooting the falls at Hanging Spear Gorge in the Adirondacks. What a rush, man. It's a seventy-five-foot drop. Great cover shot, right?"

"Is that a custom Sea Eagle? I've read about them on the web. How did it handle?" Once more, Zander had succumbed to Shaw's spell, forcing Ebony to dispatch a sharp elbow into her partner's ribs. He flinched.

Before Shaw could launch into another long-winded technical explanation, Ebony asked. "When was the last time you saw Olivia?"

A dark shadow flashed across Shaw's face, which he replaced with a tense grin. "It's hard to say. Recently." He paused, pulled out his phone, and checked his calendar. "I remember. It was three weeks ago. I was purchasing tickets online for the Adirondack Paddle Fest and Outdoor Expo when Livvie popped in. She'd been to see her folks, and after I grabbed the tix, we went to lunch down the street at Meyer's Olde Dutch. They make great burgers, if you're interested."

"How did she seem at the time? Did she mention Kyle?" Ebony asked, disinterested in his restaurant recommendation.

"Livvie was still in summer recess, so she was pretty chill. But she mentioned Kyle had postponed their wedding from Valentine's Day until springtime. Livvie can be bull-headed and short-tempered when she doesn't get her way, and his decision pissed her off. But I reminded her we had unfinished business."

Ebony nodded slowly, prodding him for details.

"Not that it applies to your investigation, but Livvie owns shares in Outfitter, and we're negotiating the buy-out." His jaw tightened as though smothering his annoyance. Ebony believed she heard his teeth scrape as he grated them. "The lawyers are taking their sweet time, and Livvie is being Livvie." Shaw's charismatic smile returned, fraudulent this time. "We'll work it out. We always do."

Shaw clearly harbored feelings for Olivia. He may try to hide them, but Ebony smelled the desire, the slow burn like the autumn bonfires in the air.

With the discovery of Shaw's intimate personal and business relationship with Olivia and her family, his involvement in Kyle's disappearance was becoming more complicated by the minute. Ebony needed to dig deeper. She needed to get her hands on the divorce papers to root out the allegations behind the divorce and the settlement between the parties.

Under the rules of the Ninth Judicial District, divorce filings were confidential, and the court restricted access to the parties only. In conjunction with the investigation, Ebony could employ other means. DA Tarrico could issue a subpoena, but there was no pending criminal case. Or

Ebony could hire an expert to get them, like PI Carey Wentworth. Sleazy Wentworth, the enthusiast of 1980s aviator sunglasses, grease-stained raincoat, and rotten teeth, had his sources, which she preferred not to know. Somehow, he always delivered the dirt when she needed it. Certainly, the divorce papers would shed light on the financial ties between Shaw and Olivia, perhaps more.

"What about Emory? When was the last time you saw him?" Zander asked, fiddling with a collapsible camping lantern.

"He also stopped by the store a few weeks back. He wanted to get Livvie a birthday present. Since she already had a ton of water gear, he selected the most expensive handcrafted leather duffle bag in the place and a matching travel backpack. He mentioned she could use them on their honeymoon." Shaw's expression remained stoic, but Ebony noticed a vague tic in his left cheek.

Oh, to be a fly on the wall during that meeting, she mused. To eavesdrop on the naïve fiancé seeking advice from the soon-to-be ex-husband about a birthday gift for Olivia. Shaw could barely control his emotions when discussing Olivia with them, and she imagined the herculean self-control he must have mustered to deal with Kyle. Kyle could be an instigator, especially when struck by jealousy. Kyle must have known about their past relationship, but their marriage was another question.

She'd witnessed Kyle's possessiveness first-hand. Years ago, she, Kyle, and Jessie had been out for burgers and beer when Jessie dropped a comment about a *New York Times* article featuring Hal's father's Manhattan real estate holdings. Kyle had exploded into a jealous tirade, bashing Hal and his family, and claiming they were ripping off desperate, unsuspecting landowners. He'd bolted from his chair, leaving Ebony and Jessie to find their own way home.

Kyle's immaturity had shocked Ebony, but he'd been Jessie's problem. She'd never understood the attraction, except he'd been Jessie's rebound guy when Hal had dumped her and married Erin. Everyone knew rebound guys rarely stuck.

But timing was everything. When Erin and Kyle had forsaken Hal and

Jessie, their unfading attraction had drawn them back together. Finally, after years apart, they would be united in marriage as they had planned long ago.

It had taken time, but after five years, Kyle and Jessie had split up. Maybe Hal's reentry into Jessie's life had prompted the break. Or perhaps Jessie realized Kyle was a schmuck. As an outsider, Ebony could only guess since Jessie never confided in her anymore. But Kyle's disappearance shed an uncomplimentary spotlight on the past and the present.

"I'll take this lantern," Zander said, approaching the register.

"Good choice. It's light-weight, and the LED will last forever," Shaw said, taking Zander's credit card and tapping it against his iPad. "Honestly, I never got the two of them. They didn't seem to have much in common, not like she and I did. Pictures speak a thousand words." He flicked his head toward the rafting photo on the wall behind the counter. "It beats me how Kyle swept Livvie off her feet."

"Her parents said it was love at first sight," Ebony said.

"It must be true because Livvie doesn't want kids, and she told me he's got one. I mean, she's a teacher and loves working with her students, but she doesn't want her own. To her credit, she worries about teens bullying each other, and organized a summer workshop for her choir. She says she sees how difficult it is to raise a kid." Shaw paused and brushed a strand of hair from his face. "Livvie's tough on the outside, but inside, she's a softie." He laughed. "Motherhood doesn't compliment her brand."

These claims were nuggets worth remembering.

"Did either of them mention their plans to paddle out on the Hudson that weekend?"

"No. It came as a shock to me." Shaw returned the card and Zander's purchase in a fancy recycled paper bag. The thick black titanium band on Shaw's left ring finger was unmistakable evidence he was still a married man. "You'd figure after all this time, nothing Livvie did could shock me."

Ebony and Zander thanked Shaw and turned to leave.

"Hey dude, wait." Shaw scribbled on Zander's receipt and handed it to him. "You almost forgot that, and I put my name and number on it. Hit me up if you ever want to go paddling."

Ebony shook her head as the men fist-bumped, and she held open Outfitters' door for her dumbstruck partner.

Chapter Twenty-Two

Back home after their stroll, Ed kissed Jessie and Lily goodbye. "Remember what I said, honey. Don't get swept up in the drama. In the end, no good will come of it." Ed crushed Jessie in a bear hug, squeezing the air from her lungs. He released her, planted a peck on her cheek, and slid into his blue Subaru parked in the driveway.

As he drove away, her father's warnings echoed in Jessie's head. They shadowed her around the kitchen and with each chop of the ingredients for dinner's stir-fry recipe. They sizzled in her cast iron wok and evaporated into the steam above the pan's searing surface.

Jessie shivered and glanced at Lily, hoping the sight of her daughter would quell her fears. In the play yard, Lily played happily among her toys and clambered to her feet, resting her chin on the playpen's top railing. Soon her one-year-old would be too tall for confinement.

As the last pink fingers of the sunset faded to indigo, her phone shimmied on the counter. It was a text from Hal.

On the way home. See you shortly. Luv u.

His greetings reminded Jessie of the earlier call from the New York City area code and the voicemail waiting to be heard. She paused her cooking, pressed play, and listened to the message.

"Good afternoon, Ms. Martin. My name is Nicole Thomas, and I am the Director of Human Resources at the Barclays Center. When you receive this message, please call me." Ms. Thomas dictated her number, thanked Jessie, and bid goodbye. The pitch of the woman's voice dropped off at the end of each sentence as if foreshadowing tragic news. Bad news the caller didn't want to leave in a voicemail.

"Crap. It must be about your medical insurance coverage," Jessie said to Lily. "I suppose we'll put you on my policy now that your daddy...." There was no way Jessie would allow Lily's coverage to lapse, especially after the mountain of medical expenses she and Kyle had incurred because of Lily's premature birth. Born six weeks early, Lily's hospitalization in the Vassar Brothers Hospital NICU had cost upward of a hundred thousand dollars, not including expenses for Jessie's near-fatal bout of eclampsia. Thankfully, insurance had covered most of their expenses.

"It's too late to call Ms. Thomas now, so I'll call her in the morning," Jessie said. "And I'll call Jeremy to place you on my policy at work."

Was no aspect of her life beyond Kyle's reach? Jessie gathered up his yearbooks and threw them on her desk in the den. By shutting the den door, she officially banished Kyle and the myriad of problems from her mind for the evening.

Hal would be home soon, and she wanted to uncork a Cabernet, enjoy a nice dinner with her family, and lavish Hal with the attention he deserved.

"Hello there, gorgeous," Hal said as he sauntered in the back door. "I thought about you all day as I banged away on my gavel." He planted his moist lips on Jessie's, and his hands slid down along the length of her back, turning her skin to gooseflesh. They came to rest on her ass, and he gently squeezed, tugging her toward him.

"No more than I have been thinking about you, my love," she said.

She slipped her hands around his neck, deepening their kiss and pulling him closer. Her hips ground into him, feeling his arousal. After a few magical moments, Lily squealed in delight, breaking the spell cast over her and prompting Jessie to withdraw from Hal's caresses.

Hal narrowed his amber eyes, and a sly grin spread over his handsome face.

Apparently, they shared similar ideas for their after-dinner activities.

The next morning, Jessie awoke feeling empty and unsatisfied. It was as if she'd gone through the motions with Hal in bed last night; her body had been in one place with him while her mind had been somewhere else. Had

Hal noticed? Why couldn't she be honest with him? Jessie didn't want to push him away for a ghost, as her father had admonished.

However, her introspection was short-lived. Ms. Thomas's message about Lily's insurance awaited her. What else could it be?

After performing her morning routine for herself and Lily, Jessie returned the call.

"Nicole Thomas's office," a young man said.

Jessie introduced herself and asked to speak with Ms. Thomas.

"Oh, yes. She's expecting your call. One minute, please. I'll see if she's available." The line clicked, and a commercial for the venue's upcoming acts played over the phone.

"Ms. Martin?" Ms. Thomas asked. "Thanks for returning my call. I'm contacting you about Kyle Emory. We were sorry to hear about Kyle's passing. It came as quite a shock to us. We all liked Kyle, and he was a valued member of our Barclays team." She paused and sighed. "Kyle was kind to the staff no matter their position in concessions, janitorial, or the visiting road crew. You could tell Kyle loved his job. He always wore a smile. He'll be missed, and we send your family our sincere condolences." Her words and tone felt genuine, reassuring.

"Thank you. It's very thoughtful of you to speak so warmly about Kyle," Jessie said.

"I'm calling because Kyle listed you as his next of kin." Ms. Thomas' voice hitched as though she'd lost more than a colleague, a close friend. She cleared her throat and continued. "I understand your family is going through a difficult time, but there are certain matters which we need to discuss, and there's paperwork to be completed. Is this a convenient time, or would you like to speak at a later date?"

"No, it's fine. How can I help you?" Jessie planted her feet on the ground, bracing herself for the impending blow.

"As a benefit of Kyle's employment, he enrolled in our group life insurance policy. The basic benefit was two-and-one-half times his salary, plus an add-on for accidental death."

Jessie wasn't expecting this bombshell. A shot of adrenaline juiced her heart, and she steadied herself against the hallway wall exhibiting a gallery of family photographs.

Ms. Thomas continued. "I hate to be crass and discuss figures, but according to the payroll department, Kyle's salary was $375,000.00 per year. If we extrapolate the life insurance proceeds according to the formula, the gross benefit is $937,500.00. With the $500,000.00 accidental death benefit, the total life insurance proceeds would be $1,437,500.00."

"Am I to understand that Kyle's life insurance proceeds are almost one-and-a-half million dollars, and he named me as the beneficiary on his life insurance?"

"Yes, and no. I'm sorry for the confusion. I suppose I didn't make myself clear. He named you as next of kin and trustee for a beneficiary, the minor, Lily Martin. I believe Lily is Kyle's daughter."

"Oh?"

There was a long silence. Ms. Thomas gulped as though she had sipped a glass of water. "There is a wrinkle, though. To satisfy the accidental death benefit, we'll need a copy of the death certificate showing Kyle's accidental death."

"Right now, the situation is unresolved, but I'm sure we can deal with that when the time comes."

Ms. Thomas didn't mention it, but most policies provided that suicide invalidated the contract. Despite Ebony's mean-spirited suggestions, Jessie believed the exclusion wasn't relevant here.

"And there is one other technicality regarding the claim."

Here it comes. The S-word.

"Kyle named a co-beneficiary on the policy, and I was wondering if you knew how I can get in touch with her."

"Her? Did Kyle leave money to his sister or his mother?"

"No, they weren't designated. He named Olivia Vargas as a one-half beneficiary."

The speech center of Jessie's brain froze. She fumbled for words as her thoughts kicked into high gear, reeling around as though a tempest had sucked her into a hellish vortex.

Olivia Vargas? The woman who Kyle had met only six months ago, who he'd asked to marry him, and who was a stranger to his family and friends? *Olivia Vargas?* The woman who had been his kayaking companion at the time of his disappearance? *Olivia Vargas?* How could Kyle cheat Lily out of three-quarters of a million dollars in favor of this stranger? This gold-digger. This social influencer.

Once again, Kyle's actions were reprehensible and irresponsible. Yet, so fucking Kyle Emory.

A white-hot rage attacked her toes and consumed her body in scorching heat all the way to her head. Her muscles quivered. Blindness robbed her of sight, and a curtain of blue haze descended over her world. Jessie gulped for air, struggling to regain control of her body, vision, and emotions.

Tender memories of Kyle—birthdays, vacations, anniversaries, and holidays — flashed in her mind, juxtaposed with the pain of the present. The loss. The betrayals. Trapped within the scenes playing inside Jessie's head, the seconds stretched on, severing her connection to reality.

The chiming of the grandfather clock drew Jessie back to the present. She concentrated on the steady rhythm of her breath, and as her sight and senses returned, her outstretched hand grazed the smooth surface of the wooden floor beside her. The soft hall carpet cradled her head and body, and her phone remained gripped in her fingers. Gingerly, she rose, clueless as to how she'd collapsed.

"Ms. Martin? Are you there?" Ms. Thomas asked.

"Yes. Sorry, I don't know what to say."

"I understand this is a shock, but are you all right?"

"I'm fine," Jessie barked, gathering her wits. "Please email me the documents with instructions, and I'll call you once I've reviewed them." Jessie blurted out her email address and ended the call in time to expel the primal scream crushing her chest. Then she doubled over and vomited on the carpet.

"MOTHER FUCKER!" she screamed, flinging her phone against Kyle's photo. From the white sandy beaches of Hilton Head, he smirked at her.

Chapter Twenty-Three

"Mama! Mama!"

Lily's bawling pierced the heart of the night, rousing Jessie from a sound sleep. Disoriented by the terrifying cries, she tossed back the covers and stumbled down the pitch-black hallway. In the nursery, Lily wobbled upright in her crib, her tear-stained face swollen. The baby's nose was runny, and her cheeks flared as crimson as cherries. Jessie scooped Lily up in her arms and discovered the child's pajamas were damp, and her diaper was full. After attending to Lily, she crept back to bed, careful not to wake Hal, who had slept through the commotion.

As sleep settled over Jessie, her phone buzzed, and the shrill ping of a text further disrupted the fitful hours of sleep.

Have news. Call me in the morning. E

Her phone said it was three in the morning. She wondered why Ebony was awake at this hour and what breaking news couldn't wait until morning. Ebony had always been a night owl, and being a cop, she could be on the night shift. And she thought with annoyance, if the matter was so urgent, Ebony should have phoned rather than texted.

The terse missive offered Jessie little reassurance and raised more questions in an investigation as stagnant as pond algae. Its mysterious implications surged through her like caffeine, hurling her jumbled thoughts into a dark abyss.

Perhaps they'd found Kyle's body, or his mangled body parts, after the propeller of a tanker trawling the Hudson had pulverized him. Maybe Kyle's filthy, weed-encrusted body had washed up ashore somewhere along

132

the three hundred miles of riverfront leading to the ocean, or a fisherman casting for shad had hooked a more macabre prize instead.

Or they had discovered Kyle alive, or stricken with amnesia from a traumatic head injury, or on life support in the hospital.

The grisly theories spun on, fueled by the stark autumn night, her imagination, and sleep deprivation.

As the soft golden streaks of dawn blazed through the bedroom curtains, sleep finally carried Jessie away. But when the box spring creaked, cutting her respite short. Hal shuffled across the bedroom floor, yawned, and slammed the bathroom door. Moments later, giggles resonated down the hallway, drawing Jessie, wrapped in her fluffy bathrobe, back to the nursery. This time, Lily greeted her with a smile and shouted, "Da!" as she entered the doorway.

In the kitchen, Jessie flipped on the coffeemaker for Hal, lit the burner underneath the teakettle, and warmed Lily's bottle. With Lily riding her hip, the aroma of percolating coffee accompanied them to the front door to fetch the newspaper.

Outside, the morning was brisk and sunny, and she startled at the figure perched on the top step of her porch. Ebony sipped from a disposable coffee cup and scrolled through a newsfeed on her phone as the swirling tendrils of steam vanished into the cool air.

"Good morning. Couldn't wait until I texted you back, huh?" Jessie asked. "It must be important if you're staked out on my doorstep before seven in the morning."

"I've only been here a few minutes, and I figured you'd be up soon." The early morning light bathed Ebony's caramel skin, hair, and sapphire cat eyes in gold as though she were a mythological goddess dressed in jeans and a motorcycle jacket. Ebony slipped her phone into her jacket and groaned as she rose, favoring her left hip. "Got a few minutes?"

"Sure, come on in. I'd offer you tea, but I see you came prepared."

"I'll take some toast if it's no bother and a refill on the tea." Ebony grabbed Lily's chubby hand and gave it a wiggle. "Good morning, missy. Is it breakfast time for you?"

Lily kicked her feet clothed in bunny-covered pajamas and squealed in delight.

Ebony trailed them into the kitchen, grabbed a chair at the table, and waited. Upstairs, the hot water pipes rattled, indicating Hal was showering, allowing Jessie and Ebony time for a brief chat without interruption or questions.

With Lily settled in her highchair, Jessie scurried around the kitchen preparing breakfast.

Filled with suspicion, Jessie's heart thrummed. She opened her mouth to speak, but Ebony began.

"About the text last night." Ebony nibbled on the toast. "There's some news." Ebony sipped on her cup and settled back into her chair.

"What the hell, Eb? What are you saying?"

"I realize my message was cryptic, but I wanted to assure you Kyle's case is never far from my mind. We still haven't located his body, but we've gathered certain details about the kayak."

"You'd said there was a defect with the kayak. What did you find?" Jessie asked impatiently.

"Forensics believes someone tampered with Kyle's kayak."

Jessie's throat tightened as if someone had socked her in the chest. Her fingers clutched the grainy butcher-block island for stability, and she lowered herself into a kitchen chair. "So there was no manufacturing defect, right? And you've found evidence to suggest tampering? What do you mean by tampering?"

"I don't understand all the technicalities. That's Zander's domain, but there's a tiny drainage plug on the top deck of the kayak, and it was missing when forensics made their inspection." Ebony extracted an envelope from her pocket and passed it to Jessie. Jessie shuffled through the photos, stopping at a close-up of the red kayak. Ebony pointed at the black hole in the center of the frame.

"What does the plug do? Could it have fallen out by itself?" Jessie asked.

"This plug keeps water out of the shell or the body of the kayak. It's about the size of a nickel, and no, it fits into the hole pretty snug and must be removed by hand."

"Who removed it? If it's that small, how did it sink the kayak?"

"We're not sure. Our forensic team believes it's possible, but we're consulting experts in the field. We don't know how or when the stopper was removed. Zander and I are interviewing witnesses about this new information."

"It is possible the plug was missing before Kyle began the trip?"

"Yes, but we don't know. Not yet."

"You're thinking there's foul play, aren't you?" Jessie understood the accusation emanating from Ebony's strained expression. "No, Eb. He didn't pull it. I've told you before, Kyle wasn't suicidal. There are a ton of witnesses who might be suspects, so interview them before you indict Kyle for killing himself. One of them must've planned to get rid of Kyle."

It felt odd to be defending Kyle, especially after all they'd been through. But since he wasn't able to speak for himself, Jessie needed to preserve Kyle's legacy for his family and Lily. It was the least she could do for her daughter's father.

"Besides, did he leave a note?" Jessie glared at Ebony, demanding an answer. "You recall how anal Kyle was about everything in his life. He would've left a note."

"At our preliminary interviews, the Vargas family stated they were close with Kyle, but we're checking into it." Ebony grabbed Jessie's hand. Her hand was warm compared to Jessie's, which had turned to ice. "I promise we'll figure out what happened to Kyle. You need to be realistic. He got caught in a storm, and the missing plug may amount to nothing, but we'll pursue every lead." Ebony squeezed Jessie's hand and smiled sympathetically. "And no, there was no note."

No suicide note. No body, and it had been over seventy-two hours since Kyle had disappeared. Jessie couldn't admit the words out loud, but in her heart, the truth was as apparent as the gaping hole in Kyle's kayak. Kyle was presumed dead.

"Isn't it odd his fiancée survived the ordeal, but Kyle didn't? It makes little sense," she shouted in frustration. "Someone's to blame for Kyle's disappearance, but who? Why can't you tell me who did it?"

Jessie needed distance from Ebony and the lightning bolt she'd tossed into Jessie's lap. She needed to think without Ebony glowering at her, trying to read her mind, or faking a feeble attempt at intimacy. Growing up, the two could have finished each other's sentences, but no longer. Too much had changed between them, but Ebony's probing expression suggested she was assessing Jessie. Was Ebony here because of their friendship or because she was a cop?

She resumed her preparation of Lily's breakfast and stirred the grainy oats, mesmerized by the grey bubbling goop. *Foul play. Murder.* Was Jessie a suspect? She and Kyle had been cordial lately, but Ebony had borne witness to their stressful, unresolved relationship.

"Am I supposed to tell his parents there was foul play? Possible murder?"

"I wouldn't mention anything to Bev and Tom until our experts report back. If you need to tell them anything, let them know we're working hard to find Kyle, and we'll pass along any news as soon as we have any." Ebony sipped on her tea.

"I think they're tired of hearing that empty response. Have you questioned the fiancée? She had direct knowledge about events leading up to their excursion."

"Olivia has been so distraught that the doctors have sedated her. We'll be speaking to Olivia and her family as soon as possible. And I'm going to ask you a favor. Please don't mention our discovery to anyone. Not even Hal. He's County Court Judge and shouldn't be privy to this ex parte information. We never know how our case is going to develop." Ebony retrieved the packet, folded it, and slipped it into her pocket. "I probably shouldn't have told you about the plug, but you're entitled to know."

"Given our relationship, Hal would recuse himself anyway, but I'll keep this between us." Jessie spooned the cereal into a bowl with a smiling cat on it. She added butter and cinnamon, placed it on the kitchen table, and blew on it.

At the sight of breakfast, Lily lit up.

"Here, please let me feed me her," Ebony said, offering to assume the breakfast duty. "It's the least I can do."

You can say that again, Jessie thought. After the interrupted sleep and the unfounded allegations against Kyle, feeding Lily was only the beginning of the payback.

As Ebony grabbed the pint-sized spoon, a warm wave of relief flooded Jessie like a shot of Kentucky bourbon. Ebony didn't suspect her of wrongdoing if she'd confided in her about the missing plug. She needed Ebony to say the words, though. Jessie needed to hear them.

"At least you don't suspect me of pulling the missing plug."

Ebony tilted her head as though weighing the evidence against Jessie. "Nope. Not this time."

Jessie wasn't convinced.

Chapter Twenty-Four

The heat, humidity, and acidic smell of chlorine hit Cindie the moment she entered the swimming pool at the James J. McCann Athletic Center at Marist College in the Town of Poughkeepsie. She shaded her eyes against the bright light reflecting off the white walls and crystal clear water of the Olympic-size pool. On the back wall, the red, white, and blue Metro Atlantic Athletic Conference banners proclaimed Marist men and women as swimming and diving champions for the past twenty years.

A group wearing wetsuits gathered at the far end of the pool, next to three diving boards, which were staggered in height. Two-thirds of the way down the pool, a moveable white bulkhead separated the swim lanes from the deep end, allowing for multiple uses of the facility at one time. Presently, a dozen divers monopolized the facility and were looking down at a woman in the water with air tanks strapped to her back. She gripped the pool ladder and pointed toward the center of the pool in front of the tallest diving board.

The water-bound speaker had to be Joanna Medina. Cindie had spoken with Dr. Medina, and they had arranged a meeting at the Marist pool, where Medina was holding a training session for the Dutchess County Sheriff's office.

Cindie gingerly traversed the slick pool deck, wishing she'd worn sneakers rather than her suede pumps, and shed her camel hair jacket and wool blazer as the humidity intensified. She joined the back of the group, listening as Medina instructed them.

"For your next exercise, I need you to break up into teams of three. One of you will play the victim in a lake simulation and will lie at the bottom of the pool. The second will be the diver. They will close their eyes, simulating the murky water conditions in the lake, and hunt for the victim by touch only. They will report their observations to the third team member on land, who will make notes and sketch the position of the body. This will test your dive team's training and communication skills. Ready? Break up into your groups, and victims and divers, put on your tanks." She addressed a young Black woman in a wetsuit printed with blue images of coral on its sleeves and calves. "Sissy, can you please give them a hand if they need it? Thanks."

The lanky, athletic woman ascended the ladder onto the pool deck, water streaming off her shiny second skin marked with red panels on her torso like a Marvel superhero. The equipped teams from the sheriff's office splashed into the water, leaving their colleagues sitting on the pool edge to record the observations. Sissy crouched beside them to supervise the exercise.

Medina removed her metallic red tanks and whipped off her mask, then squeezed the excess water from her long, silver braid. "That should keep them busy for a while," she said. She extended her wet hand to Cindie in greeting. "Joanna Medina, but you already know that."

Medina's handshake was firm, and up close, she looked older than in her website photo. In her mid-fifties, like Cindie, Medina's hair was silver, not blonde, and excessive sun and water exposure had left a topographical map of fine lines on her leathery complexion.

"Cindie Tarrico, nice to meet you." Cindie reached to shake Medina's hand, and the soles of her pumps slid on the slippery surface. "Whoa!" she shouted as Medina grabbed her arms to steady her. Cindie's hands felt moist, and she wasn't sure if it was her clumsiness, the dense air inside the natatorium, or the Aqua Woman.

"You okay?"

"Damn shoes," Cindie said, shaking off the spill. "Dr. Medina—"

"Joanna."

"Joanna. Thanks for meeting with me. Sorry to interrupt your session, but we have a situation in Poughkeepsie, and I'm hoping for your guidance." Cindie explained about the storm, the kayak, Kyle's disappearance in the Hudson, and the unsuccessful attempts of the search teams to locate the victim by boat and air.

"The accident occurred four days ago, and still no body has surfaced?" Medina asked. "That's not unusual with the Hudson. The river is three hundred feet in the center, and bodies sink to the bottom. The immense water pressure keeps them submerged, and because of the fish and debris in the river, sonar can mark a body as a large fish or sunken log, making drowning victims difficult to locate. When the body decomposes, the internal gases build up, causing the body to rise to the surface. The time depends on the clothing, body mass, depth of water, tides, water temps, and the weather." Medina unzipped the top of her suit from the back and rolled her neck in a stretching motion. "Since you're investigating an aquatic death scene, I'd recommend you don't assume the cause and manner of the death. Be careful not to diagnose it as an accident or suicide. If it is a homicide, the premature conclusion might cause you to overlook important evidence. I can't tell you how many times witness statements and behaviors reflect a tragic accident, but the authorities have completely misread an intentional death. The key questions are whether it makes sense the victim did not survive the storm and are there any red flags for foul play."

"Do you think the missing plug impacted Kyle's apparent drowning?" Cindie asked.

"Every aquatic death is different, so it's impossible to say without a complete investigation and autopsy. However, I wrote a paper on the topic and can send you some guidelines for conducting the drowning investigation. Hopefully, your investigators have already jumped on the basic forensics processing of the river crime scene, like taking notes and photos, making sketches, gathering physical evidence, and getting witness interviews. And using divers, of course. Like these guys in the pool."

The shrill tooting of a whistle echoed off the tile walls as a pack of giggling coeds streamed into the pool area and dove into the lanes at the shallow end of the deck.

"Also, engage an expert on the river currents and tides. They may give you a clue to where the body may rise," Medina added.

Medina had given her a lot to digest, and Cindie was fairly certain that Shepardson's team had covered the bases. She was about to ask whether Medina recommended engaging a crime scene reconstruction specialist when Sissy approached her partner and whispered in her ear. Medina glanced over at a diver frantically signaling to her onshore pal, a clear failure to communicate.

"I'm sorry, I've got to cut this short. We're shorthanded because my husband was supposed to be helping us with this training session, but he was called out on an emergency case in Kentucky. Anyway, you know how to reach me if you need anything. Please call me when you find your victim. I'm sure we'll have more to discuss then." Medina turned to Sissy. "Please send Cindie the article I wrote for the summer *Riptide* Magazine about the homicidal drowning. You know which one I mean, 'Brown Water and Red Flags.' I'll forward you Cindie's contact information."

"Here," Cindie said, handing Sissy her business card. "I'm looking forward to reading it, and I'm sure we'll be speaking again once the case develops."

"I don't mean to be cynical, but be suspicious. Don't let tunnel vision inhibit your evaluation of the situation. You and I have witnessed the seamier sides of human nature. And well, you know, people can be fucked up."

Medina was correct. Cindie had helped prosecute homicides and manslaughter, but they had all occurred on terra firma. Kyle's presumed drowning in the Hudson was a first.

"Keep up the good work, and thanks for your time."

The two women shook hands. Medina zipped up her wetsuit, slipped on her goggles, and dove into the water without making a splash. Only the sound of a rip.

Chapter Twenty-Five

Ebony wanted to savor every minute of her first morning off in a week. She was in heaven, chowing down on a flaky chocolate croissant at Kelly's Bakery and sipping on a frothy cappuccino, her special diet cheats. The neighborhood bistro had an industrial vibe of chrome, subway tile, and concrete, but the aromas of bittersweet chocolate and baking bread made the place feel warm, like home.

A regular patron, Ebony had grabbed her favorite table in the back corner to wait for her younger sister to arrive. Carly was perpetually late, a trait their parents attributed to her birth being two weeks after Carly's due date. In character, Ebony had been born a week early, yowling all the way.

Outside the wide mullioned windows beside her table, Ebony noticed the sky darkening in the west as angry black clouds rolled in over the Walkway on Hudson. The cloudbank appeared to swallow the pedestrian bridge as it marched eastward over the river toward her.

She willed her mind to go blank and relish the solitary moment, but the sticky residue of the week clung to her weary bones. The gravity of Kyle's missing person case, the upcoming sergeant's exam, and her sometimes-strained relationship with Drew wouldn't release her.

A spike of envy stabbed Ebony as Carly pushed open the bakery's glass door and waved to her. With ballerina grace, her sister glided across the room as though she were skating on air. Tall, exquisite Carly had been blessed with a flawless body of sepia skin, sparkling wit, and an eidetic memory. In contrast, Ebony's athletic prowess, raw determination, and intense analytical mind had served her as a cop. The women were contradictions in color, strengths, and personality, and no one ever suspected them as being related, let alone sisters.

Ebony stole a glance at her own reflection in the window, and as Carly approached, she tried not to compare her own shortcomings—the frizz tucked in a colorful African headscarf, the bland tawny complexion, and the wide nose inherited from their father— to her accomplished sister. Ebony had invested no time in primping this morning; yet leave it to Carly to wear an electric blue plaid suit and a black and white polka-dotted blouse as though she were lunching at the Plaza Hotel.

Carly loomed over her, hands on her slender hips, staring down at Ebony's snacks. "You didn't wait for me. Eb, you're a mean old big sister."

"Shut up and sit down." Ebony reached behind her, grabbed a small brown paper bag from underneath her jean jacket, and set it on the table. "What were you complaining about, you spoiled brat?"

"Spoiled brat? Remember July 13, 2005, at noon, when you had a meltdown because Mom and Dad wouldn't let you go to the movies with your friends? They were going to see *Harry Potter and the Goblet of Fire.* And Dad was pissed because you hadn't emptied the dishwasher."

"Come on, you're just showing off. Of course I don't remember, but at least I was old enough to go to the movies with my friends. You weren't even in a training bra." Ebony loved to spar with Carly.

"Ah-hem," Carly said, glancing down at her perky breasts. "It's not a problem now. Hey, shouldn't you be studying?"

They laughed and caught up with events of their lives, and Ebony expressed her frustration with Kyle's investigation.

"If we had a body, it would be different. But we've got nothing but the kayaks and the eyewitnesses' after-the-fact testimonies. The Vargases are a cagey bunch, neither exonerating nor pointing the fingers at each other."

"And the land and water searches have provided no clues to Kyle's whereabouts? I'm presuming you believe he's dead."

"We've used canine, aerial, diving, and sonar units, but no luck." Ebony shrugged. She believed Kyle was dead, but she couldn't say the words out loud. Not yet.

"It may take time, but he'll turn up. Bodies on the river usually surface a mile or so from where they went in, if they surface at all."

The finger of a frigid chill skimmed up Ebony's spine, making her shiver. She'd heard the old-timers at the station recount stories about victims who'd found their ultimate resting place in the turbulent river and about bleached human bones being washed up along the shore. She prayed this didn't happen to Kyle.

"Once you locate the body, it's still going to be challenging to process the crime scene. If Kyle's body has been submerged for over three days, his body may be bloated, decomposed, or have become fish bait. Also, he could've become the host for aquatic organisms. So you'll have to deal with external environmental evidence, too," Carly said.

Ebony studied the remnants of the creamy leaf-shaped swirl topping her cappuccino.

Carly knew what she was talking about. Her medical specialty was forensic pathology with a degree from the NYU Grossman School of Medicine. For the past two years, she'd been the assistant medical examiner for Dutchess County and an adjunct professor of clinical microbiology at Marist College, where their parents were tenured professors.

Their folks had supported their daughters' career choices, but sometimes Ebony sensed their disappointment over her entering the police academy after graduating from Marist. They should've seen it coming with her BA in criminal justice, but they'd hoped she'd pursue law school after she'd aced the LSATs and earned a GPA high enough to score admission at any school, even Yale or Harvard.

However, unlike Jessie, studying case precedent, preparing for trial, and arguing with an adversary weren't her game. Ever since Aunt Alicia's disappearance, she'd longed to wrestle with the frontline issues in the community, preventing crime, and apprehending the bad guys. To protect. To serve. And to honor an aunt she loved. Toting a gun and badge had been a perk.

After a week of spinning her wheels, Ebony struggled to suppress a twinge of underachievement that fed her jealousy. She knew it was all in her head and not anything Carly or Jessie had said, but sometimes she couldn't shake having a physician sister and a best friend attorney. But screw them. Instead of measuring herself against them or her parent's desires, she should trust in her choices and talents. She was a kick-ass homicide detective who'd helped apprehend multiple killers, who was the only female detective on the force, and who was on her way to getting a fat promotion.

Carly must have noticed Ebony's attention drift away, and she felt the sharp tips of Carly's boots dig into her shins. "Hey, we're not here to talk shop. We're here to talk about Mom and Dad's anniversary party." A fork of lightning lit up the sky, followed by a crack of thunder, which sent the vintage Edison light fixtures into a flicker. "Wow! That was close. I didn't know a storm was coming."

"Speaking of storms, Mom will have a fit if we have a party. She's insisting on a low-key family dinner," Ebony said.

"But you know Dad. He's the romantic in the family. After thirty-five years, he thinks they deserve a celebration, and—"

Another roaring clap of thunder interrupted Carly, this one more violent than the first. Her marble grey eyes pivoted toward the ceiling as if wondering whether the sky was about to fall.

The cacophony was so deafening that Ebony couldn't hear the phone ringing in her jeans pocket, but the vibration tingled against her thigh. She retrieved her phone and answered it, noticing Carly with her phone pressed to her ear and her arched brows burrowed in deep concentration.

"Detective Jones, I realize you're on the late shift, but we received a 911 call reporting a body has surfaced downtown in Upper Landing Park on North Water Street. It's your case, so I expect you and Pulaski to be at the recovery scene," Chief Shepardson said. "The duty sergeant has contacted Pulaski, forensics, and the medical examiner, and emergency services are on the way to the park to meet you."

Carly snapped her fingers to attract Ebony's attention and pointed to her phone, indicating she'd also received the grisly news.

Ebony nodded, and her gaze shifted away from her sister toward the Walkway, which towered over Upper Landing Park on the eastern shore of the Hudson, about five minutes from cozy Kelly's bakery. Fog had enshrouded the bridge, hiding it from view, and the rain pelting the windows had turned the landscape into a bleary abstract painting of slick leaves, waterlogged roadways, and trees shimmying in the storm.

"Thank you, sir. I'm on my way. Dr. Jones is with me, and it appears she's aware of the situation. I'll text Zander to meet me at Upper Landing. Do we have any other details?" As she spoke, her phone pinged with a text from Zander. She'd read his note after she finished up with the chief.

"None. So keep me posted. Good luck, Jones."

Before she could say goodbye, the chief ended the call. Her sister had already risen, packed up her tote bag, slung it over her shoulder, and grabbed her coffee to go. Carly's jaw had tightened with stress, in evidence of the horrors awaiting her at the riverside.

"Come on, let's book," Ebony said, rising from her seat. Carly had already reached the door.

Racing through the rain to her car, Ebony scanned the text.

Here at ULP. Looks like we've found him. See you soon.

Zander had beaten her to the punch.

Chapter Twenty-Six

By the time Ebony's VW turned into the ornate wrought-iron gates of Upper Landing Park, the rain had quit. Low soggy clouds remained, shrouding the park and the river in dense fog. An officer wearing a yellow slicker motioned her through the gates, and up ahead, the flashing lights of the ambulance, fire trucks, and police vehicles parked in the circular gathering area were barely visible.

In better weather, the Hudson would have stretched beyond the rocky shoreline of the park, tucked two hundred feet beneath the trestles of the Walkway Over the Hudson. Ebony would have observed the picnic tables dotting the water's edge, the Mid-Hudson Bridge to the south, and the park's history portrayed in photographs and plaques along the brick wall on the park's northern edge.

Ebony knew the tear-shaped park well, and it constantly amazed her how underutilized it was. Often in solitude, she and Drew had spent lazy summer afternoons basking in the sun on the grassy lawn and tossing sticks to Wrangler. The park was a gem hidden in the heart of Poughkeepsie and an escape from the daily grinds of their demanding lives.

Until now.

The wheels of her yellow car skidded on the wet surface and screeched to a halt in between Zander's smart car and Carly's sporty red Range Rover Discovery. Carly had put a polar fleece over her blouse and was suiting up in white disposable overalls and rubber boots. She and Zander exchanged small talk as he stepped into his coveralls and tugged them up over his black corduroys and cobalt turtleneck cashmere sweater. These two made quite a pair, dolled up for the work of fighting crime.

Zander moved closer to Carly, and she touched his forearm, her hand lingering there. Ebony stared. Were they flirting at a crime scene?

It couldn't be. Ebony shrugged it off.

Zander caught her attention and yelled, "Heads up!" and chucked her a coverall. She suited up, slipped her hood over her headscarf, yanked on her rubber boots, respirator mask, and gloves, and joined her sister and Zander.

The ghostly-looking trio marched through the mist and mud toward the deadly commotion on the riverbank. Carly veered off toward the faint yellow tape tied between the trees lining the Fall Kill Creek, which marked the tributary as a crime scene. She stopped and yelled back to Ebony. "Are there any distinguishing marks to identify the victim as Kyle Emory?"

Ebony cupped her hands around her mouth and replied, "None that we know of. Just let us know what you find."

A uniformed officer was interviewing a Black teenage boy in a camo rain poncho who was sitting on the rear steps of the ambulance. The boy had rolled his jeans to his knees, revealing skinny, mud-smeared legs that jerked up and down like he was pedaling a bike fast. His dog, a black and white pit bull, waited patiently beside his master's bare feet. The teen shivered as he motioned toward a sandbar that pointed its silty finger northward about a hundred feet into the Hudson. It was low tide and a short wade from the shoreline to the towhead, which explained the kid's filthy toes.

"There's a dead guy out there! I saw him! Somebody's got to get him," the teen shouted. "A real live dead guy is out there!"

"Sam, calm down. It'll be all right. We've got teams coming to retrieve him." Officer Victoria Robinson pushed back the hood on her yellow and silver-striped rain parka and set a comforting hand on the teen's shoulder. She introduced Ebony and Zander to the frightened teen, Sam Perkins, who lived in an apartment complex due north of the park. "Sam says that he and his dog, Malcolm, were fishing out on the sandbar in the rain when Malcolm started barking."

"Yeah, my grandpa says the rain's the best time for bass fishing, so we came to try it," Sam said, his shaky voice cracking. "Mal's a great bird-dog, so when he started barking, I thought he'd found a crane or a duck's nest in the reeds over there." Sam tipped his head toward the swampy area near the shore.

The muscular dog rose to his paws and shook off the excess water from his wiry coat. The splatter covered Ebony and Zander's white coveralls with black spots, and Mal wagged his stubby tail with exuberant joy.

"Good boy!" Sam tossed Mal a treat, which the canine caught in his large, gaping mouth. "Mal looks scary, but he's not."

Ebony estimated that if Sam was fourteen years old and Mal was approximately seven, they'd been companions for half the kid's life, explaining their unbreakable, loving bond.

Zander wasn't fond of dogs and stepped back from the canine with sharp fangs. "Sam, what did you see?" he asked.

"I was on the far end of the spit waiting for a bite. I told Mal to shut up, but he kept barking louder and faster. He wouldn't stop. I put down my rod and waded over to where he was dancing and splashing around in the water. That's when I saw the guy tangled up in the weeds, floating face down."

Ebony was a sucker for dogs and crouched to the dog's level, offering him her hand to sniff. Carefully, she scratched behind his floppy ears. "Good boy. You're a hero for finding a missing person." Mal plopped down on the wet grass and rolled onto his back, begging for a tummy rug, legs curled up in submission. If Mal had found Kyle, he deserved more than a belly rub, so she complied. "Good doggy." The dog's long pink tongue lolled out of the side of his mouth, and she believed she heard the pup sigh in pleasure as she scratched his coarse white fur.

"Vic, do you mind if we borrow Sam so he can show us what he saw?" Ebony asked.

"Be my guest," Vic said.

Trailed by the mutt, Zander, Ebony, and Sam slogged through parked emergency vehicles toward the picnic tables on the low ridge overlooking the river. To the far left, the Fall Kill Creek waterfall roared as its crystal clear water gushed over rocks and ledges on its way to the Hudson. The creek slowed as it merged with the brackish river, creating an ecosystem of weeds, fish, and wildlife before being swallowed by the open water.

Carly and three emergency services techs were wading in the creek toward the body. A contrast in heights, the rushing water covered the thighs of her assistants while it only skimmed her statuesque sister's knees. Two techs dragged along a mesh body bag, a basket stretcher with a floatation collar for extracting the body from the water, and a black duffle bag with testing equipment. It was going to be slow going since processing the body in water was more complicated than a nonaquatic recovery. They needed to collect aquatic, biological, and entomological samples and take environmental measurements at the scene while the third tech shot photos and videos documenting the recovery.

The fog, tall grasses, and saplings obstructed Ebony's view making it impossible to determine whether Kyle was the victim.

"Sam, that's where you found him, right? He hasn't moved, and you didn't touch him?" Zander asked.

"Yeah, that's where we found him in the weeds and rocks. And hell, no, I didn't want to get anywhere near him, and neither did Mal."

"Did you see anyone else around?"

Sam shook his head. "I told Officer Vic I was here alone. Earlier, I saw some crew teams practicing on the river, but that's all. Just me and Mal trying to catch some bass. Can I get my fishing stuff and go home now, please? This place is giving me the willies."

"Sorry, this is a crime scene, but we'll gather your equipment, and Officer Vic will make sure it's returned to you," Ebony said. "You did a good thing by calling 911, and we appreciate your help. Before you go, make sure Officer Vic has your phone number, email, and address."

"Hey, dude. Can you keep your discovery on the down low for the time being?" Zander asked. "We don't know who the victim is, and we don't want anybody getting the wrong idea. You'll help us with that, right?" Zander offered his fist for a pound. "Thanks, Sam." The kid complied, and in a blur of olive drab, he hightailed it back to Officer Vic, who waited by the ambulance.

"After all these years, you'd think I'd remember whether Kyle had any birthmarks or scars, but none come to mind." Ebony squeezed her eyes shut, trying to picture Kyle alive, but it was useless. She shoved her gloved hands into her coverall pockets to ward off the chill attacking them. "That guy in the water could be anybody... some jumper from a while back... or brought in by the tide from anywhere on the river. To be honest, I have mixed feelings about him being Kyle."

"Don't go beating yourself up. We'll know soon enough. And if it is Emory, we can concentrate on other aspects of our investigation. In the meantime, do you want a coffee? They've always got some in the emergency services vehicle."

"No, thanks."

"I'll be back in a few."

The wind shifted as a hazy sun peaked through the concrete ceiling of clouds overhead. The mist lifted like plumes of gray smoke from the river's surface, revealing fractured reflections of sunlight on the choppy waves.

From the ridge overlooking the creek, Ebony observed the medical examiner's team surround the prone body and collect samples of water, insects, soil, and plant life. Carly dictated to the videographer documenting the collection of evidence and the processing of the crime scene. From the looks of it, the procedure required time, patience, and finesse, because the victim was floating face down with only his shoulder blades and back visible. His appendages and head were hidden beneath the water. After the team had wrapped the victim's head, hands, and feet in nylon bags, they maneuvered the dead man into the mesh body bag. Finally, they transferred the limp body onto the floating recovery basket, and Carly peered over at her and shrugged. The protective goggles couldn't hide her sister's fatigue; she looked as though she'd aged ten years.

"God, I hope it's not Kyle," Ebony prayed aloud, thankful for the solitude. But who else could he be? To her knowledge, there had been no other reports of missing persons. If it were Kyle, she'd be making a third unwelcome visit to Jessie's house. This time, she'd be delivering the most catastrophic news possible.

Kyle was dead.

Chapter Twenty-Seven

An hour later, the medical examiner's crew had finished their work. From the ridge above the creek, Ebony observed her sister struggle up the steep, muddy embankment ahead of the stretcher transporting the dead body. Upon reaching the yellow crime scene tape on the ridge, Carly lost her footing and slid backward, landing on her ass in the Fall Kill Creek. Ebony pursed her lips, suppressing her laughter as her sister arose, dripping with brown muck, mud, and green algae.

"Goddamn, sonofabitchin'. Look at what I have to endure to get my fucking job done. And does anyone appreciate it? No!" Carly yelled, co-opting their father's favorite phrase after a Yankees' loss.

The extraction team halted in place, the stretcher jiggling as they bobbed their heads in mutual amusement.

Unable to control her laughter any longer, Ebony chortled aloud. "Nice way to break the tension, sis. I'm sure the corpse appreciated the floorshow."

"Ha!" Carly said sarcastically. She waded to shore, ripped off her muddy gloves, and wiped her filthy hands on the saturated overalls, leaving muddy handprints from her waist to her knees.

"Here, give me your hand," Ebony said, grabbing her sister's hand and guiding Carly up the slippery slope. "Good thing I was here. You could've become fish bait like your friend on the stretcher."

Carly pushed back her hood and yanked on the zipper to step from the soggy suit. "Damn, that water's cold. We measured it at sixty-eight degrees in three feet of water. That's not so bad with insulated rubber boots, but these coveralls don't withstand complete immersion. I should have worn a wetsuit."

"Well?" The high-pitched beeps of the ambulance backing up toward the recovery squad interrupted Ebony's inquiry. "What can you tell me about the victim? Is it Kyle? Can you establish the cause of death?"

"He's definitely dead," Carly replied. "It's too early to determine the cause of death or his identity. But theoretically, the victim could be Kyle because he's within a mile of the accident location, and the tide explains finding his body north of the bridge. This guy was in a tussle because there's significant bruising and discoloration on his neck and hands, but again, that's my initial observation after bagging his extremities." She leaned against a maple sapling, removed one boot, and flipped it upside down, letting the water drain out, and then repeated the technique with the other boot. "Before we make any assumptions, we have to perform an autopsy and examine the DNA, dental records, x-ray comparisons for prior injuries and surgeries, fingerprints, jewelry, birthmarks, tattoos, scars, clothing, personal effects...Hey, why am I telling you this? You're the cop; you know the drill."

"Because you're showing off again. I wondered whether the corpse had a sign around his neck saying 'Hi, I'm Kyle Emory.'"

"Don't get glib with me. So far, the sign says 'John Doe.' There's a lot of work to be done before we identify him. We don't know where he entered the river or how long he was in or the water's effect on his decomposition. And no, we've got nothing to tell Jessie." Carly paused, scrutinizing her. "Maybe you're too close to this case, and you might step back and let Zander assume the lead."

"It's not like that. Trust me. If I thought there was a conflict, I'd recuse myself, but that's not the case. Thanks for caring, though."

Zander strode toward them, the legs of his overalls rustling with each step. At the rear of the ambulance, the EMTs deflated the stretcher's flotation collar and slid the heavy basket inside. Before they slammed the door shut, a putrid, sour smell of decaying matter permeated the air. The scent of death.

"Whoa!" He pinched his nose. "Any news?"

"I'm headed to the morgue, and I'll let you know when I have anything. After we remove his clothing, I'll check for a wallet or phone. In the meantime, if you could ask Jessie or Kyle's family about any identifying information, it would be helpful," Carly said.

"How am I going to ask her intimate questions about Kyle again without raising her suspicions?"

"You're the cop. You figure it out." Carly called as she plodded away, her coveralls flapping like a tail and leaving a trail of puddles behind her.

Ebony wanted to flip her sister the bird, but she restrained herself. "It's bad enough she's got a photographic memory, but now she's bossing us around like we're her lackeys."

"So what? That's our job, isn't it?"

"Yeah, but we can't reveal they've pulled someone from the river. Not yet."

"You're kidding, right? Even though we told Sam to keep his mouth shut, it's going to be plastered all over the news and social media before we get back to the office. Perhaps not by him, but by somebody who's observed the commotion here at the park," Zander said. He jerked his thumb toward the emergency responders' vehicles. "We already have information on the witness intake forms, so let's get out of these spiffy outfits and figure out what's next."

"We'd better contact Jessie and the Emorys before the news breaks. It would be horrible to discover a body's been fished out of the water from the media and not from us."

Fortunately, Ebony knew Jessie wasn't active on Facebook. With work and Lily, Jessie had said she didn't have time to waste on social media. However, Jessie followed the news online and in print, leaving no time to waste.

"We haven't confirmed he's Kyle," Zander said. "Although realistically, who else could it be?"

The question permeated every molecule in Ebony's chilled body.

Back at the station, Ebony and Zander reviewed the items Carly had requested, and they added a few of their own. Eye color. Hair color and texture. Photographs. Eyeglass prescription.

They reviewed the file to determine the evidence already in hand. Not much.

The forensic team was examining Kyle's kayak, and they made a note to speak with the evidence division about whether they had lifted DNA and fingerprints from the vessel. Dental and medical records might prove to be more problematic since they required HIPPA releases from the next of kin or a time-consuming subpoena. Since Jessie and Kyle had purchased a house a few years ago, she might possess Kyle's Power of Attorney. Since they hadn't legally declared Kyle dead, the POA remained valid, allowing Jessie to sign the medical releases. It was a long shot, but worth pursuing.

"What about Kyle's employer, the Barclays Center?" Zander asked. "If they mandated a pre-employment physical, we could request the reports from them. Or even from his prior employer, the Mid-Hudson Civic Center."

"That's thinking outside the box, or should I say the arena?" Ebony scribbled a note to contact Barclays and the civic center about the medical records.

Fortunately, the Vargas family had provided a general description of Kyle's clothing on the day of his disappearance, but nothing significant jumped out at Ebony. He'd been wearing nondescript blue jeans, a white long-sleeve t-shirt, black quarter-zip sweatshirt, sunglasses, and sneakers. They hadn't known the brands, although Olivia might, but she was still recuperating from the shock.

With Olivia's prolonged unavailability, Jessie remained their most reliable source. Ebony was fairly certain Kyle was free of tattoos and was too macho for jewelry, but Jessie could confirm those facts as well as any scars or birthmarks.

"It looks like we're back around to Jessie again. How do you think she's going to respond to the questioning?"

"She'll catch on immediately, so we'd better be straight with her. She's realistic enough to suspect that Kyle has drowned, and she'll cooperate. Knowing Jessie, she'll want to jump headfirst into the investigation if she hasn't done so already."

Seeking Jessie's help was like opening a floodgate. Jessie would interpret the overture as an invitation to join their case or embark on her own private investigation into Kyle's death. She was smart, though. Jessie understood where the police drew their boundaries, but she'd inch up as close as possible without violating the lines.

Without the cause of death, Ebony or Zander couldn't predict whether any danger existed, but if it did, Jessie would find it.

Chapter Twenty-Eight

From the moment Jessie answered her front door, she couldn't escape a sense of dread. She knew what was coming. Kyle was dead.

One look at Ebony and Zander confirmed it. Ebony clutched the emerald charm on her necklace, seeming to finger it for comfort, while a subtle wrinkle pinched the corners of Zander's eyes. Their drooping shoulders and slack, almost pitiful, expressions were the ultimate giveaway.

Truthfully, Jessie had been expecting them. Four days had passed with no sign of Kyle, and inevitably these two messengers were going to appear on her doorstep to inform her Kyle was dead. Today was the day.

She stepped aside to admit them inside. The house was quiet, and their steps echoed on the wide plank floorboards.

"Come on into the kitchen. We can talk there," she said, leading Ebony and Zander down the hall and steeling herself for the misery about to crush her spirit. "Okay, what have you got for me?"

"I won't bullshit you, so I'll come right out and tell you. We've found a body in the Fall Kill Creek near Upper Landing Park. The medical examiner extracted him from the water, and they've transported him to their office for an autopsy," Ebony said.

Jessie's breath hitched, and she melted into a kitchen chair, gripping its solid wooden arm. "Is it—?"

"We don't know who it is. That's why we're here. We hope you can help us identify Kyle so we can compare the description to John Doe," Zander said. He recapped the conversation with Carly and extracted a page from his pocket containing the list of requested items. "We're wondering whether you can review these and let us know what objects or information you have."

"Can't his fiancée help you with this?" Jessie couldn't hide the bitterness in her tone.

"No, she's still indisposed," Ebony said with exasperation.

"Give me a fucking break."

"I agree, but time is of the essence. The ME needs to identify this person to determine a cause of death. That's why we came to you," Ebony said. Her eyes darted to Zander and back to Jessie.

"All right. I want to find out what happened as much as you do, so let me see your list." Jessie studied Ebony's scratchy handwriting, and at once the blow struck her hard. They'd reduced Kyle's life to x-rays, dental records, and scars.

Then a faint spark of hope glistened. Ebony knew Kyle, and she could recognize him unless his time in the river had disfigured him. The victim might not be Kyle. "Did you see the guy they pulled from the water?"

"No," Ebony said. "The victim was tangled in the weeds face down. Unfortunately, we didn't get a good look at him before Carly processed and bagged him." A beat. "I'm sorry. I don't mean to sound crass, but I'm telling you the facts."

My god! Ebony had described Kyle as though he was a side of beef bagged for commercial distribution. Tears welled at the image of him floating in the clear, shallow water, and Jessie blinked them away. She needed to keep her shit together; otherwise, she'd be useless to her family and the investigation.

"Do you remember what he wore that day?" Zander asked.

"Not really. Jeans and a sweatshirt? His usual uniform, nothing special."

"Do you know what sneakers he wore?" Zander asked, glancing down at his own polished Italian loafers with silver buckles.

"It's funny that you asked. He's got a sneaker collection in the basement, along with his other belongings. Kyle splurged on his shoes, but I don't remember what he was wearing. There's always mass confusion when he picks up Lily, so I didn't pay attention."

"Did Kyle have any surgeries or accidents? We're looking for his medical and dental records," Ebony asked.

This was a peculiar question because Ebony already knew the answer. Jessie would have mentioned any hospitalizations or accidents to Ebony in the course of their long friendship and normal chitchat. But she assumed the question was "on the record" as Ebony jotted notes into her phone.

"While we were together, nothing. Not even a cavity. You can contact Douglas Dental, and his primary care provider is Capstone Health. They should have his recent records. Kyle didn't discuss his life before we got together, so you'd have to check with his mother about those years. If Kyle had health issues when he was young, I'm sure his mother would have mentioned it to me. She's a talker."

"Tattoos? Birthmarks? Scars?" Zander asked.

"Yeah, right. Kyle with a tattoo? Nope. Nope. Nope. I'm not much help, am I?"

"We're eliminating open issues, so no worries," Ebony said, sharing a reassuring smile. "How about his wallet? A special key chain or anything he may have had on him."

"I can help you with those. For Christmas, I had Lily give him a leather wallet because his old one fell apart, and he was too cheap to buy a new one. It was a rustic-tanned brown leather billfold with slots for his license and credit cards. He used to carry an Amex, VISA, and MasterCard, not that he ever used them." Kyle had a habit of leaving his wallet at home, making her pay for the dinner tab. "And he owned two key chains, an old trilobite fossil that he carried for luck, and a newer silver electric guitar. A few years ago, he'd misplaced his fossil, so I bought him the guitar for his birthday. I'd engraved it with 'With love from me to you, Jessie.' After the Beatles tune."

"That helps. How about jewelry?" Zander asked.

"Yes!" she shouted, at last feeling she was being helpful. "There was a bracelet."

It had been three years ago on their third anniversary, the leather anniversary. She'd wanted to surprise him with something memorable, not a briefcase or gloves. So she'd splurged on an expensive calfskin bracelet with a sculptural silver hook clasp, and it had blown Kyle away. She recalled his embarrassment at the chintzy flowers and candy he'd given her to celebrate the milestone.

Jessie described the intricately braided black leather cord. "I can't say whether he wore it anymore, but when we were together, he never took it off. And he didn't leave it here with his stuff in the cellar."

"Now we're making progress. Is there anything else you can think of?" Zander asked.

Jessie remembered the box of Kyle's high school memorabilia but kept quiet about it. She hadn't yet completed her time travel into his youth. "I may have his old toothbrush or hairbrush if you need his DNA. I can check under the sink."

"Sure, and if you find it, bag it up for us." Ebony reached into her jacket pocket and tossed Jessie a plastic evidence bag. "One quick question before we go. When you bought your house, did Kyle give you his Power of Attorney, and did he leave a will?"

"When I found out I was pregnant with Lily, I begged Kyle to make our wills. He'd refused. I guess he didn't want to think about his own death. Even without a will, under the laws of intestacy, Lily is his sole heir."

Ebony eyebrows rose as though Jessie's inheritance concerns had been ghoulish. They weren't, though. Lily was her priority.

Now would have been the perfect time for her to mention the Barclays Center life insurance proceeds. But Jessie hesitated, considering the unwritten civil and criminal procedure rule drilled into every law student. When coaching witnesses, instruct them to limit their answers to the question. Answer only the question asked. Don't volunteer any information. Offering a spontaneous response was like tumbling down Alice's rabbit hole. There was no end.

Jessie wasn't inclined to share any further information with Ebony and Zander since her own agenda was under construction. She wasn't withholding evidence or interfering with the police investigation; she wasn't ready yet. Eventually, she'd pass along any relevant discoveries, but only after she'd gathered evidence identifying who had caused Kyle's death and after she was convinced Ebony had her and Lily's best interests at heart. Besides, from their tense body language, Zander and Ebony weren't being transparent with her either.

Nor was she ready to reveal another heart-wrenching truth about her ill-fated relationship with Kyle. When Jessie had discovered she was pregnant, she and Kyle had a terrible row. Not only because the pregnancy was unplanned, but also because Kyle had accused her of infidelity. He'd been jealous of her friendship with Terrence Butterfield. He'd demanded she submit to a paternity test to prove the child she carried was his, not Terrence's. But she'd refused. The exchange of harsh, hurtful words had been the beginning of the end. Yet, Jessie knew the truth.

A few months later, during her third trimester, Kyle abandoned her for the Barclays Center position.

Of the pain Kyle had caused and the lies he'd told, his baseless suspicious-ness had been his most monumental betrayal and the real reason she'd postponed their wedding. To this day, those scars ran so deep she'd kept them hidden from everyone, even Hal.

And, at the time, she'd wished Kyle were dead.

"Otherwise, there's nothing else," Jessie said, praying Ebony remained oblivious to the secret eating away at her heart and soul, and a deception that would make her suspect number one on Ebony's hit list.

Despite the torment, her lie would never stop her from uncovering the truth about Kyle's death.

Chapter Twenty-Nine

When Cindie checked her computer the next day, Medina's article was waiting in her email inbox. She printed a copy of "Brown Water and Red Flags" and dug into the twenty-page article, impressed by Medina's concise narrative and its potential relevance to the Kyle Emory situation. However, Cindie still wasn't convinced that Kyle's apparent drowning constituted a crime because there was no corpse. Or that the missing plug could reap such a drastic result.

Yet Medina's article suggested otherwise. She questioned whether law enforcement, dive teams, and medical personnel erroneously investigating drowning incidents as "tragic accidents" rather than as homicides contributed to homicidal drowning being overlooked. By misdiagnosing the crimes, the death investigators missed the "red flags" in the "brown water." Medina supported her theory by citing case studies of *accidental* drowning in lakes, bathtubs, and a non-swimmer found submerged off a dock in a pond. When analyzed with Medina's "do these deaths make sense" criteria, the *accident* diagnoses were disproven in all scenarios; "red flags" had been missed, and foul play had been determined too late, resulting in contaminated crime scenes. She also found evidence that the perpetrators had staged the homicides to resemble an accidental drowning, stymieing the investigators for days, weeks, or even years.

To prevent future misdiagnosis, Medina provided a blueprint for the crime scene and forensics units to process water scenes, including reconstructions, and collecting environmental samples along with the witness statements and the autopsy. In summary, the author urged caution against

163

jumping to conclusions about aquatic cases. "Once a body has been discovered in the water, it should be treated with the same professionalism as though they had it found on land," Medina wrote.

"Clever," Cindie said aloud. The fluorescent pink highlighter pen squeaked on the page as she marked the excerpt. "It's all about mindset, not hindsight. In aquatic cases, first responders don't seem to ask the right questions. They're relying on the standard incident form and can't recognize the valuable evidence involved in foul play."

"You say something, Chief?"

Cindie recognized the baritone voice of her old boss, Hal Samuels, who entered the room and craned his neck, surveying her office renovations. She flipped over Medina's treatise to thwart his curiosity.

"It's hard to believe these are my old digs. Pretty classy, Cin." Hal flashed his famous jury-pleasing, award-winning smile that was nestled within his new copper beard.

A glow of pride warmed Cindie's cheeks. She'd invested her time, creativity, and money into updating the decor, and Hal's compliment gratified her. "It's great to see you, too. It's been quiet around here without you. What brings you by? Are you homesick, your Honor?"

"Nah, I needed to stretch my legs. I'm Acting Supreme Court Judge on a commercial property line dispute, and the jury's out for deliberations on issue of liability. If you ask me, on the law and facts, the title company, the engineer, and the surveyor screwed up. But it's not my call." Hal settled into the chair facing her, his long legs stretched out and crossed at the ankles. He relaxed back with his hands supporting his head. "I'm getting the hang of the civil claims, but there's nothing like a good old murder."

Cindie had been Hal's second in command for five years, and she didn't swallow his excuse for the visit. Not for one second. The Dutchess County Supreme Court Courthouse and the DA Annex were attached through a short labyrinth of hallways, and even when walking slowly, it didn't take three minutes to get from building to building. That distance wasn't enough to stretch the kinks out of Hal's athletic legs. Hal wanted something from her.

"I always loved the view from this office. My new chambers are on the second floor with a decent view over Market Street, but nothing like this panorama."

She cocked her head and glared at him, encouraging him to get to the point.

"Oh, I'm sorry. Are you busy? Am I interrupting you?"

"Hal, there's something on your mind. Please get to the point and tell me what it is," she said, crossing her arms across her chest to contain her annoyance.

"It's Jess. Rather, it's Emory's disappearance. We have no clue what's going on with the investigation, and it's driving her crazy. Hence, me crazy. She's distracted, stressed out, and distant, which isn't Jess." Hal shifted his position. He leaned forward, resting his elbows on his knees, and wrung his hands. "I'm not requesting any favors or for you to disclose any confidential information, but what's the status of the case? Is there even a case?"

"It sounds like you have issues to discuss with Jessie, but her reaction sounds normal. For goodness sake, her kid's father is presumed dead," Cindie said, carefully selecting her words so as not to offend him. "Not officially, but it's been four days, and we haven't found his body, and we may never locate him. I believe it's a terrible accident unless the evidence proves otherwise."

"So, you're being straight with me? There's no news?" A veil of skepticism tinged the relief in his voice.

Cindie cast him an insulted, you've-got-to-be-kidding-me look. "The investigation isn't in my hands. The police are working the scene, the witnesses, and the evidence. You know the drill. If the situation changes, Jessie will be the first to know." Her mind shifted gears. "Do you know of any fatalities on the Hudson while you worked here? This seems to be a case of first impression."

"Presumed drowning, no. We had vessel collisions because of weather or operator inexperience. One time, a group of teens stole a speedboat from one of their parents, but fortunately, there were no fatalities. I'm unaware of any deaths on the river between Albany and Peekskill, but I wasn't tuned into the lower Hudson. Why?"

Cindie hesitated, unsure about mentioning Joanna Medina or asking Hal whether he'd heard of her. She realized she'd been second-guessing him as though trying to catch him in a lie. She'd been treating him like an adversary rather than an old friend or a mentor who'd graciously shared his wellspring of knowledge with her over the years.

"Even though it's not a docketed case, I've been consulting with an aquatic forensic expert named Joanna Medina." She explained Medina's experience as an expert witness in aquatic scene processing. "Ever heard of her?"

"So you suspect foul play?"

Kyle Emory's presumed drowning was Cindie's first challenge during her brief tenure as District Attorney. How she handled the case would not only affect her credibility as DA, but whether she held onto the position at election time. Every four years, the citizens elected a new DA, and they remembered the incumbent's wins and losses of headline-grabbing cases. One slip and she'd be finished before she'd even gotten started.

"No, I'm being prudent. I don't want to mishandle the investigation in case it's not an accident. And I want to protect your impartiality as the criminal court judge. Hal, I don't want to jeopardize this opportunity for you."

Hal nodded with approval as though he'd taught her well. "As you should, on both accounts. And no, I'm unfamiliar with Medina. We never required her services." He rose to leave. "Thanks for your honesty, and take care, Cin." He leaned forward to peck Cindie on the cheek. His lips were warm, but the hand squeezing hers was icy and clammy. "I appreciate your time, and please forgive my boldness. I don't mean to put you in an uncomfortable position. Jess has me worried, that's all."

Spoken like a man in love. A man who had watched his lover nearly perish in a cluster of prenatal seizures. An honorable man who never shirked his responsibilities to family, friends, and community.

"I'll call you if there's anything to report. You take care, too," she replied.

Hal waved half-heartedly and departed her office, his shoulders slumped as though resigned to a crisis beyond his control. Not a good look for

Hal Samuels, former District Attorney, County Court and Acting Supreme Court Judge.

As much as Cindie pitied Hal, she represented the People of the State of New York, and she was protecting him in the event the potential criminal case was assigned to his courtroom. She believed the less Hal knew about Kyle's case, the better, and that he should receive any updates through Jessie.

It must be a trying time in their household, living in limbo, she mused. They hadn't legally declared Kyle dead, but he wasn't alive either. Not a pleasant time at all. Hal and Jessie were a solid couple, and they'd survive this ordeal. Hopefully, it would strengthen their relationship and not tear them apart, although Hal already bore the signs of wear.

The shrill ringing of her desk phone interrupted her reverie, and she answered it.

"Yes," she whispered in a raspy voice.

"Cindie, Matt Shepardson here. We've fished a body out of the river, and we have sent him over for an autopsy."

"Do we have an ID? Is it Emory?" Cindie swallowed, clearing the crackle from her voice. "Does it look like foul play?"

"Not yet. Jones and Pulaski are gathering ID information, and I'll let you know as soon as we have anything."

She hadn't yet sent Medina's article and checklist over to Shepardson, but Jones and Pulaski were pros. "There's something I want to share with your team about processing the crime scene. I'll email it right over, and let's assume it's a crime scene, not an accident. It's best not to scrimp on the investigation, just in case. Let me know if you need anything else. I'm available 24/7."

"Got it. Thanks."

Death had finally come calling. It would be another excruciating long night.

Chapter Thirty

Jessie sighed in relief when Ebony and Zander were gone. Finally, she was alone and could process everything they'd dumped on her. Kyle's presumed drowning. The mysterious body. Her life turned upside down.

The inevitable consequences of Kyle's death swirled inside her head like a carousel, making her dizzy. Raising Lily alone. Telling Kyle's parents the news. The life insurance. Setting up trusts for Lily. The medical examiner's cause of death findings. The suspicious unavailability of Olivia Vargas. And the missing kayak plug.

Jessie needed to stop the merry-go-round and hop off, but it was no use. Grim reality juiced up her thoughts and emotions into hyper-drive, and Jessie didn't know how to decelerate.

As an attorney, she served as counselor, psychiatrist, lawyer, and mother confessor to her clients. She comforted them, empathized with them, and cajoled them into scrutinizing their problems with objectivity.

With Kyle's death, the table had turned. Being the survivor sucked. Jessie understood she needed to stop the self-pity and consider Lily's future first. "Live for the living," as her Nana Evelyn had so often preached. Take it step by step.

However, Ebony's inquiry had struck a painful chord. The nosy questions about Kyle's power of attorney and their estate planning disconcerted Jessie as a mother and an attorney. Ebony insinuated that by failing to resolve those legal issues, she'd left Lily unprotected. She'd accused Jessie of being a lousy lawyer and a neglectful parent and that her passivity had caused

Kyle to devise half of his life insurance proceeds to Olivia.

Jessie wondered about the rest of his estate—his bank accounts, his condo, and his personal property. Had his ridiculous suspicions about Lily's paternity driven him to strip Lily of her probate rights, too?

Everyone knew Lily was Kyle's daughter. The dark curly hair and creamy complexion were gifts from her father, just as Jessie's mismatched emerald eyes, elfin ears, and rosebud lips were hers. Further, Kyle's name as Lily's father was on her birth certificate, and adopting Emory as Lily's middle name was testament to her heritage.

Jessie's mouth grew dry as betrayal festered in her belly. She needed to know Lily's rights as a child born out of wedlock. Would Bev, Tom, or Kyle's siblings challenge Lily's entitlement to Kyle's estate or the life insurance proceeds? Did Lily have legal grounds to challenge being disinherited?

As hard as she tried, Jessie couldn't banish these distressing thoughts from her mind. Was it possible to mourn a man who double-crossed his own flesh and blood as he'd done to their daughter? How could she tell Lily about her father when Jessie didn't know him at all?

Jessie pulled up the New York Estate, Powers and Trust Law on her computer in the den. Except for the basics learned in law school, Jessie's legal practice hadn't touched upon the complicated area of the wills and trusts. She recalled that when a person died without a will, the rules of intestacy applied. The statute governing intestate descent and distribution stated that if there is no spouse, everything passed to the child or children.

Good, Jessie thought. Lily is protected. The knot in her gut eased slightly in relief.

However, Jessie needed to determine whether Lily was Kyle's *legal* child. The bellyache intensified as the section defining non-marital children delivered a devastating blow. Like in her religion, Judaism, the law considered Lily to be the legitimate heir of the maternal family, not the paternal. Since she and Kyle weren't married at the time of Lily's birth, then legally, Lily wasn't Kyle's child. Lily had no legal father, and Kyle lacked any rights to or responsibilities for Lily. Her daughter couldn't inherit from him *unless* the court entered an Order of Filiation declaring his paternity,

169

or she and Kyle had signed an Acknowledgment of Paternity form. Since neither party signed the birth certificate issued by the State of New York, the document failed to establish paternity.

Panic struck as her heartbeat thrashed in her ears, rendering her unable to think straight. There had been no court Order of Filiation. Any recollection of Kyle's signing an acknowledgment of his paternity was sketchy, at best.

At the time of Lily's birth, deadly eclampsia had trapped Jessie in a cluster of relentless seizures. Her ob-gyn had saved her life by administering anti-convulsant medication and delivering Lily by emergency cesarean section. For days afterward, Jessie had been sedated. She barely remembered being discharged from the hospital, or any papers she and Kyle may have signed to admit their three-pound, nine-ounce preemie into the NICU. She'd next seen Kyle six weeks later when they'd brought Lily home from the hospital, and their interaction had been brief.

For more than a year, she'd worked to banish this life-threatening experience from her memory. When she and Kyle separated, they'd never broached Lily's paternity again. In this new light, though, she'd be forced to relive this harrowing crisis and add this unresolved issue to the list of those left behind by Kyle.

While Jessie's concerns were valid, she admonished herself for berating Kyle. Kyle was dead, and despite the damning proof, her heart told her Kyle loved Lily. The problem was he loved Olivia, too, and ardor can easily manipulate a man into making irrational decisions.

She needed to dispel those thoughts and concentrate on ferreting out more about the Vargases and the kayak. If Kyle were dead, she'd deal with the fallout and her legal course of action later.

Jessie's finger grazed the shiny white shutdown key on her laptop, and she froze. There were records containing information about Kyle's interaction with the Vargases. Not Kyle's medical records, but his phone records. To save money, she and Kyle shared a mobile family plan, splitting the bill each month. And since Kyle had been neurotic about storing his text messages in the Cloud, those might be accessible, too.

Logging into their telecom provider's account, Jessie located Kyle's text and call logs for the eight months prior to his meeting Olivia. His call history included the date, time, contact number, type of call—incoming or outgoing, and whether it was from a mobile or landline. No recipient names were provided, but Jessie could cross-reference them with the transcripts of his text messages stored in the Cloud. She printed out the logs and downloaded them onto her computer into the "Household Expenses" file. It was the perfect spot to hide the data in case someone hacked into her computer.

Also, Jessie knew the password to Kyle's phone. Stupidly, it was his birthdate. Occasionally, when they'd lived together, they'd shared phones. She'd always suspected Kyle had engineered their swaps to keep tabs on her friendship with Terrence Butterfield. But the switches had proven handy when either had forgotten to charge their phones.

Since neither Ebony nor Zander mentioned Kyle's phone, she assumed the storm had washed it away, too. Yet, it was odd they hadn't broached the subject.

What she'd found was better than the phone. She held the key to Kyle's digital life, and it could lead her to a suspect for murder.

Chapter Thirty-One

"Do you think Jessie was being honest with us?" Zander asked, maneuvering their black SUV onto the arterial highway beneath the Mid-Hudson Bridge and heading toward the police station.

"Honesty isn't the point. Thoroughness is." Ebony paused as she watched the traffic flowing westward across the bridge. The afternoon sun peeked through the cutouts in the giant gleaming towers, washing the bridge in a silvery iridescence as if it was too icy to touch. "Jessie provided significant leads about the trinkets and lack of skin markings. But I sensed she wasn't completely forthcoming. I should've probed harder."

Jessie wasn't a person who could keep secrets, but her reticence suggested that there had been omissions of deeper, intimate truths relevant to the case. Ebony couldn't blame her. Their incompatible occupations had cast a pall over their sisterhood, although Kyle's disappearance seemed to have diminished the distrust between them. It was like Kyle's case was the Mid-Hudson Bridge connecting them together. Only time would tell whether they remained isolated on their respective sides or met somewhere in the middle.

"I'm thinking about the medical and dental records," Zander said.

"Yeah?"

"I understand there's no common law marriage in New York, but isn't Jessie Kyle's next of kin, even though they weren't married?"

"Because Lily is Kyle's kid, too?" Ebony paused. "And Jessie is Lily's legal guardian? That's one way to look at it."

"Couldn't Jessie request Kyle's medical and dental records on Lily's behalf?"

"If there's no Power of Attorney, then under HIPPA?" Ebony hadn't considered Jessie's legal agency on Lily's behalf, which was worth pursuing when the time came. At present, she focused on the tidbits Carly required to identify John Doe. "It's what Jessie didn't offer that makes me wonder. I suspect she's researching other avenues on her own. I'm not sure what she's up to, but something's going on. This isn't the first time I've warned her off a case, but Jessie barrels ahead anyway without considering her safety or that others worry about her."

"Sound like somebody else I know. It's no wonder you are buds. You're practically the same person."

Ebony didn't reply but bit her lips, pondering Zander's observation.

"Did you hear what I said? You and Jessie couldn't be more alike if you were—"

"Yeah, yeah. Sisters from another mother," Ebony said wistfully. Or the twin steel towers of the Mid-Hudson Bridge.

Oddly, Zander's remark rang true. As kids, she and Jessie were inseparable, mirror images of each other: dressing, talking, and walking the same, sharing the same friends, belonging to the same clubs, and playing the same sports. They would do anything for each other.

As adults, she and Jessie had grown into obstinate, passionate, intuitive, responsible, and compassionate creative thinkers and risk-takers. They both dedicated their lives to pursuing justice and upholding the law. Ebony's head had convinced her that their twin-ship was in the past, but her heart spoke otherwise. Jessie was a sister from another mother, and Ebony couldn't fail her, or Lily, in solving the mystery of Kyle's presumed drowning.

They arrived at the station, and Zander exited and slammed his car door. She sat alone in their SUV while his long, cat-like strides carried him toward the steel-reinforced door.

"Hey," she called, chasing after Zander. "Speaking of sisters, after we check in, let's report our findings to Carly and see what headway she's made."

An hour later, Ebony and Zander pushed open the glass door of the modern one-story brown brick structure housing the Dutchess County Medical Examiner's office. They flashed their badges at the receptionist through the picture window in the vestibule, and she asked who they wanted to see.

"Dr. Carly Jones," Zander replied.

"Wait here, please," the woman said in a heavy Jamaican accent. There was no reason for the woman to recognize Ebony since this was her first trip to her sister's workplace. She'd avoided the morgue like the plague, but she'd made an exception for Jessie and Lily. The receptionist picked up the phone, made a call, and hung up. "Please come through. Dr. Jones will meet you in the waiting room straight ahead."

A buzzer sounded. The door clicked open, and they entered a small waiting area. The room was painted a nondescript sage green, and someone had arranged four yellow vinyl chairs on the dull beige tile floor. A stinging odor of bleach masked by an antiseptic lilac fragrance filled the recycled air.

Ebony's shoulders relaxed when the sickening smell of death didn't greet them. Yet she swallowed hard to ingest the noxious scent in the air.

"How do they ever get used to this smell?" Zander asked. He retrieved his handkerchief and blew his nose.

"I couldn't, but this explains Carly's abuse of perfume. After working here, the chemicals have probably fried the inside of her nose."

The sound of a slamming door, accompanied by the swishing of footsteps across the tile, preceded Carly's entrance into the room. Stylish as ever, Carly topped her purple scrubs and booties with a black scrub cap printed with medical anatomy. The detailed drawings of the heart were pale pink, the brain was green, and the kidneys were mustard color. A pale green bow trailed down her back, and a matching surgeon's mask dangled from one ear.

"Nice cap," Ebony said, shivering in the refrigerated air.

"I commissioned it online." Carly grinned. "Hi, Zander. Did you find out anything?"

Ebony thought she saw him blush.

"We thought we'd check in because we have Kyle's physician and dentist info for you, but not much else. How's it going with John Doe?" Zander asked.

"We've disrobed him, but we're just starting on the autopsy. He's Caucasian, with black hair, around thirty-five to forty years of age, 5'11, and no tattoos. We don't have his accurate weight because his body is bloated, but he looks to be in good shape, not obese. There's nothing unusual about the street clothing. Gap Jeans, t-shirt, and sweatshirt. Nike sneakers. No wetsuit. The cold-water temps decreased his deterioration and slowed the rigor mortis, so we're trying to ascertain his time of death. We'll have a better idea when we open him up."

Ebony nodded. The description fit Kyle to a *T*, and she described the accessories and wallet.

"His pockets were empty, but if the storm tossed him around, he could've lost those items in the water."

"What about a cell phone?"

Carly shook her head.

So far, she and Zander hadn't uncovered one either. Ebony would have to double-check with the Vargas family and forensics to determine whether Kyle had left those items onshore before embarking on the trip.

"There's one thing Jessie mentioned. A leather bracelet. She says he never took it off."

Carly scrunched her elegant nose as if thinking. "Funny you should mention that. He was wearing a bracelet on his right wrist, but it was an eighteen carat gold chain. We had to cut it off him because his hand was bloated...." Carly paused. "We're checking it for the manufacturer's markings so we can track down. It's like the one Mom gave Dad for his fiftieth birthday. Remember, we gave him endless shit about him wearing a girlie bracelet."

The sisters giggled conspiratorially as Ebony watched Zander shake his head and shove his hand into his pocket to cover the silver chain encircling his wrist.

"If you send us a photo, we'll forward it to forensics," he said.

"Will do. Would you guys like a tour? You can suit up and attend the autopsy. That would be a real treat since you've never been here before. You might find it interesting."

"Sure, that would be—" Ebony said, but a sharp heel grinding into her boot toe interrupted her acceptance. Zander's husky blue eyes glared at her as his neck muscles tensed. "Perhaps next time, but thanks. We've got to get back to the station."

"All right. Next time. I'm holding you to it. Dad had a blast when I brought him through. He took a selfie lying on the stainless steel table in the lab." She chuckled. "That man watches too much true crime on television. Are you sure I can't persuade you?"

"As appetizing as that sounds, we'd better book it," Zander replied.

"One thing before you go, did Jessie mention Kyle having a pierced ear? Our John Doe has his left ear pierced. There was no earring, just the hole."

"Kyle with a pierced ear? No, but I'll ask her," Ebony said. "And she's looking for a toothbrush or hairbrush for us."

"Okay. Thanks. I'll call you. Later, Zander." Carly tapped her colorful surgeon's cap, pivoted on her heels, and disappeared through the door.

Conservative and cheap Kyle Emory wearing an expensive bracelet and piercing his ear? This didn't sound like the Kyle Emory she knew. Maybe the team missed the mark and John Doe was a John Doe.

Then where the hell was Kyle?

Chapter Thirty-Two

On a scale of one to a hundred, Jessie's stress level skyrocketed to ninety-five. Every muscle in her body ached with fatigue. There was nothing physically wrong with her, but the rollercoaster day had battered her body and her emotions to a pulp.

After dinner, as she and Hal were cleaning up, she immersed her hands in hot, soapy water and garnered every ounce of energy to scrub the lasagna glued to the baking dish. Out the kitchen window, the streetlights flickered on down the lane. Inside her neighbor's homes, they were eating dinner, doing homework, having bath time, and undertaking their normal nighttime rituals. Theirs were lives without traumatic events barreling down upon them like a freight train.

In her peripheral vision, she spied Hal studying her. "Go on." He snatched away the sponge. "Put Lily to bed. Take a bath. Relax. I've got this." She must have looked like crap because his steady voice quavered with concern.

He didn't have to twist her arm. In a shot, Jessie tucked Lily into bed and slipped into a steamy bath. Her aches and pains dissolved into the bubbly foam. Afterward, she'd crawl into their soft, cozy bed, maybe have a quiet conversation with Hal, download the latest thriller onto her tablet, or stream a blockbuster on the flat screen. Any distraction from the whirlwind of her life.

Twenty minutes later, Jessie climbed from the tub refreshed, and wrapped her hair and prune-like body in fluffy towels. Her phone buzzed on the granite counter. Recognizing the incoming number, she threw on her robe and answered it.

"Aunt Jessie! Aunt Jessie!" the high-pitched voices of two youngsters screamed over FaceTime. "Where's Lily? We want to see her! Put her on." The excited faces of her seven-year-old niece, Sophie, and her nine-year-old nephew, Nicholas, flashed on the screen and then vanished as they wrestled for dominance over the phone.

"Give me the phone. I want to talk to her," the boy yelled.

"No, you gimme that," the girl said.

"Sorry, Jess," her brother Ethan said, reclaiming the device from his kids. The sight of his goofy, broad grin made Jessie smile. While Jessie was the spitting image of their mother, Ethan was a hipper millennial version of their dad, with his broad shoulders and his silver-sprinkled temples. "The kids are excited about leaving Cali and coming east for Thanksgiving. It's been a while. Nice outfit, squirt. We didn't catch you at a bad time, did we?"

"No, just chillin' in the tub. It's great to see you. How's Gemma?" The grunts and groans of kids wrestling continued in the background.

"Hey, kids. Cut it out. If you're going to fight, I'm sending you to your rooms. Do you want that?" Ethan yelled. His kids whined, "no," and the flat-screen television clicked on at a loud volume. "Come on, guys. Please turn that down." They complied, and the room quieted to a dull roar.

"Good parenting, Mr. Mom."

"Shut up. Gemma's great. She's in Pilate's class. You know how it is with these Silicon Valley wives."

"Hey, why are you home with the dynamic duo? Did you get fired or something?"

"Nah, I'm starting a new gig in two weeks, so I took time off to hang with the kiddos." He pivoted his face away from the camera to check on the kids. The theme song of an animated show about crime-fighting, talking dogs came on.

It seemed like every time they spoke, Ethan was changing jobs. It happened so often Jessie couldn't keep up with her older brother's career path. An IT prodigy, the metaverse had lured Ethan away to the West Coast, and he jumped from company to company, ascending the corporate ladder. He'd told her he'd made mega-bucks in his last position managing a team of designers at a mobile phone geo-location app startup in Los Gatos. Jessie never doubted that someday Ethan would fund his own startup rather than work at one, or he'd become CEO of Google, Meta, or TikTok. Yet, she hoped he'd move back East, so their kids could know each other.

"And why are you calling me in the middle of the afternoon? Did Dad sic you on me?" Jessie shuffled into the bedroom, making herself comfortable on the bed.

"Can't a guy check up on his sister? I'm sorry I haven't called sooner. It has been crazy around here. I feel awful about what you're going through over Kyle. You know I thought you could do better, and you did with Hal, but is there any news?"

Ethan never minced his words. He didn't need to. When they were growing up, he'd always been her go-to guy. Seven years older than she, he'd always watched out for his little sister. She told him everything, because he wouldn't bullshit her. Although a continent away and with families of their own, Jessie still sought the counsel of her older brother.

Jessie brought Ethan up to speed on the events, "...and he was engaged to be married," she said flatly.

Ethan's jaw dropped open in shock. "What? You're shitting me? Dad didn't mention that."

"Yeah, he proposed to some hot social influencer-slash-music teacher who's twenty-nine years old."

"Whoa. My man's a player, after all." Ethan paused. "Just kidding, squirt."

"I know, but I'm baffled. The police are stonewalling us. Kyle's folks are horrified. And I'm worried about Lily. She and Kyle were getting attached." She paused. "I've been lucky, though. Hal's been great about everything, but my emotions are all over the place."

"By the cops, I'm assuming you're referring to your bestie."

"Uh-huh," she replied, feeling like a grade-schooler who had been called out for brawling in the schoolyard.

"Jess, I feel for you, but I can help. When I was working at ThreeDee Innovations, I was the contact person on a deal with a custom kayak builder. He was pursuing the possibility of producing a kayak using our 3D technology. Nothing came to pass, but I'm sure I can find his contact info. I know nothing about kayaks, but this man's a leader in the field. Would you like me to send it along?"

"Sure. It wouldn't hurt to talk to him. I've been digging around because, as I mentioned, we're not getting much information from the police."

Ethan laughed. "I bet you have. And no doubt you've been stepping onto Ebony's toes. It's crazy how you two argue like sisters. And I'd better see her at your wedding next summer. Otherwise, I'll be pissed."

"Yeah. We've reached a truce. She and her partner are the lead investigators, and I'm trying to help from the sidelines."

"You never stand on the sidelines, you jump right in. Just do me a favor and stay safe." The sound of a crash and a cry coming from the couch interrupted Ethan. "What's happening over there, Nick? Soph?" The wailing grew louder, as if someone had committed a bloody murder. "Jess, I've got to go. I'll send along the info. Love you. Bye."

Before she could return the farewell, the screen turned black.

A half-hour later, exotic sports cars raced around the hairpin curves of Rome on her television, and snipers fired from the red tile rooftops. Stuntman jumped off bridges, and missiles exploded, when a text from Ethan arrived.

Nick OK. Just a scrape on his knee. He'll survive. Here's the deets. Good luck. Best to Hal. XOXO E

Merritt Hanson, Esopus Custom Kayaks. www.escustomkayaks.com. merritt@escustomkayaks.com.

She texted a smiling face and a heart, and then fell asleep.

The next morning, Jessie woke up early, and she popped up in bed. It was pitch black except for the silvery moonlight seeping through the bedroom curtains. The time on her phone read five o'clock, and beside her, Hal softly snored.

In the darkness, Jessie slipped from the covers, grabbed her phone, and set her feet on the chilly wooden floorboards, which creaked, making Hal stir. She froze, but then padded from the room, closed the bedroom door, and proceeded downstairs to the den.

On her laptop, she searched for EsCustomKayaks.com, and a website popped up purveying "Exceptional Designs for the Discerning Boat Builder. Celebrating Twenty Years." A collage of technical drawings of kayaks streamed by on the title page, along with the history of kayak construction, a gallery of projects, a blog, and ordering information. Jessie clicked on the gallery, and dozens of handcrafted wooden kayaks were on display. The variations in color and the striations of wood elevated these watercraft to another level, pieces worthy of an art exhibition in a museum. There was no mention of using 3D technology, but there was a link to the Hudson River Maritime Museum in Kingston, N.Y., where the owner, Hanson, taught classes on woodworking and building skin-on-frame canoes.

Hanson had also posted a selfie of him kayaking on the Hudson. His athletic arms brandished a handmade paddle above his head, and he wore a broad-brimmed canvas hat and sunglasses. Hanson, shirtless beneath his life vest, looked to be in his fifties.

From Hanson's credentials, Ethan had done her a solid. Not only was Hanson a master shipwright, his workshop was twenty minutes north in Esopus, N.Y., on the other side of the river.

Despite the late hour, Jessie sent off an email to Hanson.

Mr. Hanson, my name is Jessica Martin, Esq., and I'm a local attorney working on a personal injury case involving a defective kayak. To prepare my case, I'm seeking an expert on boat building, and my brother, Ethan Martin, recommended you. Your expertise would be greatly appreciated. Can you please advise if you are interested, and, if so, when you are available to meet? Thank you. Jessica Martin, Esq.

Her words weren't exactly the truth or a lie either. Kyle had been injured, and she needed to figure out whether there had been a defect with his kayak. Jessie hoped Hanson would respond and that he knew his way around the cheap plastic versions like Kyle's. Otherwise, she was stumped.

She was about to sign off on her computer when she received an email notification.

Jessica: How's noon today at the Hudson River Maritime Museum?
Merritt

Chapter Thirty-Three

Jessie nudged open the door of the Hudson River Maritime Museum on the Rondout Creek wharf. She stopped to admire the tall-masted sailboats and expensive cabin cruisers docked along the narrow tributary flowing into the Hudson. Off-shore, in the middle of the river, she spied the Rondout lighthouse, one of the remaining lighthouses on the Hudson River. Accessible only by water, the century-old brick house standing guard over the river now belonged to the museum and the City of Kingston.

"Hey, can you shut the door, please? It's chilly outside," a woman behind the reception desk called out.

"Sure, sorry. I was admiring the view," Jessie said. She entered the building and approached the receptionist. The woman was in her late forties, with dark hair and wild, shocking streaks of gray framing her round face. Behind her, on blue clapboard, a makeshift gift shop displayed posters, postcards, books, and nautical-themed gear and home goods. To the left was the main entrance into the museum celebrating the maritime history of the Hudson and its tributaries through maps, paintings, and ship models.

"That happens all the time. The lighthouse has an amazing history. Did you know it had one of the first women lighthouse keepers in history? During the Civil War, Catherine Murdock assumed the job when her husband, George, died, and she operated the beacon for over fifty years. It's fascinating to think about Catherine's life when there were no highways, and the Hudson was a busy commercial route." The woman sighed wistfully as though being a keeper was her dream job. "Sorry, how can I help you?"

"I'm here to meet Merritt Hanson. Is he around?"

"My husband's next door at the Wooden Boat School, finishing up with a woodworking class." Ms. Hanson smiled. "It's out the door, to your right, toward the river."

Jessie thanked Ms. Hanson and walked toward a gray building she recalled had once been a Mexican restaurant. A massive carved sign stating "The Wooden Boat School" hung over the door. She entered, and the smell of fresh-cut trees and sawdust filled the workshop. The room buzzed with a cacophony of saws and machinery, and students planed planks of lumber at worktables and hammered on the shells of boats.

She walked over to a young girl chiseling a piece of wood outlined with a name framed by feathers at the ends. It looked like a signboard for a boat. The girl didn't look up.

"Excuse me. I'm looking for Merritt Hanson."

The girl stopped her handiwork and looked up. "Oh, hi. Sorry. I was in the zone. What did you say?"

Jessie repeated her request, and the girl aimed her chisel at the corner, where a tall, muscular man with sun-bleached hair instructed a group of teens crafting kayak paddles. Jessie walked over to the group and watched them sandpaper their semi-finished projects.

"Kids, it's quitting time. Clean up your workspaces, gather your gear, and I'll see you next week when we'll apply the varnish. Great job, everyone."

As the kids followed his instructions, Hanson approached Jessie.

"Jessica Martin? Hi. How's Ethan doing? Your brother's a great guy. It's too bad we couldn't work together. As you can see, I'm a traditionalist." He extended his hand, and Jessie shook it. His skin was as rough as the sandpaper the kids had been using.

"Thanks for meeting me. Is there somewhere we can talk?" Jessie had to raise her voice above the din echoing off the studio's rafters.

"Follow me."

Hanson led her into a classroom attached to the noisy workshop. The walls displayed nautical charts and photos of the seven lighthouses that dotted the Hudson from the Statute of Liberty to Hudson, New York.

"The museum holds our maritime training classes in here. Please take a seat and tell me what's on your mind."

Jessie and Hanson sat at a long white table set up in the room. She swallowed to ease the tightness in her chest. "I may have misled you about my case, but I urgently need your help." She launched into the story about Kyle's drowning and the kayak's missing plug.

Hanson folded his arms across his chest as he listened. "I heard about the accident but not the details. What a tragedy. The kayaker, Kyle Emory, was your former partner, and he's the father of your child? My condolences, and I appreciate your need to find out what happened. You need closure. Wait a second." Hanson rose and searched through a cabinet, extracting a rolled tube of paper.

Jessie studied Hanson. He was her father's age, but his weathered skin and ruddy cheeks made him look older. He probably had his own kids, maybe grandkids, and being a kayaker, perhaps he'd lost loved ones in dangerous waters. When she'd told him the truth about her visit, Hanson could have dismissed her, but she felt his sincere sympathy and his willingness to help her solve the mystery of Kyle's death.

He set the tube on the table and unfurled it. It was a series of drawings with white lines, letters, and markings on an indigo background, the blueprint of a kayak and paddle. She noticed it was a US patent application with Hanson's name listed as the inventor, and it was dated March 2000, almost twenty-five years ago.

"As you can see, this is mine. One of my first kayaks. It's quite simple, but it will help illustrate the mechanics of a boat." Hanson tapped on Figure 1, the lengthwise side view of a kayak with its bony curved lines outlining the boat's skeleton. "This patent is for a wooden boat, not the plastic kind your friend used. The principles are the same, though. On the top deck, there are scupper holes, or drainage holes. They're inserted above the waterline and allow the boat to drain water off the deck surface. If one is missing, it doesn't impact the safety of the boat. A missing drain hole alone couldn't have caused a kayak to capsize."

He pointed to Figure 4, a drawing of the top deck of the kayak with a gaping cockpit in the center. "The cockpit is the largest hole in the boat, big enough to accommodate a kayaker sitting inside the craft. In most of my kayaks, the space is open from bow to stern." On the drawing, the cockpit monopolized a third of the length of the boat. "An open cockpit is the real danger when the water gets rough, and most sea kayaks have a nylon skirt attached around the opening to keep out water. It tightens around the kayaker's waist to seal the cockpit. Recreational kayaks don't have the skirts because they are meant for paddling in lakes and ponds, not the open water."

"Does the skirt allow the kayakers to do those fancy rolls in the rapids?"

"Exactly. But it can present a danger when someone doesn't know how to exit their kayak."

"This may be a stupid question, but does a kayak sink?" She'd wondered why they'd found Kyle's kayak capsized rather than submerged in the river.

"No. It doesn't. Even a fully flooded kayak won't sink. The kind your friend had, the Pelican, has a foam block inside the stern. That creates a watertight and airtight compartment in the hull and keeps the boat afloat. Kayaks capsize; they don't sink."

She didn't want to appear like an attorney interrogating a witness, so she took a deep breath and prioritized the questions she wanted answered. "What should someone do if they fall out of the boat?"

"The prudent thing would be to stay with your boat or hang onto the bungee cords until help arrives. They shouldn't try to climb back in because they could get dumped back into the water, or they could drag the boat deeper beneath the surface."

Her shoulders slumped in response to his answers. Hanson seemed like he was being honest with her, giving her the facts, not bullshit.

"From what you've told me, Kyle wasn't wearing a life vest. He was wearing street clothing, the waves were high, the water was cold, and it was windy. From my experience, ninety percent of water-related deaths are attributable to not wearing a life jacket. Without knowing the exact details, I'm sorry to say Kyle's lack of skills, unsuitable clothing and equipment, and his cold shock and panic contributed to his death. More so than a hole."

186

Jessie knew where this conversation was leading. Human error killed Kyle, not the missing plug. Yet, the blame couldn't be Kyle's alone. Olivia accompanied him on the trip, and Jessie wondered about her responsibility for the disaster. "Would his companion have been able to save him?"

"Was she an experienced kayaker? Was she knowledgeable about rescues? Remember, there was wind and rain, and she could have drifted away from him. Even if she'd tried, she might not have been able to save Kyle."

"If I send you the details, would you put your opinion in writing? This information may be helpful to the police. It's been helpful to me."

"I'm glad, and I'm sorry for your loss. Sure, send it along." He rolled up the blueprint and snapped a rubber band around the paper roll. "It's too bad your friend ignored the first safety rule about staying with your kayak. He may have been able to hang on until help arrived."

Jessie felt like her heart was shrinking. If only she could reverse time and warn Kyle about the storm. Even if Kyle had put himself in danger, someone had intended to hurt him. Somebody pulled the plug, and Jessie wouldn't rest until she found the culprit. There was more to Kyle's story than his death.

"Yeah, it's a shame."

Chapter Thirty-Four

For the past five years, Ebony and Zander had worked side by side. But they were as opposite as night and day, hot and cold, or sweet and sour. Ebony had concluded that Chief Shepardson had partnered them as a teaching moment, a bizarre experiment designed to make the rookie detectives either sink or swim. Ebony and Zander had outsmarted the chief, though. Over time, they'd sorted out their incompatibilities. Their combination of smarts and ingenuity had proven to be deadly, contributing to their docketing more felony collars than anyone on the force.

With the sergeants' exams looming on the horizon, Ebony had been analyzing their partnership, and its highs and lows, especially the drug bust which had plugged a bullet into her hip. When the chief had announced only one vacancy for sergeant, Zander had opted to transfer to the Dutchess County Sheriff. If he passed the exam, he'd undertake a newly created position to develop a countywide crime database. Sadly, they were embarking on parallel paths, unlikely to cross again.

During their tenure, Ebony had assumed the role of the partner with bat-shit crazy ideas. She believed rules were to be tested, not broken, and she'd fine-tuned the art of quickly assessing the boundaries. She was a maverick. A rock n' roll loving, blue-jean and leather-wearing cop. The "bad ass" during the interrogations.

Zander, the straight-laced arm of the pair, was the conformist. He pretended to be hip and trendy, but the sartorial conservatism of his shiny Italian loafers, British raincoat, and jacket and tie made him stand out like a Super Bowl ad. A closet techie, Zander was organized and analytical, and he served as Ebony's conscience to ensure she colored within the lines. He was always the Boy Scout, the "good" cop.

Most likely, Kyle's case was to be their final major investigation together. From the moment the chief had dispatched them to Upper Landing Park, Ebony had known the truth. This case was their last hurrah, and Ebony struggled to accept her partnership with Zander was about to end.

Neither had spoken about their imminent split. Instead, they'd thrown themselves into Kyle's case with greater fervor than any other assignment. Yet, it hung over them like the fog over the Hudson.

Zander perched on the edge of Ebony's desk, his arms crossed over the brass buttons of the navy blazer he'd purchased at the designer outlets. He breathed on the face of his smartwatch, shining it on his trouser leg.

"Can you look at this? I want to make sure we've covered all the bases in Emory's case." Zander dragged a spare chair next to his so they could share his computer screen, and he cleared a space for her at his desk. The computer was open to a spreadsheet of Kyle's case that listed the witnesses, dates, times, and summaries of the interviews, the evidence transmitted to forensics for analysis, and a catalog of scene videos, photographs, and drawings. He'd left empty spaces for the autopsy, and ME's environmental reports. "Your database of local municipalities in the Bennett case inspired me."

Her face warmed at his unexpected compliment.

He pointed at the screen. "We've interviewed Carlos and Viv Vargas, Cody Shaw, Jessie, and Tom and Bev Emory. That leaves Max and Ana Vargas, Auggie Vargas, Serena and Andrew White, and Olivia, of course."

When viewed in black and white, it was obvious they hadn't accomplished a lot during the week since the accident. The witnesses had shoveled a ton of bullshit, leaving them with no leads about who'd pulled the plug or whether John Doe was Kyle Emory. They were stuck, treading in dark, stagnant water.

If Kyle's demise wasn't an accident or suicide, then somebody killed him. But who? And what was their motive? Even if it was a long shot, there had to be a clue.

"Cody mentioned a tiff between Kyle and Auggie, and Auggie lives at White Oaks, where they'd stored the kayaks. He's worth a return trip to the compound, and maybe Olivia will finally be ready for a chat," Ebony said. She cracked her knuckles in anticipation.

"I'm a step ahead of you. I called Auggie and made an appointment for an hour from now." Zander glanced at his watch. "We should arrive in time."

"Come on, let's go. It'll take us about forty-five minutes to get there. I'll grab my notes and meet you at the car. We don't want to be late." Ebony patted his shoulder. "Great job on the spreadsheet. Let's see what Augusto Vargas has to say."

Zander took the highway to Garrison rather than the scenic drive along the Hudson. "See, we made it here in plenty of time," he said, turning onto the winding side road that led to White Oaks.

Ahead, a metallic white Mercedes convertible with a black ragtop sped toward them from the opposite direction. It swerved across the faded double yellow line into their lane, racing toward them head-on. Ebony gasped as it skidded back into the proper lane within feet of their bumper. She listened to the screeching tires resonate through the silent mountain pass as the sports car fishtailed, kicking up a trail of dust, dry leaves, and gravel as it whizzed by. It had vanity plates that read *BETMAN13*.

Zander stamped on the brakes, jolting them forward in their seats. "Did you see that? The jerk could have killed us. He must be going seventy miles an hour."

Ebony's head lashed backward against her headrest. She rubbed the tender spot on the back of her skull, and he studied her with concern.

"Sorry. Are you all right?" he asked.

"Yeah. That car was parked in front of Hudson Outfitters the other day. I bet it's Auggie's car. I'll call it in." She radioed in the plate numbers and waited for a reply as Zander cranked the steering wheel, flipped on their blue emergency lights and the dashboard camera, and raced after the speeding roadster in hot pursuit.

The winding road was slick with wet leaves from an early morning shower, and the tires of their SUV spun and skidded on the slippery surface. Zander pressed on. They spied the Mercedes ahead on a long straightaway, but then it disappeared around a sharp curve, only to reappear ahead on the road. Never veering onto the unpaved side roads, the roadster followed the main paved road, accelerated, and sped away.

Their quarry led them down a steep incline toward the river route into Garrison Village, the tiny riverside community where Max and his wife lived. Suddenly, the car veered north on Route 9, which ran parallel to the Metro-North commuter line linking Manhattan to Poughkeepsie.

The clunky SUV was no match for the sleek, exotic speedster up ahead. As it tried to catch up with the rocketing car, the old motor groaned and whined. The Mercedes shot into a dark tunnel carved into a mammoth shale mountain and vanished from sight again. The narrow passageway was barely wide enough to accommodate one car, yet the roadster raced onward at more than twice the posted speed limit of thirty miles per hour.

The tunnel was no challenge for the aerodynamic roadster, and Ebony held her breath as they plummeted into the black nothingness. She wondered whether their bulky vehicle would become a victim of the ancient manmade passage, imagining deep scrapes on the door panels or lost side view mirrors. In the gloom, Ebony gripped the side handles until her muscles trembled, waiting for confirmation of the plates.

A crackle came over the line as they descended into the darkness, but as they roared deeper into the cavern, the signal vanished. The SUV headlights flicked on, illuminating the slender roadway and reflecting off the red taillights of the sports car, growing more distant with passing each second.

"Come on, step on it," Ebony said. The roaring motor downshifted, slowing their car as though Zander had eased up on the gas. "We're losing him."

"He's not going anywhere. There are no exits off this route, and there's flat roadway on the far side of the tunnel. Besides, I don't want to kill us, and I'll make up the time once we're back in daylight." His voice quavered as he spoke. In the dashboard lights, his knuckles clutched the steering wheel, glowing ghostly white. Zander's expression turned hard, determined to catch the speeder.

As they returned to the blinding light of day, the blackness disappeared, making them blink as their eyesight adjusted. Zander had been correct. They were still trailing their quarry. Beneath them, their car growled as it shifted into a higher, faster gear. The speedometer read eight-five miles an hour as they flew along the pristine blacktop surface.

Crackling over the radio returned. "Car 29, can you hear me? I have a vehicle identification," the dispatcher said.

"Yes, copy. Standing by," Ebony replied, depressing the speaker button.

"The plates are registered to Carlos Vargas and Augusto Vargas. Do you copy?" The dispatcher spelled out the last name. "V-A-R-G-A-S. Do you copy Car 29?"

"That's affirmative. Over," Ebony said, ending the call.

"That son-of-a-bitch. Where does he think he's going?" Zander paused. "I have his number on my phone from this morning. Grab it from my jacket pocket and call him. Let's see if he answers." His concentration remained glued to the road as their speedometer climbed to ninety-five miles per hour. Slowly, the distance between the two cars shrank as though by his sheer will, leaving only a few hundred yards between them.

Ebony hit the redial button on Zander's cell. The number rang and went directly to voicemail. "He must have it turned off."

The Mercedes banked sharply, turning left onto a two-lane road skimming the shoreline of the Hudson. The bumpy road ran between the broad river on the left side and the Metro- North train tracks on the right. The water's edge was so close that the waves from a passing barge washed over the rocky shore, spilling onto the macadam surface. Beyond the tracks, the cliffs from the Breakneck Mountain Range rose sharply overhead. There was no escape for the sports car, and Zander and Ebony were gaining ground.

Zander followed suit. He jerked the steering wheel to avoid an uneven storm drain, but the front passenger tire clipped the edge of the steel cover, sending the SUV sailing through the air. "Hold on," he said as they landed with a jolt. The clamor of metal scraping across the black tar pierced

Ebony's ears, making her wince.

Zander continued to gain ground on the white car as they bounced along the wet, uneven pavement.

"Listen!" Ebony heard the distant whistle of a train and the clanging of a bell outside her window. Then, approaching from the south along the shoreline, the glittering headlight of a battered blue and silver Metro-North locomotive came into view. Their car quaked from the turbulent vibrations, announcing the advancing engine. Her body followed suit, and she grabbed onto the overhead handle for safety.

A short distance ahead, the road intersected with the tracks, and she spied the white car flying toward the crossing. The red lights on the rail crossing sign flashed in warning, and the black and white gate sluggishly lowered to block the entrance into the railroad junction. Barreling toward them at twenty-five miles an hour, the train would be on them within minutes. Again, the hollow train whistle sounded in forewarning.

"Do you think Auggie is crazy enough to beat the train?" Ebony asked. The Mercedes edged closer to the crossing, not appearing to stop. "Look, they're trying to maneuver around the gates."

"They'll never make it. If there's a collision, this could spell a major disaster. Not just for the car. They'd be putting the engineer and passengers in danger, too."

"And us. If the train derails and flips on its side, we're goners. There's no place for us to escape, either." Ebony glanced toward the river lapping up on the rocks, and the track and shale wall on her right. A fine layer of perspiration tickled her upper lip as she clutched the overhead handle, and her fingernails dug into her palms.

This wasn't what she expected today. She never envisioned the possibility of her own death. The air inside the car's cabin grew electric as the drama unfolded in slow motion, not in real-time. Her heart pounded against the ribs, feeling as though she were colliding with the train, the rocks, the mountain, and her destiny.

They watched and waited as they drove on.

The sports car inched its nose past the gates, its tires resting against the outside rail. Then, it stopped. The driver must have reconsidered the foolhardy death wish, and he reversed, coming to rest on the roadway safely out of the path of the speeding train.

Ebony exhaled the breath she didn't realize she was holding, and her grip relaxed. She shook her stiff hands to return their circulation as her pulse slowed.

The train tooted as it passed by, and the engineer waved.

Zander screeched to a halt behind the idling vehicle, threw the car into park, and he bolted out the door, breaking into a run. The blue lights pulsated through the SUV's grill in time to his galloping footsteps. Before following him, Ebony double-checked the blinking red light of the onboard camera to make sure it was recording the scene about to go down. Satisfied, Ebony darted toward Zander and the metallic white Mercedes. Even though her bum hip ached, she was still able to keep up with him.

Zander's face glowed as red as the crossing's flashing warning lights. He clenched his fists, prepared to fight. Ebony had never seen him so enraged, and she worried about the fate of the sports car driver. Luckily, she was present to intercede.

Competing with the deafening thunder of the train, the whooshing of the air through its mighty wheels, and the clanging of the warning signal, Zander drummed his fists on the gray-tinted window of the driver's door and windshield. "Police, open up. Goddamnit. Police. Open the door. Now!"

The train pulled away, and a silence filled the air. The bell ceased, and the gate returned to its upright position, paving the way for travel across the tracks.

The sound of tussling and the whispers of irritated voices filtered outside the car.

Ebony glanced at Zander and shrugged, her hand resting on the holster of her Glock.

Zander reached into his utility belt, extracted a badge, and smashed it against the window. "I'm warning you. Either you open the door, or I'll smash the window. I'm counting to five. One...two...three..."

CHAPTER THIRTY-FOUR

The click of the driver's door stopped his counting.

The door slowly opened, and before she could intercept him, Zander seized the shoulder of the driver camouflaged in an oversized black hoodie and sweatpants.

Ebony squeezed his arm and whispered in his ear. "Stop! The dashcam's still on!"

Zander froze, and his arms dropped to his side. But it was too late.

Chapter Thirty-Five

Cindie Tarrico hadn't become the Dutchess County District Attorney by being unprepared. She believed in preventative law as much as she did in preventative medicine. If a crisis raised its ugly head on the horizon, there was no reason to wait to address it.

The disappearance of Kyle Emory shimmered like a mirage on the infinite sea. Each day, his mystery floated toward her, intensifying. It wouldn't hurt to coordinate her team—the aquatic expert, the medical examiner, the lead detectives, and her staffers—before the investigation bore down on her like an oil tanker on a dinghy.

She'd sent an update to Joanna Medina and checked her off the list. Next was Carly Jones, MD.

Cindie was old school. She preferred books fanned across her desk open to the statutes or case law rather than researching on her computer. Somehow, rummaging among the stacks of musty treatises was easier than navigating the digital screens and websites. Leave the tech stuff to the younger legal cubs, not the lioness.

Unsure where Carly fit into the puzzle, she'd splayed open the blue and red leatherette volumes to the statutes governing County Coroners, Coroner's Physicians, and Medical Examiners, and their duties, reports, and record-keeping procedures.

The law empowered the district attorney and medical examiner with separate and distinct responsibilities in the drama starring John Doe. Carly Jones, MD, was entrusted to take possession of the body, identify him, seek confirmation from the next of kin, and perform an autopsy to establish the cause, the manner, and time of death. Under New York State law, Carly's clout extended far beyond examining fingerprints, DNA, dental records, and X-rays. The medical examiner could also investigate the essential facts surrounding the death, such as interviewing witnesses, issuing subpoenas, examining witnesses under oath, and seizing property, which may prove useful in determining the cause of death. If the ME discovered evidence of a crime, they had to deliver copies of their reports to the DA.

Cindie's responsibilities kicked in upon a finding of foul play by prosecuting the perpetrators of the suspicious death. And she'd never seen one more suspicious or frustrating than Kyle Emory's. The DA's powers permitted her to request the ME to make findings of facts related to John Doe's death, and, guided by Medina, Cindie prepared a lengthy demand to Carly's boss, Dutchess County Medical Examiner Frank Mailer, MD. He was a pompous ass, who flaunted his green hospital scrubs around town like a badge of honor, but Mailer was accurate and reliable. She inquired about any underlying illness or injury that could have contributed to John Doe's demise and whether he'd died of natural causes, accident, suicide, or homicide.

A nagging uncertainty suggested the latter, and Cindie wanted to ensure that the responsible party paid for their crime. On the one hand, she could rely upon Carly Jones to provide a meticulous conclusion. However, on the other, with their conservative reputations, the MEs might label this death as an accident, not a homicide. Medina had warned her about snap judgments leading to false conclusions, tainted evidence, and letting a killer go free.

Surrounded by onionskin annotated with purple sticky notes and legal pads marked with scribbles, Cindie longed for the cigarettes she'd quit three decades ago. Her knees grazed against the wooden panel beneath her center desk drawer, and her clothing snagged on the rough surface, making her feel claustrophobic. She needed to adjust her seat before she lost her mind.

Cindie rose and crouched beside the chair, fiddling with the height knob. She couldn't get the damn chair right. It was either too high or too low. She swore under her breath and leapt up with a groan to test her latest setting.

"Need any help?" Carly Jones asked. She leaned against the doorjamb, inspecting the office. "This is quite an improvement from your predecessors. Slick furniture and curtains."

"Thanks, I'll fix it later," she said, returning to her desk chair and knocking her knees against her bottom drawer again. "Damn chair!"

Carly's serious expression contradicted her playful Barbie pink pantsuit and navy blouse. Tall and statuesque with a wild mane of black hair, Carly looked more like a fashion reporter than a pathologist. And her perfume, Lilies of the Valley!

"What have you got?" Cindie said, gesturing for her visitor to take a seat across from her desk.

"No thanks. I'll stand." Carly paused, her eyes locking onto Cindie's. "I wanted to tell you in person. We're still working on the autopsy, but we have an ID. It's Kyle Emory. The initial cause of death is drowning, and I'll have more details tomorrow."

Although Cindie had expected the verdict, she slumped back in her chair.

"We need to examine the environmental evidence collected at the scene and inspect his organs before I submit our report. The aquatic nature of the death complicates the autopsy. However, we identified him through his dental records, DNA, and a scar."

"I'm sorry to hear that. Our paths crossed last year when he was a witness in a murder trial. He seemed like a decent, if not misguided, fellow, but his untimely death is going to affect so many people, especially his child. It's a shame."

"I know. Our jobs aren't easy, but at least we care about the dead who can't speak for themselves and about their survivors." Carly knotted her fingers and stretched her hot pink-clad arms over her head. "God, I'm tired. It's been a long few days."

"I understand he'd moved out of the area, so where did you get his DNA?"

"The dentals came from his dentist's office, and Jessie Martin provided his toothbrush and hairbrush. She also remembered that he'd had stitches beneath his chin from a swimming accident. Luckily, we identified him from those sources. I'm glad I'm not the one who's going to break the news to Jessie." She paused, slouching against the doorway. "I'll leave that to my sister. We all grew up together, and anyway, it will be less awkward coming from Ebony."

"Yes." Cindie's chest tightened. She'd promised to notify Hal of any developments, and she considered whether to fulfill the vow or follow protocol with Ebony taking the heat. "Have you told Ebony?"

"Not yet," she said. "I tried her a couple times, and her phone went to voicemail. I'm on my way to alert the chief about our preliminary findings. You were my first stop."

"Off the record, have you found any evidence of foul play?"

"It's too early to say. When we removed his clothing, I noticed significant lacerations and contusions on his neck and upper torso, but until I dig in, please pardon the pun, I can't draw any conclusions about head trauma. And his submersion in frigid water delayed the onset of rigor mortis and the decaying process. Therefore, we have additional factors to deal with in determining the cause of death. Although, preliminarily, it's drowning."

"I don't want to interfere with your process, but I've been in touch with Joanna Medina."

Carly straightened her shoulders. "The Joanna Medina? The Statute of Liberty Joanna Medina? How, what, made you get in touch with her? She's one of the top aquatic forensic experts in the world."

"Yes, she's impressive. We might want to engage her expertise, especially if this is a homicide. It would be helpful to have her in our corner in case there's a fight."

"Isn't there always a fight?" Carly chuckled.

"A drain plug was missing from the kayak, and the victim and her relatives had access to the craft. If the defect contributed to Kyle's death, we have several high-profile suspects on our watch list. Olivia's father is a pharmaceutical executive, and her mother, a renowned artist."

"I'm not an expert on kayaking accidents. I'm a forensic pathologist who deals with everything in the kitchen sink. This case requires an expert, so let's meet with Medina as soon as possible. Perhaps she can consult on the autopsy."

"That may present a problem. Joanna's on the road, but I'll call her."

"She could attend virtually, but I'm getting ahead of myself. Medina might not be interested in our case."

"Oh, she's interested," Cindie said with assurance. With an awkward silence passing between the two women, the conversation had reached its natural conclusion. "Before you go, let's call Matt Shepardson. It will save you the trip."

"Sounds good to me."

Cindie's clammy palms reached for her desk phone and pressed the chief's number on speed dial. The phone rang, and he answered.

"Matt, hi. It's Cindie, and I'm here with Dr. Carly Jones. She has news—"

Chapter Thirty-Six

Ebony and Zander stepped back from the Mercedes speedster as the wide-angle lens of the dashboard camera recorded their every movement. After a decade on the force, neither of them had ever been accused of brutality nor abuse of power, and Ebony aspired to keep it that way. She and Zander were honest cops, and she trusted that he felt the same way, too.

Zander bent down to look inside the car. He appeared to be controlling his temper, but Ebony anticipated an imminent volcanic explosion. The red inflammation of anger spread from his cheeks to his face and neck and migrated down into his clutched fists.

A young woman disguised in a baggy black sweatsuit slumped over the leather steering wheel of the Mercedes speedster. To hide her identity, she tugged the hood over her head as though retreating into a shell like a turtle.

"Olivia Vargas," Zander said through gritted teeth. "License, insurance, and registration, please." The scarlet flare on his face faded to its normal hue, and Ebony relaxed.

Olivia was not alone in the vehicle.

"Officer," a man said, thrusting his arm over Olivia from the passenger's seat to present the documents to Zander.

Ebony bent over to steal a better look inside the car. Zander snatched the paperwork, ignoring the passenger, Auggie Vargas. "Ms. Vargas, please exit the vehicle, and place your hands where I can see them."

Ebony walked around to the far door and opened it. "Mr. Vargas, get out, please."

"Detective, I told her to stop, but she wouldn't listen to me." His features twisted in annoyance, and he slipped out of the cockpit and punched the black canvas ragtop. "Olivia snatched the keys out of my hand and took off with them. I couldn't let her steal my car, could I? She wasn't fit to drive." His jaw clamped shut in apparent recognition that he may have incriminated his sister for additional wrongdoings.

"Calm down. We'll deal with you in a minute. Please step away from the vehicle and wait over there while we speak with Olivia," Ebony said. She gestured toward a massive table-shaped boulder by the side of the road.

"In Oli's defense, all she did was speed. Nobody got hurt." Auggie went to join his sister, but he halted when Ebony raised her arm to stop him.

"I told you to wait by the rock. Olivia has broken more laws than speeding. Reckless driving and resisting arrest... to name two. But I said to hold on. We'll speak with you soon."

Auggie sauntered over to the boulder, tinted green with dried lichen, hopped up on its flat top, and retrieved his phone from the pocket of his bomber jacket.

Ebony rejoined Zander, who was patting down Olivia. At first, the woman complied with her limp arms and legs splayed like a starfish. Then Olivia shielded her face and flinched at his touch. "No wallet, license, or weapons. Only this." He opened his palm to reveal an orange prescription bottle containing 10-milligram tablets of Valium. Five days ago, the doctor had prescribed ninety pills to be taken three times a day, yet the bottle was almost empty.

"Ms. Vargas. Can you tell us the last time you took the medication and how much you took?" Ebony asked. No reply. "Have you ingested any other drugs or alcohol?"

Olivia's arms dropped to her sides, and she remained silent. Her hooded head lolled forward like a rag-doll, and she wobbled on her feet.

"Ms. Vargas, we're going to ask you to perform a simple field sobriety test. Can you walk in a line, please?" Ebony asked.

There was still no response, although the brusque manner in which her head snapped up and she retreated from Zander proved her alertness.

"Ms. Vargas, are you all right? Do you need medical attention?" Ebony grew concerned about Olivia's silence. They might have to transport her to the hospital for a chemical blood test. Though first, they needed her consent, and they had to provide warnings about the repercussions if she refused. If she declined, Olivia could face a one-year mandatory revocation of her driver's license. Ebony hated to pursue this hard line, but it might be necessary. "Ms. Vargas, I'm going to ask you again, do you need to see a doctor?"

"I'm fine." Olivia sneered. "I've got nothing to say to you." She looked past Ebony's shoulder, mesmerized by the flashing lights in the grill of their car.

"Zander, let's put her in the back seat and interview her brother. Maybe we'll get the answers out of him."

They supported Olivia beneath her arms, and she moaned and struggled against their touch.

"Hey, get off of me. Will you?" Olivia cried as they led her down the road to their SUV. Her sunglasses slid to the edge of her short nose, and she pushed them back up with her middle finger.

"Ms. Vargas, you're in enough trouble as it is, and we suggest you cooperate with us. We'll be taking you in for questioning."

"Questioning about what? Are you trying to bully me? I told you I've got nothing to say, but get your hands off me!" she shouted, trying to break free. "Stop brutalizing me. Can't you see I'm in mourning?"

What a spoiled bitch, Ebony thought. Olivia had put everyone's lives in danger and was acting as though she and Zander were at fault. Ebony shook her head to dispel the hostile thoughts creeping into her mind as Zander glared at Olivia as though he was ready to smack her.

With tensions and tempers inflamed, and since Olivia didn't appear to need immediate medical attention, it was best to ignore her erratic behavior.

"We'll discuss everything when you get to the station," Ebony said.

"Or maybe not." Olivia's body stiffened as they neared their car, forcing them to drag her through the dirt.

Ebony's own legs felt rubbery as they placed the woman in the back seat and locked the door.

When they approached Auggie, he was on the phone, rattling away in Spanish and waving his arms in excitement. Ebony recognized a few words dropped during his animated conversation: "Olivia," "*mi coche*," "*la policía*" and "Pápa," and gathered the gist of the exchange. Auggie peered up at them, said, "*Luego te llamo*," and hung up.

"*A quién llamará más tarde?*" Ebony paused and smirked. At that moment, her phone buzzed in her pocket, and she ignored it. "Who will you call later?"

Ebony and Zander already knew the answer. Carlos Vargas was never out of reach to his children.

Auggie jerked his head back in surprise. "I'm assuming you're taking us to the police station? My father and our attorney will meet us there. He's advised us not to speak to you until they arrive."

"We understand. Your sister is already in the car, and we ask you to join her in the rear seat. If you give us your keys, we'll move your car to the side of the road so it's not blocking traffic. Someone can gather it later for you. Do we have your permission to move the vehicle?" Zander asked.

"Yes. The keys are still in the ignition. Please be careful. It's an expensive car."

Auggie probably hadn't meant to be insulting, but rich kids like him were used to getting his own way. Ebony would respect his property, but she and Zander needed answers.

"Are we under arrest?"

"Not at the present time, but we have questions for you."

"Like I said, we've been advised—"

"Understood, but please get in the car," Zander said, opening the rear door.

They discovered Olivia curled up asleep on the backbench, and they buckled Auggie in alongside his unconscious sister. After relocating Auggie's car, Ebony and Zander drove back to the station, unloaded their passengers into an interrogation room, and waited for Carlos and his attorney to arrive.

It didn't take long. Forty-five minutes later, Carlos Vargas arrived in the police station foyer. Composed and well-dressed in his jacket and tie, his rigid body betrayed fear. A slender, middle-aged Latina woman uniformed in a navy suit, crisp white blouse, heavy gold jewelry, and carrying a designer briefcase accompanied him. The jet-black glossy mane cut below her shoulders swayed as she marched into the station with an air of determination. This lawyer meant business.

Bypassing the duty sergeant's desk, the lawyer rapped on the glass door leading into the station's beehive. "Excuse me, I'd like to see my clients, please." Her voice was harsh and demanding.

Anticipating their arrival, Ebony had been on watch, waiting for them at the glass door. Zander had remained at his desk, processing the Vargas siblings' paperwork.

The attorney pressed her identification card against the glass. "I'd like to see my clients, Olivia and Augusto Vargas, right away."

Ebony pressed the keypad and admitted them into the station. "I'm Detective Jones, one of the arresting officers." She extended her hand in greeting, but neither Carlos nor his representative accepted it. "I'll show you to the interrogation room, where you can confer with them. We're quite eager to speak with them when you're done."

Carlos refused to make eye contact and deferred to his companion.

"We'll see about that," the woman snapped and grimaced. From the vertical line between her plucked brows and the deep marionette creases around her mouth, Ebony surmised the frown was a permanent fixture on the attorney's face. "I advised them not to speak with you, and I trust you didn't violate their rights. Have you given them their Miranda Rights?"

"This way, please," Ebony said politely.

She led them through the central beehive to Interrogation Room Three, a roomy cubicle that could easily accommodate the Vargas family, their attorney, Zander, herself, and a stenographer. A metal table with four chairs occupied the center of the room, and a whiteboard hung on the far wall. The siblings sat at the table, and Olivia sprang into her father's arms at the sight of him.

"Oh, Pápa," she said, burying her face in his chest. She sobbed.

Crocodile tears, Ebony thought. Olivia was playing it up big time for her audience.

"*Mi pobrecita,*" he replied softly, stroking her head. "Everything will be all right."

"Dad," Auggie said sternly, almost embarrassed.

Carlos tersely acknowledged his son as though blaming him for the present debacle.

"Make yourself comfortable, and I'll check back on you in a while," Ebony said.

The attorney harrumphed, and the door behind Ebony slammed as she left.

Zander pulled her aside in the hallway outside the room. He stood so close she could see the gold flecks in his wolf-blue irises. "Do you know who that is?" he whispered and continued, not giving her time to answer. "That's Gloria Reyes Castellano, the civil rights advocate. She represents the famous rappers Gottya Going, Mayhem Duo, and Shortie Tall, who are pushing for a state bill that prohibits music lyrics from being used as evidence against a defendant in a criminal proceeding. Supposedly, the sponsors in the Assembly enlisted her to draft the law. And the rumor is she's running for Congress next term, representing the Bronx."

"Yeah, so?"

"She's hot shit, that's all, and she's here on behalf of the Vargas kids. I'd say Carlos has a bit of sway."

"Everyone's for sale, Z, especially lawyers. What's impressive is Carlos has the coin to pay her retainer."

Zander shrugged. "We'd better let the chief know what's going on. The press and social media follow every move Castellano makes, and we don't want to get caught unprepared."

"Great. Just what we need... attention to Kyle's case."

"Crap. What are we going to do? We need to interview these two while they're in custody. With this traffic incident, we may be screwed." Zander scratched the back of his neck.

CHAPTER THIRTY-SIX

"The traffic case has nothing to do with the drowning." Ebony scoffed.

"Not if Gloria Castellano has anything to do with it. She's a vocal proponent of defunding the police force, and she'll twist both cases into civil rights violations. You know, cops versus Latinos."

"That's ridiculous. Neither case has any association with human rights. Except poor Kyle's. And he's probably dead. Come on, let's run it by the chief." She tugged at his blazer sleeve, and he trailed her through the bustling beehive. The hum of phones ringing and the buzz of their colleagues debating cases echoed off the pasty beige cinderblock walls. Zander glanced back at the interrogation room suspiciously.

"Don't worry, they won't bolt. They're curious about our intentions," she said.

Ebony and Zander discovered Chief Shepardson leaning against the wall outside his suite, conversing with the harried duty sergeant and his lieutenant. They couldn't hear the content, but the lieutenant crossed his arms over his chest and listened as his assistant spoke in a hushed tone.

The duty sergeant crooked his nicotine-stained thumb at Ebony in accusation. "Detective Jones let them enter without following protocol. How are we expected to do our jobs when the plain-clothes don't follow the rules?"

"Marc, I'm sure Detective Jones didn't mean any disrespect, but I'll take care of this. Jones, Pulaski. My office, please."

Inside the chief's office, Zander and Ebony took seats across from the chief after he'd lowered himself into his burnished leather chair. "Well, for a change, you two have created quite a ruckus around here. What's going on?"

Ebony's phone buzzed in her jean pocket. Unnerved by the impending tongue-lashing from the chief, she ignored it.

They informed Shepardson of their findings about Cody Shaw, his relationship to Olivia, Auggie Vargas, and his disagreement with Kyle, the high-speed car chase, and their intended interviews with Auggie and Olivia.

"You've been busy," the chief said, picking up a ballpoint pen and clicking it. "From your description, you have probable cause for speeding, failure to obey a traffic control device, reckless driving, reckless endangerment, resisting arrest, and driving while impaired. The state has regulations regarding railroad crossings, which they've also violated. Have you arrested the Vargas siblings on any of the charges?"

"Not yet. Olivia had been unavailable since the kayaking accident, and she could be helpful in identifying the corpse in the morgue. And we need her first-hand statement as a surviving victim. With the evidence of foul play, or at least kayak tampering, she and Auggie have become persons of interest," Zander said.

"We're in a tough spot. We need their cooperation, and if we cite them, it might blow our investigation," Ebony said.

"I see your dilemma. What about the attorney who ignored the desk sergeant? Man, is he pissed off." The chief raised a thick, white eyebrow at her, acknowledging the source of the duty sergeant's anger. "He'll get over it."

The knot between her shoulders relaxed. She'd dodged the bullet.

"She's Gloria Reyes Castellano, a Bronx heavy-hitter. Gloria's their legal guard dog, and we won't be able to get close to the Vargases if we issue traffic summonses to them," Zander said. "And as I mentioned to Ebony, she likes to stir the pot with the police."

"Not a lover, huh?" the chief paused and scratched his thinning white hair with the pen. "There are a couple of ways you can play it. You can throw the book at them and negotiate their cooperation as part of a plea deal. Or negotiate with the attorney up-front before you issue your charges. Or you can look the other way and not issue any citations. After all, the incidents occurred outside our jurisdiction."

"They almost killed us, and besides, we have state-wide jurisdiction where there's probable cause, which we have here," Zander said, his voice failing to temper his annoyance.

"Is there a dashcam recording? We're under scrutiny more than ever these days. Everything has to be by the book," the chief said.

"Yeah, there is. We started it the moment we took off on the chase. We haven't reviewed it yet," Ebony said.

"Checking the video should be your first move. It's going to be used as evidence on any charges you issue, so make sure it supports your position. Make a backup in case we need to send it to the district attorney, and be sure to establish your chain of custody. Treat it like any other evidence. Fill out your paperwork. Log it. File it with the property department. You know the drill. Even if you don't intend to bring charges." He paused. "The decision is yours. Just consider whether issuing traffic tickets justifies mucking up a potential homicide investigation." He raised his hands up in question and shrugged. "Keep me in the loop."

The chief's desk phone rang, and they rose to leave. He answered the line, furrowed his bushy brows, and gestured for them to remain.

Ebony glanced at her phone, noticing two missed calls from her sister. Carly rarely texted, claiming that after speaking to the dead all day, she craved interaction with live humans. Ebony showed her phone to Zander, and he shrugged.

"Yes," the chief said and listened. "Hmm. Yes, they're here. I'll let them know. Thanks, Cindie." The chief hung up the phone and shook his head. "That was the district attorney. We have an ID on the body."

Shit. When it fucking rains, it pours, Ebony thought.

Chapter Thirty-Seven

Ebony leaned over Zander's shoulder, watching him download the dashboard camera video to his desktop computer. He opened the video folder, and a file emerged with the date and time stamp on it. "See, we've got it. Here it is." Zander clicked on the movie, opened it in the video player program, and pressed the start arrow. The angle and the clarity of the video were as crystal clear as any 4K movie streaming on a flat screen.

"The picture looks good, but the audio's muffled," he remarked. "Dashcam microphones can capture sound about twelve feet away, and we parked farther away than that from Auggie's car. The sound isn't as audible as I'd like, but it'll work. Maybe I can play around with the settings and beef it up."

"No, don't do anything. We're not making a blockbuster film; we have to play by the book."

Zander frowned. "All right."

They watched in silence as the video replayed every bump and turn through the countryside and along the shoreline and their encounters with Olivia and Auggie. The seconds on the time clock embedded in the upper right-hand corner of the image spun by. They'd chased the Mercedes for a half-hour before it stopped at the railroad crossing, and their dealings with the siblings had lasted another fifteen minutes. In total, the video lasted forty-five minutes.

As Ebony recalled it, their conduct had been above reproach. The traffic case was open and shut. At the scene, they had treated Olivia with respect, but on the video review, their recorded interactions with Olivia appeared distorted.

It was as though Olivia had staged acts of police brutality for the camera. They watched Zander smack his badge against the window and pounce on Olivia behind the wheel. She shielded her face with her arms and writhed as Zander frisked her, suggesting the use of excessive force. Later in the video, just prior to her being led to their vehicle, Olivia glanced over her shoulder and stared into the camera lens, breaking the fourth wall. She addressed the audience as if to say, "Watch this!" When they seized Olivia's arms to take her into custody, she jerked her head back, thrashed about, and yanked her forearms away from them melodramatically. It was a stunt designed to portray her as the victim. At the movie's climax, Olivia collapsed to the ground, forcing Ebony and Zander to drag her to their SUV.

Ebony also observed that Olivia had pivoted away from the camera, so it hadn't captured her middle finger gesture.

"She set us up," Zander said, rerunning Olivia's portion of the video. "The film doesn't depict what happened at all." He paused. "After Shaw mentioned Olivia's cosmetic gig, I checked out her social media reels and feeds. She's got over a hundred thousand followers and growing. She's a pro at playing to the camera, and she must have known about the dashcam and its limited microphone range, too. I should've known better and been more careful, but I didn't think about it. I was too crazed about the wild goose chase and her endangering our lives."

"You can't blame yourself. We know the truth, but it's bizarre how different the event plays out on film. It's like an alternate reality. Can you run the last section again, please?"

Zander replayed the portion where he'd frisked Olivia and discovered the prescription bottle in her sweatshirt pocket.

"Stop here," she insisted.

Zander paused on the frame where Olivia had shielded her head with her arms, and he narrowed his eyes. Olivia had crossed the black sleeves of her sweatshirt over her face in a defensive act of protection against an imaginary beating.

"Castellano could have a field day with this frame. I can see the news headline—*Cops Abuse Grieving Fiancée.* Civil rights abuse. Illegal search and seizure. Excessive police force. We're screwed," Ebony said.

"But the car chase and our dealings with Auggie would stick." Zander gnawed on a cuticle, and realizing his actions, he slipped his hands into his pockets.

"Big deal. We'd have to release the entire video, not just his portion. Besides, at best, Auggie's an accessory. He'd argued he wasn't resisting arrest; he'd tried to stop Olivia. She'd stolen his car, and he won't press felony grand larceny charges against his sister. And if the underlying charges against Olivia don't stick, neither will his."

"But Olivia was speeding and driving recklessly. She crossed a gated railroad crossing." Zander's voice reflected a mixture of frustration and desperation.

"I understand. Do we want to jeopardize the drowning investigation over a speeding violation?"

He smacked the table with his open palm. "Shit!" He winced and rubbed it.

"What do we do now?" Ebony's question was rhetorical. Olivia had pigeonholed them into ignoring her vehicular infractions. At least she wasn't getting away with murder.

A few moments later, Ebony knocked on the door of the interrogation room to announce their entry, and she and Zander entered.

Carlos Vargas paced in front of the whiteboard on the far wall and stopped as they entered. Auggie and Gloria Reyes Castellano sat at the table with their head together, whispering conspiratorially, and Olivia sniffled in the seat beside her brother. Her hood was pushed back, and her puffy eyes flared red.

Castellano glanced up at them. Her features hardened into her trademark scowl as though she were mad at the world, especially Ebony and Zander. "My clients are quite upset about being detained. Either you press charges or release them. Otherwise, we'll be starting an action for harassment, among other violations of their civil rights."

"Ms. Castellano, may we speak with you outside, please?" Ebony asked.

"You can speak freely in front of my clients."

"I'm afraid that's not possible," Ebony said. "Ms. Castellano?" She gestured toward the door.

Castellano glanced at Carlos, who shrugged and then nodded. Auggie and Olivia observed in silence.

"I'll be right back," Castellano said, trailing Ebony and Zander from the room. Once outside, she continued in a tone as abrasive as steel wool. "What's this all about? What couldn't you tell me in front of the Vargases?"

"I'm sure you know that last week Olivia and her fiancé, Kyle Emory, got caught in a storm on the Hudson, and that Mr. Emory's kayak capsized." Ebony sketched out the details of their investigation, those available to the public.

"Yes, I'm aware of the accident, but what does that have to do with my client's arrest?" Castellano remained arrogant, confident.

"First, Auggie and Olivia aren't under arrest. Earlier today, we were in transit to interview Auggie about the accident when the car chase waylaid our meeting," Zander said. "There's been a recent development in the case, and we require your clients' cooperation with our criminal investigation. That's our priority."

Outwardly, Zander spoke calmly, but Ebony knew the decision not to prosecute the siblings was killing him. With the identification of Kyle's body, their priorities were clearer than ever. Find out what happened to Kyle and who tampered with the kayak.

"So, you're not pursuing the vehicle violations? But you believe it's foul play, and my clients are now suspects in a homicide investigation."

"We believe they may have information relevant to the presumed drowning case. Olivia is a survivor of the accident, and Auggie had independent dealings with Kyle, so their input would be helpful," Zander said.

Ebony cleared her throat and steeled herself for the admission she'd dreaded since she'd first been called to the scene. "As Detective Pulaski said, vital information has come to light, which we need to share with you. It is not for publication, but you may share it with the Vargas family as it affects them." Ebony inhaled and exhaled a long breath as Castellano's intensity bored into her. "We've recovered a body from the Hudson, and we have identified it as Kyle Emory."

Castellano placed her hand over her heart. Her aggressive demeanor softened, and she became solemn. "Does Olivia know?"

"We received the confirmation minutes ago. The question is whether we can speak with her about the incident before she gets the news or afterward?"

"The cause of death?"

"Uncertain. The autopsy is pending," Zander replied.

"Will she be required to identify the body?"

"We'll be contacting Kyle's parents. We think that's best. Despite what occurred today, Olivia has been through enough trauma." Ebony paused. The homicide case depended on Olivia and Auggie's cooperation, and now it was up to Castellano to make the call. "We could interview Auggie now and postpone Olivia for another day. However, her parents have stonewalled our contacting her. They've been... overprotective."

Castellano remained quiet for a few moments and stepped away from them.

Ebony couldn't tell whether Castellano was stalling for time or weighing the ramifications of their news. If Castellano refused to cooperate, the DA could subpoena Auggie and Olivia, which would be time-consuming. Ebony preferred a conciliatory approach, but if pressed, she'd rush to court for the judge's signature.

Castellano rejoined them. She thrust her shoulders back and elongated her neck. "My primary concern is for my clients, and I won't compromise their rights under any circumstances."

This pronouncement reflected shades of Jessie Martin. Why did lawyers always think cops were out to screw their clients?

"Detectives, I will agree, but with conditions. First, you cannot interview my clients without my being present, and I will schedule their interviews based upon our mutual availability," Castellano said. "Next, I will break the tragic news to the Vargases. They are old family friends, and I'm sure they would prefer to hear the sad news from me. Obviously, we will postpone Olivia's interview for a few days. Arrangements will need to be made, and I'm sure you appreciate her delicate situation and her mental health."

Ebony bit her lip to prevent chuckling at the last statement. Olivia was anything but delicate.

"Finally, Augusto will be interviewed today. You will limit his questioning to the Kyle Emory case. Carlos will take Olivia home, and I will remain with Augusto to supervise the conversation. We will receive a transcript of his interview. And I will coordinate all future communications with the Vargas family through my office. Understood?"

Zander and Ebony nodded.

"And we'd like the keys to Augusto's car."

"Here's the receipt. Auggie can retrieve them from the property department before you leave," Ebony said, handing her a slip of paper.

"Give me twenty minutes, and we'll be ready to proceed." Castellano swiveled away, brushed the wrinkles from her navy blazer, opened the interrogation room, and disappeared inside.

"Let us know if you need anything," Zander called to the slamming door.

Chapter Thirty-Eight

Auggie Vargas stood when Ebony, Zander, and the pretty strawberry-blonde stenographer entered the room. His handshake was firm, leaving Ebony's fingers with a mild buzzing sensation in its aftermath. It was the practiced grip of a salesman, or a conman, who relied on his grasp to seal the deal.

His trendy suede bomber jacket hung over the back of his chair. The short sleeves of his navy polo shirt displayed the guns of a strength trainer, and his thigh muscles strained against the legs of his jeans. Auggie Vargas was short, compact, and strong enough to kick someone's ass.

The four of them waited in silence while the stenographer prepared her computer. The steno was a civilian in her twenties, and her hands trembled as she tested her gear.

As was their habit, Ebony let Zander assume the lead with the soft questioning, and toward the end of the interview, she'd chime in with the tougher questions. With Castellano present, she'd need to temper her aggressive routine to ensure the slick gatekeeper didn't cut her off.

Auggie fidgeted in his chair, exuding the nervous energy of a puppy trying to sit still on command. He bounced one knee as he crossed and uncrossed his arms.

The stenographer began when Zander signaled her, and he made the introductions. "Augusto Vargas, we appreciate you staying to speak with us today. We note that your counsel, Gloria Reyes Castellano, accompanies you, and Detective Ebony Jones and myself, Detective Alexandre Pulaski, will conduct this interview regarding the drowning death of Kyle Emory.

We're sorry for your loss. Please signify your consents on the record."

Ebony smiled to herself at the sound of Zander's complete name. He rarely spoke it, but when he did, he proudly announced it in recognition of his relatives, one of the first Polish settlers in the City of Poughkeepsie. His name carried weight in the community, and he'd often boasted about the north side park with a swimming pool bearing his surname.

"I do," Auggie replied. Castellano agreed.

"Thank you. How did Olivia take the news?" Zander asked.

Auggie glanced at Castellano. "Not well. Oli's health was improving, but Kyle's confirmed death will set her back. She'd stopped taking the sedatives that were making her sleep all day. Now, who knows? I feel bad for her and wish there was some way to help."

"Do you know where Olivia was driving after she took your keys?"

"Don't answer that. Detective, we are limiting your questions to the drowning," Castellano said.

"*Tia* Gloria?" Auggie asked and whispered in her ear.

Tia translated to aunt, a sign of affection, although not necessarily a reference to blood relations. As Ebony suspected, there was depth to the relationship between the Vargas family and Gloria Reyes Castellano.

"You may repeat the question," Castellano said, and Zander did.

"She's been stuck in the house for a week now and has been begging my parents to let her visit Kaal Rock Park to find Kyle. Oli believes Kyle might magically appear if she returns to the park. This morning, Oli insisted she needed to see where Kyle had disappeared. My folks refused to let her go and took her keys away. When I refused to take her, she became hysterical, and we argued. Oli grabbed mine out of my hand and ran out the door. I had to go after her. That's when we encountered you."

Broken hearts make people do foolish things, Ebony thought.

"Since she's been indisposed, we haven't been able to speak with her about the day of the accident. That's why your statement is important. Let's start at the beginning." Zander paused, tapping his pen on the table. "According to your statement given to Officer Robinson at the accident scene, you were standing on the riverbank at the time Olivia and Kyle embarked on their river journey. Correct?"

"Yes."

Can you tell us what you observed when they set off?"

"They left in two separate kayaks. Oli in the blue one, and Kyle in the red, which was weird because they'd switched kayaks. They paddled from the sandy pebble beach south of the picnic area while the rest of us hung out on the lawn."

This was news. Kyle and Olivia had switched kayaks. Hers, the red one, had been the one with the missing plug.

"Did they mention their destination and when they would return?"

"They were going to paddle north along the shoreline, skirting past Waryas Park to the Walkway, and come back. They said they'd be back in fifteen minutes. But then I noticed them veer off toward the middle of the Hudson. They were both experienced kayakers, so we thought nothing of it. I tried to call Oli to find out what was going on, but she didn't answer her phone."

"Where were you situated onshore?" Ebony asked.

"My dad, Max, Serena, Andrew, and I were sitting around a picnic table, talking, snacking, and drinking. My mother and Anna were playing with Kyle's daughter, Lily, who was in her stroller."

"When the storm hit, how long had Kyle and Olivia been on the water?" Zander asked.

Auggie rested his elbows on the table and knitted his fingers into a tent. "I'd say about fifteen minutes. They were about three-quarters of the way to the stanchion when the sky turned black, and the wind kicked up. The storm came out of nowhere, and they couldn't make it back to shore in time." He shook his head. "Max and I ran down to the water. It was windy, and we figured they couldn't hear us, but we yelled and waved our phone flashlights anyway. We watched them paddle through the whitecaps toward the bridge for cover. We were worried they wouldn't reach the bridge in time, but there was nothing we could do. I called Oli again but got no answer." His voice broke off, and he stared at his hands. When he spoke again, it was in a raspy whisper. "That was the last time I saw them together."

Castellano nudged Auggie's arm. "It's okay. I know this is difficult. If you prefer, we can take a break."

Auggie shook his head. "No, I want to get this over with. I want to help if I can."

"And then what happened?" Ebony was getting antsy. She didn't want to rush Auggie, but she wanted to move the interview along. She and Zander had read the reports, and Auggie wasn't contributing any fresh insight except about the switched boats.

"When the rain and the wind had stopped, we came out of the pavilion. The guys ran down to the waterfront, and we heard Oli screaming and saw her paddling toward us. We were in shock because she was alone. In the distance, we saw Kyle's kayak, but we couldn't tell if he was in the water." He exhaled and then continued. "The first safety rule is do not leave your kayak. Stay there until help arrives, and we thought Oli was coming in for help. A few minutes later, Oli pulled back into the beach and stumbled out of her kayak, shivering. She called 911 and collapsed on the grass, screaming Kyle's name."

"Why didn't anyone call 911 when the storm began?" Ebony asked.

"We thought they'd be okay sheltering beneath the bridge. As I said, Kyle and Oli were experienced kayakers and had safety training. No one thought there was an emergency. Olivia and Kyle had their phones, and we'd assumed they'd make the call if things got rough."

"Did Olivia explain what happened out on the river?"

Ebony inched her butt to the edge of the seat, listening. They were getting to the core of the matter.

"No, she was in shock. She was wailing and crying." Auggie dragged his fingers through his short, dark hair, and his eyes grew watery. He blinked and sniffled. "It was awful. We couldn't do anything until the police and the boats arrived."

Ebony felt little sympathy for the Vargases, but Auggie's grief-stricken face reminded her they were all survivors. The Vargases had been helpless to prevent the weather's wrath and could only watch the tragedy unfold before them. The shadow of trauma would haunt them for the rest of their lives. Especially Olivia.

How does anyone survive the inconsolable loss of a loved one? How do you rise every day, knowing you'll never see them again? That they disappeared beneath the waves before your eyes? And you were helpless to save them?

However, the empty drain hole was evidence that someone had orchestrated the loss. It was her and Zander's job to uncover who and why. Unfortunately, they were no closer to uncovering the truth.

When asked, Auggie confirmed Kyle's nondescript, dark clothing and that Olivia had given Kyle a fancy gold bracelet after their engagement.

"She showed me the engraving inside *'Te amaré por siempre,'* 'I'll love you forever.'" He glanced at Castellano, seeking reassurance.

The bracelet sounded like an ostentatious upgrade from Jessie's leather and silver anniversary gift. Ebony remembered Kyle proudly flashing the symbol of love as unpretentious and unique as Jessie. Did he cherish Olivia's gift as he had Jessie's?

Auggie also corroborated that Kyle and Olivia weren't wearing wet suits, only street clothing. "They'd intended to keep close to shore where the water was shallow, so they didn't wear vests either. They'd left them in the trunk."

In response, one corner of Zander's eyebrow shot up.

If New York State law required kayakers to wear U.S. Coast-Guard approved personal floatation devices, why hadn't they worn them? Also, it had been a warm September, and Carly had noted the water temperature had been a brisk sixty-eight degrees. Why hadn't they worn wet suits, even for a quick jaunt?

Only Olivia had the answers, so she and Zander would have to wait.

"Do you remember whether Kyle left his wallet and phone on shore before he and Olivia set out?" Ebony asked.

"Yeah. Before they took off, Kyle asked me to hold his wallet and the electronic keys to my father's BMW. He and I had taken my father's car to pick up his daughter before our gang met up at Kelly's bakery." He paused. "My father had driven Kyle's car with the kayaks on top, so he had Kyle's keys."

Ebony made a note to request Kyle's keys from Castellano. Presently, Kyle's rusty BMW sat in the impound lot, awaiting a forensics inspection. If Dr. Vargas had the keys, why hadn't he offered them during their interview at White Oaks? Had it been an oversight, or was it intentional?

"What about Kyle's phone?"

Auggie cracked his knuckles as though trying to conjure up the image of Kyle's actions on that fateful day. "I think he stowed it in the storage compartment in the kayak. He said he wanted to snap pictures from the middle of the river. He'd mounted a waterproof SportsPro camera on the front of Olivia's kayak in case she wanted action shots for her social media."

"Are you sure? We didn't find either device when we salvaged the boat from the river."

"I'm sure. I helped him install the camera mount after dinner the night before. The base was an industrial-strength suction cup, and when we tugged on it, it didn't come off. It wasn't going anywhere."

Ebony added the missing items to the list on her phone. She'd double-check with forensics later.

Right now, it was time to ratchet up the pressure. But she wondered how far she could go before Castellano reeled in her questions.

"Auggie, we've heard that you and Kyle had a disagreement and weren't on speaking terms. If so, why did you help him with the camera?"

"I don't know where you heard that, but it's incorrect. I'd asked him for a favor, and he couldn't help me out." Auggie squirmed in the metal chair, which screeched on the linoleum tile floor. He cast his eyes toward Castellano and then toward the door as though planning to escape. "No big deal or hard feelings."

His attorney's manicured fingers twirled an M&M-sized diamond stud in her ear, and her expression remained hardened. "Wait one minute. We're getting off track. I thought this was an accident investigation, and now you're asking my client questions about his relationship with Kyle Emory. Are you investigating an accident or a homicide?"

"Ms. Castellano, we are fact-finding about the events that resulted in a drowning on the Hudson River. There is no evidence to suggest it was homicide, but the relationships may guide our investigation going forward," Zander said.

"It's okay, I have nothing to hide," Auggie said.

Castellano patted his arm in a show of support. "All right. Proceed."

"What kind of favor?" Ebony asked.

"I work for an online sports book, and Kyle is, was, my bro. I asked him to introduce me to some of the Barclays' acts and players, and he wasn't able to do it. That's all."

"Your request sounds suspicious to me. It's no wonder he refused," Zander said.

"No, it's not what it sounds like. Online sports betting is expanding, and it's becoming more sophisticated by targeting consumers with digital marketing campaigns. Betting companies are expanding into podcasts, social media content, and talent deals for celebrities and athletes, where they produce original content for websites and social media. Some firms pay as much as mid-eight figures for the right talent." He whipped out his phone and showed them the website for GoTo Sportsbook. "This is what I'm talking about. I wanted to talk to the Nets and Liberty players about their interest in our platform. You know, strike a deal to pitch for us. We're trying to build content and audience."

Zander whistled. "So the sportsbook and casino websites are more than about placing the bets."

"They're only two of the revenue streams. People pay attention when a celebrity speaks. They like to watch programs starring their favorite celebs, and those celebs influence their buying habits. There's also a secondary market for streaming services for these programs, which increases the nationwide and international reach of our online profile. Raul, I mean Cody, is the perfect example. He earns nice coin promoting sporting goods equipment on his show, on social media, and in videos. Olivia, too. She has a cosmetic line she promotes. Honey Face. It's the same principle."

This kid may look young, but he's slick, Ebony thought. He had the jargon and his elevator pitch down. Wisely, Auggie had invested in Hudson

222

Outfitter, which benefitted from Cody Shaw's media notoriety. Ebony scribbled another note about Olivia's shilling.

"What's the deal with Cody and your sister? Are they still close?" Ebony asked.

Castellano's eyes sharpened and slid over to Ebony. She opened her mouth to speak, then stopped.

"Yeah. Cody carries a torch for her. I think she's stringing him along. He's always been in love with her and probably always will be. The jerk still wears his wedding ring, even though she filed divorce papers." Auggie stopped and stared at them as though realizing something. "If Kyle is dead, and I'm sorry he is because I love him, but I wonder if she'll go through with the divorce. Oli doesn't like to be alone."

"Cody mentioned that you, he, and Olivia, are partners in Hudson Outfitters. What's Olivia's and your position in the business?" Zander asked.

"We've been partners for about five years. Cody is the face of the business and knows about the products, but he can't add a column of numbers to save his life. Plus, with my marketing background, I'm able to monetize Cody's celebrity. He's the president of the company, and I'm VP and treasurer. Oli is secretary and holds a minority shareholder stake. Cody gave her shares as a wedding gift, and I'm sure he wants them back now." He chuckled. "Poor sap. Good luck with that."

"Is the business profitable?"

"Detective, how is this question relevant to the drowning?" Castellano asked.

Zander's foot nudged Ebony's under the table. They were thinking the same thing. These three were tight, and money and revenge were prime motivators for criminal action. If Cody and Olivia were married and never intended to divorce, they might have been running a con on Kyle. They could've plotted to steal his money to support a struggling business with Auggie as a co-conspirator. He was a gambler, someone used to playing the odds. Or had he embezzled money from their business and conspired with his sister to wangle money out of Kyle?

The ideas were speculation, Ebony thought, ones saved for a later time. She nudged him back.

"I'll withdraw the question," Zander said.

"Returning to Kyle," Ebony said. "Did he explain why he couldn't make the Barclays introductions?"

"Kyle said he was still getting settled into his new job and didn't want to press it. It was no big deal either way," Auggie said. His jaw tightened, and his black irises enlarged, leaving a thin strip of brown coloring around the edges.

Auggie's eyes were the windows into his soul, and his dilating pupils hinted at the lie he'd told. The Barclays' leads had meant more to Auggie than he was letting on, and the disagreement between the men was more heated, too. Further, Carlos, Viv, and Auggie could have fabricated their close relationships with Kyle to mislead the investigation. The Vargases were a tight-knit bunch, and they could've viewed their son-in-law-to-be's refusal to help Auggie as the ultimate treachery, setting the stage for revenge. Like pulling a plug. Or murder.

Chapter Thirty-Nine

The mounds of evidence on Ebony and Zander's desks were becoming unmanageable. In a few short days, they had collected crime scene photos, forensic reports, the medical examiner's preliminary reports, maps, and dozens of interviews. With a growing cast of suspects, the hill would soon become a mountain.

Ebony easily digested the materials, but she was a visual person. It was time to create the evidence board where she could analyze each suspect, piece of evidence, and photo side by side, and where hidden clues revealed themselves like magic. Often, the victim's pleading expression egged her on to solve the mystery of their death. She was a pushover for the desperate, forlorn eyes like those on the missing persons' posters on the station's bulletin board. They haunted her. Ebony could never look away.

She and Zander were gathering the material into a carton when Officer Vic Robinson interrupted them. The full-figured officer smacked her lips and shook her head in disapproval.

"Hmm, hmm. Detectives, you sure know how to make a mess," Vic said. She carried a sealed manila envelope marked "URGENT" and held it out to Ebony. "Here, let me add to it. It's a package from the DA's office, and it looks important."

Ebony seized the envelope and withdrew its contents, the autopsy for Kyle Emory. The DA had attached a note on her official stationery to the thick package bound by a heavy-duty black clip. *Please call me after you read this. We have lots to discuss. Cindie T.*

"Someone is here to see you. He's waiting in the hallway," Vic said.

"Can you tell us who's here?" Zander asked, annoyed.

"Nope. It's dull around here, so give the girl some fun."

"Thanks. Tell our mystery guest we'll be available in a minute. We need to review this before we do anything else," Ebony said.

Vic left, and Zander and Ebony thumbed through the autopsy report, which contained tissue analysis, postmortem forensic imaging, a toxicology report, and environmental studies before examining the document titled *Report of Investigation by the Dutchess County Medical Examiner*. The form, a concise one-sheet report, included the decedent's name, address, phone number, incident location, time of death, and type of death. There was a comprehensive description of the body's characteristics, such as height, weight and hair color, and the stage of rigor mortis. The report also had a section for noting the injuries found, and frontal and rear diagrams of the human body for identifying unique features such as scars and tattoos and injuries. Toward the bottom of the report, it stated the probable cause of death, the manner of death, and the disposition of the case.

Ebony read the latter section aloud: "Ante-mortem trauma and hemorrhaging of the decedent's head, neck, shoulders, and arms were not self-inflicted, and postmortem lacerations and abrasions were found from his scraping along the rough surface of the Hudson River. The skin on the decedent's hands was shriveled and whitened from being submerged in the water, the airways and stomach contained a bloody froth, and the decedent exhibited cerebral edema. On further analysis, the bloody froth consisted of fresh-water, microscopic algae, and silt in his lungs. The lungs were swollen, and because of the water retention, they had increased from the normal weight of 470 grams to 600 grams. Cold preservation of oxyhemoglobin in his face, head, and neck region caused the bright pink hue of the decedent's skin."

"Come on, get to the point. What did he die from, and was he murdered?" Zander asked.

"Hold on. I'm getting there. My sister can be long-winded." She jumped to the bottom of the page above Carly's signature line. "Probable cause of death: Drowning. The manner of death: the antemortem physical injuries contributed to the victim's death, possible homicide."

Ebony knew that asphyxiation by water was a diagnosis of exclusion based on ruling out other causes of death from the medical and physical evidence. While Kyle drowned, Carly concluded from the autopsy that Kyle also sustained blunt force trauma, but how and why? The questions now became how did Kyle sustain the trauma, and did the trauma cause Kyle to lose consciousness so that he drowned in the river? The ME concluded that his pre-death injuries were separate from his drowning and had not been self-inflicted.

"There was another player on the scene, but when were the injuries sustained?" Ebony asked. "At the picnic? The night before?"

"And who caused them? Auggie? Cody? Carlos? Olivia? Who was angry enough to assault and batter Emory?" Zander returned the papers to the envelope and slipped it into the carton.

"The report doesn't give us any more leads. If anything, it complicates our case. I feel like we're beating our heads against the wall. We're not making any progress."

"Come on, chill. Let's call Carly and the DA later. We've got a visitor, and maybe we'll get some answers."

Ebony recognized the well-heeled visitor as Carlos Vargas. He sat outside an interrogation room inspecting his tan suede loafers as though searching for scuffs. Carlos was so absorbed in his examination that he failed to notice their approach. "Carlos, what brings you in to visit us today?"

"It's time," Carlos whispered.

"Time?" Zander asked.

"Yes. It's time for Olivia to tell her story. It's eating her up, and she's ready to get it off her chest." He gestured toward the closed door next to him.

Zander peeked in the small window on the door. "She's here with Ms. Castellano, I see."

"Yes, as you know, Gloria has been our family's advisor for decades, and we feel it's best if she's present during the interview."

"That's fine. We're glad Olivia is feeling well enough to come in. Will you be joining us?" Ebony asked.

"It's best if I don't," Carlos said and hesitated. "She's fragile, so please be careful with her."

They thanked Carlos and entered the room, where Olivia and Castellano awaited them. Dressed in a low-cut black mini-dress with a lace bodice and sleeves, Olivia appeared camera-ready. She'd plaited her long sleek hair into a French braid, flawlessly applied makeup to disguise the dark circles beneath her eyes, and painted her long nails white, with the letter *K* inside a heart on her thumbs. Her hazel eyes were downcast, but they flicked up, bright and clear, to greet them.

"Detectives, sorry for appearing without prior notice, but Olivia insisted on coming today," Castellano said. "I hope we're not catching you at a bad time. Olivia is prepared to make her statement, hoping to help you put Kyle's accident to rest. Everyone needs to move on from this tragedy."

"Not at all, and we appreciate your cooperation. Do you mind if we contact the District Attorney and have her present?"

"I believe once you hear Ms. Vargas, it won't be necessary. But if you wish."

Zander and Ebony exchanged glances. If anything suspicious appeared on the record, they could recall Olivia for questioning, either voluntarily or under subpoena.

"For expediency's sake, we'd like to proceed," Zander replied. "Do you mind if we use a videographer to record the interview?"

Castellano cast her gaze sideways at Olivia, who smiled. "Not at all. So long as we get a copy."

Image meant everything to Olivia Vargas, and her life was open to the public on social media. So far, they'd succeeded in controlling the flow of information, and Ebony needed to ensure that Olivia didn't jeopardize their work by releasing the interview on the internet or in the media. Castellano and Olivia had to sign an NDA, or it was a no-go. "This is an ongoing accident investigation, and to circumvent any leaks of confidential information, we're requesting you and your client sign NDAs. They will include Ms. Vargas agreeing not to post on any aspect of the investigation on social media."

Castellano and Olivia agreed.

Ebony and Zander sat at the metal table across from Olivia and Castellano, with the videographer setting up his equipment in the room's corner to capture Olivia close up and personal. Ebony's heart raced as the tension grew inside the cubicle.

After the introductions and the administration of the oath, the videotaping began. As usual, Zander took the lead. This time, she and Zander would be on alert for any manipulations by the melodramatic Olivia Vargas.

"Miss Vargas, we're sorry for your loss, and if at any time you need to take a break, please let us know," Zander said. Olivia extracted a tissue from her boxy patent leather designer bag and dabbed her eyes. "Let's start with the night before the accident. Were you and Mr. Emory together that evening?"

"Yes, we'd planned an early departure the next morning for our picnic at Kaal Rock Park and apple-picking in Milton, so our family stayed together at White Oaks."

"You mentioned a picnic and apple-picking. What about the kayaking?"

"That was Kyle's idea. It was a last-minute decision. He'd checked Saturday's weather, and since it was going to be beautiful, he decided we should go out on the river. He and my brothers, Auggie and Max, loaded the kayaks onto Kyle's car after dinner."

"Did you perform a safety check of the kayaks before you loaded them?"

"Yes. There's not much to check, but we examined them for damage and made sure the bungees and storage unit covers were secure."

"What time did you leave White Oaks for your picnic?"

"Kyle and Auggie left in my father's car around nine. It was Kyle's weekend with his darling daughter, Lily, so they took my dad's car to pick her up at her mother's house." A hint of resentment seeped into her voice. "My parents and I drove in Kyle's car, and my cousin Serena and her husband, Andrew, and Max and Ana, drove their own cars. We left after Kyle."

"What were the plans to meet up with Kyle and your cousins?"

"At ten, we were to grab a coffee at Kelly's Bakery and then drive to Kaal Rock. Things went smoothly until we got to the park."

"What do you mean?" Zander crossed his arms across his chest and leaned back in his chair.

"Well, Kyle was having a difficult time with Lily. She was cranky and cried for her mother. Kyle considered canceling our day trip until my mother and Serena settled her down. They love babies." Olivia's mouth pinched, and she demurely placed her hands in her lap.

"What time did you and Kyle set off on your kayaking trip?"

"First, we had a disagreement." Olivia paused, and she blinked rapidly, perhaps realizing she'd revealed a weakness in their relationship. "Only, a minor one, like most couples do," she corrected. "I wanted to paddle along the eastern shore of the river. You know, up past Waryas Park to see the new apartments they were building north of the Walkway Over the Hudson. But Kyle wanted to race to the farthest pier of the Mid-Hudson Bridge. It's about a thousand feet off the shoreline, not too far. Since he's a history buff, he was interested in the suspension bridge's construction. He'd had a beer with the boys and was in terrific spirits, and I didn't want to ruin his fun, so I agreed. Kyle thought it would be a rush to take photos in the middle of the river. He craved adventure, or maybe he was showing off for my family."

And the pics would make slick posts for Olivia's social accounts, Ebony thought.

"What time was this?" Zander asked.

"Oh, about eleven." Olivia's hazel eyes darted toward Castellano, seeking approval. Castellano nodded.

"How was the weather? Had you checked it?"

"I'd rechecked the weather app on my phone, and it looked clear, so we set off."

"Did you notice anything unusual about Kyle's kayak?" Zander asked.

Zander was finally piercing the heart of the day's events. The room was so quiet Ebony believed the others could hear her heart pounding against her ribs. She held her breath, anticipating Olivia's response.

"No, not really. He wanted to carry more gear than his kayak could accommodate in the compartments, so we switched boats."

CHAPTER THIRTY-NINE

"You and Kyle switched kayaks?"

"Yes. He wanted to bring a seat cushion, paddle, and cooler bag with beer, which wouldn't fit in his kayak, so we switched."

"Then what happened?"

Olivia sighed. The smile she'd plastered on for the camera wavered as she continued. "We paddled out to the bridge pier, and, as we were returning, the weather turned ugly, and we were stuck out near the pier. We took off because Kyle wanted to go back. He wanted the thrill of riding the choppy waves, but the white caps were too big, and they crashed over our kayaks. I'd done white water kayaking before and knew how to handle it, but Kyle didn't. His boat flooded with water and capsized. He fell into the frigid water without a life jacket or proper clothing, and he'd been drinking. I didn't know what to do."

Olivia paused. She covered her mouth with her hands as if to contain the unspeakable pain. Castellano slid her arm around Olivia's shoulder, and Olivia cuddled against her. The older woman whispered Spanish words of comfort to the grieving survivor.

"Would you like a minute? We can take a break?" Ebony asked. The real-life horror of the asphyxiation consumed the room, sucking the air from the space as it had from Kyle's lungs. She felt lightheaded, as though balancing on a tightrope with her arms spread out to stabilize her inner turmoil. Not only was Ebony reliving the shocking death of a victim, she was reliving the death of an acquaintance.

Ebony feared they couldn't confine Olivia's sorrowful tale to this room. She was duty-bound to share it with the chief, the district attorney, and, worst of all, with Jessie and Kyle's family.

Olivia exhaled and straightened up. "It's too horrible to describe. It's hard to believe that I watched Kyle disappear. For as long as he could, Kyle held onto his paddle and seat cushion. I tried to grab him, but I couldn't. Kyle yelled for me to call 911, but I was struggling to keep myself afloat. I tried to reach him, but the wind and the current pushed us farther apart. After calling out to him, I lost sight of him in the wind, rain, and waves. I don't know what happened next other than Kyle was gone." Tears streamed down Olivia's beautiful face, which emitted a picture-perfect glow. She stared into the camera, basking in the cinematic attention and preserving her survival story for posterity.

"You mentioned your experience in turbulent water. Can you estimate the height of the waves?" Zander asked, with pride in his nautical expertise.

"They were over my head, about four feet. It was terrifying. I've whitewater kayaked and rafted, but I've experienced nothing like this before."

Ebony wondered how Olivia's hubby and adrenaline junkie, Cody Shaw, would have handled the unexpected tempest. He was the opposite of boring, worker bee Kyle Emory, who was a guy who followed the rules but didn't break them.

"How long was your fiancé in the water before you lost sight of him? What did you do then?" Zander asked.

"I don't know. I lost track of time. I was in survival mode." She paused. "After I couldn't find Kyle, I paddled back. By the time I reached the shore, the storm had passed. I was cold, tired, drenched, and crazed about losing Kyle. As soon as I landed on shore, I called 911. About fifteen minutes after, he went missing."

"Why did you wait so long?"

"I was scared for my own life... that I might drown in the river."

"Ms. Vargas, doesn't New York State law require kayakers to wear lifejackets offshore?"

"I object," Castellano interjected. "How is my client supposed to know what the state law requires?"

"I'll rephrase the question. Ms. Vargas, do you know whether New York State requires kayakers to wear lifejackets when they are offshore?"

"Yes, it requires that we wear a floatation device approved by the Coast Guard."

"Were you wearing a life vest?"

"No."

"Kyle wasn't wearing one either, was he?"

Olivia shrugged. "As I mentioned, Kyle took risks. He either overesti-

232

mated his kayaking ability or underestimated the dangers of the river. He would still be alive if he'd been wearing one."

"And his blue kayak had a cockpit skirt to prevent water entering, but your red one didn't. Right?"

"Uh-huh," she sniffled. "I never should've switched with him. This is all my fault."

"No, honey. It wasn't your fault. You can't blame yourself," Castellano said, squeezing Olivia's hand. "This was an awful accident."

"I wanted to marry Kyle and have a family with him. We had plans. What am I going to do now? Oh, god!" Olivia shed a waterfall of tears, and her shoulders violently shook as she gasped for breath. "This is all my fault."

"No, sweetheart. No," Castellano whispered. She turned toward Ebony. "Ms. Vargas is the survivor of a terrible ordeal. I believe you have enough to establish Mr. Emory's drowning was an accidental death."

"Ms. Castellano, we have a few more questions. Please, let's take a five-minute break so Ms. Vargas can compose herself," Ebony said. "I promise, we're almost finished."

"Well, I hope so. Ms. Vargas is voluntarily making her supplementary statement, even though she gave one at the scene of the accident," Castellano said. "She isn't obligated to be here, so please wrap this up. As I've said, you have sufficient evidence to conclude that the couple got caught in a pop-up storm, and Olivia's fiancé's death was no one's fault."

Sufficient evidence? Ebony was just getting started.

Chapter Forty

J essie arrived at the police station, clutching a manila envelope to her chest. The papers crinkled, announcing their importance to Kyle's case. As surely as she knew anything, Jessie believed the damning evidence rested within Kyle's phone records. Friends and foes would be revealed. Without those logs, Ebony and Zander were blundering the investigation and waiting for the call logs from the phone company. But luckily, Jessie held them in her hands.

Officer Victoria Robinson accompanied her to the familiar hallway inside the police station. The cheap, uncomfortable metal chairs lined the dingy beige walls outside the interrogation rooms. Previously, she'd occupied those rooms as an accused or accuser, and today she was merely a visitor. A well-dressed gentleman staring at his shoes straddled a chair, and she wondered whether he was awaiting interrogation by Ebony and Zander. The man smiled as Jessie settled in, but then his admiration returned to his expensive footwear.

Inside the envelope, Jessie clasped the last three months of Kyle's telephonic existence: logs of incoming and outgoing calls and text messages and transcripts of the texts. Except for Kyle's family and her own, she didn't recognize any numbers. The unfamiliar contacts represented yet another symbol of the gulf between their lives.

She'd felt like an intruder, a voyeur, scrutinizing the texts about Kyle's blossoming connection to the Vargas family. His relationship with Olivia appeared intense yet stormy, with the spats often being initiated by Olivia.

There had also been a series of heated conversations with Olivia's brother,

Auggie, over a failed business venture. However, a text from someone named Cody Shaw frightened Jessie the most. A day or two before Kyle's disappearance, Shaw had sounded possessive, even threatening, in a message suggesting Kyle's inability to satisfy Olivia. Perhaps Jessie was being paranoid, reading malice where none existed, but she planned to insist that Ebony and Zander consider this man as a person of interest. In her mind, these two connections to Olivia Vargas represented dangers to Kyle. Dangers discovered too late. Although, not too late to investigate.

Jessie glanced at the time on her phone. It was almost four o'clock. She still had marketing to do and couldn't wait much longer. A few minutes later, the interrogation room door opened, and Ebony and Zander stepped outside. The sound of sobs coming from inside the room floated into the hallway, and the waiting man sprang to his feet and raced into the room.

Still clutching the envelope, Jessie stood and peeked inside the slender opening in the doorway. A stunning Latina woman in her late twenties with a long dark braid dabbed her cheeks with a handkerchief. At the metal table, an older woman slid her chair over to allow the man to comfort the distraught woman.

"Oli, my darling. Are you all right? Hush. Hush. Everything will be fine," the man said. The crying subsided. "Gloria, is she finished yet? This must be such an ordeal."

Ebony slammed the door and stared at Jessie as though catching her committing a crime.

"Is that her?" Jessie asked. Her voice cracked.

Ebony bobbed her head.

"She's gorgeous. I can see Kyle's attraction to her." Jessie waved her hands over herself as though comparing the older model to the newer one.

"Don't go putting yourself down. This one's a piece of work," Zander said, nodding toward the door.

Ebony's eyes darted to Zander, and they widened as if to censor his further comments on the topic.

"I'm here to drop off Kyle's phone and text messages. I thought you could use them." Jessie explained the phone plan shared with Kyle and her access to the cloud storage of his messages. "There are several threatening messages from Auggie Vargas and Cody Shaw which bear a closer examination. I've highlighted them for you," she said, presenting the package to Ebony.

"Thanks. We haven't heard from telecoms, so this information will help." Accepting the envelope, Ebony continued. "What do you mean, threats?"

"Threats. Menacing messages, like 'I'm going to get you' statements. You'll see. The content appears suspicious, and I urge you to follow up with these guys. They seem to carry a grudge against Kyle, and one or both may have acted upon it."

Jessie caught a flash of recognition between the two detectives. Her new announcement hadn't come as a surprise.

"Who is Cody Shaw?" she asked.

"Cody Shaw is Raul Esperanza's pseudonym. His stage name." Ebony tapped her fingers on the back of the metal chair and studied Jessie for a reaction. "Well?"

Ebony was testing her, and Jessie bit the inside of her cheek to quell her mild guilt over withholding the discoveries of the life insurance proceeds, the kayak construction, and obtaining PI Wentworth's report. "How am I supposed to know that?"

Ebony scowled at her, waiting her out, but two could play this game of cat and mouse. Jessie glared back. She was a legal gladiator, and there was no way Ebony could intimidate her or warn her off. Not when her mind was set. They'd been down that road before. It hadn't worked then and wouldn't work now.

Ebony eyes narrowed. "You initially didn't seem upset about Olivia committing bigamy with Kyle, and you still don't." She paused. "What's going on here? Is there anything else you'd like to share with us?" Ebony's nostrils flared as her tone sharpened, and she gritted her teeth.

"I've got nothing. But you should be more hospitable and less accusatory. I brought you documents that might break the case open," Jessie said, feeling drained by the situation. She wanted to go home. "I'll think twice next time."

Ebony shifted her weight from one leg to the other and winced. "Damn it, Jessie, you'd better not interfere. Why can't you let us do our job? You've been lucky before, but there's no guarantee that whoever murdered Kyle wouldn't come after you. If you're not worried about your safety, think about Lily, Hal, and your family...." Ebony was keyed up. "And me. We can't be responsible if anything happens to you."

Jessie locked onto her friend's blue topaz eyes and held them for a long moment. Without saying a word, she marched out of the station. She had a killer to catch.

Chapter Forty-One

As Jessie strode away down the corridor, Ebony squeezed the rough texture of the envelope in her hands. Sure, she'd wanted to hug Jessie and thank her for Kyle's records, but Jessie had a propensity for the dramatic. Everything was a big deal. Everyone was a suspect. She couldn't deal with Jessie and her moods right now.

"Before we go back in, should we review these phone records? I know you don't want to admit it, but Jessie's intuition usually hits the mark. I have to give her props for that." Zander shrugged an apology for siding with Ebony's frenemy. "They may provide ammunition for questioning Olivia. Come on, let's take a look."

Ebony hated to admit it, but Zander was right. She had to quash her cattiness and concentrate on the prize. Finding Kyle's killer. While Ebony predicted that Olivia might not have pulled the plug, she was certain that Olivia sat at the heart of Kyle's case. Olivia Vargas was the bull's-eye in the target and, ultimately, the instigator of Kyle's death. But how? And why? Had Olivia cast a spell over Auggie and Cody, making them her co-conspirators in the death plot?

"I'll inform Castellano we'll return in a few minutes, and I'll meet you at your desk," she replied.

A few minutes later, she discovered Zander leaning back in the desk chair and gazing at the ceiling with his hands clasped behind his head. His new brown Chelsea boots, the style with the fancy elastic sides and no zippers, rested on his bottom desk drawer like a footrest. Ebony recognized his thinking pose, the one he struck to block out the tumult of the station and mull over a problem.

Zander rarely cogitated. Once his judgmental mind was set, he became obstinate, bullish. Of all his quirks, this one bugged her the most, but it would be the one she'd miss after he transferred to the sheriff's department. She enjoyed the prodding, the banter, the cajoling, and his yielding to her whims—most of the time.

"So?" she asked. "Did you read the logs?"

He sat up straight and stamped his feet on the floor, startling Ebony. "Let's review the facts. I consider three people to be suspects. First, there's Olivia. Kyle and Olivia go kayaking after switching boats, and they get caught in the storm. Kyle drowns, but she survives. The kayak she's using has a skirt to prevent water from entering. We discover a missing plug on Olivia's kayak, the one Kyle is paddling. Olivia says the trip was Kyle's idea. She's clearly trying to defer the blame for Kyle's death onto him. Although she's still married to Raul/Cody, she's rushing Kyle to the altar. And she's Cody's business partner and co-owner in his real estate."

As he spoke, Zander's vision seemed to skitter around the room. He wasn't speaking to her; rather, he was babbling aloud. There was no stopping him.

"We also know she has the lucrative side gig of pimping cosmetics on social media. She plays the damsel in distress, but she's an actress and manipulative. Just look at the way she has Carlos wrapped around her pinky."

Zander paused, and Ebony jumped in. "Cody said that Olivia's not as tough as she seems. She's super-involved with her students and school. Maybe the situation has stressed her out to the point of breakage." She twirled the gold hoop dangling from her ear lobe. "Then there's Auggie's. He's in business with Cody and Olivia in the store. We don't have the financials on the business, but we should get them because there might have been money issues affecting their relationship. Also, he was hustling Kyle about his sportsbook cross-promotion idea, and Kyle's refusal didn't sit well with him."

"The texts show Auggie was pleading with Kyle for the introductions.

And saying that his job was in jeopardy if he didn't score any big-name influencers. With his fancy car, he pretends he's loaded, but is he? Was he under money pressure? Does he have gambling debts?" Zander asked.

"What do Shaw's text messages say?" Ebony asked.

"Before we get there, Shaw's still married to Olivia. The dude still wears his wedding ring even though the divorce is pending. The night before the accident, he and Auggie had access to sabotage the kayaks at White Oaks. Are Olivia and Cody in cahoots, but what's the motive? If they are conspiring, does Cody need Kyle out of the picture? Suppose he doesn't want Kyle to marry Olivia, then he has a motive? Right?"

Ebony's mind raced, searching for answers. They were missing something. Perhaps the answers were in the texts.

"Can you tell me what the texts say?"

There were three piles of logs and transcripts on the desk, one for each suspect.

"Jessie did a great job of highlighting the suspicious messages. Let's start with Auggie." He flipped the pages to a series of messages sent one week before Kyle's death.

Kyle, let's meet up after work tonite to discuss my proposal. It's important. How's the Blue Piano Bar at 7?

Kyle replied he was busy. So, Auggie persisted.

I'll be there if you name the time.

Kyle didn't respond to Auggie's text, and the tone of the texts grew more insistent.

Come on, dude. We're family. Do me a solid and meet me. What've you got to lose?

From the texts, it appeared the two had met up, and the conversation hadn't gone as Auggie wanted. Kyle declined Auggie's request for introductions to his sports and music celebrities.

Bro, please reconsider your decision. It's a win-win. My boss has given me until 5. If you don't come thru I'm fucked. I may lose everything.

Auggie's desperation was palpable. But a threat of murder? Ebony read on.

Hey, if I'm fucked, so are you. You'd better watch your back. I can make your life miserable.

"That sounds like a threat. But what harm can he cause Kyle? Poison Olivia against him? Sic Cody, or Max, or Carlos on him?"

"Auggie must have had something on Kyle. But what could it be?" Ebony asked. "Auggie knew about his sister's marriage to Raul, but suppose Kyle didn't. Would he tell Kyle about Olivia and Cody? Could Auggie stand by and let the wedding happen, trapping Kyle in the bigamy plot? What do you think?" She paused, stroking the emerald necklace around her throat, a gift from her beloved, deceased Aunt Alicia. "Or Auggie killed Kyle in revenge, but it seems to be a stretch. Killing your soon-to-be brother-in-law because he refused a favor? Does that seem plausible to you?"

"We can't rule him out. Auggie developed a grudge against Kyle, but there's no evidence he acted upon it. Besides Auggie, there's only one text from Cody. Look, its tone is malicious."

Quit talking shit about me to her. She's a big girl and can make up her own mind. It's none of your business who she hangs out with. Leave us alone or you'll regret it. I mean it.

"What prompted this nastygram?" Ebony asked.

"It came out of nowhere. Suppose Cody had confronted Kyle about Olivia, or Olivia had instigated the trouble. There's nothing to explain it."

"We have two credible threats against Kyle. But did either suspect act on them?" A sudden coldness struck Ebony's core. If they'd known about these threats, perhaps they could've saved Kyle's life. Though Kyle never would've reported them to the police or asked for help. He'd been a proud man. A guy who isolated his emotions, the source of his rift with Jessie.

"I know what you're thinking. Don't blame yourself. You're wondering if you missed clues, but you didn't. We couldn't have stopped Kyle's death from occurring."

"Yeah, but I feel sorry for Kyle, Jessie, and Lily. What about Olivia's texts?"

"She sounded clingy and made demands on his time," Zander said. "Often, Kyle claimed he was too busy at work to see her, and Olivia complained about his schedule at Barclays and seeing Lily on his days off. She whined and referred back to their fling at her cousin's wedding. They'd argue. Then Kyle would take her out to dinner or a show to make up. Then it would start all over again. It could have been Olivia's immaturity or her insistence on getting her own way."

Zander was a player and seemed to understand about keeping the ladies happy. At thirty-four, he'd often argued he was too young to settle down. He preferred to think of himself as a bee, flitting from blossom to blossom, rather than pollinating the mature blooms. Zander was a true *gamophobe*, afraid of commitment and marriage.

His laid-back attitude raised the alarm bells whenever he ogled her sister. But Carly was a big girl. She could take of herself. Of the two, Zander was the one who needed to beware.

Olivia appeared to be the opposite. She loved being married so much that she'd conspired to commit bigamy.

It was Ebony's job to investigate a murder, not pass judgment on other people's relationships. Yet, it provided insight into the woman waiting inside the interrogation room. "This generates more questions for Olivia. If she'd been demanding and sexually permissive with Cody, he might have become addicted to her."

"Men get hooked on crazy shit, Eb. It doesn't need to be drugs, booze, or gambling. Sex is a strong obsession. Some guys might even kill for it."

As Ebony had thought, Olivia was the luminous blue zone of the flame; the combustible outer layer generated a deadly heat. Cody, Kyle, and Auggie were the moths attracted to the dangerous flame, and it was time to extinguish the fire before anyone else got burned.

Chapter Forty-Two

J essie buttoned her faded denim jacket, grabbed the canvas sack of groceries from her Jeep's hatchback, and strode up the garden path, appreciating the last vestiges of Black-Eyed Susans, hydrangeas, and dahlias. The late afternoon sun had shifted westward, swathing her backyard in forest green shadows, and the breeze had tossed a handful of maple leaves earthbound onto the dense lawn.

Before the market, she'd delivered Kyle's phone records to Ebony at the police station. While Ebony's genuine interest in Jessie's finds had eased her mind, she remained reticent about sharing her other discoveries about Olivia, Kyle's past, and the insurance policy with Ebony, Zander, or even Hal. Eventually, she would, but not until she'd completed her investigation.

In the yard, Hal and Lena laughed as Lily pulled herself up on the arm of an Adirondack chair, toddled for a split second, and then landed on her rump, cushioned by the layers of pants and a diaper. The breeze captured Lily's giggles and carried them to greet Jessie.

"Hey, sweets. Need help?" Hal called as Jessie strolled up the walk to join them. She shook her head. He scooped up Lily and met Jessie halfway, leaning in for a kiss. "How was your day?"

"Fine," she replied. Jessie kissed Lily on her cheek and Hal on the mouth. "What a gorgeous afternoon. I love these days, cool in the morning and evening, and warm during the day."

"It's even better now that you're here." He enclosed her in his arms so that the three formed a tight, unbreakable circle.

"I can see my babysitting services are no longer required. Your father is expecting me, so I'd better get going," Lena said. "Oh, I heard you spoke with Ethan and the kids yesterday." Nothing escaped her mother. "I hate that Ethan and his family live so far away. I wish they'd move back, but at least I have you, my Lilybean." Lena's voice cracked, and she caressed Lily's chubby hand. "I'm looking forward to having the whole family together for Thanksgiving. I can't wait for Lily to meet her Uncle Ethan, Aunt Gemma, and cousins Nicky and Sophie."

Lena planted a farewell kiss on Lily's cheek and patted Jessie's arm. "I'll talk to you tomorrow, sweetheart." Lena waved at her granddaughter as she strode toward the driveway, then slid into her sporty Audi hatchback and drove away.

"Why didn't you mention Ethan called and that his family was coming to visit?" Hal broke away from their embrace and carried Lily toward the back porch.

"It wasn't worth mentioning. He called to find out about Kyle. That's all." Jessie tried to avoid mentioning Kyle to Hal. It felt awkward discussing her dead ex with him, especially since Hal had vociferously opposed her "meddling in police matters."

Yet Jessie's self-imposed cone of silence had become oppressive and torturous. Secrets, lies, and omissions had destroyed her relationship with Kyle, and she'd become entrenched in a similar cycle of deceit with Hal. From the first moment she'd learned about Kyle's disappearance, an invisible wall had been erected, separating her from Hal. It was tearing Jessie in two—pulling her toward her past with Kyle and pushing her away from the present with Hal.

Worse yet, she felt like she was cheating on Hal by discussing her past. Investigating the past. Uncovering Kyle's secrets.

Ever since they'd met in law school, Hal had the power to read her mind and heart. Lately, she'd been distant, and this time, she knew from his furrowed brow he wouldn't let the topic go.

Hal held the kitchen door open for her, and Bono, his whiskers covered in cobwebs, scooted inside behind her before the door slammed shut.

"I know Kyle's situation is bothering you, and I want you to feel you can discuss him with me. He's an important part of your life and Lily's." The soft gleam in Hal's eyes reflected his love for her. "I'd never ask you to forget about the father of your child. And I know you'd never ask me to disregard my marriage to Erin. These memories are important. They made us who we are, and we need to preserve them for our kids."

Jessie set her sack on the counter while Hal set Lily into her highchair and fastened a bib around her neck. "You know, just as Kyle stopped being an interloper in our relationship, he returned, literally, from the dead. I don't want his death to overshadow our life."

"So don't let it."

"It's hard not to. His life and death are a frustrating puzzle, which I can't solve. I'm convinced someone contributed to Kyle's drowning, but I'm powerless to discover who or why?"

"Contributed? That's an odd assumption."

Jessie grabbed the jars of baby food and scooped the contents into a silicone bowl, and popped it into the microwave.

"I think someone either plotted, or acted, or failed to prevent Kyle's death," she said.

"That's quite a conspiracy theory, Jess. It makes you sound paranoid, and you have no absolute proof. You need to accept Kyle's death was an accident caused by a storm. Not treachery."

"You're wrong. Kyle was a strong swimmer and an experienced kayaker. How can you explain why he died, but Olivia survived?" The microwave timer dinged, and impulsively, Jessie grabbed the meal. The heated bowl burned her fingertips, and she slammed it on the counter. "Crap!"

"Are you okay?"

"Just peachy," Jessie said, turning on the cold water and immersing her scorned fingers in the icy flow.

"Can I do anything to help?" He ran to her side.

"No! Leave me alone. I'll be fine," she shouted above the running water. Her body tensed at his proximity, and she gave him a dismissive wave.

"You're not acting fine." He stalked away and grabbed a pint-sized spoon from the drawer, and stirred the hot food in Lily's bowl, watching the steam

245

rise. "We've been down this road before, and you can't blunder around, placing yourself in danger. It's irresponsible. Leave the heroics to Ebony and Zander. That's their job. You're a lawyer, not a private investigator."

"I don't know what you're talking about."

"Yes, you do."

Jessie wondered whether he'd detected her furtive activities or whether she'd left any clues behind. Her thoughts turned to the stack of Kyle's yearbooks in the den.

"This time, it's personal." She snapped off the faucet and wiped her hands on a ragged Mickey Mouse dishtowel, a souvenir from a Disney World trip with Kyle. She clenched her teeth, and the muscles in her jaw tensed.

"Terrence Butterfield wasn't personal?" He seemed to be constantly throwing her misadventures and near-death experiences in her face.

"It's a matter of degree, and you know it. You don't understand. Kyle is… was family." Jessie glanced at Lily, who gnawed on a pink rubber block of the letter Z. She couldn't help being reminded of Kyle every time she looked at their daughter.

"I do. Kyle was your family, but he relinquished the right when he abandoned you when you were seven months pregnant. And you seem to forget how he incriminated you in Ryan's murder." He paused, blew across Lily's bowl, and tested the temperature with his pinky. "He's Lily's father, but you can't make excuses for him because he's deceased."

"I'll do that." Jessie snatched the spoon from Hal. "You have no idea what I'm going through and there's no way you could. I need to work things out in my own way."

"Just keep Kyle's death in perspective. That's all I'm asking you." Hal glared at her, but she refused contact with his soft amber eyes wounded by her dismissive attitude.

As she fed Lily, her mind drifted. Her father's warnings echoed in Hal's remarks. Kyle had been a lousy father, an unreliable partner, and dishonest about his past and present. Yet, something compelled her to investigate the drowning. Call it suspicion. Misplaced loyalty. Love. Stupidity. A desire to solve the mystery. She couldn't quit now. A microscopic corner of her heart would always belong to Kyle.

As long as she remained aware of the danger, there was no reason to stop. Not until she discovered evidence of foul play. Given the admonitions from Hal, Ed, and Ebony, Jessie needed to continue on the sly. She didn't want any of them, especially Hal, to believe she'd become obsessed.

Or had she? Was it too late?

Chapter Forty-Three

All heads swiveled toward Ebony and Zander as they entered the interrogation room. Adrenaline coursed through Ebony's veins, making her pulse race. She was far from finished with interviewing Olivia Vargas, and she was stoked. As was their routine, Zander had lofted softballs at their witness, and it was Ebony's turn to pitch the fastballs a hundred miles an hour over the plate.

She didn't buy Olivia's grieving widow routine. She'd witnessed the deep, heartfelt grief of the loss of a spouse, partner, and relative, and Olivia's crocodile tears didn't come close. Though before Ebony executed her kill shot, she needed to understand what had happened out on the river and what part Olivia had played in the disaster.

Olivia fingered a diamond crucifix dangling around her throat, and an air of arrogance had replaced the innocence she'd previously displayed. Armed with her overprotective father and attorney, Olivia seemed prepared for a fight. Perhaps the fight of her life.

"Detectives, as you can see, Ms. Vargas is extremely upset. We'd appreciate it if you keep your questions to a minimum," the attorney said acerbically. Castellano flicked her hair away from her shoulders and straightened her spine to dominate the room.

Two could play at this game, Ebony thought.

"We will oblige your client as best as possible, but our investigation has shifted its focus from an accident to a brutal homicide investigation," Ebony said.

"A homicide? No. That can't be," Olivia cried. She looked from her father to Castellano as the color drained from her face.

"That's impossible. Kyle's death was an accident. He drowned," Carlos said, his voice shaky. "Who would want to hurt Kyle?"

"We don't know, but we're afraid it wasn't an accident. We need to proceed with the interview to get to the bottom of this. Ms. Vargas' information is essential to uncovering the truth behind Mr. Emory's death, and we're confident she seeks to bring the perpetrator to justice as much as we do."

Zander signaled at the videographer, and the green light blinked.

"Oh, yes. Of course." Carlos Vargas said, clasping his daughter's hand. He remained seated, displaying no signs of departure. "Oli, are you all right?"

Olivia's body grew rigid, but she smiled weakly and stroked her necklace.

"My client is the victim in this passion play you're staging, and she's innocent of any wrongdoing in connection with Kyle Emory's death. Let's move this interview along so she can go home," Castellano said.

"We never said she wasn't, but her statement can help us identify who may be responsible," Ebony said.

"Good. We're agreed," Castellano replied.

Ebony studied Olivia's heart-shaped face, demeanor, and body language. Olivia's jaw was set. Her posture was stick-straight, and she'd drawn back her shoulders to expose the diamond cross nestled at the base of her long neck. There was no better time to plunge into the deep water.

"Ms. Vargas, can you please tell us about your relationship with Kyle Emory? We know you recently became engaged, but you're not wearing an engagement ring. Did Kyle give you one?"

Olivia examined the space on her left ring finger. "He said there was a family heirloom, his grandmother's ring, that he wanted to give me. But he had to get it back from his former fiancée, who refused to return it."

"Are you referring to Jessie Martin, the woman with whom he shares a child?"

"Yes, Lily. What a delightful baby, but Kyle told me the mother is a real shrew. She only cared about his money and his taking Lily off her hands, and they were always fighting. He couldn't stand it, and I had to pick up the pieces every time. It's a wonder how those two ever got together. He said Jessie never appreciated him." Olivia waved her hand dismissively.

"How would you describe your relationship? Were you happy?" Ebony asked.

"Oh, we were terribly happy and compatible. Kyle was so loving, understanding, and kind. We enjoyed hiking and attending concerts and sporting events. Since he worked at the Barclays Center, we enjoyed the best seats at every venue. The Garden. Yankee Stadium. Broadway. His name and connections got us into the VIP lounges and backstage to meet the performers. Harry Styles has very soft, warm hands."

Ebony raised her eyebrows, wondering what that meant. Had she had sex with Harry, too?

"I mean when we shook hands. They were warm and soft. He has the loveliest smile, and when he said my name in his lovely British accent, I thought I was in heaven," Olivia bragged.

"Did you and Kyle ever fight?"

"No, there was nothing to fight about, except he had a dark side." Olivia gave a pregnant pause and lowered her voice to a hush. "He made me perform sexual acts that made me uncomfortable, and he made sex tapes." She winced and shivered. "I felt pressured to have sex with him, even though I enjoyed it. He was *so* good at it. He wanted me to be someone that I wasn't." A flush crept across her cheeks, and she glanced at Zander, who squirmed in sympathy with her discomfort. "Kyle was so much older and more experienced than me, and I wanted to please him, make him happy, so I did whatever he wanted. I loved him. I still love him. I wanted to marry Kyle and have his babies. And now he's gone," she cried. Olivia turned toward her father, and Carlos rubbed her back and smiled in understanding.

If Ebony hadn't read Kyle's text messages, she would have believed Olivia and the erratic behavior she'd incorrectly attributed as a motive for Kyle's suicide. Castellano and Carlos seemed to buy into Olivia's victimization, but Ebony had learned her lesson with this bitch. After the high-speed chase, the phone messages, and the dash-cam video, Ebony suspected that this wily witness plotted and planned every breath she inhaled.

"If you felt uncomfortable, why didn't you break up with him?" Ebony prodded.

"I told you I loved him." Olivia's voice choked. A single rehearsed tear trickled down her cheek. "He meant the world to me. I would've done anything for him. Anything..."

Ebony swallowed hard to contain her anger. She hungered to accuse Olivia outright of treachery, but without evidence, there was no crime. There was still more ground to cover. "Ms. Vargas, our records show you are already married to Raul Esperanza. Yet, you're engaged to Kyle Emory?"

"Yes, but a divorce is pending."

"That's true. I can confirm that the final judgment of divorce is awaiting the judge's signature," Castellano said. "We're expecting them to be signed any day now. I have copies if you'd like them."

"That would be helpful. Thank you. Was Kyle aware of the marriage?"

"My marriage to Raul wasn't a genuine marriage. I grew up with him. He's more like a brother to me than a husband."

The photos on the Hudson Outfitters' walls portrayed a different story. Olivia's adoring gazes at Raul. The way they'd groped each other, not in brotherly love. In "I'm-hot-for-you-and-can't-keep-my-hands-off-you" heat.

"You're also business partners with Raul in Hudson Outfitters and also in land, correct?"

The witness nodded.

"Do your divorce papers divide your personal property and other assets?"

Olivia scoffed, and Carlos clicked his tongue in apparent disgust.

"I don't see how Olivia and Raul's financial relationship applies to your drowning investigation," Castellano said. "The parties are in negotiations, if you must know."

"So you and Raul remain business partners, but have no other personal relationship?" Zander asked. He'd remained mute up to this point, although he tapped his boots madly on the linoleum tiles. Ebony could tell Zander was losing his patience and wanted to move the interview along.

"We're still friends, not that it's any of your concern."

"This line of questioning is absurd," Carlos said. "Raul is like a member of the family."

"I recall you mentioning the same thing about Kyle. Do you say that about all of your daughter's lovers?" Zander asked.

Ebony kicked Zander under the table, attempting to shut him down. He glared at her, his mouth pinched in resentment.

"Dr. Vargas is not a party to this present interview. I demand you exercise decorum; otherwise, I'll end this meeting," Castellano said.

"Had you and Kyle set a wedding date?" Ebony asked, resuming control of the runaway train.

"Originally, we'd picked Valentine's Day. However, Kyle postponed it until late spring. He wanted his daughter to participate as the flower girl. She's only a year old now, but she'll be walking by then."

"Did the delay upset you?" Ebony's tone was light but assertive.

"I wasn't thrilled about it, but I felt like we were married already. The wedding was a formality. I spent so much time with him at his condo; we were practically living together already. And anyway, I was moving in after Christmas when my lease expired. We'd opened a joint bank account, and Kyle was speaking with HR about naming me as his life partner on their paperwork."

Ebony typed "Barclays HR" into her phone and then pulled up the *Honey Face* website. She held it up for Olivia and her entourage to view. Olivia's fresh, smiling face greeted them, and her video commercial streamed. Ebony paused the advertisement. "Ms. Vargas, you seem to be quite a successful pitch person for *Honey Face Cosmetics*."

"Oh, yes," Olivia purred. "I love their products. It's a fantastic startup, and I'm proud to help them build their brand. They've only been around for two years and started from scratch. I've built 100,000 subscribers across my platforms, and their sales have skyrocketed. In fact, we have a live-stream shopping event planned for Black Friday Weekend. And they've offered me stock for my sweat equity. Soon I'll be an owner and a social influencer."

"Detective, again, I'm questioning the relevance of this inquiry," Castellano replied.

"I guess it's fortunate Kyle never posted your sex tapes or photos online, isn't it?" Zander posed, intimating that a whiff of immorality could kill her future with *Honey Face* or any other company. A fine line of perspiration shimmered across Olivia's upper lip, and she wiped it away. "Did you or Kyle take any photos on the day of the accident?"

"We took a bunch before the storm hit, which I posted on my social media platforms. I don't know what Kyle did with his. They were probably on his phone."

"Do you know what happened to Kyle's phone?" Ebony asked.

"I assume he had it when he fell into the water." Olivia paused. "Oh, god. He's gone. I'll never see him again. How am I going to live without him? How can I return to teaching and face my classes? They adored him as much as I did." Her French-manicured fingernails flew up to hide her face, and she sobbed.

A grand finale equal to an Oscar-winning performance, Ebony thought.

Zander wrinkled his brow as though weighing the truth of Olivia's speech.

"I think we're done here," Castellano said.

"I hope you're happy," Carlos said, stroking his daughter's bowed head. "You've upset my daughter, and who knows what irreparable damage you've caused?"

"Ms. Vargas, thank you for coming in and speaking with us. Again, please accept our condolences for your loss," Ebony said.

The videographer stopped the recording and began dismantling his equipment.

Ebony and Zander remained seated as Castellano, Olivia, and Carlos rose to leave. Olivia and her father departed while Castellano lingered on the threshold.

"Don't forget to supply me with a copy of this video, and please let me know when you've wrapped up the case. We truly hope you apprehend Kyle's killer."

"Of course. We'll send along an NDA. Thank you for your cooperation," Zander replied. He rose, shutting the door behind Castellano. When he'd returned to the table, he drummed his long fingers along the metal top. "Well, what do you think?" His taps became louder, more frantic.

"Can you please stop tapping? I can't think straight." Ebony paused. "Olivia was under oath, so we have to review her statement for perjury. But did she commit murder or manslaughter? Not sure. Her proximity to Kyle makes her a suspect, but so are Auggie and Cody. They all had the opportunity, but their motives, attempts, and commission of the crime remain unclear. There are no clear-cut threads."

"Let's review the logs again. I can't help feeling something is staring us in the face. Yet, what could their motives be? Money? Sex? Revenge? Jealousy?" Zander asked.

"Beats the shit out of me," Ebony said.

Chapter Forty-Four

There was one place that wasn't considered a crime scene: Kyle's condo in Brooklyn. Jessie had never been, and with her attorney's mind working overtime, she decided more clues to the murder might lie within. Thus, the condo deserved an examination.

The mid-morning traffic had been light on the RFK Bridge into Brooklyn, and it had taken her less than two hours to reach Kyle's apartment. It was in the Crown Heights Section of Brooklyn, a walkable distance from the Barclays Center. Earlier that morning, Jessie had spoken with the building manager, explained the situation, and after overcoming the woman's initial hesitation, she met Jessie outside the slim, modern gray brick building on Pacific Street.

Kyle's unit was on the second floor, and totting Lily up the steps, Jessie's fingers trembled as she pressed the electronic key on the keypad. As the door swung open, Jessie didn't know what to expect. She stepped into the foyer of a magnificent duplex with white walls, a built-in wine cellar, a cascading crystal chandelier, and gleaming oak herringbone floors.

"Wow! This place must have set Daddy back a few million dollars," Jessie said, setting the toddler on the floor. "Let's look around."

On the first floor of the apartment, two bedrooms were to their left, and ahead a wooden staircase with a glass banister led upstairs. Lily trailed her past the laundry room and spa-like bathroom into the rear of the unit. A state-of-the-art kitchen with white quartz countertops opened into a living room, which was an interior designer's dream. Natural light flooded the spacious room through the wall of windows overlooking a deck and a tiny courtyard.

"Why didn't you tell me Daddy lived like the King of Brooklyn?"

Lily lost her balance, tumbled onto the thick white living room rug, and giggled.

Jessie swept Lily up in her arms and carried her upstairs to investigate the second story. The stairs led beyond the master bedroom and en suite bath to a private roof deck on the third story of the house. She slid open the glass doors and took in the sparkling blue skies above the Manhattan skyline. The city felt so close. It was as if Jessie could reach out and touch United Nations, Empire State, and Chrysler Buildings.

"This view must be amazing at night," Jessie said.

Lily yawned in response, signaling it was time for her mid-morning nap, and returning downstairs, Jessie discovered a nursery in a first-floor bedroom. It was simply set up—a crib, dresser-changing table, rocking chair, and a few stuffed animals—but it would do. Settling Lily in her crib, Jessie shut the door, ready to search the rest of the unit.

First, Jessie tiptoed upstairs to check the master suite. The tidy room was decorated in the crisp, modern furnishings of a five-star hotel, with a king-size bed with an upholstered headboard, two comfortable high-back chairs next to the window, and a massive gold mirror hung over the oak dresser. On the dresser sat two photos—one of Kyle and Olivia at a wedding and the other of Jessie, Kyle, and Lily at Lily's first Christmas. Jessie opened the dresser drawers and rummaged through clothing and underwear she'd spent years washing, drying, and folding. From the frilly lingerie, crop tops, and ripped designer jeans she discovered in a bottom drawer, Olivia had moved in.

Inside the closet, Kyle's new dress shirts and suits hung beside a woman's silk kimono bathrobe, and on the floor were Kyle's shoes and Olivia's stilettos and sandals. On Kyle's bedside table, Jessie hunted for the smartwatch she'd given him for his birthday two years ago. It was missing. He may have worn it on the date of his accident.

Discovering nothing of interest in the master bedroom, she returned downstairs to the second bedroom, which Kyle had converted into a guest room/office. Lightness filled her chest at the sight of his computer on the desk and the thought that Olivia hadn't snatched it. Jessie imagined the clues hidden inside it as she packed the laptop into her tote bag. While eager to view them, she'd explore them when she reached home.

Beside the computer lay a folder with an attorney's correspondence clipped on top. The letterhead read Gloria Reyes Castellano, Attorney at Law, White Plains, N.Y., but Jessie didn't recognize the name.

"What the fuck?" Jessie gasped, her face warming with anger as she flipped through the documents. It was an unsigned deed, transferring one-half of the condominium to Olivia Vargas as joint tenants with right of survivorship. That meant that Olivia would own the entire apartment if something happened to Kyle. Had Kyle intended to give Olivia the apartment and cheat Lily? What was he thinking? Why had he turned against his own flesh and blood?

Jessie's muscles quivered as she snapped photos of the paperwork and left them on the desk.

As her fingertips gripped the desk drawer, she heard the front door open and footsteps striding across the hardwood floors toward the kitchen. A female voice laughed, talked on her phone, and dropped something on the kitchen island.

Jessie stood in the doorway and listened.

"Yes, Daddy. I made it to Kyle's apartment. I'm going to grab my things, and I'll be right home. Yes, I promise. Yes, I'm feeling fine. I can handle being here." Olivia paused. "I love you, too, and I'll be home in a couple of hours."

The patter of footsteps grew louder, and Jessie froze. Where was she going to go? At first, she felt like a thief, but then she realized she had the legal right to be in the townhouse, unlike the intruder.

"What are *you* doing here, Jessie?" Olivia snapped. She must have recognized Jessie from the dresser photo. Olivia, with a duffle bag slung over her shoulder, charged at Jessie, forcing Jessie against the bedroom wall. She stood so close Jessie saw the precise lines of the eye makeup masking Olivia's messy life.

"I could ask you the same question." Jessie's voice quavered. Her first thought was of Lily asleep in the nursery next door. She needed to get to her, protect her. Jessie shoved Olivia aside and dashed out of the room.

Olivia dropped the duffle and followed in pursuit.

"I live here now." Olivia's attention slid to the closed nursery door, and a smirk crossed her haughty face. "Oh, I see *mi preciosa hijastra*. My precious stepdaughter, Lily, is here. We are old friends. How she loves her sweets."

Jessie ignored the jab. "This is Kyle's home, not yours. Get out."

"I've stayed here so often that he wanted it to be my engagement present. Because he loved me."

Something about Olivia's taunting didn't ring true. During Jessie's years with Kyle, she would never have described him as generous, especially with expensive property. Money had been a constant issue between them. To stem Kyle's complaints about her extravagances like wine, dining out, and vacations, she'd contributed more than her fair share. And before his death, his support and house payments had been chronically late.

"Please grab your things and give me the key. You're no longer welcome here." Jessie held out her hand, her palm uplifted. "Oh, and I'm demanding that you cease and desist any postings about Kyle. You need Lily's permission to use his name and image, and as Lily's mother, I'm demanding you stop. It's disgusting and degrades his memory."

"You're not in the position to demand anything, are you? Aren't you an attorney? Isn't your fiancé a judge?" Olivia balled her hands into fists and inched toward Jessie.

Jessie shuffled backward through the open door of the spare bedroom, and the bed's edge pressed against her calves. There was nowhere to go.

"I don't know what you mean," Jessie said.

Olivia's face twisted in determination. Her gaze darted toward the empty desk space where the computer had been, toward Jessie's tote bag on the bed, and settled on the letter and deed. "First, I've made Kyle a celebrity through his death. He's famous now, and people all over the world are mourning him. Lily should be proud of him."

"Your posts aren't for Kyle. They enhance your image, your publicity, and sell whatever products you hawk." Jessie fought the urge to grab a fistful of Olivia's glistening black hair and yank it out by its root.

"The world knows what Kyle meant to me, and my suffering. The publicity may rub off on me, but I'm grieving for Kyle, which is more than I can say about you. You should be ashamed, coming here to steal his personal property. I should call the cops." Olivia's face flushed as crimson as her skintight t-shirt.

Good luck with that, Jessie thought.

"And as I was saying," Olivia said, "the public is very fickle. Critical reviews of judges and lawyers can ruin their careers. Can't they? Wouldn't it be a shame if someone complained about your competency and ethics, and about Judge Samuel's prejudicial behavior?"

Unfortunately, the New York State ethics rules prohibited attorneys from defending any frivolous claims made by internet trolls. Their only remedy was to deny the spurious claim and turn the other cheek.

Jessie studied the Gen Xer, wondering whether she meant to fulfill her vile threats. With Olivia's growing legions of followers, she could incite an internet flash mob against Jessie and Hal, and an onslaught of troll reviews. Olivia was a dangerous force in the digital world, but Jessie doubted whether her clients, colleagues, family, and friends would believe the bitch in the real world.

"I'm not asking you," Jessie said with force. Her focus never left the attractive young adversary. "I'm telling you to delete the posts, give me the keys, and get the hell out of here. You have five minutes to clear out your shit. After that, I'm calling the police." She paused. "I'll be in the kitchen, and please be quiet. My daughter is sleeping."

"Whatever. You'd better watch your back, *puta*." Olivia huffed, swiveled on her heels, and scampered upstairs to the master bedroom.

Her heart racing, Jessie returned to the kitchen and paced the floor. She glanced at the time on her phone, wishing the minutes would speed up. As the deadline arrived, Olivia tromped down the steps to the foyer, grumbling and making as much noise as possible. Clothes overflowed from her bag, and she tried to zip it, but couldn't. "Fuck!"

"The key?" Jessie asked, approaching Olivia.

Face pinched in anger, Olivia pitched the key to the floor. She grabbed a bottle of champagne from the foyer's wine refrigerator and stomped to the door. *"Puta!"* she yelled, slamming the door behind her.

A deep, satisfying sigh escaped from Jessie's lips. "Good riddance," she said.

On legs weak with relief, Jessie wobbled down the hallway and peeked inside the nursery. Lily was asleep in her crib. For good measure, she glanced inside the office. The letter, deed, and folder had vanished.

Chapter Forty-Five

The spindly branches of the rosebushes scratched against Jessie's bedroom window awakening her from a fitful night's sleep. Jessie's bleary vision shifted from the panes toward the silvery ceiling overhead. From the shadows on the surface, she could tell it was after midnight. Hounded by the howling wind and repetitive snapping on the glass, she found it impossible to return to sleep. Sliding from the covers, Jessie tiptoed toward the bay window across the room and drew the filmy curtains aside to watch the trees bow and sway in the glow of the full moon.

"Is everything okay?" Hal asked.

"Sorry, I didn't mean to wake you."

"You didn't. The racket woke me up, too. I've been lying here, not wanting to disturb you." He threw back the comforter, inviting her into his side of the king-size bed. "Come here. You must be freezing."

Jessie hadn't thought about the frigid bedroom, but at his mention of it, a chill shot from her bare feet up to her neck, making her shiver. She darted toward Hal and snuggled in close, his body radiating comforting warmth.

"That's better, isn't it?" he asked, tucking the down comforter around them.

"Mmm," she replied. His t-shirt was soft against her cheek, and as he wrapped his arms around her, she pressed her ear to his chest, listening to the steady beat of his heart.

"Jess?"

"Uh-huh," she murmured.

"We need to talk." His grip tightened. "The two of us have been so busy lately, we never seem to connect, even when we're sitting in the same room. I'm worrying about work, and you're thinking about Lily, and…. It's only natural you're concerned about Kyle."

Jessie's body stiffened, and she tried to wiggle free, but he'd trapped her within his embrace. "Do you really want to talk about this now?"

"We never seem to have the time, and I get the impression you're carrying around a monstrous weight. So talk to me, Jess. Please tell me what's going on. Let me in. Your silence, your alienation, is scaring me."

"That's not my intention. I'm trying to sort things out in my mind, but it's like I'm trapped in a maze, and I can't escape."

"You shouldn't be navigating the labyrinth alone. We're partners, lovers, and friends. We're here for each other. I'm sorry I've been tied up at work, but I'm still settling into the judgeship. Regardless, I'm here for you. Whatever you need. Whenever you need it. I don't want you to slip away from me. Never again."

"Me, neither," she whispered. They'd spent seven long years, a lifetime, apart. Then, less than a year ago, they'd found their way back to each other, and Jessie refused to jeopardize their new life together. From the choked sound of tears in his voice, Hal felt the same.

"You need to tell me what's going on. Please."

Jessie hadn't wanted to burden Hal with her problems about Kyle, but she'd inadvertently wounded him. But did Hal want to know the truth? Once he heard it, would his feelings for her change? Hal was ready to listen, but was she ready to tell him everything?

"I need to sit up." She rose, climbed over him to her side of the bed, and switched on the nightstand light. Hal's worried eyes followed Jessie as she pushed the pillows against the headboard and leaned back. "Kyle's drowning has created an awkward situation all the way around. It's uncomfortable dealing with his parents, my parents, Ebony, and especially you. I'm juggling everyone, trying to portray positivity and keep everyone's spirits up when my nerves are frayed beyond belief. Plus, there's the added craziness of the surprise fiancée. It has hit me from all angles… and then there's Lily."

"You don't have to handle Kyle's death alone," Hal said, sitting beside her with their shoulders touching. "If I can speak honestly, I know you've been up to something. I didn't know what it was, but you are hiding something from me. And it hurts to think you had to." Pain filled his handsome face, and a frown deepened the vertical line between his brows. "You are not alone." Hal entwined his fingers with hers and squeezed. "Do you understand me? You are not alone."

Jessie felt like shit. She didn't deserve this wonderful, compassionate man. Someone who would sacrifice his life for her. Do anything she asked of him. Believe in her and love her unconditionally. How could she have mistreated him?

"I'm sorry. I should've shared with you, but I didn't want you to accuse me of interfering with police procedures or worry I was becoming obsessive about Kyle's life and death or weak in the face of this tragedy. And I couldn't compromise your position as a criminal court judge." A tear trickled down her cheek, and he wiped it away with his thumb. His soft lips kissed the wet trail on her skin.

"I would never think those things."

"Well, maybe after I tell you the entire story, you might change your mind."

Hal tilted his head to the side and raised an eyebrow. "We'll never know until you spill the dirt."

"Okay. I'm ready to dish," Jessie said. She inhaled a deep breath and blew it out. The tale of her suspicions and recent exploits slipped off the tongue. Once she began, she couldn't stop. Afraid Hal's response would inhibit her, Jessie stared out the window into the night. Hal remained silent, listening.

As her story spun on, the exit to the hellish maze revealed itself to her. Its bright red light pointed the way home and back to Hal.

When Jessie had finished, her shoulders dropped away from her ears, and the knot in her neck relaxed. The ten-ton weight crushing her heart had vanished, and lightness filled her soul.

She fixed her gaze on Hal as she waited for his response.

A wide smile spread across his loving face. "Shit, Jess. You've been dragged over the coals. Isn't it better now that you've gotten it off your chest?"

"So, you're not mad, angry, or disappointed with me? As I listened to myself, I doubted my sanity. But I'm not crazy, right?"

"I wouldn't go that far," Hal joked. "And no, I'm not mad or angry or whatever at you. Kyle's drowning raises some valid concerns about foul play, and now we can address them together. We might not find all the answers, but we'll try. You, Lily, and his family deserve justice." He paused. "And I know what you're thinking. I'll recuse myself if the case gets assigned to my criminal docket." His eyes locked onto hers. "Jess, you... our family... will always come first."

Jessie kissed him. His warm lips were inviting. "Can we please go to sleep now?"

"Sure, we'll work this out in the morning," he said, kissing her again. This time, his lips trailed down her neck and came to rest at her collarbone. The heat of his breath turned her skin to gooseflesh, and her nipples grew hard as he fondled her breasts beneath the thin layer of her nightgown. "But we are awake now."

"Yes, we are," Jessie murmured, absorbing the pleasure of his tongue and nimble fingers exploring her body.

Jessie never wanted him to stop. She shuddered with pleasure, succumbing to their carnal desires as the pink rays of the sunrise streamed into the window.

Chapter Forty-Six

Jessie and Hal walked beneath a futuristic oval oculus, supported by a spectacular steel canopy, to enter the Barclays Center. Hand in hand, they stopped and peered up through the opening at the piercing blue September sky. Above their heads, the words "Eleven Trains. One destination. The Barclays Center" swirled by on a screen looping the interior face of the oculus. The building's undulating roof reminded Jessie of a weathered metal-mesh bean pod planted on three-square city blocks within the heart of Brooklyn. Across the plaza, commuters trickled out of the shiny new subway station, which serviced the arena and the local community.

A bald-headed guard greeted them at the glass doors. After reviewing their identification and scanning them through the security, he directed them toward the concourse on their right, toward the human relations department, where the director, Nicole Thomas, waited.

Their shoes squeaked across the polished marble floor of the empty lobby. The two-story atrium exuded an azure glow, reflecting the backlit blue glass banner installed above the electronic billboard that promoted upcoming events. Running along their right, a wall of box office windows hailed HELLO BROOKLYN, and straight ahead, a walkway led into the arena.

Jessie tugged on the sleeve of Hal's jacket. "Come on. Let's take a peek. When will we ever get another chance to have the place all to ourselves?"

Without a soul in sight, they strolled down the passageway to a railing. Behind them, seats ascended toward the ceiling, and below them, more seats and a steep staircase descended to the shiny basketball court. The floor, displaying the Brooklyn Nets logo at center court, was almost a full story below street level. Above center court, the massive four-sided electronic scoreboard was dark, enhancing the eerie silence of the massive space.

Jessie had been here once before to see a concert, the show of a lifetime. When the arena had first opened a few years ago, Barry Levy, Kyle's former boss, and the Barclays' new general manager, had invited them to see Barbra Streisand. Levy had given them fifteenth-row orchestra seats, but when the producers had relocated the soundboard to their section, he'd invited them to join him in the owner's suite.

Jessie still recalled the orchestra tuning up. A hush fell over the audience as the lights dimmed. A single spotlight lit an empty center-stage microphone. As the strains of violins played, Barbra rose from beneath the stage like Venus De Milo from the sea, belting out one word. The signature word prickled Jessie's skin with goosebumps. *"Peo-ple."* Nineteen thousand Barbra fans screamed as tears streamed down Jessie's cheeks. She'd heard the voice of an angel.

Back then, she and Kyle had been good together. No fights. No secrets. Jessie preferred to remember him in the bloom of their relationship rather than in its withered and deceitful state.

Jessie didn't know how long she'd been staring at the polished floorboards, but Hal's sharp tug on her arm returned her to the present.

"We can't keep Ms. Thomas waiting," Hal urged, glancing at a text on his phone. He'd cleared his calendar for the day, but he was always on duty. Jessie squeezed his arm in appreciation and acknowledgment. There was no need to delay the inevitable.

"Ms. Thomas said she'd have the paperwork ready when we arrived. But I want copies of all the documents Kyle signed: his employment agreement, health and dental insurance applications, 401K, life insurance, and any other benefits owed to Lily. I need to keep track of his benefits package, because I can't let Lily's health insurance lapse."

"Don't worry. We'll figure everything out. Lily will be taken care of."

Hal slid his arm through hers, and his touch reassured her they were taking the journey together. Forever. If she'd leveled with Hal from the start, it would have saved her endless stomachaches and sleepless nights.

The smell of French fries and stale beer wafted through the concourse as they passed the shuttered vendors from popular Brooklyn eateries. When they reached the administrative offices, Hal pushed the door open and stood aside to admit Jessie. To their left sat a pert receptionist wearing a fitted Barclays Center navy blazer. "Ms. Martin?" she asked and smiled. "Ms. Thomas is expecting you. Please take a seat. She'll be with you momentarily."

Jessie's eyes glided across the room. On a modern white sofa beneath the schematic drawings of the stadium, Ebony sat studying her phone. She glanced up at them, her body turning rigid, and she scowled.

Before Jessie and Hal could sit down, Ms. Thomas appeared. Unlike Ebony's exotic biracial appearance, there was nothing distinctive about Nicole Thomas. In her mid-forties, Thomas was the epitome of the corporate culture in a navy suit bearing the Barclays' logo, white silk blouse, and her dark hair pulled into a ponytail. Her warm smile improved her features as nondescript as the windowless white office.

"Ms. Martin, it's nice to meet you. As I mentioned on the phone, Kyle will be missed here." As Jessie introduced Hal, Thomas' curious eyes alighted upon Ebony, but returned to Jessie. "If you'd like to follow me."

Jessie and Hal pivoted to follow Ms. Thomas into her office but stopped. "We'd like Detective Jones to join us, please. She's investigating the cause of Kyle's drowning, and I'm sure she has questions as well." Ebony saluted and flashed her badge.

Inside the office of the HR Director, Hal and Jessie settled into the two chairs facing Thomas' desk. Ebony's shoulders relaxed as she took a seat beside the door.

"I'm sorry you had to travel down from Poughkeepsie. I could have sent the packet to you via Federal Express," Thomas said.

"You'd mentioned you were sending the documents that required my signature. However, I'd also like copies of Kyle's complete HR file, like his employment contract and insurance forms." Jessie's gut clenched at the memory of the shocking Barclays employment agreement. Kyle had hidden it from her, and she'd found it inside the pocket of the blazer she was taking to the dry cleaners. "Both Hal and I are attorneys, and we'd like to make sure everything is in order before I sign the papers."

"These documents might provide background for our investigation, so could you please make a duplicate set for me if Jessie consents?" Ebony asked.

Jessie consented. Although she didn't understand the connection between the documents and Kyle's killer, she suspected Ebony must have a lead. Otherwise, she wouldn't have made the request.

"No problem. I understand. We want to ensure the same thing." Thomas dialed her phone and asked her assistant to make copies of the file.

"If I might ask," Jessie said. "When did you first know about the life insurance change of the beneficiary?"

"What change of beneficiary?" Ebony blurted out.

"I'm sorry, Detective. I thought you knew. Kyle added Olivia Vargas as his co-beneficiary with his daughter, Lily. They share in a policy worth a million and a half dollars."

Ebony leaned forward in her chair. "Olivia Vargas stands to receive seven hundred and fifty thousand dollars?" She paused. "We have an ongoing murder investigation involving Kyle's drowning, and nobody thought this information might be important?"

Thomas shrugged. "We weren't aware of anything of the kind, Detective. If I had known—"

"But Jessie, you knew. Why didn't you mention this to me?" Ebony asked.

Jessie remained quiet for a few moments. Should her response be defensive or offensive? What were her priorities, her stake in the situation? Hands down, she owed a duty to herself, her child, and Kyle's family rather than to Ebony.

Jessie tried to be a good friend, an ally, but their relentless friction burdened her like a metal choker around her neck. With each altercation, the screw tightened, strangling her. She'd delivered the phone records and was trying to help, but Ebony wanted more. Always. Ebony's endless badgering wore thin, and Jessie needed to assert her independence.

"For one second, put yourself in my position. Kyle's death has created a stressful and complicated scenario for my family. I've been bombarded with information I never expected, and I'm coping with Kyle's drowning as best I can." Jessie paused, but once she spoke, she couldn't resist. "I resent your attitude and your insistence that I owe you anything just because you're a cop. Well, I'm an attorney and am entitled to withhold client information until the appropriate time. I would've told you about the insurance after gathering all the relevant facts and discussing them with Kyle's family." Jessie faced heated, and Hal's hold on her forearm warned her to stop. The HR Department wasn't the appropriate venue for airing her issues with Ebony.

"Ebony, we can discuss this later," Hal said. "I don't think we should impose on Ms. Thomas with our personal concerns. Returning to the topic, we'd like to know when Kyle changed the policy, and I'm sure you would, too."

Ebony's jaw tightened. She crossed one leg over the other and slipped her hands into her pockets.

Jessie thought they were past the arguing, the polarization, and the rivalry, but apparently not.

Nicole Thomas squirmed in her chair and cleared her throat. "About two months ago, Kyle and I spoke, and he mentioned he was getting married in the new year and wanted to review the health and life insurance forms. He didn't seem to be in a hurry since the wedding wasn't until the spring. Then, about a month ago, I received the completed paperwork and transmitted them to be processed. I didn't know the contents until just prior to my conversation with Ms. Martin last week."

"Kyle named Olivia Vargas on both policies?" Jessie asked.

"Yes, the health insurance, life insurance, and his 401K. Since he joined the staff a year ago, the 401K has accumulated little value, but Ms. Vargas shares the account with his daughter."

"Has Ms. Vargas been in touch with you?" Hal asked.

"Yes, Ms. Vargas contacted me about the benefits last week. Performing our annual health insurance review has left me swamped, and I haven't sent the paperwork to her yet." Thomas sighed in exasperation and gestured toward the cartons on the floor next to her desk. "My assistant director is out on maternity leave, so we're scrambling for help in preparing our projections for the coming year. We have over twelve hundred employees, and it's a nightmare."

Hal whistled. "That's quite an organization."

"It's a massive undertaking to operate a facility of this magnitude. As senior vice president of business ops, Kyle helped coordinate all of the departments. He did a terrific job and left tremendous shoes to fill."

There was a knock on the door, and the receptionist entered the room, handed two stacks of manila envelopes to her boss, and disappeared. Thomas distributed them to Jessie and Ebony. "I wish there was more we could do. Can you please let us know when the funeral is being held? Our management and staff have expressed their desire to pay their respects to Kyle's family and you, of course."

This was the first time Jessie considered the immensity of Kyle's new position. He'd gone from managing an antiquated three thousand-seat convention center in Poughkeepsie to operating the half-billion-dollar, nineteen thousand-seat home of the NBA and WNBA. Perhaps she hadn't understood his daily pressures, but Kyle should've been more candid with her about his life.

Another tap on the door caused Thomas to spring to her feet. Jessie, Hal, and Ebony's attention shifted toward the doorway and the visitor.

A slender, gray-haired man dressed in a tailored blue pinstripe suit entered the office. Jessie immediately recognized Kyle's boss and mentor, Barry Levy.

"Nicole, please sit down," Levy said as he approached Jessie. He clasped Jessie's hands in both of his. They were soft and welcoming. "Jessie, I heard you were in the building and wanted to give you my condolences in person. When you're finished with Nicole, could you please stop by my office?"

"I believe we're finished here, Mr. Levy. Ms. Martin, if you have more questions, please contact me. Again, our thoughts and prayers are with you."

"Ms. Thomas, can we impose upon you to postpone any action on the life insurance until after Jessie and I, and of course, Detective Jones, have reviewed the documents?" Hal asked.

Thomas glanced at her boss, who nodded. "Of course. Please keep in touch."

Chapter Forty-Seven

With its deep indigo carpet, tweed furnishings, and soft blue walls, Barry Levy's office was even more luxurious than the owner's skybox that Jessie recalled from the Streisand show. On the top floor of the facility, the office featured one glass wall offering a bird's-eye view of the arena, while another displayed a bank of flat screens monitoring the lobby, the ticket office, and the empty basketball court. Signed photos of Levy with the Nets, the Liberty, the Rolling Stones, Adele, Jay-Z and Beyoncé, and other entertainment and sports legends graced the walls above his ebony wood credenza. Below them, crystal awards naming Barclays as "Venue of the Year" glinted in the overhead lights.

Levy gestured toward the sofa, chairs, and coffee table next to the broad window, and Jessie, Hal, and Ebony followed him. Mercifully, the tension over the insurance beneficiary had dissipated momentarily, but its trace lingered in the air.

"Can I offer you some refreshments?" His staff had set a catered spread out on the black granite bar next to the couch.

They declined, and Jessie spoke. "Mr. Levy—"

Levy interrupted her. "Please call me Barry."

"Barry, I'd like to introduce my fiancé, Hal Samuels, and Detective Ebony Jones of the Poughkeepsie Police Department."

Levy shook hands with her companions. "Samuels? Are you related to the real estate investor Harold Samuels? We partnered with him on the construction of the Nets' new state-of-the-art training facility at Industry City."

"Yes, he's my father. I'm not affiliated with the firm, though." Hal tried to mask his discomfort at the mention of his estranged father's name, but Jessie noticed.

"Hal's a criminal court judge for Dutchess County," Jessie added.

"Impressive, just like your father. When we were developing the project, your father pitched us an old, rundown warehouse that used to produce Topps Baseball cards," Levy said. "At first, we were skeptical. After his firm prepared the architectural renderings, his creativity astounded us. We purchased the space and renovated it into a spectacular facility with practice courts, lounges, a theater, and an outdoor terrace. You'll have to ask your father to take you on a tour." Levy's gray eyes crinkled at the corner. "When you speak with him, please send my regards."

Hal smiled weakly. "I certainly will."

Hal had mentioned that his father had developed the Nets' practice center jointly with his ex-wife Erin's father. Blaming Hal's divorce for a lawsuit stemming from the project, Hal's father had sparked a family feud, alienating Hal from his mother and older brothers.

Levy clasped his hands and placed them in his lap as his smile softened and his shoulders drooped. "Jessie, I can't tell you how shocked we were to hear about Kyle's accident. I've known Kyle for ten years, ever since he was my intern at the Garden. Man, he loved the music business and knew more about the biz than any person I know." Levy flattened his tie sprinkled with the tiny white eagles on a navy background, the Barclays' logo. "He sacrificed a shining future at MSG when he moved upstate to Poughkeepsie for the job at the Mid-Hudson Civic Center. But, the things we do for love."

Jessie's cheeks warmed. Hal squeezed her hands, which had turned so icy she'd lost sensation in them.

"For years, I tried to convince Kyle to return to MSG, and then later to join me here when I opened the facility. He stubbornly refused, and despite my best efforts to entice him, he held off for a long time. I was thrilled when Kyle finally accepted the senior ops position. He mentioned you had a baby on the way, and he was ready to make a career change."

A twinge of guilt squeezed Jessie's heart.

"And then, when Kyle mentioned he was getting married, I was thrilled for you both. It wasn't until Nicole mentioned the life insurance policy that I noticed the change in his circumstances. Although I considered Kyle a friend, he was tight-lipped about his personal life. But he showed me pictures of your adorable daughter." Levy twisted the gold signet ring on his pinky. "I'm going to miss him." His voice choked.

Jessie couldn't bring herself to speak. She felt like crap, having misjudged Kyle's sacrifices and his intentions for accepting the Barclays' job. Jessie still wouldn't have abandoned her life, her job, and her family and moved to Brooklyn. However, they could've compromised if Kyle hadn't been such a jerk.

Hal would never have acted so selfishly. Not in a thousand lifetimes.

"We will all miss Kyle. We're going to do our best to make sure Lily knows what a terrific guy he was," Hal said.

Ebony had been sitting quietly, but she fidgeted in the club chair as though she desired to intercede in the conversation. Something was on her mind. "Barry, can you confirm whether Kyle spoke with you about Go-To Sportsbook's requesting introductions to your teams and entertainers? Did he mention someone named Augusto Vargas?"

Ebony's sharp detour about sports betting and Augusto Vargas caught Jessie off-guard. Wentworth's report noted that Augusto worked in business development for Go-To, but how did this relate to Kyle's drowning? Was Augusto a suspect in Kyle's demise? Had he pulled the plug on the kayak?

"Yes. Kyle did. I thought the request was impertinent. Even more so, now knowing the shared last name with Kyle's beneficiary. It's more than a coincidence. I'm assuming the two are related."

"Yes, they're siblings, and Ms. Vargas had accompanied Kyle kayaking on the Hudson at the time of the drowning," Ebony said. Her attention was laser-focused on Barry Levy.

"Kyle came to me about a month ago. He'd said Vargas had made overtures to him on behalf of Go-To Sportsbook. They sought access to our teams and acts to represent their franchise in creating original video content for their platforms. I told Kyle that the Barclays Center is a family brand, and it would be inappropriate for us to be associated with the betting or gaming industry. With the legalization of online betting, it's a growing business and could mean big bucks for the players and acts, but it's not in our lane."

"How did Kyle react?" Ebony asked.

"He didn't seem to care about the refusal. Kyle confided he disliked the idea, too, but thought it was worth mentioning." Levy rose and went to the window and gazed down on the empty basketball court several stories below. He spoke in a faraway voice, facing away from them. "Kyle struck me as being uncomfortable about the conversation. Like he was under pressure to present it. He loosened up once we agreed to reject the idea."

"Did Vargas ever submit a written proposal to you or Kyle?"

Levy turned to address them and straightened his shoulders. "No, there was nothing in writing. After our initial discussion, Kyle never mentioned the pitch again. We were planning next year's team and tour calendars, so we moved on to the business at hand." He approached Jessie, extending his hand to her. She rose from the sofa, recognizing the end of their meeting. "I'm glad I could see you today. Please give Kyle's family my regards, and if you ever want tickets to the arena, please let me know. You're part of the Barclays family." To emphasize his sincerity, he clasped Jessie's hand tightly, his ring digging into her moist palm.

The audience over, Hal, Jessie, and Ebony filed out of the office into the private elevator that would take them to the first floor. Jessie and Hal held hands in silence as an unnerving specter hovered over them all the way to the lobby.

Chapter Forty-Eight

The Manhattan-bound train chugged into the Croton Harmon station, blocking Ebony's view of the river and mountains from the platform. Zander's train was on time, and she spied him careening out of the last car, sucking on a straw attached to a white cup. A dental appointment had prevented him from joining her earlier at the Barclays Center, but he'd refused to miss out on their meeting at Go-To Sportsbook in White Plains.

She waved, and, catching his attention, he wove toward her through the crowd in slow motion, probably half-stoned on pain meds. Zander drank a pink smoothie, and a thin line of liquid dribbled into the stubble on his chin. When he smiled, only half of his face seemed to work.

"What the hell happened to you?" she asked.

"I had to have a cap repla-th on a molar, and the novocaine ha-th-n't worn off yet. I wouldn't feel a thing if I took a bullet in my cheek." His tongue wasn't functioning either.

Ebony took his words as an invitation and pinched his left cheek. Zander didn't flinch.

"Th-ee what I mean? It should wear off th-oon, and I'm looking forward to no more pain." He rubbed his jaw.

"I'm glad you made it. When we get into the car, I'll fill you in."

During the twenty-minute ride to White Plains, Ebony's banana yellow VW bobbed and weaved through the frenetic afternoon traffic. Ebony pressed her foot on the accelerator and darted in between two semi-tractor trailers, then scooted over into the far lane, bypassing a slower Cadillac.

There was no time to spare.

"Watch where you're going!" Zander yelled as she plunged back into the center lane, cutting off a school bus. A deep, annoyed horn blared. "Your driving sucks. It's why I don't let you drive our SUV. You'd kill us before we arrived anywhere."

Ebony scoffed, ignoring Zander's death grip on the door handle, and described the meetings with HR and Barry Levy and the insurance windfall awaiting Olivia Vargas. She reached behind her seat, making the car swerve as she handed him the envelope. "We may find the motive we were looking for when we examine these documents."

"Damn it, Eb. Keep both hands on the wheel and use your blinker. We'll look at them later, if we make it."

They turned off the highway and followed the driving app's directions to Go-To Sportsbook Betting, Inc. At the entrance of a sprawling industrial complex, Ebony pulled up to the business directory. Zander confirmed that Go-To was in Building C, Suite 104, in the far reaches of the development. They drove on.

The sun was setting, and the corrugated metal face of Building C seemed to emit a tangerine warmth from within. In the center of the building, as massive as a department store, they observed a sign on a black metal door denoting only Suite 104. Ebony and Zander parked, approached the door, pressed the buzzer, and waited.

"Can I help you?" a disembodied voice asked. A green light flashed above a security camera to the left of the door.

"We're here to see Sharif Hamedi. We're from the City of Poughkeepsie Police Department." Ebony and Zander flashed their badges at the camera, and the door lock clicked.

They followed a long empty hallway to the end, where they encountered a second black door. The name Go-To Sportsbook Betting, Inc. was engraved on a tiny brass plaque above a video doorbell. They rang the bell, flashed their badges again, and the door opened.

Ebony and Zander stepped from the industrial hallway into a gaming facility unlike any casino they'd ever seen. There were no colorful neon signs enticing gamers to place bets or comfy armchairs set before gigantic screens live streaming golf, basketball, baseball, horseracing, soccer, and odds boards while slot machines chimed in the background. No half-naked waitresses sashayed by to comp their drinks. The setup was closer to Wall Street than the Vegas Strip.

Along the perimeter of the sterile white room, men and women hunched over their keyboards at stark Ikea-like workstations, watching numbers flash on their multiple screens. The employees either spoke on phones, answered phones, or entered data into their desktop computers. Beneath the desks, garbage cans overflowed with fast food bags and water bottles, and paper towels, papers, and disinfectant wipes jammed the rolling baskets set on the cheap linoleum flooring. The walls were bare, and the only splurge in the office appeared to be the expensive ergonomic chairs supplied to the workers.

As far Ebony could see, the room connected to similar rooms in both directions. If Go-To occupied the entire building, the size of the operation and the amount of money gambled over the lines would be mind-blowing. She heard that for the Super Bowl alone, fifty million people had placed sixteen billion dollars worth of bets.

From the doorway on the right, a thirty-something man of Middle Eastern descent walked toward them. He was dressed casually in an oversized grey hoodie, jeans, and sneakers. "I'm Sharif Hamedi, president and CEO of Go-To. Detectives, how can I help you?" He scratched his dark, close-trimmed beard.

"We'd like to speak with you about one of your employees, Auggie Vargas. Is there someplace that's more private?" Ebony asked.

Zander massaged his jaw and winced. The anesthetic must be wearing off.

They followed Hamedi through seven identical rooms until they reached a glass conference area. Ebony and Zander joined Hamedi around the conference table, and their host leaned back in his chair and shut the door.

"We wanted to confirm that Augusto Vargas is an employee of Go-To Sports Betting. How long has Auggie worked for you?" Ebony asked.

"Is Auggie in any trouble? I hope not. He's a cool dude and a hard worker." Hamedi paused, momentarily distracted by the green neon numbers and letters on the black screens along the back wall. Then he continued. "Auggie jumped on board right at the beginning, so for about five years. He was right out of college and helped me launch this lean startup."

"Is Auggie a shareholder in the company?" Ebony asked.

"Go-To is a startup, so we offer stock options to our employees for their sweat equity. He's held several positions in our organization and has vested a stockpile of options, but I haven't checked whether he's redeemed them. He should because he'll get in for pennies on the dollar. If we're acquired, he could become rich."

Ebony had several college friends who'd hit pay dirt when their artificial intelligence and e-commerce incubators had been gobbled up by Google, iHeartMedia, and private equity firms. From them, she'd learned that to be an attractive acquisition, a tech startup needed to create a unique idea, get into an accelerator, obtain seed financing from venture capitalists, and skyrocket its valuation. Go-To Sportsbook was prettying itself up for a suitor.

"Your company seems to be doing well. Is it possible that Go-To could be sold soon?"

"We're in stealth mode. There's been interest from our sector, but we're up again the big boys like Caesars, DraftKings, and MGM," Hamedi said. "We're taking measures to diversify our business model to increase our gross margins."

Hamedi was acting coy, but Auggie's scheme would certainly tie in with Hamedi's expansion aspirations.

"Was Auggie involved in Go-To's diversification plans?" Ebony asked.

The heels of Hamedi's sneakers bounced in a nervous fury. "We've received our Series B funding, and Auggie was instrumental in our growth hacking. But our plans are proprietary."

Hamedi was growing cagey about giving them any details, and his tech-speak was getting on Ebony's nerves. Why couldn't these nerds speak English? She'd had enough of his gamesmanship.

"How about we tell you about Go-To's connection to a murder investigation? And about Auggie contacting our murder victim, Kyle Emory, to make a pitch to his boss at the Barclays Center? Specifically about introductions to their NBA and WNBA teams and the performers so Go-To could enlist them as influencers. Does that sound like proprietary information to you? Or does it sound like fraud? Maybe undue influence or contractual interference? Or how about when Barclays refused Auggie's overtures became a motive for murder?"

"Murder? Hold on a second. I had nothing to do with his idea or any murder. I never authorized Auggie to make the proposal and knew nothing until afterward. But he's chief of business development, an aggressive guy, and I rely upon him to make it rain. Like I said, he helped this business launch."

"Was Auggie under any pressure to perform? Was a prospective buyer forcing your diversification as a purchase contingency?"

"I don't know what you're talking about," Hamedi replied in a challenging tone.

The slick CEO appeared to be keeping things on the down low. However, pressure must be mounting on Hamedi and Auggie to produce, expand their slice of the pie, and return the investments to their VC investors. Go-To's financing wouldn't last forever, and with these vast offices, flocks of employees, truckloads of hardware and software, their start-up stash was being gambled away like the bets of their customers.

They were losing Hamedi's cooperation, and before he dismissed them, Ebony changed the course back to Augusto Vargas, inquiring about any recent changes in his personality.

"No. He's an unfiltered, high-energy person, although, during the past month, he's been more subdued. But we all have lots of shit going on, don't we?" Hamedi asked.

Some more than others, Ebony thought.

"What's your policy about an employee opening a betting account here?" Zander asked. "Is it possible?"

"Absolutely not," Hamedi said. "It's one of my cardinal rules. I don't want my employees indebted to Go-To. They can't shit where they eat. Plus, the New York State Gaming Commission regulates us. To maintain our license, we need to keep our house clean. However, that doesn't prevent our employees from gaming elsewhere, and I wouldn't know if they did."

"That's interesting," Ebony said. Auggie couldn't bet at Go-To, but he could wager on other websites. Or he could have opened an account under a different name.

Zander raised his eyebrows in mutual understanding. "I don't think we have any more questions. If we have any others, we'll be in touch," he said, handing Hamedi his card.

"Before we go, can you direct me to the restroom?" Ebony asked.

"It's down the hall in the second room on the right," Sharif replied.

* * *

On her way down the corridor, Ebony passed the executive offices, and Auggie's name appeared on the door marked "Business Development." The door was ajar, and since she was alone in the corridor, she slipped inside.

The sterile office contained only a white desk and chair, a credenza, and a video monitor on the wall displaying a constantly changing chart of numbers. A multi-screen desktop computer played sports videos to an empty room, and beside it sat piles of folders and binders. Ebony rifled through a stack of white folders containing correspondences, and when nothing drew her attention, she moved onto another pile. Again, there was nothing of interest.

She thought she heard footsteps in the hallway and froze, but it was the sound of her heart beating in her chest. Time was running out, and Ebony needed to get back to Hamedi before someone discovered her inside Auggie's office. But she wasn't finished. Not yet.

Ebony tried to open the center desk drawer, but it wouldn't budge. She tugged on it again, and, after the third try, it creaked open. Inside, a printout of the upcoming Barclays schedule lay on top of other papers. A handwritten note from Auggie to Hamedi was clipped to the packet.

"S: What do you think? How about some star power for Go-To? My brother-in-law works there. Think about what the Mannings did for Caesars. Could work for us. A"

"A: Hit him up. Projections for the fourth quarter are weak. If we don't raise cash soon, we're fucked. Get it done. If you can't, we need to talk. S"

Ebony snapped photos of the documents and notes, and slid the drawer shut. She popped her head out of the doorway and, discovering the hallway clear, slipped out of the office and returned to the conference area.

The CEO guided them back through the gambling complex to the entry room. "Hey, you never mentioned whether Auggie is a murder suspect?"

"Sorry, Mr. Hamedi. We're in stealth mode," Ebony said.

In her mind, Sharif had morphed from a sleazy bookie into an outright thief and liar. He had known about Auggie's scheme, the company was financially stressed, and Auggie's job was on the line. She'd caught the Go-To boys in a web of lies, but were they a motive for murder?

Chapter Forty-Nine

Ebony drove homeward on the Taconic State Parkway, a scenic north-south route designed by Franklin Delano Roosevelt in 1925. Completed in 1965, the picturesque highway meandered through the Hudson Valley's hills and farms, midway between the Hudson River and the Connecticut and Massachusetts state lines. Concentrating on the rush hour traffic, she wasn't paying attention to Zander's fiddling with the car radio.

He'd switched from her indie rock station to NPR, where a nationally syndicated news program was ending, and a banjo piece reminiscent of the *Deliverance* movie theme came on the air.

"Listen, it's *The Hudson Outsider* show. Let's see if Cody Shaw knows what he's talking about this week," Zander said, cranking up the volume.

"Where do they broadcast from?"

"Beacon, why?"

The timing couldn't have been better if Ebony had planned it. The Cold Spring exit off of the Taconic was approaching, and it would be a quick detour up the river to Beacon. "We have one more stop before we go home."

"Got it. We should be there before Cody signs off the air," Zander said.

Cody's laid-back hipster voice slithered out of the car speakers as they veered onto the next exit and followed the road to Beacon. The public radio station, WMMC, was located downtown in a converted brick Victorian house. Modern white clapboard additions sprouted from each side of the house like unwieldy oblong wings.

For the third time today, they rang a video doorbell, flashed their shields, and a door lock buzzed. They entered the main parlor, which the station owners had converted into the reception area decorated with gold records, music festival posters, and memorabilia. The reception desk was empty, and behind it, a locked frosted glass door led to the broadcast studios. Cody's mellow tones rained on them from the circular speakers mounted into the ceiling.

The glass door opened, and a young woman entered the reception area. Ebony's heart squeezed. The woman possessed the identical doe eyes, black curly hair, crooked mouth, and creamy complexion as Kyle Emory. She could've been Kyle Emory's female doppelgänger except she had multiple piercings along her ears and eyebrows.

Ebony shook off the prickle on the back of her neck. It felt like she'd entered a time warp, peeking into the past at Kyle or into the future at Lily as a grown woman.

"Ebony, what are you doing here?" the apparition asked.

Ebony examined the person again. Then she remembered. "Dani? You gave me a fright. I thought I'd seen a ghost." She winced at her insensitivity. "I'm sorry about your brother." She approached Danielle Emory, Kyle's younger sister and the twin to their brother, Peter, and gathered her into a hug.

"Thanks. I keep forgetting how much I resemble Kyle. These days, I can see the pain on my parents' faces, and it only makes matters worst." Dani's looked down at her black suede sneakers.

Ebony introduced Zander, who also expressed his condolences. "Dani and I have shared a few meals and bottles of wine at Jessie and Kyle's house, but that was a while ago." Ebony paused. "I don't know if Jessie or your folks mentioned it, but we're assigned to Kyle's case. We stopped by to interview Cody, but what are you doing here? I thought you worked in a sound recording studio in White Plains?"

"This is my side gig. Cody twisted my arm to help him out with this show and his podcast." Dani brushed a stray curl away from her round face. "Hey, what does Cody have to do with Kyle's drowning?"

"We're sorry, but we can't go into specifics. We have questions for him, that's all," Ebony said. She hated to be evasive with a member of Kyle's family, but maybe she'd have more answers after their conversation with Cody.

"He'll be signing off in a few minutes. You can wait here or come in and check out the studio."

"Sure," Zander said, "let's see the studio."

Zander's man-crush on Cody already annoyed her, but the level of his man-love would blow through the roof after observing Cody on the air.

Dani led them along a short hallway flanked by the large picture windows of the deserted studios. She ticked them off as they passed by. "That's the news department, the AM studio, one FM studio, and the production studios. They mostly rebroadcast satellite transmissions these days. Cody's show is one of the few remaining live programs." Sadness registered in her voice at the prospect of the dying art form. "Here we are."

A red *On Air* light flashed in the studio window where Cody was broadcasting, prohibiting their entry inside. The studio was a large boxy room, with an *L*-shaped counter dominating the space. Speakers and a video screen playing cable news hung from the walls covered in black spongy honeycomb material designed to absorb the sound. The counter was crammed with adjustable metal microphone booms, computers, a soundboard with glowing dials and levers, and multiple screens. The state-of-the-art tech reminded Ebony of the command center inside the communications vehicle they'd used during a recent homicide investigation.

Ebony glanced at Zander, and his face beamed with the excitement of a kid on Christmas morning. She sighed and shook her head, resigned to seizing control of this interview.

Cody stood behind the console wearing headphones, watching the video monitors, and talking into a microphone. He glanced at the wall clock, which read six o'clock, and turned a knob on the soundboard.

"See ya next week," he said, "and always let the North Star guide you home." His voice faded away as his hillbilly theme song grew louder. The *On Air* light flicked off, and Cody removed the headphones.

Dani pushed open the studio door and poked her head inside. "You've got company," she said, gesturing toward Ebony and Zander. The background music ended, followed by a taped program featuring Pete Seeger's Sloop Clearwater and its educational programs protecting the Hudson River ecosystem.

"Thanks, babe." Cody clasped Zander's hand and they bumped shoulders. "Dude. This is a surprise. How's the camping light working out?"

Zander's face flushed, and words seemed to fail him.

Cody turned to Ebony. "Detective, how are you doing?" He rolled down the sleeves of his plaid flannel shirt and shook out his mane.

Ebony cleared her throat. "Cody, do you have a few minutes? We have questions about your relationship with Kyle Emory."

"Sure enough. Let's go into the break room. I could use a cup of caffeine."

The break room comprised the dwelling's former kitchen, and from the avocado and gold Formica countertops, the galley dated back to the 1980s. Cody poured four ceramic mugs of coffee, and the group settled into chairs around the scarred wooden table, which were of more recent flea market vintage.

"Dani, are you sure you want to take part in this conversation? I don't want to make you uncomfortable," Ebony said.

"If Cody has no problem with me staying, I'm good." She shook her arm, causing a leather bracelet with a silver clasp to slide to her wrist. It was the one Jessie had described as a gift to Kyle.

"No worries. How can I help?" Cody slung his arm over the back of his chair and crossed one leg over his knee in a laid-back style.

Ebony and Zander had a job to do, and they couldn't allow Dani's presence to censor their investigation. They had evidence of Cody's violent threat against Kyle, his access to the kayak, and his relationship with Olivia. Until they had answers, Cody was a person of interest in Kyle's drowning. His vibe was chill and carefree, but killers, especially psychopaths, were masters of disguise. Cody was ambitious, athletic, and capable of causing bodily harm or death.

Ebony dove right in. "What is your relationship with Olivia Vargas? We understand you're still married, but are you two still romantically involved?"

"Hell, no. Livvie and I have been friends since we were kids. Everybody expected us to get married, so we did. And it didn't work."

"But are you still involved?"

"Just as friends. Like I said, we grew up together."

Dani pursed her lips.

"Why don't we believe you, Cody?"

"Beats me, but it's the truth." He looked toward Dani as though seeking her forgiveness. "I swear. It's over with Livvie."

"Someone tampered with Kyle's kayak before he set off at Kaal Rock Park. You had access to the kayak during the evening before he set out, and we have Kyle's phone records. Two days before his death, you sent him a text. A very threatening text telling him to mind his own business about your relationship with Olivia."

Dani squirmed in her chair as she glared at Cody. "What are they talking about?"

"What? Can you show me the text, please?"

They showed Cody the text.

Quit talking shit about me to her. She's a big girl and can make up her own mind. It's none of your business who she hangs out with. Leave us alone, or you'll regret it. I mean it.

Dani leaned over Cody's shoulder as he read the message, and then he turned to her. "I didn't want to upset you, but Kyle called me. He'd found out about us, and I know how protective you are of our privacy."

"Not that it's anyone's business but ours," Dani said. "I resent when other people stick their noses where they don't belong."

"Livvie's the opposite. Everything is out in the public. And when she's pissed off, she can be vindictive, and we're going through a hassle right now over our property settlement. So she must've snitched to Kyle about our relationship and my rough times with drugs, drinking, and partying. When I was growing up, I acted young and stupid, but Carlos straightened me out. Don't we all make mistakes, man?" Cody conspiratorially winked at Zander. "Kyle was furious, and he laid into me about Dani. He accused me of being Peter Pan. Said I wasn't good enough for his sister and to leave her alone."

"How did you respond to Kyle?" Zander asked.

"I let him blow off steam and didn't react. Later, I thought about it, got ticked, and wrote the text. It was stupid. I should've left it alone."

"Did Kyle call you or come see you?" Ebony asked.

Cody shook his head. "I didn't speak with him again until the night before the trip. Neither of us brought up the conversation. Everything was cool." He clasped Dani's hand and brought it to his lips. "Babe, I'm sorry. I should've mentioned it, but I swear to you, I had nothing to do with your brother's death."

"What about your access to the kayak? The plug was missing, and you had the opportunity to remove it," Ebony said.

"First, we all had access to the kayaks at White Oaks. Me, Auggie, Kyle, Max, Livvie, and Carlos set them into the car rack the night before their trip. I'd loaned Kyle my SportsPro camera suction mount, which he, Auggie, and I installed. Everyone had their hands on the kayaks."

"Do you have any idea why they switched boats? Kyle taking the red one and Olivia taking the blue?"

"No idea," Cody said with a shrug. "And second, I'd never mess with anyone's gear. You've got to respect the equipment, and it will respect you. Finally, about the plug, well, a missing plug alone wouldn't sink a kayak."

Ebony studied him. Cody caught her gaze and seized it in a test of wills. He tossed his head back, leaned back in his chair, and crossed his arms across his broad chest. Cody Shaw was an expert in the field. He'd kayaked white water rapids, waterfalls, and open sea expeditions, and he knew the equipment better than anyone. But was he covering his ass or speaking the truth?

"What about the wedding ring? You're still wearing it," Zander said.

"I've developed arthritis in my hands, and they're so swollen, I can't remove the damn thing. Next week, I'm going to a hand specialist to have the ring cut off before it permanently damages my circulation." Cody held up his swollen left hand and wiggled the finger where the black ring cut into his flesh, irritating his skin. "I want to make sure this irreplaceable hardware isn't ruined."

She wondered whether he was referring to the ring or his digit.

"Did Auggie ever mention anything to you about asking Kyle for a favor?"

Cody sipped on his coffee. "What kind of favor?"

"Work-related," Zander said dryly.

"No. But he didn't seem as keen on Kyle as he'd been when Livvie and Kyle first met."

"What do you mean?"

"I couldn't put my finger on it, but there was tension between them." Cody twisted his head as though trying to recollect something. "I don't know if this is related, but Auggie had promised to help me raise the capital to purchase Livvie's share in the business. He's going to loan me the dough to buy her shares so I can keep my majority ownership of Outfitters. Until I resolve this mess with her, I'm overextended."

The recurrent theme of Auggie's financial desperation recycled throughout every conversation. Was it possible Auggie needed the Go-To sales commissions for the Hudson Outfitter stock purchase rather than for a gambling debt? But Kyle stood in his way? Auggie wouldn't directly benefit from Kyle's death unless the sister and brother had conspired against Cody. By purchasing Olivia's shares, Auggie could become an equal partner with Cody. Or they could force Cody to sell out to them. Were Olivia and Auggie out to swindle Cody, too?

"Do you know whether Olivia or Auggie informed Kyle about your marriage to Olivia?"

"I have absolutely no idea, but it was old news. There's nothing worth talking about. It was long over." Cody massaged his tender red finger. "I get how this looks, but it's over with Livvie. She married Raul Esperanza, but I'm a different guy now. I'm Cody Shaw."

The rosy hue in Dani's cheeks had paled, but she leaned over and kissed him. "Cody, I know who you are and that you wouldn't hurt anyone. I wish you'd told me the truth about Kyle."

"I was going to, but Kyle died. As far as I was concerned, our disagreement died with him."

"We're going to need you to come to Poughkeepsie to make a formal statement about your relationship with Olivia, Auggie, the kayak, and the message to Kyle."

With one hand, Cody knotted the fingers with Dani's and placed them over his heart. Signaling their solidarity, Dani lovingly combed his long, shiny hair. "I want to make a clean sweep so Dani and I can move on. Is tomorrow soon enough?"

Cody and Dani were of one heart and mind, indivisible by Olivia Vargas.

Chapter Fifty

Ebony's hand gripped the stick shift of her VW bug. Deep in thought, she upshifted into fourth gear, and the motor whined as they sped homeward along the Taconic Parkway. It was unusual for her to misread a suspect, but she had with Cody Shaw. The worst part was that Zander's admiration of Cody had been justified. Or was it? Shaw seemed to have an answer to every question they'd thrown at him, but she believed there was still a five percent chance that he'd lied to them. She wasn't striking him from the list until she'd been completely convinced of his innocence.

Shaw had reminded her of something they'd overlooked—the SportsPro camera case in the barn. Kyle had attached the camera to the front deck of the red kayak, but no one found it when they'd fished the boat from the river. The device and mount were drowned in the storm, like Kyle. Stuck in the river's muddy surface or washed out to sea.

"Do you know anything about SportsPros?" she asked.

"So, you were wrong about Shaw, weren't you?"

Zander was baiting her, tempting her to wipe the smugness from his face by clocking ninety on her speedometer. Her foot pressed the gas pedal but then eased up.

"Concentrate, will you? SportsPros. Is there any way to store the photos or videos in the cloud?"

"I don't see why not. Let me check." Zander extracted his phone from his pocket and searched the web. "There's an app you can download onto your phone. The upload directions are easy, but you must have a SportsPro subscription. Even if Kyle had the app and uploaded his content into it, his phone is gone."

"But the cloud isn't. It's a long shot, but we know someone who has access to his cloud."

"Do you think Jessie will cooperate with us after the incident at Barclays? You slammed her pretty hard."

Ebony's ears warmed at her unbridled rudeness to Jessie in Nicole Thomas' office. Sometimes, Jessie got under her skin and made her crazy. Neither jealousy nor hatred sparked these feelings; rather, it was her frustration with Jessie's stubborn independence and lack of concern for her own safety. "Jessie acted okay when we met with Levy… There's only one way to find out."

Zander snorted. "Right."

Despite everything, Jessie's phone number remained on Ebony's speed dial. Number three on her favorites, after Carly and her parents, and before Drew. Ebony pressed the button, and the phone's ringing blasted over the car's speakers.

Brring. Brring. Brring. The phone defaulted to voicemail. Ebony tried again with the same result. She wouldn't be surprised if Jessie never spoke to her again.

"Give me her number. Maybe she'll speak to me."

Zander snatched her phone and, while he punched the numbers into his cell, Ebony's phone rang, and he answered it.

"It must be urgent if you're calling me." The wintry timbre of Jessie's voice resonated throughout the VW's cabin. "I couldn't answer the phone before. I was busy with Lily. What do you want?"

The time was ripe to apologize. Not just for the sake of the investigation but because of her stupidity. Jessie was entitled to her privacy, especially during this period of grief. If Ebony didn't make the overtures now, at this moment, she might forever sever the fragile ties binding them.

She spoke before she could change her mind. "Jessie, I'm sorry about the way I spoke to you in Thomas's office. I was out of line. You're going through a difficult time, and I've been selfish and inconsiderate. I acted like

292

an asshole, and I hope you'll forgive me."

The profound sense of loss penetrated Ebony's core, weakening her control over the steering wheel. If she lost Jessie for good, she'd lose part of herself—the part originating in her childhood, which had shaped her into who she was today. Jessie had encouraged her to take risks and always be true to herself. These traits made her a good cop, a dutiful sister, a caring daughter, and a best friend.

Jessie had also taught her about kindness. Lately, Ebony had been a bully to Jessie, but she wanted Jessie in her life. Now more than ever. She needed Jessie's spark, love, and loyalty. And she prayed her best friend accepted her plea for forgiveness.

A long, static silence infiltrated the line. Zander mimed a "thumbs up" as they waited for a response.

Finally, Jessie sniffled. "I appreciate your apology, but we need to have a longer conversation about our friendship. For now, I'll call a truce." She paused and blew her nose. "I know you called for another reason."

"Can you meet us at the station now?"

"We're putting Lily to bed. Why don't you and Zander stop by in a half-hour? That would work for us."

"Okay. We'll see you then, and thanks."

"See you shortly." Jessie hung up.

"That went well," Zander said awkwardly. His stomach growled, and he coughed to disguise the racket. "With the dental appointment, I haven't eaten all day. Since we have time to kill, let's grab some grub."

"Thinking with your stomach, huh?" Ebony chuckled.

They stopped at a red light on Route 9 in Wappingers Falls, a few miles from the station. The seductive billboards of the fast-food joints beckoned them to stop for a bite to eat. When the light changed to green, Ebony pulled into a drive-through burger joint.

A half-hour later, Ebony and Zander exited the yellow VW onto Jessie's gravel driveway. It was seven-thirty, and the quiet residential neighborhood was pitch dark except for the old-fashioned street lamps dotting the street. Jessie's front porch lamp directed its welcoming glow over the leaf-covered

293

sidewalk, and soft lights streamed from the downstairs windows.

The cool air smelled sweet from damp dirt and withering hydrangeas and hostas. An undertone of wood-smoked hickory filled Ebony's nostrils. Soon the pumpkins and mums would be gone, and the winter holidays would arrive. Time was flying by, and they still hadn't identified Kyle's killer.

Their case was like the plum tree rotting in Jessie's front yard. Like Kyle, its trunk and branches had been vital and strong, but now the limbs were thin and bare. Without a substantial lead, their case would be as dead and cold as the decaying old tree.

If they were lucky, one more clue could lie within Jessie's homey cottage on Platt Street. A lead that could break Kyle's case wide open. Otherwise, their case was as dead as the dried leaves crunching beneath their shoes.

* * *

Jessie watched Ebony and Zander marching up the walk, and she rushed to open the front door before the bell woke Lily. Their bent postures and wrinkled foreheads foreshadowed more bad news.

"Hi. Come on into the kitchen. I'll open a Pinot Noir," she said. Her throat felt tight. "Or a beer?"

Dressed in sweats and socks, Hal leaned against the kitchen counter and opened the fridge. He grabbed two beers and handed Zander a frosty IPA. Then he flicked his head at Jessie, signaling it was time to come clean to their guests.

Jessie's clammy fingers slipped as she wrangled two wine glasses to set on the table. Her pulse thrummed in her ears, rivaling the thunderous pop of the wine cork being expelled from the green bottle. Once she fessed up, anger, as fiery red as the Merlot in the bottle, would replace their sour expressions. Bracing herself, she selected the chair beside Hal. The moment of reckoning had arrived.

"Before you get started—," Jessie said, her trembling hands pouring generous portions of wine into each glass. Ebony grabbed her glass and took a protracted gulp. "I owe you an apology, too. I haven't been totally honest with you about my activities or the information I've obtained." She gathered the stack of Kyle's high school yearbooks from the counter and set them before Ebony. Her canvas tote bag sat at her feet on the tile floor. "Early on, you'd implied that Kyle could have committed suicide…."

"Jessie," Ebony interrupted.

"Here's evidence you're wrong." Jessie opened to the swim team pages. "When Kyle was a kid, he loved the water and was captain of his high school swim team, a state champion swimmer, and a lifeguard. There's no way he would have killed himself in the water."

While Ebony and Zander thumbed through the books, Jessie slid a manila folder across the table.

"Also, I'd contacted Carey Wentworth to prepare a background report on Olivia Vargas. Here's a copy for you. I'm sure you've performed your own, but having this one might help. As you know, Carey's a wizard in digging up secrets."

Ebony's intense gaze flicked up from the team photos, and she remained silent. Hal sipped on his beer and leaned back in his chair, listening, unfazed. Zander's attention lingered on the yearbooks, clearly avoiding the storm brewing between Jessie and Ebony.

"Finally, my brother, Ethan, put me in touch with Merritt Hanson, a shipwright who constructs custom kayaks in Esopus. I met with Merritt, and he told me that by itself, it was highly improbable the missing plug caused Kyle's kayak to sink. There must have been other reasons for him to capsize, like the thunderstorm. His expert opinion is inside the folder, too."

Jessie further recounted her trip to Kyle's apartment, her confrontation with Olivia, and the missing deed to Kyle's condo. "While I was there, I retrieved his computer. I've written the password on top. Here, I haven't opened it or booted it up." She retrieved the laptop from her bag and handed it to Ebony.

Ebony drained her wineglass and shifted in her chair, grimacing. It was difficult to read whether Ebony had winced in pain or in disgust with her. Most likely, a combination of the two.

"You've been busy," Ebony said in a sarcastic, controlled tone. "It would have been nice—"

"Ladies, this is a challenging situation, so let's get practical." Hal straightened up in his chair. "I'm giving you advice from my years in the DA's office. I may be restating the obvious, but every case hinges upon the evidence and the credibility of the witnesses. It's whether you can convince the jury that the defendant has violated the law pertinent to a specific crime. You must meet the elements of a crime to win a conviction. And you have to ensure the evidence was collected legally. There can be no fruits of the poisonous tree."

Hal paused, rubbing the stubble on his chin. "I've never handled an aquatic homicide, but they're tricky, and forensics and DNA will only accomplish so much. It's going to take every shred of evidence to identify the culprit and succeed. By pooling your talents and resources, the DA will have more evidence to mount her prosecution. But you have to follow the rules for evidence collection, and the evidence must be persuasive beyond a reasonable doubt." He leaned forward with his elbows on the table. "I don't mean to lecture, but sometimes it helps to be reminded of the legal parameters of the system. And from the judicial perspective, if this case appears on my docket, I'll recuse myself. I'm too involved in the case." He glanced at Jessie and Ebony. Zander's head remained buried in the yearbook. "Regardless, you need to put aside your disagreements and make it as easy as possible for the judge and jury to convict the suspect."

Hal had given them a polite dressing down. It was up to Ebony to make the next move.

Ebony flipped her empty glass upside down and set it on the table. "I guess there's only one choice. We want to nail this sucker, whoever they are." She launched into a summary of their interviews with the witnesses, their alibis, the autopsy results, and the video camera.

Jessie couldn't fathom what she was hearing. The autopsy indicated that Kyle's body had been beaten black and blue. "You're telling us Kyle was attacked before he drowned? When? By who?"

"We're not sure. It's possible the injuries were sustained during the storm.

That's why we're interested in the lost SportsPro camera that was attached to Kyle's kayak. It may provide some answers." Ebony paused. "When you accessed his text messages through the cloud, did you notice whether he'd uploaded any photos or videos from the day of the accident?"

"I can't say I did, although it's easy to check on my laptop. It's in the den," Jessie replied. "Or on Kyle's."

"Hold on, Jess. Let's use yours so we can preserve the chain of custody on Kyle's. There could be valuable information, and we don't want to taint it," Hal said.

Jessie smiled in acknowledgment.

"Good. Pulaski and I will grab yours," Hal said, laying a hand on Zander's shoulder. "Let's give the ladies a minute."

"Yes, sir. I mean, Your Honor," Zander replied.

Hal led Zander toward the den door at the far end of the hallway, leaving Ebony and Jessie alone in the kitchen.

Jessie and Ebony stared at each other. For the first time in ages, Jessie saw her best friend, Ebony Jones, standing before her. Not Detective Ebony Jones. Not an accuser. Or a skeptic or a naysayer. Only her best friend. Light-heartedness spread throughout her, relieving the fear, guilt, and insecurity she'd carried for so long. Now, the joy of reconciliation, possibility, and hope bubbled within her, helping her regain a part of herself, too. The part reserved for Ebony.

"Well, aren't we the assholes," Ebony said.

"Yep, we are. We're too much alike. Too stubborn. Too ambitious. Too proud and...."

"Too damn smart for our own good." Ebony's eyes grew watery, as did Jessie's. The long-awaited state of peace between them simmered with the promise of endless talks, apologies, and flowing tears.

"Come here," Jessie said. They fell into each other's arms.

"I'm sorry," they murmured in unison between the sniffles. They separated as Hal and Zander reentered the kitchen. Jessie wiped her damp face on her shirt sleeve, and Ebony pivoted her face away to hide the red streaks on her cheeks.

"Are we ready to watch home movies?" Hal asked, propping the laptop on the kitchen table as the group gathered around.

Jessie signed into her joint iCloud with Kyle, her heart pounding in anticipation as the tiny rainbow wheel churned. The icons of her computer applications populated the white screen, but not one for SportsPro.

She clicked on the photos folder, and, within seconds, thousands of pictures appeared, the most recent being last weekend of Lily with her parents at the petting zoo. Then, as if by magic, Kyle's kayaking pictures materialized. Ten in all. There were photos of Kyle, Lily, and Olivia posing on the lawn at Kaal Rock Park, a group photo of the Vargas family enjoying snacks, and Olivia baring a shoulder as she loaded the blue kayak into the river. Others featured Olivia grinning and paddling toward the Mid-Hudson Bridge, a shot of the eastern shoreline from the middle of the Hudson, and another view facing south over the water. In the foreground of the last photo, a SportsPro was mounted to the kayak's front deck, clearly in sight. However, no recent videos had been added to the library.

"Please enlarge the front deck just past the bungee cords," Zander requested, pointing at the screen. "There, beyond the SportsPro, you can see the drain plug is missing."

Jessie enlarged the picture, revealing the tiny, round black hole close to the tip of the red kayak's bow. "Even if it was gone, Hanson's report states the missing plug wasn't the cause of the drowning."

"Can you email these to me and print them out? They could be helpful," Zander asked. "What about the SportsPro subscription?"

She pushed the button, sending the request to the printer in the den. "I have another idea. Do you have the instructions for downloading media from the camera?"

Zander pulled up the camera's website and read the instructions aloud. "We're looking in the wrong place. Kyle didn't upload his SportsPro videos to the iCloud. He'd uploaded them to his SportsPro subscription account. They're on a different cloud server. Here, shove over."

"Sure." Jessie slid aside, allowing Zander to take her place. His fingers flew across the keyboard, locating the application, downloading it onto her laptop, and reaching the account sign-in page.

"Password?" he asked.

Within the password keeper on Jessie's phone, she typed in SportsPro. Kyle's password popped up. *Lilybean0905&*. Lily's birthdate. Jessie repeated the letters and digits aloud while Zander typed them in.

Zander posed his fingers over the "enter" button. "Ready?" Four sets of steady eyes watched the computer screen.

Jessie dug her fingernails into Hal's arm, eager to open the application's library. What would they find? Would it reveal Kyle's killer?

Before she could stop herself, she heard her voice scream, "Stop!"

Chapter Fifty-One

Jessie shut the front door behind Ebony and Zander, and through the sidelights, she tracked Ebony's car racing away down the street. Hal's warm hands encircled her waist, spun her around, and pulled her close. She tucked her head against his vintage Rolling Stones sweatshirt, listening to the reassuring beat of his heart.

"I understand this is difficult. Who knows what we'll find on the camera, so I want you to be prepared. It could get ugly," he said.

"That's not the reason I stopped Zander." Jessie jerked her head backward and gazed into Hal's eyes. "If we're undertaking this step, we should adhere to the legal procedures under the supervision of the DA and the chief at the police station. As you suggested, we might uncover crucial evidence, and I wanted to preserve the chain of custody of the files. We don't want any accusations of evidence tampering to arise."

Jessie's mind had switched into criminal defense attorney mode. She foresaw the tricks her wily brethren could employ to dismiss murder charges like the ones her former-nemesis-turned-law-partner, Jeremy Kaplan, had played on her during Butterfield's murder trial. She refused to allow the past to repeat itself, especially with Kyle's investigation at stake.

And although Jessie would never admit it, a tiny part of her required time to prepare for the potential horror show embedded within the camera's files.

"I'm surprised Ebony and Zander didn't consider the consequences. But they were amenable to meeting tomorrow for the big reveal." He pinched a fluff of lint from Jessie's hair and tucked a stray curl behind her ear. "I'm embarrassed, though. I'd only considered preserving the integrity of the hardware and software, but not the cloud. The chase blinded us, but it's fortunate you were thinking clearly. I must be getting soft in the head, or it's your effect on me, Ms. Martin?"

"Good thing you're no longer the DA." Jessie yawned. "It's been a long day, and my mind has melted. Let's go upstairs and relax, maybe watch a movie, or...."

"Or?" He cocked his head and raised an eyebrow.

"Read a book?" Jessie knotted her fingers in Hal's, and they climbed the stairs to the bedroom.

* * *

At noon the next day, Jessie arrived at the police station to meet Ebony and Zander to review Kyle's SportsPro files. "Hey," she said to Ebony, juggling a tote bag jammed with her computer and files. "Hal and the DA should be here shortly. They'll join us during their lunchtime recesses."

"Good. The chief, too. Come on, follow me." Ebony nudged open the greasy glass door to the central station with her shoulder and led Jessie to the interrogation room where they'd installed the murder board. "Are you nervous?"

"I wasn't until you mentioned it. And until I saw your handiwork on the whiteboard."

Photos of Kyle, Olivia, and two Hispanic men identified as Augusto Vargas and Carlos Vargas, and another brawny fellow named Raul Esperanza, aka Cody Shaw, had been taped to the board. Jessie recognized the names from Wentworth's report and their previous discussions. The wall was a hodgepodge of evidence—photos of the kayaks, the Mid-Hudson Bridge, the crime scene, maps of the Hudson River, crime scene sketches, aerial photographs, and Kyle's phone logs and text messages.

"Wait here. We'll be with you in a moment," Ebony said. "You'll be okay, right?"

Jessie nodded. The icy fingers of death extended to her, prickling her spine. She'd been in this situation before with different crimes and suspects, but with the identical goal of catching a ruthless killer. This time, the victim was someone she'd loved.

She diverted her eyes from the photos of Kyle, bloated and floating in Wallkill Creek, and lying prone on a stainless steel slab in the morgue. Her limbs shuddered at the proof that Kyle was undeniably dead. The truth was hard to deny when it was staring at her in full color.

Jessie didn't want to remember Kyle as a corpse, only full of life. Instead, she focused on his victim photo, which she recognized from his dresser. He looked handsome in his beige sports jacket, navy slacks, and an open-collared sports shirt. Olivia must have selected a happy memory from their brief life together, as evidenced by the sliver of her bare shoulders and long dark hair intruding into the scene. None of Kyle's pictures, either in death or life, were going to ruffle her. Jessie had more important issues on her mind.

Jessie plugged in her computer, arranged the envelope bearing the Barclays logo next to her keyboard, and waited in the empty room. Ten minutes later, Ebony, Zander, Chief Shepardson, Cindie Tarrico, and Hal arrived. A photographer and stenographer shuffled inside, and the steno situated her computer on the table.

"Sorry to keep you waiting," the chief said. "We appreciate you coming in and bringing your computer. Forensics is examining Kyle's laptop for fingerprints and hacking, but we needed to get into your cloud drive as soon as possible. We believe you should make your statement under oath. Do you agree?"

"Should I have brought my attorney?" Jessie joked, throwing Hal a quizzical look. He furrowed his brows and shook his head.

"No, it's a formality to establish the chain of custody of the digital evidence. We may need to impound your computer, but Detective Pulaski will download any evidence onto an external hard drive. We'll make the call after we've completed the data collection."

"I understand. Let's begin, please," she said, her hands turning clammy.

Zander attached a cellphone-size black box to a port on Jessie's computer.

"I've programmed it to recognize and extract only the SportsPro cloud's data. It won't copy or compromise any other files on your hard drive." Then he plugged a cable into another computer port and typed a few strokes on Jessie's keyboard. "I've connected your computer to the video monitor on the far wall. That way, we can all watch the images streaming from the cloud."

Cindie Tarrico removed her camel blazer and hung it over the back of her chair. Two-carat diamond studs sparkled in her ears as she made the introductions on the record. The DA smiled, and soft crow's feet crinkled the corners of her eyes. "Ms. Martin, we want to confirm that you are the sole owner of a MacBook Pro Laptop computer, IOS Operating System, and Serial Number—" Jessie located the operating system and serial number and dictated them to Cindie. "And since your meeting with Detectives Jones and Pulaski yesterday, you have not entered the application, the cloud, or Kyle Emory's subscription for the SportsPro camera on this or any other device, correct?"

"That's correct." The knot in Jessie's stomach eased. It was empowering to be the star witness rather than the interrogator or the suspect.

"Ms. Martin, when did you first discover the application?"

"Last night with Detectives Jones and Pulaski, and Judge Hal Samuels was also present."

"Did any of you enter Kyle Emory's account on the SportsPro website?"

"No, none of us did. We entered the password but did not access any files," Jessie said.

"Does anyone other than yourself have access to the computer?"

"Only Judge Samuels, but neither of us touched the computer after the detectives left our home last night around eight-thirty."

"To your knowledge, does anyone else have the password to the cloud server you share with Mr. Emory? Or his SportsPro cloud?"

"No."

"Ms. Martin, we are going to request you retrieve Mr. Emory's files, and we're going to document all actions taken on your computer. Can you please boot it up?" Cindie asked.

"You want me to do it? I thought the detectives would conduct the search of my computer. I give them my permission to do so."

"Yes, but it's your computer. We believe it's best if you log on."

"All right." Jessie shrugged.

Cindie waved at the photographer, a young uniformed officer with ash-colored hair. He moved closer to Jessie, and the odor of his citrus cologne filled the air. The stern officer photographed the screen and made notes of the date and time of the operation.

Recalling the simple steps Zander had undertaken during the previous evening, Jessie mimicked them: locating the website, finding the sub-scription login, and entering the password stored on her cellphone. The unnerving sound of the camera shutter accompanying each stage made her fingers fumble. At last, she stabbed the "enter" button, letting out a huge breath.

The familiar rainbow disc swirled as a faint image populated the screens of her computer and the wall monitor. "It might take a few moments to download the files," Jessie said. The camera aperture continued to open and shut, documenting her every movement.

Then the library loaded. The little black storage unit emitted a whirring sound and a blinking white light. The download had begun. Kyle had uploaded one file into the SportsPro cloud. It was a ninety-minute video, time-stamped with the date of his drowning.

Jessie gritted her teeth, clicked on the video, and let it play.

The room was dead silent; everyone's eyes were locked on the screen.

Kyle's SportsPro camera must have activated during the boat's unloading from the roof of his car, as the wide-angle movie began with the kayak being unloaded and carried to the picnic area at the park. No faces were visible, just unrecognizable voices laughing and talking, with multiple hands tossing the red kayak from person to person.

They set the kayak on the ground facing northward toward the Mid-Hudson Bridge with the picnic table in full view. The sky was blue and cloudless, and the morning sun glinted off the dark, calm surface of the Hudson. Kyle, Olivia, Lily, and the Vargas family reveled in the warm weather, removing their jackets and flinging them into the deep green grass. The guys tossed around a ball in a game of touch football while the women gathered around the table, gossiping and showering Lily with attention.

Viv opened a bottle of white wine and took a swig from the bottle. The women giggled at the matriarch. Olivia snatched the bottle from her mother and wiped the top with the hem of her fuchsia sweater. She pulled out her phone, gathered her hair into a low ponytail, puckered her lips, and held the bottle up to her cheek as she snapped a picture. Olivia took a drink as she posted the pic on her social media.

"What are you two, animals? Can't you wait until I unpack the cups?" Max's wife Ana joked. Olivia snuck a second swig and doubled over in laughter, spitting the wine on the grass.

"My followers love to see me act on the spur of the moment," Olivia purred. "I've reached ninety thousand of them. That's a big deal!"

"Yeah. Yeah," the women replied, unimpressed.

Jessie squirmed in her chair, her fists clenching at the sight of her daughter being manhandled by complete strangers. Drinking strangers. Hal rested his hand on her shoulder, urging her to relax. They would get through this ordeal together.

"Okay, they're at Kaal Rock Park. The time stamp says ten-forty a.m. Kyle and Olivia should be leaving soon on their river excursion," Ebony said.

Moments later, the football game appeared to get rough. Although the audio was sketchy, the video was crystal clear. Auggie walked up to Kyle, pitched the football to the ground, and shoved him with both hands. After an exchange of words, Kyle held up his hands in surrender and stalked away. Auggie took a few steps in pursuit, yelling at him, but then he doubled back toward the other guys.

"Hey, Oli, are you ready to go out on the water?" Kyle asked.

God, it was weird to hear Kyle's voice. Perhaps one of the last words Jessie would ever hear him speak.

"Sure, honey," Olivia replied. She rose from the table and disappeared from view.

"We'd better get going if we want to make apple-picking this afternoon.

It can only be a quick trip," he said.

"Kyle, let's change things up today. I'm going to try out your kayak. Okay?"

"Sure. Are you ready?"

There was no reply.

Next, the red kayak seemed to have sprung wings, reeled like a drunkard, and landed on a soft, sandy beach on the shoreline. The kayak rocked as Kyle climbed in and pushed off. His paddle rhythmically splashed the brackish water as the boat swam away from the shore.

Kyle called to Olivia. "Hey, where do you want to go? How about north along the shore toward Waryas Park? We might see some eagles. It's that time of year."

"The bridge doesn't look that far," Olivia said, paddling alongside. "I'll race you there and back. The winner gets the sexual favor of their choice. How's that for an incentive?"

"Oli, I'm an old man, and you wear me out sometimes, but you're on."

The sound of female giggles filled the screen. Kyle paddled hard, but Olivia shot into the lead as they raced toward the first stanchion of the Mid-Hudson Bridge. Water splashed, sprinkling the camera lens, and Kyle wheezed with each stroke.

"Come on," Olivia taunted. "Catch me, old man!" She laughed and stopped paddling just shy of the bridge pier. "I'll count to five and give you a chance to catch up."

Kyle's breath labored as the blade of his paddle severed the river, grunting as he pulled. Olivia counted, snapped photos, and at five, she sped through the water, glancing over her shoulder at Kyle struggling to reach her.

Out of nowhere, the wind kicked up, and the sunlight vanished. A whooshing sound swirled around Kyle, and the grey water grew choppy. On the western shore, a line of black storm clouds marched over purple mountains toward Kyle and Olivia.

"Hey, Olivia. We'd better turn back. A storm is blowing in. Olivia!" Kyle screamed into the howling wind.

As Olivia reached the bridge, the raindrops fell. The storm grew virulent, and a fog descended over the bridge and the river, decreasing Kyle's visibility. The wind-driven rain pelted Kyle and his boat, leaving a watery, psychedelic sheen on the camera's lens. Tall white caps fractured the river's surface, dousing the kayak and submerging its tapered red bow.

A crack of lightning illuminated the western bank, and thunder rolled through the valley like a herd of wild deer. "Jesus!" Kyle's voice filled with panic. "Olivia, are you okay?" He panted as he paddled toward Olivia, who was beneath the bridge.

"Let's pause the video for a moment and analyze what we've observed so far," Cindie said. "We could all use a breather."

Jessie's heart had been pounding like a horse's hooves, and she tapped the pause button. A sharp muscle spasm squeezed her forehead, and she rubbed the skin between her brows, seeking relief. The worst part of the journey lay ahead.

"It looks like the weather took them by surprise," Ebony said. "But the video contradicts Olivia's testimony about Kyle instigating the race to the bridge and his drinking. Olivia also stated she wanted to turn back to shore when the rain started."

"It was the opposite. She'd been drinking. Not much, but we need to determine whether forensics tested her blood alcohol level," Zander said. "There's also the switcheroo with the kayaks. That was Olivia's idea, too."

"Do you think she heard Kyle's warning about turning back?" the chief asked.

"Who knows? It's hard to estimate their distance apart, plus there was the wind," Zander said. "I'm thinking they were thirty yards from each other, which is far on the water." He paused. "Further, neither craft was suitable for river use. Their kayaks were for recreational use on lakes, not the open water of the Hudson River."

"Olivia was reckless, speeding off as she did. And did you notice that neither wore a life jacket? They were experienced boaters and should have known the safety protocol. Yet, they were irresponsible and violated the law," the chief said. He glanced around the room at the solemn faces. "Any other comments, or are we ready to move on?"

The room grew silent in assent.

Jessie wanted to flee, but her legs had become leaden. Kyle hadn't known it, but his last moments loomed on the horizon. However, this audience did. They were about to witness Kyle's life slip away. His body would grow exhausted from fighting the storm, and water would fill his lungs, depriving him of air and life. If asphyxiation didn't get him, hypothermia would.

What a horrific way to die, Jessie thought. Trapped in a tempest with no escape except for Olivia.

Jessie pressed the button, and the video began. All eyes shifted back to the wall monitor.

Battered by the wind and rain, Kyle paddled across the south-running waves, dissecting them with each stroke. Another battery of tall waves washed over Kyle's head onto the kayak's front deck and into the open drain hole. "Olivia, Olivia! Are you all right?" he screamed. "Don't move. I'll come get you."

Kyle stroked toward her, a carpet of white foam surrounding him. A forceful gust of wind lifted the stern of his kayak, tipping the boat forward and skidding it sideways, parallel to the waves. Kyle was about six feet away from Olivia when another massive wave broadsided his kayak. The audio had captured the sloshing sound of icy water entering the open cockpit around his body and feet. "Oh, god, I'm sinking! Olivia, help me!"

Olivia's fingers clung to the rocky surface of the bridge stanchion. Drenched and shivering, she blinked away the water streaming into her eyes, holding firm to the bridge's surface.

The bow of Kyle's kayak pitched skyward as water filled the cockpit, sinking the stern. The camera recorded Kyle abandoning the ship, his powerful arms taking long, methodical strokes toward Olivia. He clung onto his flimsy paddle as his only flotation device. Upon reaching Olivia, he attempted to grab onto the bungee rigging on her boat's deck.

"No. Get away!" she cried, swatting him away.

"Olivia!" Kyle screamed, with one hand wrapped around the paddle and the other outstretched toward her, pleading. "For god's sake, help me! Call 911!"

Olivia reached toward him. She grabbed Kyle's bobbing head and forcefully dunked him in the roiling river. Then she snatched his paddle away from his weakened grip. Kyle burst through the surface, gasping for air and thrashing about in the violent river. Shock and fear washed over his face like the undertow pulling him under.

"Olivia? Help me!" he pleaded, struggling to keep afloat.

One corner of Olivia's mouth curled into a smirk as she watched Kyle fighting for his life. And did nothing.

Jessie recognized the pure evil oozing from Kyle's fiancée and knew what was coming. "Watch out!" she shouted at the screen as Olivia lifted the paddle's metal shaft above her head and swung the blade downward. Once, twice, three times. Kyle floundered in the frigid, turbulent river, fighting off the blows to his head, shoulders, and chest. His arms flailed, attempting to reach Olivia to make her stop.

"No," Olivia screamed, shoving the blade's end into Kyle's chest and pushing him away into the swirling foam.

An aggressive two-foot whitecap proved too much for Kyle, propelling him into the swift current streaming toward the center channel of the Hudson and toward his death.

"Help! Help!" Kyle's voice faded as he vanished from the camera's eye.

Olivia pitched Kyle's paddle into the water and reached inside the cockpit skirt of the blue kayak. She withdrew a slender black package and, within seconds, inflated a life vest and slipped it on as she watched Kyle disappear beneath the choppy surface.

The howling winds of the tempest replaced Kyle's pitiful cries.

The picture on the screen rotated upside down, then turned greenish-grey as the camera sank below the surface, ending the video.

Chapter Fifty-Two

Jessie wanted to puke. The acidic taste of bile burned the back of her throat, and she swallowed hard to keep the liquid from rising. Emotions flooded through her, making her vacillate between sadness and anger. Anguish and revenge.

Around her, everyone stared in disbelief at the dark, blank screen as though seeking an explanation for the horror they'd witnessed. As champions of the criminal justice system, they'd become hardened by death. Daily, they wrestled with the bloody aftermath of man's heinous crimes against man. Over the decades, they had investigated and prosecuted every imaginable variation on the theme.

Not Jessie. Until recently, homicide had been an abstract concept studied in law school and casebooks. As a novice criminal defense attorney, death's skeletal fingers seemed to reach out to her, tapping her on the shoulder. First with Ryan Paige. Now Kyle's murder had unfolded on her computer screen.

The youthful photographer snapped additional photos of the black screen while tears streamed down the stenographer's face. "That was awful," she said.

Jessie's vision blurred in a rage as crimson the blood she wanted from Olivia. Olivia. Kyle's cold-blooded killer. Every fiber of her being demanded Olivia pay for her sins. She wanted blood for blood.

"That wasn't just awful," Jessie shouted, her voice quivering. "That was murder. Olivia killed Kyle. Charge her with second-degree premeditated murder."

All heads snapped toward her.

"Before we jump the gun, let's replay the video," Cindie said, apparently trying to manage the situation before it erupted into chaos.

"I don't need to watch it again. The ending won't change. Olivia killed Kyle. She whacked him over the head and killed him," Jessie replied.

"During the showing, I jotted down notes," Ebony said, scanning her phone. "They're basic, but let's examine the facts. Before Kyle and Olivia set off, Auggie was pissed at Kyle and pushed him. Afterward, Kyle and Olivia departed on their kayaking trip around eleven. Olivia shoved off in Kyle's blue kayak with a cockpit skirt that prevented water from entering the hull. Kyle had taken Olivia's red kayak without a skirt and with a missing drain plug."

Ebony reviewed her notes aloud. The events had captured Olivia's cold, calculating essence.

"And somewhere along the line, Olivia ditched the vest because it was never found," Zander said, "but we traced a cash receipt we found in the barn at White Oaks. She'd purchased one in a store in Westchester." He rose and tapped on Auggie's photo on the whiteboard. "Auggie had money issues, and his grudge against Kyle serves as a motive for pulling the plug."

"You're jumping ahead," Ebony said. "Besides, Hanson's report states the missing plug alone wasn't the cause of the drowning. It was one factor but not the cause. There's no evidence linking Auggie to the plug." Ebony leaned back in her chair and stretched. "Every Vargas had a chance at the plug."

"Kyle was still alive after Olivia attacked him and sent him adrift," Cindie said.

Jessie's mind raced, dissecting the scenario as if it were a law school essay question. If a person physically harmed a victim, who doesn't die from the harm inflicted, is the perpetrator responsible for the eventual death? What is the threshold of their liability? Can the perpetrator benefit from the victim's death? What defenses are available to the perpetrator? Did a correct answer exist in this bizarre situation?

Certainly, if Olivia had aided Kyle and called 911, Kyle might still be alive.

Her assault on Kyle, pushing him into the current, and her failure to save him unequivocally led to Kyle's drowning. Case closed.

"The video shows Olivia clinging to the bridge for her life. It's possible she was in a deranged state of mind and lacked the mental capacity to understand her actions. She might have been panic-stricken." Cindie argued as the devil's advocate.

"Olivia Vargas is adept at playing to the camera. Her hysteria could have been an act. Remember how she set us up when we tried to ticket her for speeding?" Zander replied.

"Pulaski, your argument doesn't stand. How would Vargas have known the SportsPro was recording?" the chief asked. "If she did know, would she have attacked him that way?"

Zander pursed his lips. "We don't, but Chief, she's devious. Olivia knew about the camera. They'd mounted it on her kayak's deck."

"It's something to consider, but I'm unconvinced."

Cindie leaned her elbows on the table, resting her chin on her fists. "Also, why didn't Olivia call 911 from the river? She watched Kyle drown and waited until she returned to shore before reporting his disappearance. Even in a storm, it would have only taken minutes for *Marine 1* to be deployed to save him." She paused and glanced at the whiteboard in the front of the room. "Unfortunately, the autopsy isn't clear about a few key items. It mentions pattern-bruising suggesting that Kyle was struck by some type of object. It could've been the paddle, or he could have collided with his kayak or river debris. Also, it doesn't establish how long Kyle struggled in the water or when hypothermia set in. He was in the water too long to make those conclusions. But they've declared drowning as the formal cause of death. How long did it take Olivia to make the call?"

They replayed the video. The time stamp showed Kyle floating off camera at eleven-twenty-three.

Cindie ruffled through papers in a folder on the table. "Emergency services clocked her phone call at eleven-forty-seven. She made the call twenty minutes after the current had swept Kyle away."

"Under normal conditions, with water temps around sixty-eight degrees, hypothermia sets in around thirty minutes. But Kyle had the storm, the waves, the injuries, fatigue, and the current working against him." Zander held up a hypothermia table he'd pulled up on his phone at kayak.org. "He couldn't survive without Olivia's help."

"Officer Robinson's initial interview shows Olivia in shock but not incompetent. According to Olivia's statement, she was cogent and could've made the call from the river," Cindie said.

"What about premeditation?" Jessie asked. "Olivia switched kayaks and had a life vest hidden away. Doesn't that count for anything?"

"If we charge her, we have to be prepared for a fight. The Vargas family attorney, Gloria Reyes Castellano, has made a career as a legal tiger. She'd argue Olivia acted in self-defense in pushing Kyle away or that she was too emotionally disturbed to call 911. And the kayak switch and life vest are irrelevant because Kyle died from exposure to the elements," Zander said.

"But Kyle wouldn't have drowned if Olivia hadn't pushed him off. We must hold her responsible for her actions. That's the justice system." Jessie couldn't believe she needed to restate the law to the law enforcement team. They should have known that the New York Penal Law provided that where a person acts with depraved indifference to human life and causes the death of another or acts in such a manner that creates a grave risk of death to another, the perpetrator is guilty of second-degree murder. It didn't get any clearer than that. Based on the video, Olivia had committed second-degree murder, a felony carrying life imprisonment without parole. No one could argue that Olivia's actions didn't hasten Kyle's demise. Or that something had motivated her. She had seven hundred fifty thousand reasons to be motivated.

Jessie's cheeks warmed in frustration and anger. She couldn't comprehend why the others struggled to reach the obvious conclusion. "Why are you waffling? The law is clear." But in reality, the law wasn't black and white. It encompassed as many gradations of gray as the Hudson's waters. "You honestly believe a murder charge won't stick? What's the alternative, manslaughter? Reckless endangerment? Olivia's actions went far beyond intentionally injuring Kyle. She killed him." As fervently as Jessie argued, the ultimate decision belonged to Cindie.

Either of the alternate choices would be a gift to Olivia, a slap on her wrist. Manslaughter, where a serious injury results in someone's death, was a Class B or C Felony, carrying a maximum twenty-five years incarceration. Reckless endangerment, creating the risk of serious injury or death, was a Class A Misdemeanor with up to one year in jail. It was possible Olivia could serve no time at all.

Hal cleared his throat in a judicial manner. "There's no reason to make an immediate decision. Olivia Vargas doesn't appear to be a flight risk. She's easy enough to track through her parents or her social media accounts." Hal directed his remarks at his successor, Cindie. "You have cartons of evidence to review that will allow you to make a case against either Olivia or her brother, Auggie. Both had the opportunity and the motivation to kill Kyle. Just make your case ironclad. Consider how a judge and a jury would review the case, and how the decision would stand up on appeal. No matter which Vargas you arrest, you'll be sparring with Gloria Castellano. You know her. She picks her battles and refuses to quit."

Cindie crossed her arms over her flowered silk blouse and studied the anxious faces in the room. Her eyes lit on Jessie's and held them for a moment. "Jessie, I appreciate your fervor, but I must act in the best interest of the People of the State of New York. I'll let everyone know my decision in the morning, but be prepared to execute an arrest tomorrow."

The evidence glared from the screen — a shot of Olivia, her hands gripping the metal paddle above her head, ready to strike a blow that would send Kyle drifting off to his death.

"Please consider all the factors before making your decision," Jessie pleaded. Sadly, the truth appeared to be slipping away like Kyle had beneath the murky surface.

But she couldn't let it go. Not without a fight.

Chapter Fifty-Three

The group disbanded, leaving Jessie alone with Ebony and Zander in the interrogation room.

The spasm between Jessie's eyes hadn't lessened. If anything, it had intensified with the DA's mentioning the potential weaknesses in prosecuting Olivia for Kyle's murder. She tried to make sense of the situation by replaying the video in her mind. Jessie wondered how the DA could reach a conclusion other than homicide.

"Can I ask you something? What did you observe in the video?" she asked.

"We saw what you saw," Ebony said. "Olivia didn't hold Kyle's head underneath the water and drown him, but she did the next best thing. She didn't help him in his moment of need and set him adrift to his death."

Jessie read the sympathy in Ebony's expression and heard it in her words. But could she or would she take action to punish Olivia for her sins?

Zander slapped his palm on the tabletop and kicked the leg of the table. "And she lied about everything—the kayaks, the race, the life vest, the storm. We have it all on tape, and I'm as frustrated as you."

"We could debate the facts all day, but the manner of prosecution isn't our decision. It's up to the DA. You, Zander, and I know the truth, but sometimes justice is perverted," Ebony replied.

"I don't accept that. The investigation can't end this way. Olivia can't get away with murder." Jessie paused. She blinked back the tears welling in her eyes and wiped her cheek on her sleeve. "There's one more thing that's bothering me."

"What are you talking about?" Ebony asked.

"Did you examine the Barclays insurance papers? Something's not right with them. Here, take a peek. What do you think? My eyes might have played tricks on me."

Jessie retrieved the stack of wrinkled documents from the Barclays' envelope. Disbelieving their content, she'd scrutinized them over a dozen times and had stared at them until the words ran together. She flipped to the signature page marked with a paper clip and pointed to the bottom of the page. "I don't believe that Kyle's signature. It's an amazing copy, but I'm certain it's not his."

She extracted another document and placed it alongside the insurance form. "Here's a copy of our house deed as proof of his true handwriting. His signature was notarized on the deed but not on the insurance forms. Anyone could have executed these forms."

Ebony leaned over the papers, seized her phone, and snapped on the flashlight, directing its beam on the documents. "You're right. They look identical, but something's off."

"Let me grab my magnifying glass so we can inspect them," Zander said. He reached into his pocket and recovered his Swiss Army knife. He unfolded the dozen miniature tools until he came to a round magnifying glass. "I never go anywhere without this baby. You never know when it will be useful."

"You should know the half of it," Ebony said with light sarcasm.

Zander held his lens over the signature, and they leaned closer.

"Shine your light over here on the deed. You can notice that Kyle's writing is like chicken scratch. He wrote straight up and down, leaving lines like on a lie detector or EKG. Check it out." Jessie dragged her finger beneath the vertical scrawl of Kyle's signature on the deed. "And Kyle was left-handed."

"I didn't know that. His letters almost blend together, and they're all the same height on the line," Ebony said. "Here, on the insurance form, they're tilted toward the right. It's subtle, but you can notice it in the light. Lefties tilt toward the left."

"Look at the Y on the insurance forms. It's got a loop on the bottom.

There's no loop on the *Y* in the deed. I've seen Kyle sign papers a thousand times, and this is not his signature. And this proves it."

"There is a forgery, but how do we figure out who did it?" Zander asked. "What does this mean to our investigation?"

"Well, we now have two crimes: homicide and forgery. It suggests that Olivia either forged the docs herself or she had a co-conspirator. She cooked the plot, but was she swindling Kyle from the start? Did she murder him to get the money? And who else was involved?" Ebony asked.

"Even if the documents were valid, New York has 'The Slayer's Law.' No one can benefit financially from committing a crime. That means Olivia can't receive the insurance monies after killing off Kyle. And even if she did sign his name, we're back to square one if Cindie doesn't prosecute," Jessie said. Her mouth grew dry, and she licked her parched lips.

"Not necessarily, because Olivia contacted Barclays about the status of the forms. Somehow, she's involved," Zander said, raising an eyebrow. "And remember, Auggie is obsessed with money."

"Let us review our file. We should have copies of our witnesses' driver's licenses, and we can compare their signatures with Kyle's. We can also ask forensics for a handwriting evaluation. I promise you were not giving up," Ebony said. "We'll let you know if we need any other writing samples."

"I've still got his boxes in the basement," Jessie said. "Let me know, and I'll check."

A sense of calm washed over Jessie. She'd inched the needle closer to catching Kyle's killer and a forger. Two crimes were perpetrated on Kyle and linked to one person, Olivia Vargas. She wasn't driven by a personal vendetta against Olivia. Rather, she was, and would always be, impassioned by pursuing truth and justice.

Chapter Fifty-Four

At seven the next morning, the alarm on Cindie's phone buzzed like a saw slicing through her brain. "No, it can't be," she moaned, slamming the snooze button and burrowing her head deeper beneath the covers.

She'd spent the better part of last night with her team digesting the evidence in Kyle's case. Fueled by coffee and pizza, they had sparred over the tsunami of forensic evidence strewn across the conference room table. They had debated criminal law and procedure, case law precedents, and statutory interpretations until their voices turned hoarse.

Finally, at three o'clock, the heads of her assistants had drooped to the table, forcing Cindie to call it a night. "Go home," she'd ordered the five attorneys, two investigators, and three paralegals. "We have a handle on it, and I'll alert the police chief in the morning." She turned toward the paralegals. "First thing in the morning, prepare the arrest and search warrants and hand-deliver them to the city court judge. Don't leave until you have their signature. Then make copies and shuttle them downstairs to Chief Shepardson. I need the warrants in my possession by nine."

The trio of paralegals yawned in unison.

"You've all done me proud. Now, go home," Cindie said.

For the four fleeting hours beneath the duvet, Cindie's mind had whirred. Were they ready to proceed? Had they correctly identified Kyle's killer? Did they have the evidence and the law to substantiate the charges? What was the worst that could happen on her first major outing as the DA? Lose her job?

There were worse things, she considered groggily as she rose from bed and showered. Like illness and death. Thankfully, she and her family were healthy, but with death, no one ever knew.

By eight o'clock, Cindie was perched across from Matt Shepardson in his office at the police station. His collection of citations and photos on display always intimidated her, especially his portrait with Supreme Court Justice Sonia Sotomayor. Sotomayor's feisty smile sparkled at Cindie. *Don't fuck up*, she taunted.

Shaking the delusion from her brain, Cindie blathered on, justifying her decision. The chief listened.

"I respect your judgment," he said. "It's your call, and we'll provide the backup necessary to ensure a conviction. I'm glad this matter is being put to rest, and I'm confident the Emory family will be grateful, too. I know this wasn't easy for you." The chief's icy glare softened into sympathy. "I'll alert Jones and Pulaski to proceed once the warrants arrive, and I'll advise you once we make the arrest."

"Thanks. We couldn't have achieved our goals without your officers. Please thank them for their exceptional dedication."

There was a knock on the door.

"You can tell the detectives yourself," the chief said as Ebony and Zander stuck their heads into the office.

"Any news?" Ebony asked.

"DA Tarrico will fill you in. Please come in and shut the door."

* * *

Ebony and Zander received their orders and waited. An excruciating hour later, with the warrants in hand, they rushed toward their SUV in the station's parking lot. Two black and white patrol cars awaited them.

"The plan is to make the bust at White Oaks, so let's book," Ebony said.

"It's early, so everyone should be home." Zander's phone pinged. "Wait, I set up notifications for activity on Olivia's Instagram, Twitter, and Facebook accounts, and I just received one. You won't believe this."

Music streamed from Zander's phone as Ebony plucked it away from him and examined the Facebook video. "Castellano agreed Olivia wouldn't post anything about the case. The damn shyster screwed us again. If you scroll through her profile, you'll see she's been posting about Kyle all along. And her following has grown to one hundred seventy-five thousand followers. This time, Olivia has written a love ballad for Kyle, and she's singing it on a video. There's also a public invitation to a riverfront vigil she's holding for Kyle at Kaal Rock Park. It's this morning at ten. That's now."

In the video, Olivia tearfully warbled a song entitled "I'll Love You Forever." Standing in a dark room lit by candelabras, Olivia swayed as she crooned her hymn. The soft candlelight reflected off the satiny sheen of her flowing white gown as a trio of violins and a solo classical guitarist accompanied her tribute to Kyle and their endless love.

I'll love you until the end of time
Until the river runs dry
It will always be you and I
Forever.
I'll love you forever.
My love.

"We better bolt. We have fifteen minutes before the memorial starts, and with her thousands of followers, this could turn into a flash mob," Zander said, bolting toward their car.

"I'll notify dispatch. We're going to need backup."

Zander switched on the flashing blue and red lights and the siren, and pressed his foot on the accelerator. The patrol cars followed close behind. The group sped to the bottom of Main Street near the train station and made a sharp right onto Rinaldi Boulevard, where Kaal Rock Park lay off a side street three-quarters of a mile ahead. Rinaldi Boulevard was the only thoroughfare leading to the park entrance, and Olivia's siren song had brought traffic to a standstill. On both sides of the road, every parking spot was occupied, and in both directions, cars lined up bumper-to-bumper along the narrow boulevard.

"What should we do?" Zander asked. "It's impossible to drive to the park."

"We'll have to walk or run from here. There's no time to waste." Ebony stowed the warrants in the breast pocket of her tactical vest and radioed her escorts. "Traffic deadlocked. Lock your cars and proceed on foot. Let's go. Copy?"

"Copy," they replied.

"If we get separated, meet me at the door to the pavilion," Ebony said. She slipped on her jacket with POLICE written in large white letters and clipped her shield onto a lanyard around her neck.

"Don't worry. I'll be right beside you," Zander said. He tugged on his tactical vest. "Remember, we're here to make the arrest. Let's go."

They jumped out of their car and raced beside the four officers toward the park. Angry horns beeped as the team darted in and out of the line of stalled traffic.

Each step toward Kaal Rock Park delivered a fresh wave of scorching pain into Ebony's left hip. But she couldn't stop or slow down; she was in a race to catch a killer. A half block down, the screeching of tires rang in her ears, and she glanced over her shoulder to investigate. When she turned back, Zander was neither beside her nor behind her. He'd disappeared.

She thought she saw him sprinting up ahead but couldn't be certain. The crowd had thickened as folks abandoned their vehicles and joined the mass flowing down the street toward the park. Although surrounded by hundreds of souls, Ebony was alone. She had to trust that Zander would meet her at the pavilion and that they'd executed the warrants together.

This was the second time they'd ever been separated on the job. The first time had occurred during their late-night pursuit of a drug dealer about three years ago. She'd taken a slug in her hip, and Zander had watched her writhing in pain in the middle of the street. Ebony had urged him to carry on, make the collar, which he'd done. He'd followed his instincts and overcome his fears of working without her. Now it was her turn.

"Detective Jones. Over here," a voice called out.

Out of the crowd, two of the uniformed officers, Vic Robinson and her partner, Melanie Prisciandaro, appeared and hovered at her shoulder. "Vic, Mel, please run up ahead to the park's entrance, check the status of backup, and see if you can get control over the traffic. Also, confirm the Vargas family is at the park and text me. No matter what happens, don't let them leave. I'll be there as soon as I can."

"Are you sure, ma'am?" Officer Prisciandaro asked. "We can stick with you."

"No, it will be quicker if we split up. I'm meeting Pulaski in the park. Get going!"

Vic and Mel vanished from sight, and Ebony looked around, assessing the best route down to the waterfront. Ahead, the road was a swamp of vehicles and their former passengers were packed as tightly as the bullets in her holster. On the other side of the road, a ravine leading to the train tracks dropped off sharply beyond the parked cars, and to her right, blocks of apartments and townhouses lined the boulevard and the side streets. The only path lay straight ahead.

Setting one foot in front of the other, Ebony gained speed, weaving her way through the crowd. Despite the Taser-like zinging in her hip, the doubts they'd catch the killer in time, and the dark waters waiting at the bottom of the hill, she plodded onward.

Self-reliance wasn't such a terrible thing. Every agonizing step, every labored breath, motivated her to get the job done for Jessie, Lily, Kyle, and herself.

Chapter Fifty-Five

Since Ebony and Zander had arrived on the scene, the number of mourners had swollen from a trickle to a river of humanity. Hauling bouquets, candles, and other symbols of grief, the crowd flowed toward the entrance to Kaal Rock Park and the loud music. Ebony dove in, swimming along with the bustling throng. Zander remained lost, but they'd made plans. Meet near the pavilion.

At the park's narrow gates, bodies crushed together, sweeping downhill toward the Hudson. Near the shoreline, Ebony spied a riser and tall speakers mounted on poles and a memorial. Olivia caressed a microphone on the makeshift stage, singing the *a cappella* version of her ballad. Her black hair shimmered in the morning light, and the sheen of her white satin gown exuded an ethereal, angelic quality. The sweetness of her voice and luminescent persona had enchanted the audience.

When Olivia came to the final chorus, the mourners joined in. Hundreds of voices echoed off the massive shale cliffs of Kaal Rock, reverberating like a choir in a cathedral. When they completed the last line— *I'll love you forever, my love*— the crowd paused in a moment of silence. An eerie wind whistled through the framework of the suspension bridge overhead. The steady pulse of the bridge traffic replaced the missing heartbeat of the lost soul, Kyle Emory.

As though paying his or her respects, everyone, except Ebony, had stopped in place. There was no time to waste. She had a job to accomplish. Elbowing her way through the compacted strangers, sharp limbs poked her side, booted feet trampled hers, and aggressive hands tore at her clothing.

Indignant voices shouted, spitting obscenities as she shouldered her way through the pack like a quarterback.

All the time, she searched for Zander and her team members. Toward the front of the audience, she spotted the blue uniforms closing in on the stage, but since Zander wore street clothes, he remained another indistinctive body in the crowd. He could be anywhere.

Her fingers patted her vest pocket, grazing the valuable warrants. They were still there. Her mind eased. Still, if she didn't find Zander, and if the Vargases were making a run, Ebony would need to act. Zander had stressed they were here to make the arrest together. That was their mission. Her mission. Betraying Zander and violating their orders would sting. He might never speak to her again, and the chief might pull her badge and gun, but the most important thing was to stop the perps. Apprehend the people responsible for Kyle's death.

Breaking through the crowd, Ebony finally reached the Hudson's rocky shoreline. A few hundred yards to the north, the Vargas family huddled beside the stage. Officers Vic Robinson and Mel Prisciandaro waited close by. The two other officers in their team, Steiner and Harper, remained unaccounted for, along with Zander. The air was electric was a reprise of Olivia's song blasting through the loudspeakers.

The only unobstructed path toward Ebony's target was through a field of rugged pebbles, rocks, and boulders hugging the coastline. She stared across the jagged landscape and down into the swirling river below. Trapped between the lapping water and the army of Olivia's worshipers, one false move would send her plummeting into the murky, dangerous waters or impale her on the knife-like rock ledges.

Lacking options, Ebony embarked on the hazardous journey. Her fingers clutched the slick, uneven surfaces, and each scramble tweaked her already-aching body. She scaled the heights of an abandoned concrete dock covered with rusty steel bars. On reaching the top, Ebony couldn't get traction, and her sneakers slipped on its moss-covered surface.

"Shit!" Ebony cried. Her fingers grabbed at the mushy lichen, but it deteriorated in her hands. Gravity prevailed as she lost her balance and tumbled backward. She plunged into the river, landing on her feet in the slushy silt beneath the opaque water. Her sodden feet turned to ice as the mud seeped through the fabric of her pant legs, socks, and sneakers, gluing her to the river's floor. Within seconds, the mucky sludge sucked her downward like quicksand; the water rising from her ankles to her knees to her thighs, while the hot sweat of panic surged through her.

With Olivia's anthem playing, even if she cried out, no one would hear her.

"Help! Help!" She was correct. Her words vanished across the water on the wind.

Thrashing around wildly, uselessly, Ebony's worst nightmare was coming true. She was going to be swallowed alive by the frigid, black water. She'd drown, and no one would find her. The current would wash her lifeless body out to sea, or her bones would wash up on the shore decades from today.

She had never felt so alone in her life. No partner was coming to her aid. Ebony had to save herself.

The more she struggled, the deeper she sank until the water hit her waist. She glanced up at the dock towering over her and spied a moldy, gray rope dangling from the rotted rebar. It was just beyond her reach. Her trembling arms reached up, and her wet fingers skimmed along its frayed surface. The weight of her body dragged her deeper into the Hudson, submerging her up to her chest.

The older cops had warned Ebony that the Hudson kept her secrets. She was about to become one of them.

She pushed on her toes and stretched her arm skyward again. This time, her fingers grabbed a thin strand of the tattered rope, but she felt it slipping away. Her fingernails dug into the fine thread, and she pulled. Then something warm and strong grabbed her wrist.

"Hold on, will ya? I've got you," Zander shouted. His head popped over the edge of the concrete slab and joined by Officers Vic and Mel, they leaned over the dock's slippery edge, seized Ebony's wrists, and hauled her out of the river to safety.

Icy, brackish water and mud streamed down her body, and she shivered uncontrollably.

"It's a bit late in the season to go for a swim," Zander said, shaking his head. "I turn my back for one minute, and—"

"I turned my back, and you were gone. What the hell, Z?"

"I was here when it counted, so shut it."

Ebony wanted to thank him for saving her life. Throw her arms around his neck and tell him he was the best partner in the world. But there was unfinished business. The sentimentality would have to wait.

"Hon, seriously, are you okay? We'd better get you dried off." Officer Vic gathered her up in an embrace, and the warmth emitted by the bulky body made Ebony want to remain there forever.

"No, I'm good. Or I'll check to see if I'm fine later," she said, breaking away. "We've got to get moving." Officer Mel threw her police jacket around Ebony's shoulders. "Thanks, and thanks for pulling me out of the river. Come on."

Water dripping down her ruined clothing, Ebony dashed alongside Zander and the patrol officers toward the shoreline where the Vargases had gathered. Olivia clutched a wreath of red roses with a white satin sash displaying Kyle's name in gold lettering. The team came to a stop as Olivia kissed the wreath and tossed it into the water. Caught up in the swift current, the roses drifted toward the river's center as a pair of gulls cried and circled overhead.

"Detectives, what are you doing here? What happened to you?" Carlos asked.

Ebony marched past him. "Olivia Vargas, you are under arrest for the murder of Kyle Emory."

Olivia stared at Ebony in stunned silence.

"You have the right to remain silent...." Zander launched into the Miranda Rights.

From the gallery, scores of phones focused their cameras on Olivia and the Vargas family. Olivia reached into the pocket of her gown and retrieved her phone, and checked it. A victorious grin kissed her lips while Officer

Vic snapped handcuffs on Olivia's slender wrists.

"Detective, there must be some mistake," Viv Vargas said. "My daughter isn't capable of murder. She's in shock. She can hardly function." Her gaze grew distant and flinty as she jumped to protect her offspring.

Carlos whipped out his phone and stalked away from his family.

"Oli?" Auggie said. "What is she talking about? What did you do?"

Max and Ana ran to Olivia's side, and Olivia tossed her head back, shaking her long tresses, and thrust back her shoulders.

"You don't understand. Thanks to Kyle, I've got five million followers. They'll be even more now. Kyle's death gave me a new life, a new brand."

"Olivia, no!" Viv said.

"I loved Kyle, but I wanted him gone. I felt trapped, and I wanted to be free." Olivia's soft voice oozed with the venom of a rattlesnake on the attack.

The cameras continued to record away.

"I let him go. I pushed him away. I wanted him to drown so I could be free. It was my destiny," Olivia said with pride.

Shit! Olivia just admitted her crime, and Ebony needed to react quickly. "Vic, Mel, get the names and addresses of the people with cameras. Have them text the videos to you. Otherwise, impound their phones. Hurry before things turn ugly."

Vic and Mel disappeared into the crowd.

A gasp rippled through the crowd as they realized something was awry. A few voices chanted, "*Olivia! Olivia!*" The cries grew louder as others joined in.

Ebony hadn't considered it before, but an unsympathetic mob could easily morph into a stampede. If the crowd supported the bewitching Olivia and believed in her innocence, then Ebony, Zander, and their team could be in life-threatening danger.

Her racing heart settled when the imposing figure of Officer Steiner climbed onto the stage and seized the microphone. Built like an NBA All-Star, his grapefruit-sized fist made the microphone look like a toy.

"Ladies and gentlemen, we would appreciate your cooperation in evacuating the park. There's no danger, but we need to clear the area for police activities," Steiner said in a deep, authoritative voice. A chorus of boos echoed in response. "Please proceed in a calm and orderly fashion, so no one gets hurt. Officers are available at the park's entrance to help anyone who requires assistance. Thank you for coming."

Ebony hoped Steiner wasn't bluffing about the backup. The crowd turned toward the entrance and leisurely slogged uphill. Minutes later, her tense shoulders relaxed at the reassuring sound of approaching police sirens.

Cody Shaw nudged his way past Max and Ana. "Livvie? Livvie?" His eyes grew watery, and he caressed her manacled hands. "*Mi amor*, no, no, no. *Por favor*, no."

"Cody Shaw, aka Raul Esperanza, you are under arrest for the forgery of Kyle Emory's signature and insurance fraud. You have the right to remain silent..." she said.

Zander slipped the handcuffs on Shaw's wrists.

"What's going on here?" Viv asked. "You think you can interrupt a private family memorial and wreak havoc by arresting everyone? Who's next? Me? Carlos?"

Carlos placed a hand on her arm to silence her. "Viv, *silencio!* Gloria is on the way. She advises us to keep quiet until she arrives. Gloria will meet us at the police station."

Ear-piercing sirens accompanied the flashing lights at the top of the hill. The crowd parted, and a parade of police cars, followed by an ambulance, swarmed the park.

"And you, Dr. Vargas. There's no record of you obtaining a permit for this gathering. Your family can expect additional charges for violating the City of Poughkeepsie Code," Ebony said.

"That's ridiculous. This is a public park. Tell them, Carlos." Viv scoffed.

Ebony wouldn't argue with the belligerent woman. She and Zander had made their collars because the law was the law. The chief, the DA, Hal, and Jessie would have been proud.

A fleet of black and white police cars parked haphazardly around the park, and Ebony, Zander, and their team led Olivia and Shaw to separate vehicles.

Before entering the back seat, Olivia fluffed her locks, puckered her lips, and posed for one last photo. Her *Honey Face* portrayed haughtiness and confidence. Shaw slid into his back seat, heartbroken and forlorn.

Ebony shut the door behind Olivia and tapped on the patrol car's roof. The vehicle departed through hangers-on.

Zander rested on one of the picnic benches. "This had been quite a day."

"You can say that again," Ebony replied and shivered. "I've got to change out of these wet clothes."

"Stinky, too." Officer Vic held her nose and elbowed Ebony's shoulder.

A female paramedic advanced toward Ebony and set her black bag on the ground. "I heard you took a tumble into the water. Let me examine your bumps and bruises," she said.

"Sounds good. Ouch!" Ebony winced when the EMT examined the scrapes on her hands and legs. "And when you're done, can you give my partner and me a lift home?"

"I believe I can arrange that."

Ebony tossed Zander's car keys to Vic and Mel and let the paramedic get down to work.

Chapter Fifty-Six

Two days after Olivia's arrest, Ebony clocked in at the police station and made a beeline for her desk. The heels of her knee-high suede boots clicked across the linoleum floor as she entered the detective's area. She stopped dead in her tracks at the sight of the visitor lingering suspiciously close to Zander, who roosted on the edge of his desk, laughing at a joke.

"I'm surprised to see you here," Ebony said.

"Just because we're sisters doesn't mean I have to report my every move to you," Carly said. She looked fetching in a pumpkin orange cable-knit sweater with black leather pants and boots, the perfect ensemble for an autumn day. "You look nice. I'm glad to see you survived the public dunking."

Ebony brushed the wrinkles out of her black turtleneck midi-dress and adjusted her new leather belt. "Thanks, but isn't it a bit early for Halloween?" Ebony struggled to suppress any hint of sibling rivalry in her tone.

Lately, there seemed to be no part of her life that was off-limits to Carly. And was this cozy tête-à-tête proof of a hookup between her partner and her sister? She was clearly Zander's type: tall, attractive, intelligent, and available.

"I stopped by to see how Zander was doing. Do you have a problem with that? Besides, it's none of your business," Carly said.

Thou doth protest too much, little sister, Ebony thought.

"Hey, why are you dressed in black?" Zander asked. "Going to a funeral?"

"Yes, I am. I'm on my way to Kyle's memorial ceremony at the Unitarian

Fellowship. Jessie invited you, but I declined on your behalf. I didn't want you to feel compelled to go. It's mostly family, anyway."

"And we know you're as close as family." Zander smirked.

"Sisters from another mother," Ebony and Carly sang in unison.

"How's Jessie doing?" he asked. "It must have come as a shock to discover that Shaw had forged Kyle's signature on the insurance papers."

"A bit." Ebony turned toward her sister. "Listen to this. We'd all suspected Auggie was the culprit until Zander produced the receipt from his lantern purchase at Hudson Outfitters, and forensics analyzed Shaw's handwriting on it, and…BINGO! My partner, Alexandre Pulaski, saved the day."

Carly gave him a peck on the cheek. "Our hero."

A flush crept across his cheeks, and he rubbed the back of his neck.

"From what Zander told me, Olivia Vargas was a black widow, seducing men, stealing their money, and killing them. For Shaw to be a willing participant in her scheme, she must've had ironclad control over him." Carly paused. "Wasn't she divorcing him? I wonder why she didn't rob him blind and off him, too."

"She needed a minion to do her dirty work," Zander said. "I bet they were still getting it on. The guy wasn't thinking with his brain."

"Shaw admitted that Olivia had promised to transfer her stock in Hudson Outfitters and all their land holdings if he cooperated. However, for Olivia, it was about more than the bucks. She also wanted attention and power. Olivia was obsessed with her followers and boosting her profile. Look at her music video and the crowd that gathered at the park for the memorial service. They adored her and were at her command. It was scary," Ebony said.

"I disagree," Zander replied. "She was all about the Benjamins. Her Facebook and Instagram followers skyrocketed from seventy-five thousand to five million by the time we arrested her. The more followers, the more money." He paused for a beat. "I'm surprised she wasn't selling merch at the event."

"Or it could have been a way to escape her helicopter parents. They seemed awfully invested in her life." Ebony shrugged one shoulder. "We'll never know, at least not until Olivia gives her first media interview." They chuckled.

"Poor Kyle. In a way, social media caused his death. That's a sick commentary about our society," Carly said.

"You're right," Ebony said. "I'm not on any platforms. Especially as a cop, I value my privacy too much to give anyone access to my personal information. It's nobody's business." She paused. Then another culprit sprang to mind. "And the suckers who buy into charlatans like Olivia are also to blame. They fed the machine that emboldened Olivia's greed and thirst for power without considering the consequences. She really used Kyle."

"His first, deadly mistake was getting mixed up with a Looney Tunes woman," Zander said.

Ebony's eyes darted between him and her sister. "Let's hope the DA can make the murder charges against Olivia and Shaw stick."

"What about the rest of her family? Were they involved in the plot?" Carly asked.

"No," Zander continued, "we issued summonses to Carlos and Viv for illegally holding a community event in a city park. They didn't apply for a permit, get insurance, or take any of the steps necessary to protect the attendees' safety." He shook his head in apparent disbelief. "They'll pay a hefty fine for those violations, but on the more serious misdemeanor reckless endangerment charges, they could face jail time."

"Kyle's memorial could have erupted into mayhem, and fortunately, it didn't. But I'm sure Castellano will come to their rescue. She'll make a lot of noise and contest their responsibility to provide security and crowd control," Ebony said. "The DA will be tied up with the Vargas crew for quite a while."

"And the younger brother, Auggie?" Carly asked.

"Although he was their partner in Hudson Outfitter, he was blindsided by Olivia and Shaw's arrests, and knew nothing about what they were up to," Ebony said. "Auggie was too focused on keeping his job at Go-To and running the store." She extracted lip gloss from her shoulder bag and applied it, smacking her lips.

"From what you're saying, he comes off looking like a fool if the crimes were committed under this nose," Carly said.

"Maybe, maybe not," Ebony replied. "In the end, the facts revealed him to be a harmless guy who could be gambling his future and wasting his talents on a sketchy start-up. For his sake, I hope his boss doesn't screw him over."

Despite everything, she still liked Auggie. While his all-consuming pursuit of wealth might cause his downfall, she believed he had a good heart and cared about his family, especially his felonious sister.

"Between the video, Shaw's testimony, Olivia's admissions, the physical evidence, and the autopsy results, the cases against Olivia and Shaw seem rock solid," Carly said.

"You never know whether Lady Justice is going to fuck up or get it right. We can only do our best to help the system along." Ebony glanced at her phone, checking the time. "Z, I've got to go. I'll call you later." She turned toward Carly. "And you, too!"

* * *

Ebony joined the small gathering of friends and family attending the celebration of Kyle's life at the Unitarian Fellowship. Not a Vargas was in sight. Inside the octagonal building with a peaked ceiling, they'd arranged chairs in a semi-circle around the pulpit. Kyle's father, Tom, led the service and invited speakers to eulogize his son.

She sat in the last row alongside Barry Levy, Nicole Thomas, and the Barclays staff. Barry extolled his friend's virtues, praying Kyle's soul was at rest in a better place.

Kyle's siblings, aunt, and uncle, also spoke, but Jessie was the last speaker. She rose from the front row, where her parents, Kyle's family, and Hal flanked her. Hal balanced Lily on his knee as he watched Jessie climb the steps to the pulpit.

Jessie's mossy green eyes grew glassy, and her voice cracked as she spoke.

"Kyle and I shared a life. It wasn't a perfect life, but together we created our beautiful daughter. Lily is Kyle's legacy, and he will live on through her. He will also live on in our memories and our hearts. I promise you, his loved ones, that Lily will know her wonderful father, his loving nature, and how dedicated he'd been to her in his own special way. Kyle wouldn't want us to be sad today; he would want us to blast the rock 'n roll and celebrate a life lived to the fullest in a short period. Kyle, we love you. May you rest in peace."

To end the ceremony, Tom Emory's deep baritone crooned a bible verse accompanied by Dani on electric piano. It was from Ecclesiastes, or as Ebony recognized from her parents' playlist, "Turn, Turn, Turn" by the Byrds. Afterward, Dani performed John Lennon's "Imagine" as Tom wished everyone to go in peace, signaling the ceremony's conclusion. The celebrants rose and streamed toward the door.

"Ebony! Ebony!" a voice called.

She heard her name and turned to discover Jessie rushing toward her.

"Thanks for coming," Jessie said. "Can I speak with you for a minute?" Without waiting for an answer, she grabbed Ebony's elbow and led her to a quiet corner of the room. "Please let me speak before you say anything. I realized after Kyle's death that life is too short. We take the people we love for granted, thinking there's always tomorrow. Tomorrow is the day we can make amends. We can talk to them tomorrow. Tomorrow we can celebrate joy. Kyle's death has taught me that's not a given."

"I was expecting to see Kyle when he brought Lily home. I expected to have him involved in Lily's life, have him walk her down the aisle, and share grandchildren with him. We spent too much time arguing over nothing, and I didn't begrudge him from moving on. I only wish he'd been more open with me about his life because we would've gotten along better. Perhaps I would have appreciated the good in him rather than assuming the negative. I never should've believed he'd betray Lily, his flesh and blood."

Tears streamed down Jessie's cheek, and she sniffled. "And I've acted the same way toward you. I let my prejudices about your career and life choices stand in the way of our friendship. Despite our differences, we've proven we can work together. We are an unstoppable duo. I want to start fresh today. I don't want to wait for tomorrow."

"That's all I want, too," Ebony said. Her cheeks burned from the salt on her tender skin. "We've both been assholes, and it's time we stopped it. Don't you think?"

The two women fell into each other's arms, and their bodies shook with the teary happiness of reconciliation.

Hal approached, toting Lily in his arms. He laughed and shook his head. "I'm glad you two have patched things up. It's about time for 'the sisters from another mother' to act like sisters again."

Ebony and Jessie broke apart, laughed, and wiped their wet faces.

"We're having everyone back to the house. I hope you can come. It will be nice to chat over a glass of wine."

"Make that a gallon of rosé, and you're on," Ebony said.

Chapter Fifty-Seven

The light from the Tiffany lamp cast a soft, warm glow over Cindie's office desk. It was late November, and she needed the added illumination because of the shortening daylight hours and the harsh overhead lights that irritated her eyes. The holidays were around the corner, and she found it difficult to believe she'd been the DA for over two months. Where had the time gone?

The cartons in the *People vs. Vargas* murder case were piled shoulder-high on her credenza. Cindie was meeting Joanna Medina for breakfast tomorrow to discuss whether to reenact the murder on the river this late in the year. Medina had recommended the accident reconstruction because she asserted that the missing plug had caused Kyle's kayak to capsize. The theory conflicted with shipwright Merritt Hanson's opinion, and the re-creation would prove her hypothesis. However, the conditions needed to be identical to the day of the incident. With unpredictable weather and the possibility of snow, Cindie suspected they'd have to wait until the spring for better conditions. And anyhow, the case would still be in the pretrial phase.

Still, there was always more preparation for the media-grabbing case. Print, internet, cable, and broadcast reporters had flocked to Poughkeepsie, seeking interviews with Olivia Vargas and Detectives Jones and Pulaski, and shining a spotlight on Cindie and the prosecution team.

She glanced at the *Vargas* cartons and sighed. Her staff was fending off attacks volleyed from all sides. Castellano was motioning her to death to suppress Olivia's admission of guilt and all evidence seized through the search warrants, to seek the right to inspect the grand jury minutes, and to dismiss the case for violation of Olivia's constitutional rights. Meanwhile, the press sought open, uncensored access to Cindie's files and to the defendant. The contests kept her assistants busy from dawn to dusk.

Hal had warned her about the typhoon of paperwork involved in the job, but Cindie didn't mind. Unlike him, she'd never been a brilliant orator who could charm a judge and jury and bend them to her will. Cindie was strictly a second chair at the prosecutor's table, but she could organize a trial workbook, exhibits, investigators, and witnesses even if she was blindfolded. Management suited her.

Cindie slid a slender folder marked *Medina* into her leather tote bag and was preparing to tug the chain on her desk lamp when she heard a soft rapping on the door. She glanced up to find Gloria Reyes Castellano standing in her doorjamb.

"I'm sorry to stop by so late. I was in the neighborhood and thought I'd pop by," Castellano said. Not waiting to be invited inside, the attorney entered the room and settled into her sofa. "It's been a terribly long day." Castellano kicked off her high heels and rubbed her feet.

Cindie was used to the way Gloria Castellano made herself at home. The two women had known each other ever since Pace University Law School. She and Gloria had been working moms, juggling evenings and weekend classes, jobs, and families. As the most mature students in their class, they had bonded over coffee and study groups. Castellano had been a successful real estate broker in the Bronx. Then, a stray bullet had gunned down her teenage son while he'd played street basketball with his buddies. In an instant, Castellano's life changed. In her grief, she'd transformed her rage into legal activism.

Cindie never understood how Gloria coped with her unfathomable loss, and although Gloria seemed to have survived the trial, the heart-breaking sadness never faded from her friend's intense expression.

"You're always welcome in my office, Glo." Cindie paused, narrowing her eyes. "Why are you really here?"

"I just came to visit, *mi amiga*. To see how you're settling into this beautiful office and to serve you with my affidavit supporting the media's right to interview my client." Gloria reached into her bag, produced a document, and handed it to Cindie.

"Ah, it's about that *20/20* interview, isn't it? Your client wants to continue to build her brand from behind bars. No doubt she's lost her lucrative sponsorships."

"A girl's got to eat. We both know you're going to have trouble making the second-degree murder charges stick. With the stormy weather, Kyle's assumption of risk, and Olivia's emotional state, it will be a miracle if you can even persuade a jury that Olivia committed first- or second-degree manslaughter," Gloria replied. "Even if you do, she won't be in jail forever. Maybe a year or two."

Gloria seemed to ignore the insurance fraud, conspiracy, and criminal possession of a forged instrument charges stemming from Shaw's forgery of Kyle's signature. Shaw and Olivia had engineered a plot to make her a beneficiary on Kyle's life insurance policy to swindle Lily out of the fortune. Pretending to be Kyle, Shaw had requested the documents from Barclays. Olivia had intercepted the forms, had Shaw sign them, and returned them to Nicole Thomas. Shaw hadn't known about his wife's plans to expedite Kyle's death to inherit the wealth. Or so he claimed when he turned state's witness against her.

Cindie suspected Olivia had played her devoted husband, as she played everyone else, including Gloria.

"I won't comment on our proceedings, but Olivia's admission bolsters our case. She removed the plug. She snatched Emory's paddle away while he was in the water and admitted she wanted him dead."

Cindie retrieved the Affidavit of Detective Ebony Jones from the folder on her desk and read aloud,

> "Q- *Did you want Kyle dead and to drown? A-Yes, I did. I wanted to be free of Kyle.*
>
> Q-*When did you remove the plug? A-I took it out at my parents' house the night before our trip. I stashed it in my dresser so no one*

would find it.

Q-Olivia, did you intentionally remove the plug from Kyle's kayak and take his paddle so that he would drown? A-Yes, I did.

Q-Deep down in your heart, did you think you could have helped him or saved him from drowning in the Hudson River? A- Yes, but I didn't want to.

Q- If you wanted Kyle gone from your life, why didn't you break up with him? A-He would never truly be gone. I would always carry my love for him with me.

Q-Why did you do it, pull the plug? A-I wanted to get married immediately and have kids with Kyle. He kept postponing the wedding.

Q-Did you argue before the trip? A-We always argued about getting married.

Q-Why did you switch kayaks? A-Kyle's had a skirt and I could hide my life vest inside. He would never know the difference.

Q-What if you hadn't had the opportunity to get rid of Kyle during the storm? A-Kyle's dying was just a matter of time. It would have happened another time, another way.

Q-Olivia, how do you feel now that Kyle is dead? A-Fine."

Castellano waved her hands dismissively. "If we get Olivia's interview suppressed, you've got nothing. You have no proof Olivia caused the injuries found in Emory's autopsy."

"We'll let the video of Olivia beating Emory to a pulp speak for itself. The jury will clearly see that Olivia targeted Kyle and plotted to kill him." Cindie smiled with confidence, although her insecurities over the ambiguous evidence never left her mind. As the DA, she would keep them concealed, especially from her duplicitous adversary. "Gloria, I've always admired your dedication to the cause, but we're not making a deal. We're going all the way with this one."

"We'll see. Maybe we'll be lucky, and our psychiatrists will declare my client unfit to stand trial. Or I wonder if you're racially profiling Olivia." Gloria batted her dark lashes. "In the meantime, can you agree to allow the press to interview Olivia? Give the girl a break."

"I know she's like family to you, but Olivia's a manipulative, cold-blooded killer. She'll have plenty of time behind bars to write a memoir. You can pitch her story to the magazines and publishing companies then."

Gloria clicked her tongue and replaced her shoes. "I guess we'll be seeing a lot of each other, *mi amiga*. Maybe we can grab coffee the next time I'm in town? It would be nice to catch up."

Gloria Reyes Castellano was as slippery as Hal's former legal nemesis, Jeremy Kaplan. Illness had mellowed Jessie's law partner, but Gloria would always remain a bitch. Gloria was all sweetness and light on the outside, masking the cunning, calculating, sharp-tongued, and persistent nature underneath the surface. Gloria and Olivia were two of a kind. They both believed they were smarter than everyone else, but Cindie and her team would decimate them both.

"Just like old times, *mi querida*," Cindie replied, watching Gloria trot out of the door.

Cindie's phone buzzed, and she answered it. It was her husband, Paul. "Hi, darling. Yes, I'm on the way. An old friend unexpectedly stopped by, but she's gone." He explained that their daughter was coming up from the city tonight with her fiancé. "Terrific. I suppose they have more wedding plans to discuss with us. I'll stop at the bakery to pick up her favorite coffee cake. See you soon. Love you."

She would prepare her troops for the war against Olivia Vargas, her family, and Gloria Reyes Castellano. The legal battles would be bloody and arduous, but wars didn't last forever. The court system saw to that. No matter, Olivia Vargas would serve jail time for her sins against Kyle Emory, Jessie, and Lily Martin, Kyle's family, and society. As the DA, Cindie would ensure that Olivia's imprisonment was long and miserable.

Fortunately, there was more to life than the prosecution of Olivia Vargas and Cody Shaw. Cindie had a wedding to help plan.

Chapter Fifty-Eight

J essie had always believed her comfortable house was large enough, but when it bustled with her family and Kyle's, it was bursting at the seams. She smiled at the beautiful Thanksgiving chaos burgeoning around her. Her seven-year-old niece and nine-year-old nephew, and Hal's son, Tyler, weaved in and out of the adults yelling, "Tag!" Dani and her twin Pete had dragged Kyle's electric piano and guitar up from the basement and played rock tunes in the living room, and Lena, Ed, and Tom, and Bev entertained their granddaughter.

In the kitchen, her brother Ethan and sister-in-law Gemma mashed the potatoes while Hal checked the twenty-two-pound turkey roasting in the oven. Jessie put the final touches on the table and lit the white candles in her grandmother's candelabras. The crystal gleamed, the silver sparkled, and the wine was ready to be poured.

A sense of anticipation electrified the loving atmosphere inside her home. The walls seemed to pulsate in appreciation of the uniqueness of the day. Nothing made Jessie happier than to be surrounded by her loved ones on this holiday of giving thanks. While tragedy and loss had infiltrated the year, there was much to be grateful for. Her family was gathered together for the first time in years, and Jessie intended to relish every moment.

When dinner was about to be served, Jessie cued her father.

Ed rose at the head of the dining table, surveyed the attentive audience staring at him, and raised his wine glass. "There is nothing more important than family. We are blessed to be celebrating Thanksgiving with three generations of our family, including Ethan's from California, and the

Emorys, who are a part of our extended family. We have a lot to be thankful for, but we need to remember our loved ones who are gone. I toast those of us gathered around the table and those who are forever in our hearts."

"Here! Here!" the adults shouted.

"Let's eat," the kids responded.

From her high chair stationed between Jessie and Lena, Lily squealed with joy.

Platters of sliced turkey and the trimmings were passed around the table as the family piled their plates high. Glasses clinked as libations were poured. Laughter, stories, and conversation circulated as well. There was only one rule at the table—no talking politics.

"Save room for dessert," Jessie warned Tyler, who loaded his plate for the second time. "We have an extra special surprise after dinner."

"Yeah, I know. My dad told me."

Jessie studied the boy inquisitively, wondering what Hal had mentioned.

"Homemade pumpkin pie with whipped cream!"

Jessie smiled and ruffled Tyler's blonde hair. "So, save room."

At the meal's conclusion, the doorbell rang.

Jessie answered the door, and Ebony and Drew, and Zander and Carly were waiting on the front porch. Ebony pressed two bottles of champagne into Jessie's hands.

"For later," Ebony said and smirked.

"Glad you could make it." Jessie offered her cheek to the quartet for air kisses.

Zander slipped his arm around Carly's waist, guiding her inside, and Jessie thought she recognized a spark between the couple.

She was about to close the door when she spied Jeremy and Gayle Kaplan curbside, wrangling their unruly twins. "Hey, come on in. You're in time for dessert." The teenage boys raced up the front walk at the mention of food. Jeremy and Gayle brought up the rear.

* * *

"You've got a full house tonight. Thanks for inviting us," Ebony whispered in her ear.

"Just the way I love it," Jessie said, discarding her apron and slinging it over the back of a kitchen chair.

Dani carried another platter of leftovers into the kitchen and set it on the butcher's block island. The light glinted off the silver and leather bracelet around Dani's wrist.

"I'm glad you're wearing it," Jessie said.

"Kyle loved it but felt weird wearing it. I guess we now know why, but I adore it." Dani held up her arm to admire the jewelry. "It reminds me of him and my gorgeous niece."

"I'm glad." Jessie gave Dani a quick hug. "We're all family."

"Aren't those the pearl earrings Kyle gave you?" Dani asked.

Jessie brushed aside the curls to reveal the purple-grey South Sea pearl studs in her ears. "Yeah. He splurged for my twenty-ninth birthday. I thought I'd lost them, but I found them buried among some documents in my jewelry box. I decided to wear them today in Kyle's memory."

She'd also found Lily's birth certificate and the Acknowledgment of Paternity, designating Lily as Kyle's official heir. What a relief off her mind.

"Hey, sorry about Cody. You looked like you were hitting it off," Ebony said.

"It's okay, we'd only been hanging out for a couple of weeks, and I wasn't that into him," Dani said. "But once I heard about the forgery business, I figured he must have been using me to gather intel for Olivia. What an egotistical jerk and he deserves whatever he gets."

Jessie laughed. "Tell it like it is, sister."

"I mean, come on. Who wears his wedding band when he's getting divorced? The bit about the ring being stuck on his finger was bullshit," Dani said.

"From what Zander told me, Olivia and Shaw sounded like total nut jobs. I can't believe Kyle fell for her and wanted to marry her," Carly said, sashaying into the kitchen, brandishing a glass of red wine.

Dani grew silent.

"Sorry," Carly said. "I didn't mean to be insensitive."

"No worries. They'll get theirs. Let's be happy we're together, and they are going to rot in hell," Dani said.

The women's voices raised in whoops and hollers, and they exchanged high-fives all around.

Hal stuck his head into the kitchen. "Before we have dessert, can everyone please come into the living room?" He winked at Jessie, making her heart flutter.

Jessie trailed Hal from room to room, and when no one seemed to pay attention to his announcement, she whispered into Pete's ear. He picked up the guitar and plucked a disharmonious chord. The house grew quiet.

Hal slipped his arm around Jessie's waist. "As I was trying to say, please join us in the living room."

Family and friends jostled for positions inside the crowded living room, hallway, and foyer. As a hush fell over the room, Ethan joined Jessie and Hal at the hearth. Beside Jessie stood Ebony, and Ed waited at Hal's shoulder. Tyler sat on the carpet at their feet. Behind them hung the antique English landscape Hal had given Jessie when they'd first met, and along the mantelpiece stood photos of their life together.

Ethan cleared his throat, ruffled a piece of paper, and began. "We are gathered here today to join Jessica Grace Martin and Harold Samuels III in holy matrimony."

A gasp of excitement trickled through the house.

Ed grinned at Lena, who cuddled Lily in her arms next to the sofa, and Lena beamed.

Jessie faced Hal. Her face warmed as he clasped her hands in his. Jessie saw their future as bright as the gold flecks in his loving eyes. Hal had always been the one man she'd ever truly loved. She'd known it ever since her first day at NYU Law School when she stumbled into the school's foyer and spied him lording over his classmates. She'd know it when they'd reconnected in the law library during the Butterfield case. And she knew it now as they were about to become husband and wife.

344

They could have waited until June, as they'd planned, for a big summer wedding. The dress. The tuxedo. The flowers. The party. All of it. But Kyle's death had taught them life was precious. There was not a minute to waste.

Thanksgiving had blended their family and friends together for a time of celebration. In this room with their loved ones, they desired to share the truth and love they'd always felt in their hearts. She and Hal would be a family.

Hal squeezed her hands. They were soft, confident, and would catch her when she fell. She smiled and blinked back her tears, hoping he understood she loved him with every breath she took and every beat of her heart.

"Jessie, do you take Hal to be your husband, for richer or poorer, in sickness and in health, until death do you part?" Ethan asked.

"I do," she said, giggling with the nerves bubbling up inside.

"Hal, do you take Jessie to be your husband, for richer or poorer, in sickness and in health, until death do you part?"

"I do. Forever and ever," Hal said, eliciting a titter from the audience. He turned toward Tyler. "Bud, do you have the rings?"

"Oh, yeah. Here they are, Dad." The boy reached into his pants pocket and handed a navy leather box to Ed. Ed distributed the simple platinum bands to Jessie and Hal, and they exchanged their vows and slipped the rings on their lover's fingers.

Ethan glanced from Hal to Jessie and beamed. "By the powers vested in me by the State of New York, I now pronounce you husband and wife. Jessie, you may kiss your husband."

As their families cheered, Jessie threw her arms around Hal's neck and sealed the deal with a kiss to end all kisses.

Chapter Fifty-Nine

Ebony wrapped a fluffy blanket around her shoulders, warding off the November chill. Indian summer was over, the trees were bare, and although the nighttime temperatures had dipped below freezing, Drew refused to turn up the heat. He insisted the cold invigorated her mind and concentration. Her promotion exam was the day after tomorrow, and she was tired of being as frozen as green peas. She jumped off the couch, cranked up the thermostat, buried her icy nose in the sergeant's exam study guide, and waited for the heat to rise.

The door to Ebony's apartment burst open, and a gangly German Shepard bounded across the wooden floor, jumped onto the couch, and into Ebony's lap. Despite his hundred pounds and two years of age, Wrangler believed he was still a pup. He licked her face and shook the dried leaves that were tangled in his dappled coat all over her.

"Get down, boy," Drew yelled.

The pointy ears snapped to attention, then lowered in shame.

"Good boy," Ebony said. "Did Daddy take you for a nice, long walk?" The dog's tail thumped on the sofa cushion. "Now, get down and let Mommy study."

"How was your study session with Zander?" Drew asked, grabbing Wrangler by the collar and setting him on the floor. "Good boy." He gave the dog a pat on head, and Wrangler scrambled away toward his water bowl.

"We're both burned out." Ebony shuffled the pile of textbooks and notepads on the couch. "I've studied as much as I can, but it's been challenging. I'll do the best I can when I take the test."

Drew kissed her head. "You'll do fine because you're a genius."

She laughed. "Babe, you must be confusing me with my sister. She's the one with identic memory. Me, I'm like the rest of the humans."

Drew looked around their cramped apartment, from Ebony on the pullout couch to the narrow galley kitchen to the alcove bedroom. Then the baskets of clean clothes stacked along the wall and the café table that served double-duty for dining and as a workstation seemed to draw his interest. "This isn't the best time to talk about it, but we need a bigger place."

"Are you talking about renting a house?" Ebony had been up since dawn studying, and she welcomed the distraction from her life of crime.

"Sugar, I think it's time we bought one. We could use a den for you, a workshop for me, a yard for Wrangler and a garage. I'm still not used to the Northeast's winter ice and snow. We both make good livings and are committed to our careers. Maybe it's time to settle down." He plopped down on the sofa beside her and propped up his feet on the coffee table.

Ebony's pulse raced. This was the closest Drew had come to mentioning a future together. When they'd met in a bar three years ago, he'd been traveling around the country in an RV. What had been a one-night stand had blossomed into Drew's commitment to her and the City of Poughkeepsie as a firefighter.

All their quarrels, his late-night flights to the firehouse, and living separate lives vanished. Including their current tussle over the heat.

"Lieutenant Tim Decatur is retiring, and there's an opening at the Hooker Avenue firehouse. The hours and pay are better, and I'd be the ranking officer for *Marine 1*. Life wouldn't be so crazy. What do you think?"

"Who are you? And what have you done with Drew?" Ebony nudged him playfully.

"I've been considering this for a while. But with our schedules, we haven't talked. If you want to mull it over, I understand. I want you to know I'm all in. You're my family now." He pulled her into a tight embrace, and the warmth of his lips on hers made her knees quiver.

When Drew spoke, his words meant something to her. Ever since his parents died in a car wreck, he'd been alone in the world. After putting himself through college and grad school for engineering and working for Boeing in Charleston, South Carolina for five years, he'd quit. He'd cashed in his stock, bought an RV, and wandered around the country until he met Ebony. Their diverse backgrounds, race, and music choices hadn't dissuaded him from pursuing her until she'd relented.

She'd warned herself against dreaming beyond tomorrow with Drew. But with his pleading puppy dog eyes and their drooling Shepard at his knee, Drew was proposing a future. Their future. He wasn't proposing marriage, but she was ready to take the next step with Drew by her side.

"Okay," she whispered, pulling away. "Let's call a real estate agent and get this party started, but…. Can it please wait until next week?"

"Sugar, for you, I'd wait a lifetime."

His lips found hers, and she never wanted their celebratory kiss to end.

* * *

Ebony met Zander on the broad front steps of the public safety building on Main Street in Poughkeepsie. The solid brick structure with arched windows and granite sills housed the fire department, three large bays for fire trucks, and community meeting rooms. The civil service exams for police sergeant and deputy sheriff were being administered in the meeting rooms, and scores of nervous applicants representing every race, religion, and persuasion pursuing their dreams of public service jostled Ebony and Zander as they passed by.

"I thought we were the only ones taking tests today," Zander said.

"They are the candidates for every position, not only ours. It's great that so many people are interested in public service. We need more diversity in our ranks." She watched him twirl his car keys on his pointer finger. "To get our promotions, we need the top scores. So do your best."

"Eb, do you have any regrets about seeking your promotion?" His voice quavered.

For months, she'd pondered the question. To protect their community, they'd dedicated long, hard hours to dangerous assignments, but they'd done it together as partners. They'd had each other's backs, saved each other's lives, and covered each other's butt more times than she could count. Zander was her perfect work partner.

With their promotions, Ebony would be an administrator, supervising the city detectives in her department. Zander would manage a new special crimes operation for the sheriff's department, coordinating the towns and cities across the valley to create a centralized crime-reporting unit. Neither would need a partner anymore.

Ebony would miss Zander. However, these changes were part of the trajectory of her career. Five years ago, she'd become the first detective of her color and sex, so why not the first female police chief in the Hudson Valley? Ebony could taste her sweet desire for the top position, and although she'd never expressed it to Zander, she figured he knew. So did Chief Shepardson, which was the reason he pushed Ebony so hard.

If Ebony aced the test and secured the promotion, she was on her way. Nothing could stop her except herself.

She grasped Zander's shoulders and stared into his sharp eyes, refusing to become emotional. "No. We've had a great run. We've nabbed a jail full of felons, risked our lives, and earned this opportunity. It's time to see what else we can accomplish. Z, you're a great cop, and I'm proud to be your partner. Go kick ass and get the promotion you deserve."

They climbed the granite steps, and at the top, Zander held the door open for her. Ebony marched briskly past him, and she didn't look back.

349

Acknowledgements

As my readers may know, several notorious Hudson Valley true crimes have inspired my "Queen City Crimes" series. The shocking murder committed by my Forbus Junior High School history teacher, Albert Fentress, formed the basis for *The Midnight Call*, and the brutal serial killer of prostitutes, Kendall Francois, served as model for Duvall Bennett in *Hooker Avenue*.

This novel presented a unique challenge to me in that the true crime that served as the inspiration, the Angelika Graswald murder of Vincent Viafore, raised no question as to who perpetrated the crime. The legal questions involved the degree to which Graswald's reckless disregard of Viafore's life contributed to his drowning, and whether her malicious actions disqualified her from receiving Viafore's life insurance benefits from his estate. The challenge of writing "The Empty Kayak" involved creating murder suspects where none existed, finding different local settings, and transferring the mystery from land into the murky depths of the Hudson River.

The 2016 Graswald case had attracted international media attention, so I began my research with the print and media coverage of the tragedy, and with the examination of the court records for the criminal case and the subsequent civil wrongful death action. My investigation took me on an interesting journey into deep, dangerous waters I'd never treaded before, and meeting with physicians, firefighters, aquatic experts, and outdoorsmen from across the country.

First, I needed to understand exactly what had happened to the drowning victim on the Hudson, so my initial step involved researching the aquatic recovery of bodies. This led me to New York State Trooper Rell, Sr. Diver for the New York State Police Underwater Recovery Team, who sparked my interest in the underwater recovery of bodies in the Hudson.

Trooper Rell referred me to Andrea Zaferes of Team Lifeguard Systems Inc., the internationally renowned aquatic homicide expert, who had served as a consultant on the Graswald case. Ms. Zaferes was extremely knowledgeable on the subject of homicidal drowning, and was persuasive in her opinions about the truth behind the Viafore crime. She encouraged me to make sure that my detective apprehended the killer, as opposed to the questionable resolution of the Graswald matter.

Former City of Poughkeepsie Fire Chief Mark Johnson and Captain Steve Stuka offered me insights into the life-saving operations of the *Marine 1* rescue boat and the Poughkeepsie Fire Department in the event of an aquatic incident, and the hidden secrets that lay within the depths of the Hudson. Michelle Jorden, MD of the County of Santa Clara Medical Examiners Office reviewed Kyle's autopsy report for accuracy for the type of death and injuries he sustained.

My friends at Marist College, never fail me when I need assistance, and thanks to Chris DelGiorno, V.P. of College Advancement, and Tim Murray, Director of Athletics, for allowing me to wander around the James J. McCann Athletic Center Natatorium and have the place to myself.

I had never been kayaking before writing this book, let alone on the Hudson. My husband, son and I worked with Marshall Seddon at The River Connection in Hyde Park, NY to paddle on the river so I could understand the challenges faced by my characters before and after the storm, and to appreciate the importance of your equipment.

A very special thanks goes to kayaking expert and enthusiast, Eric Hawkinson, who helped me choreograph the storm sequence to insure its accuracy.

It was interesting that while Ms. Zaferes believed that the missing kayak plug contributed to the victim's death, both Mr. Seddon and Mr. Hawkinson, the kayakers, disputed this conclusion.

My editor, Lindsay Flanagan, and I worked together on "The Midnight Call," and she was the first call I made for help polishing "The Empty Kayak." Despite her jammed schedule, Lindsay came through like a champ, and I look forward to working with her on my future projects. My story coach,

Laurie Sanders, always nudges me in the right direction. I appreciate her candor and brutal honesty in making me dig deeper when I'm creating my characters and stories, and that she's never shy about editing out my literary babble.

My beta-readers street team, Dave Lowrie, Joy Dyson, Margaret King, Nalaini and Rajan Sriskandarajah, and Maureen Cockburn, have been my supporters since the beginning, and their feedback reminds me that writing about isn't always about writing, it's about reading, too.

The amazing Dames of Detection at Level Best Books, Verena Rose, Shawn Simmons, and my primary editor, Harriette Sackler, have cheered me on along the way. This is our third adventure together, and this book would not have taken shape or been on the bookshelves without their support. Thank you.

This time around, the cover of *The Empty Kayak* was an experiment that Shawn Simmons and I undertook together. We enlisted the assistance of Dall-E-2 from OpenAI in creating the cover, and after typing in a few keywords and making a series of adjustments, the cover was born. I believe that artificial intelligence is a tool to assist us, not replace us. However, the technology is developing faster than we can understand it, so, watch out for the bots!

My friend, and business associate, Jess Taylor, is always available to listen to me kvetch, no matter where he is traveling. Thanks, Jess. My amazing promotional teams of Meryl Moss Media, Kristen O'Connor, Jennifer Musico, Partners In Crime, and Storygram also deserve kudos in helping spread the word about my projects. And my assistant, Ella Diamond, was truly hands-on when it came to crunch time.

Readers may not appreciate that writing a book can take a toll on your body, especially to your hands from typing, and to your back from sitting for extended periods. I couldn't have made it through the long days at the desk without help from the staffs at Melissa Bertolozzi, PT and Patrick Clough, New York Hand and Physical Therapy. My healthy hands and back are indebted to you both.

I am overwhelmed by the support and interest that readers have taken in my stories. As I travel and speak about my books, I appreciate people sharing their personal connections to these true crime and their suggestions about other bizarre ones, which they believe I might find interesting. I'm excited that readers are drawn to my series and have a vested interest in the lives of Jessie, Hal and Ebony. They would love it, too.

You may have noticed that several pets appear in this novel. Cats and dogs bring us great joy and comfort, and my cat, Dougal, was no exception. He was my writing buddy, my constant companion, and distraction when I needed it during the writing of my books. I couldn't have written this series without him. Rest in peace, kitty boy.

Finally, and without comparison, my thanks and love goes out to my family. Special thanks goes to my mother, Ellin, for suggesting the title, *The Empty Kayak*. An avid reader, her instinct was spot-on. My husband, Mike, says I have to be "a little nuts" to write crime fiction. This nut doesn't fall far from our family tree. I hope my children and grandchildren are as proud of me as I am of them and their accomplishments. I would not be here without them.

About the Author

Jodé Millman is the acclaimed author of *Hooker Avenue,* which won the Independent Press Award for Crime Fiction, and was a finalist for the Clue and American Fiction Awards, and *The Midnight Call,* which won the Independent Press, American Fiction, and Independent Publisher Bronze IPPY Awards for Legal Thriller. She's an attorney, a reviewer for Booktrib.com, the host/producer of *The Backstage with the Bardavon* podcast, and the creator of The Writer's Law School. Jodé lives with her family in the Hudson Valley, where she is at work on the next installment of her "Queen City Crimes" series—novels inspired by true crimes in the region she calls home.

SOCIAL MEDIA HANDLES:
 Facebook: @JodeMillman
 Goodreads: @JodeMillman
 Twitter: @ worldseats
 Bookbub: @JodeMillmanAuthor
 Instagram: @JodeWrites

AUTHOR WEBSITE:
www.jodemillman.com

Also by Jodé Millman

The Midnight Call (2022, Level Best Books, 2019)

Hooker Avenue (2022, Level Best Books)

Seats: New York —180 Seating Plans to New York Metro Area Theatres, Concert Halls and Sports Stadiums (2nd & 3rd Editions) (2002, 2008, Applause Theatre and Cinema Books)

Seats: Chicago—125 Seating Plans to Chicago/Milwaukee Metro Area Theatres, Concert Halls and Sports Stadiums (2004, Applause Theatre and Cinema Books)

The Midnight Call is also available on Audiobook at www.Audible.com

9 781685 122874